Dear Reader,

When I first sat down to pen HIDEAWAY, I could not imagine writing more than a dozen titles in what has become an ongoing saga of incredible possibilities.

For those of you who've been asking for out-of-print titles in this series, your requests have been duly noted. The second installment of the HIDEAWAY collector's series will offer *Heaven Sent* and *Harvest Moon*.

However, in *Heaven Sent* you will find a discrepancy with M.J.'s birthday as indicated in the subsequent prequel, *Best Kept Secrets*. I had no idea when I created David and Serena's story that I would ever write about his mother. Please forgive the faux pas and enjoy.

Yours in romance,

Rochelle Alers

ROCHELLE ALERS

HIDEAWAY LEGACY

ARABESQUE®

HIDEAWAY LEGACY

An Arabesque novel published by Kimani Press 2007

Copyright © 2007 by Kimani Press

ISBN-13: 978-0-373-83065-7
ISBN-10:   0-373-83065-3

The publisher acknowledges the copyright holder
of the individual works as follows:

HEAVEN SENT
First published by Pinnacle Books in 1998
Copyright © 1998 by Rochelle Alers

HARVEST MOON
First published by BET Publications, LLC in 1999
Copyright © 1999 by Rochelle Alers

www.kimanipress.com

Printed in U.S.A.

CONTENTS

HEAVEN SENT

CHAPTER 1

June 14
San José, Costa Rica

David Claridge Cole felt the jet losing altitude, but he did not stir. He sat, eyes closed, his chest rising and falling heavily from the change of pressure within the descending aircraft. The set of his strong jaw and the vertical lines between his eyes marred the normally attractive face of the musician-turned-businessman. He wanted to be anywhere but on a plane flying to Costa Rica in the middle of June.

A slow, crooked smile replaced his frown as he recalled the prior evening's festivities. It had been a long time, too long, since he had enjoyed a night filled with music, sumptuous food, and celebrating that lasted until pinpoints of light from the rising sun pierced the cover of the nighttime sky.

He had been the best man in a wedding party, and the reveling following the ceremony had reminded him of how much he missed a life-style that had been a never-ending party. As the percussionist for the popular jazz band Night Mood, he lived nights and days measured by recording sessions, live performances, and promotional parties and tours. He'd been on a dizzying merry-go-round that he never wanted to get off.

But it all stopped when his older brother Martin resigned as CEO of ColeDiz International Ltd. to embark on a political career. He had been expected to take over the responsibility of the day-to-day operation of the family-owned export company. He'd even surprised himself, once he learned all of the laws and regulations regarding export tariffs as well as environmental sanctions and controls.

He'd assumed control of ColeDiz at twenty-seven and now, at thirty-six, he wanted out. Running ColeDiz for nine years had offered him the experience he needed for a future undertaking. It wasn't that he minded being a businessman. However, he didn't want to have to concern himself with the fluctuating prices of bananas or coffee. What he wanted to do was focus his energies on discovering new musical talent. The idea of setting up his own recording company had come to him more than a year ago, and the notion grew stronger each time he boarded the corporate jet for a business trip.

His last meeting with Interior Minister Raul Cordero-Vega had not gone well. What should have been a civil meeting ended with a hostile verbal confrontation. David hadn't waited for the corporate jet to fly him back to Florida, but had taken a commercial flight instead. Vega had threatened to increase the tariffs on bananas for the second time in less than a decade, because he claimed the plastic casings used to protect the fruit during harvesting were found in the digestive tracts of turtles washed up along the Costa Rican coastline. Environmentalists were pressuring the government to fine or expel the foreign-owned companies, and Vega's solution was to double the already enormously high tariffs.

Martin Cole's last act as CEO had been to transfer many of the ColeDiz ventures to Belize, while leaving the conglomerate's most productive banana plantation near Puerto Limón. And after conferring with Martin and his father Samuel, David was given the go-ahead to negotiate the sale of their one remaining Costa Rican business enterprise.

He opened his eyes, his smile widening. This was to be his last trip to the Central American country. Under another set of circumstances he would have enjoyed the lush nation filled with more than fifty active volcanoes, because the region was beautiful and so were its people. They were a warm, polite, and friendly exotic mix of native Indians, Spanish, and people of African descent.

Estimating it would take him less than two weeks to conclude his business dealings with Vega, he felt some of his resentment waning as the sight of the San José airport came into view.

Pain, frustration, and fatigue were clearly etched on the face of Interior Minister Raul Cordero-Vega, aging the man. Two weeks before, anyone glancing at the tall, erect, graying man would not have taken him for sixty-two. Now he appeared to be ten years older. That morning he'd received a telephone call telling him that his only child, a son, had been arrested and charged with drug trafficking and the murder of a United States DEA agent. This bit of news had torn his world asunder.

Gabriel Diego Vega was locked away in a U.S. prison and denied bail because the prosecutor feared he would leave the States and not return for his trial. Not even the high-priced lawyer Raul had retained to handle his son's case could get the judge to change his decision, though he pleaded that Gabriel would willingly surrender his Costa Rican passport.

So much for American justice, Raul seethed silently. A surge of rage darkened his brown face at the same time his hands tightened into fists. While his son languished in the bowels of an American prison, other known criminals ran rampant through the streets thumbing their noses at U.S. justice. Men who were known to openly engage in illegal activities felt the warmth of the morning sun and enjoyed the smell of fresh air while Gabriel lay in a small concrete jail cell on a narrow cot inhaling the stench from his open commode.

"Not my son!" he whispered to the empty room. Not the child he'd waited thirty-six years to father.

A sharp knock on the door disturbed his turbulent thoughts. "Come in!" There was no mistaking the harshness in the command. The door opened slowly and his eyes widened in surprise. She had disobeyed him. He'd told her not to come to Costa Rica. She was to have remained in the States—with Gabriel. She was all his son had there.

Large, clear-brown eyes took in the thunderous expression on the face of the tall, white-haired man. At one time that expression would've sent her running from his celebrated temper, but no longer. She was thirty years old, a grown woman. The tyrant she had once feared was gone forever, and in his place a broken man. Serena could see her stepfather hurting. What he was feeling at that moment, she also felt. Raul had lost a son and she her half brother.

Holding out her arms, she walked slowly into his study. "Poppa." Her normally husky voice shook with raw emotion. "I had to come."

Raul crossed the room and pulled her gently to his chest. Burying his face in her wealth of unruly curls, he held her close, feeling the trembling in her tiny body. "I told you to stay, *Chica.* I told you to stay because Gabriel needs you."

Pulling back slightly, Serena blinked back the tears flooding her large round eyes. "Gabe wouldn't see me."

Raul frowned. "What do you mean?"

"He refuses to see me."

His frown deepened. "Why?"

Serena shook her head, a riot of reddish-brown curls moving as if they'd had taken on a life of their own. "I don't know. I spoke to his attorney, and he says that Gabe doesn't want to talk to anyone except those who are his legal counsel." She sniffled, bringing a tissue to her pert nose. "I'm his sister, and he won't see or talk to me."

Embracing her again, Raul brought her head to his chest. "Whatever you do, don't breathe a word of this to your mother."

"How is she holding up?"

"Not well. She won't leave her room."

Extracting herself, Serena paced the length of the carpeting lining the expansive room. "I don't understand any of it, Poppa. Gabe called me and said he was going down to the Keys—"

"What keys?" Raul interrupted.

Remembering that her stepfather was not an American, and that he was not familiar with the terminology, she smiled for the first time in two weeks.

"The Florida Keys. He told me that he and a friend were going on a sailing expedition down to the Caribbean. They had planned to pick up a few more people in the Bahamas before returning to the States. On their return trip they were intercepted by the United States Coast Guard. What followed is a jumble of confusion, and U.S. officials claim that the boat they were on was filled with drugs, and that Gabe and his fellow passengers are smugglers."

"That's a lie!" Raul shouted.

She stopped pacing. "We both know that! If that boat was carrying drugs, then Gabe knew nothing about it. He had to have been set up."

"And I know who set him up."

Serena arched a delicate eyebrow. "Who, Poppa?"

Raul gave her a long, penetrating look before his heavy eyelids lowered, concealing the hatred and distrust burning within them. *"Los Estados Unidos."*

Her jaw dropped as she stared back at her stepfather. "Why the United States?"

"Because I won't permit them to rape my country. Because I make them pay for the destruction they leave behind when they take what they want from Costa Rica. These Americans grow rich and stuff their already swollen bellies…"

"Do you actually believe the United States would blackmail Gabe because of you?"

He nodded, unable to disclose the political machinations going on between Costa Rica and other foreign powers about business ventures. Foreign companies were responsible for the slow, but methodic destruction of the rain forest and its indigenous wildlife. If left unchecked, the foreigners would make the land uninhabitable, make it impossible for Costa Ricans to survive in their own country. Their nation would fare no better than the people and the vanishing wildlife of the Brazilian Amazon.

"I don't believe that," Serena countered angrily.

"That's because you are an American, *Chica*. I expect you to defend your country."

Swallowing, she chose her words carefully. "We'll talk about this later. I must see my mother."

She loved her stepfather because he was the only father she'd ever known. However, Serena could never understand his virulent dislike of Americans. She found this hard to fathom because he'd married her mother, who had never given up her American citizenship.

He inclined his near-white head. "Yes. We'll talk later." He waited and he wasn't disappointed when she walked over to him and rose on tiptoe to kiss his cheek. Cupping the back of her head, he pressed his lips to her forehead. *"Te amo, Chica."*

"And I love you, too, Poppa," she whispered then turned and made her way out of the room.

Raul waited as the door opened and closed behind his step-daughter's retreating figure. He was still staring at the door when it opened slightly and his driver stepped into the room.

"What is it?" he snapped. Rodrigo knew better than to enter his study without knocking.

"Señor Cole has arrived in San José and is waiting for you."

Raul's scowl deepened quickly. David Cole had returned to Costa Rica. The last time he and the brash young man met they'd traded words—words that had left a bitter taste in his mouth. Words he never would've permitted another man to utter in his presence. Words that David Cole would find himself swallowing and choking on.

"Tell Señor Cole that I cannot leave Puerto Limón at this time. If he refuses to come, then bring him here—either standing or reclining. The choice will be his. That will be all, Rodrigo."

"*Sí*, Señor Vega."

Raul waited for the door to close, a feral smile curling his upper lip. The United States government held his son prisoner, and now he wanted Samuel Cole to feel the same pain when he imprisoned his last born.

"An eye for an eye, and a son for a son."

His threat, though spoken softly, carried throughout the space and lingered like a musical note before fading into a hushed silence.

CHAPTER 2

Serena Morris took a back staircase up to her mother's bedroom. Heaviness weighed on her narrow shoulders like a leaded blanket. She had felt so helpless once she realized there was nothing she could do to change her brother's mind. Her letters were returned and her calls went unanswered. It was as if Gabriel Vega had divorced his family.

His eyes—she would never forget the vacant, haunted look in his dark eyes when their gazes met across the space in the Florida courtroom. His glance was furtive before he turned his head and stared ahead while pleading innocent to the formal charges of drug trafficking and murder. When he was led out of the courtroom he refused to meet her gaze again.

She and Gabe were only four years apart, yet she'd always felt much older. When her mother had come home from the hospital with the baby, she held her arms out and said firmly, "Mine."

Juanita Morris-Vega had glanced at her beaming husband, then placed the sleeping, three-day-old infant boy in his half sister's outstretched arms. The little girl and boy, who uncannily shared the same birthday, bonded instantly, and over the years had become inseparable.

Marking her way down the cool, wide hallway, Serena realized she had almost forgotten how beautiful the house in Limón was. A white, two-story, stucco structure built on a hill overlooking the lush rain forest, it claimed expansive hallways, arched entrances, highly waxed mahogany floors, and whitewashed walls. It was a home designed in the manner of a spacious Spanish *hacienda.* She had once called the house home, but now her one-bedroom apartment in a teeming New York City neighborhood was home.

Her stepfather had named the house *La Montaña.* Her mother much preferred their smaller residence in San José because of the capital city's cooler temperatures. Serena never tired of coming to *La Montaña.* She was never bothered by the heat.

Knocking lightly on the solid mahogany door, she pushed it open. The lengthening morning shadows shrouded the petite figure of Juanita Vega reclining on a massive, antique four-poster bed. Moving closer, Serena watched for movement which would indicate that her mother was awake.

"Mother?" she whispered.

Juanita sat up and stared at her daughter as if she were an apparition. "Serena!" There was no mistaking the elation in her voice.

Seconds later Serena found herself in her mother's embrace, inhaling the familiar fragrance of Joy. Her mother had worn the perfume since the first time Raul had given it to her, after the birth of Gabriel.

"I knew you would come. I prayed you'd come," Juanita said softly.

"I couldn't stay away, Mother. You need me and I need you."

Juanita pulled back and stared at a face so much like her own. Her daughter claimed a perfectly round face with large eyes that barely slanted upward at the corners. Her hair and eyes were an exact match: a warm brown with gold highlights. As she smiled, her gaze inched over Serena's short, pert nose and full, pouting mouth.

It was hard to believe that her oldest child was thirty years old, because everything about her appearance was so delicately and delightfully young. Perhaps if she secured her crinkling hair in a severe chignon it would detract from her youthful appearance, but she doubted it. Her daughter had inherited her dominant genes. At fifty-eight, Juanita could easily pass for a woman in her early forties.

Serena stared back at her mother, noting the evidence of strain on her delicate face. Her eyes were swollen from what she knew had been constant weeping, and her cheekbones were more pronounced, indicating that she had lost weight she could not afford to lose. Juanita Vega was an inch shorter than her own five-foot-four inches, and weighed no more than one hundred ten pounds. She estimated that the older woman's weight now hovered closer to one hundred.

"You've lost weight, Mother." A disapproving frown accompanied the accusation.

Juanita closed her eyes. "I can't eat or sleep. The thought that my son is accused of being a murderer haunts me day and night. I can believe anything except that he murdered someone."

"Gabe must not have known about the drugs being on that boat, and the story about him shooting that DEA agent with his own gun is preposterous. Law enforcement people are trained to apprehend and subdue a suspect, not let themselves be overpowered so that their own lives are at risk."

"That doesn't change the charge of murder," Juanita argued, her eyes filling with tears.

"No, it doesn't," Serena acknowledged, "but something tells me that Gabe will not be found guilty of any of the charges."

"Right now I'm not as confident as you are." She dabbed her eyes with an embroidered linen handkerchief. "What I can't understand is what he was doing hanging around with the son of a drug lord."

"You know he and Guillermo Barranda are friends. Ex-college roommates."

Running a fragile hand over her face, Juanita shook her head. "Of all of the people to form a friendship with, he had to find the spawn of the most ruthless man in the Western Hemisphere. I should've listened to Raul—"

"Don't say it, Mother," Serena interrupted. "It's too late to say what you should've said or done. Gabe wanted to go to an American college, and he did. And if he hadn't, who's to say that he wouldn't have met Guillermo Barranda at another time or another place? Poppa made certain that he has the best defense attorney in the state of Florida, and it's only a matter of time before Gabe will come back home." She prayed silently that she was right.

Smiling, she pressed a kiss to her mother's forehead. "I'm here now, and it's my turn to take care of you."

Stiffening in Serena's embrace, Juanita held her breath before letting it out slowly. "How long do you intend to stay?"

"I've taken a three-month leave of absence."

Juanita pulled back and stared at her daughter, knowing that Serena had waged a long and bitter battle for a promotion as nursing supervisor at a prestigious New York City hospital. Now, a week after obtaining the job title, she had taken a leave of absence.

Holding up her hand Serena said softly, "Don't say anything. I know what I'm doing. *Mi familia* comes before my career."

La familia. It was something Juanita had come to cherish as she had matured. Her husband and her children were her only earthly treasures.

The roles reversed themselves as Serena sat on the bed with Juanita, holding her gently to her heart and easing the pain her mother had carried for the past two weeks.

David Cole lay across the large bed in his hotel room waiting for the telephone call which would inform him that Raul Vega would meet with him. Their prearranged meeting for four o'clock that afternoon had been canceled, and the delay had not improved his disposition.

Two weeks—fourteen—days was all he'd allowed himself to negotiate and close on the sale of the banana plantation.

Resting his head on folded arms, he closed his eyes. Only now that he lay on the bed did he realize how exhausted he was. Eating rich foods, drinking alcoholic concoctions, and dancing until dawn had taken its toll. His head was throbbing and his mouth was unnaturally dry.

There were times when he'd engaged in two- to three-day binges of nonstop performing, drinking, and dancing, collapsing only when his debilitated body refused to remain in an upright position.

Now that he was experiencing the lingering effects of the prior night's carnival-like reveling he wondered if he really did miss his former lifestyle. A slow, crooked smile creased his sun-browned face as deep dimples winked boyishly in each of his lean cheeks. "I do," he whispered to the silent space. And he did.

He'd barely drifted off to sleep before the telephone on the bedside table rang loudly.

Picking up before the second ring, David spoke into the receiver. "Cole."

"Señor Cole, I've been instructed to take you to Señor Vega. He has offered you the hospitality of his home for your stay in Costa Rica."

As he registered the unfamiliar male voice a slight frown creased David's forehead. "Tell Señor Vega that I thank him for his generosity, but I prefer the hospitality of my own hotel suite." He did not want to give Vega the advantage of home court. As it was, *he* was a foreigner in the man's country.

"But, Señor Cole, he insists."

"And I insist on remaining at my hotel."

"I'll tell Señor Vega."

"You do just that," David countered angrily before hanging up.

Swinging his trousered legs over the side of the bed, he stood up. Going back to sleep was impossible after the phone call. Raul Cordero-Vega had become his nemesis. He was willing to sell the banana plantation—at a sizable loss if necessary—and still Vega continued to harass him. The Interior Minister would never see or treat him as an equal. David did not care anymore. Vega would come to him, on his terms, or he would let the bananas fall off the trees and rot where they lay.

Unbuttoning his shirt, he pulled it off and flung it on a chair in the opulently decorated bedroom. Minutes later his trousers and underwear followed. He would shower, change clothes, then order something to eat from room service.

Making his way into the bathroom, he turned on and adjusted the water temperature in the shower stall until it was a refreshing lukewarm. Standing under the spray of the water was invigorating. It rained down on his liberally gray-streaked black hair, plastering the short strands to his scalp. Turning his face up to the force of water coming from the showerhead, he closed his eyes. He waited a full minute, opened his eyes, then adjusted the water temperature, letting it run cold until icy, stinging fingers massaged his body.

He felt the chill, then a surge of warmth, but when he turned to his right it was too late. The figure of a man stood at his side, arm raised above his head.

David moved quickly, but not quickly enough. A huge fist cradling a small object came down alongside his temple. He felt blinding heat explode over his left eye before everything faded as he slumped lifelessly to the floor of the shower stall, his right leg twisted awkwardly under his body.

The man, who stood more than half a foot taller than David Cole's six-foot-two and outweighed him by more than sixty pounds, leaned over and turned off the water. Bending down, he lifted David effortlessly from the floor of the shower stall as if he weighed no more than a small child. Returning to the bedroom, he laid the inert body on the bed, wrapped him in a sheet, then zipped him into a ventilated body bag.

Two other men gathered everything belonging to David Cole. Within minutes the lifeless man, his luggage, and his captors rode a freight elevator to the basement and made their way out of the hotel to an awaiting van. The encroaching darkness shadowed their movements, and if anyone saw them they would be identified as hotel staff, because their coveralls bore the name and insignia of the Hotel L'Ambiance.

David Claridge Cole was on his way to Puerto Limón—reclining.

CHAPTER 3

Puerto Limón, Costa Rica

Rodrigo knocked on the door to his boss's study, his heart pounding loudly in his ears. The abduction had not gone well. Señor Cole was now in Limón, but he doubted whether Raul Cordero-Vega would be pleased with the man's condition.

"*Sí,*" Raul barked behind the door.

Rodrigo pushed it open and stepped into the room. Raul sat in the dark, his back to the door. The only light coming into the large room was from a full moon.

"There is a problem, Señor."

"What kind of a problem?" Raul asked, not turning around.

"He has arrived."

"Where is he?"

"He's—he's in the van, Señor."

"In the van where?"

"Along the road leading to *La Montaña*. We had a flat tire."

"Did you walk here, Rodrigo?" Raul's voice was dangerously quiet.

"*Sí,* Señor Vega."

"Señor Cole is younger and stronger than you are, Rodrigo. There should not be a problem for him to make it up the road."

"*Pero—*"

"But what?" Raul still did not stir from his sitting position.

"He has been injured."

Raul stiffened, but did not stand. "Injured how?"

"A head wound, Señor Vega."

"How serious?"

"He needs a doctor."

The chair clattered noisily to the floor as Raul sprang to his feet. "Fools and idiots! I'm surrounded by complete idiots! I don't care how you do it, but get him up to the house, then go get the doctor! And let me remind you that if he dies—"

"*Sí,* Señor Vega," Rodrigo said quickly as he closed the door softly, shutting out the sound of his boss's ranting.

Raul walked over to the sliding French doors leading out to the gallery, and stared into the silvery moonlight. Rodrigo and the men he had hired to abduct David Cole had bungled it. Shaking his head slowly, he prayed that the American wasn't seriously injured. He needed a live body to trade for a live body. David Cole would be of no use to him dead.

Forty-five minutes had elapsed when Rodrigo knocked on the door and informed Raul that David Cole was at *La Montaña.*

"He is in the bedroom at the back of the house," Rodrigo said softly. "The doctor is on his way."

"Have someone get rid of the van and pay the men so much money that they'll forget their own mother's names if they are questioned by anyone," Raul ordered.

Rodrigo nodded, backed out of the room, and closed the door. He had managed to redeem himself.

Raul crossed the room and opened the door. His footsteps were muffled by the carpeted runner along the length of the wide hallway as he took the back staircase to the room which was to become David Cole's prison cell. A cell much better than the one where Gabriel now resided.

He did not realize how rapidly his heart was pumping when he stepped into the bedroom and stared at the motionless body of the arrogant young man who had openly insulted him during their last encounter.

Soft, golden light shone on David's handsome face, but it wasn't until he stood over the prone figure that Raul saw the damage to the left side of his face. His eye was swollen shut and the blood pooling in his ear had drained out onto the pillow cradling his head.

Swallowing back the bile rising in his throat, Raul turned quickly and left the room. Minutes later, he knocked on the door of his stepdaughter's bedroom. He had ordered her not to return to Costa Rica, but was thankful that she had disobeyed him.

"*Chica,* I need you." His voice came out in a harsh whisper. He didn't want to wake up his wife, who was now resting comfortably in a room at the opposite end of the hallway.

Serena laid aside the book she'd been reading and scrambled from her bed when she heard her father's voice, pushing her arms into the sleeves of a silken robe. Not bothering to put on her slippers, she opened the door and found him pacing back and forth.

"What's the matter, Poppa?"

Raul grabbed her hand. "Someone is injured and he needs immediate medical assistance."

As they raced along the hallway, Serena's pulse quickened. "Where is his injury?"

"His head."

Raul watched Serena move into the bedroom where David lay motionless on a large four-poster bed. Turning a switch on a lamp, she flooded the space with more light.

Holding the lamp aloft, she stared at the face of the man sprawled on the bed. She didn't notice the sensual perfection of his generous mouth, the arching curve of jet-black eyebrows, and the stubborn set of a strong chin. But she did see that his nose seemed too long and too delicate for his arresting face. Thick black lashes lay on his high cheekbones like brushes of silk, while the hair covering his scalp reminded her of the shimmering feathers on the wings of a large gray and black bird. And just for a brief moment she wondered what color his eyes were.

Would they be as dark as his hair, or would they be a compelling lighter contrast to his sun-browned, olive skin?

She sat down on the side of the bed and picked up his hand, measuring his pulse. It fluttered weakly under her fingertips. He was still alive! Placing a hand on his forehead, she pulled it away quickly. His flesh was hot and dry.

"Hold the lamp, Poppa, while I take a better look."

Raul moved closer and took the lamp from her. He averted his gaze as Serena's fingers moved gently over David's head and cheek.

"He needs a doctor," she concluded. "He's going to need sutures to close the wound along his temple. He also must have antibiotics to combat any infections that may have set in. His fever is probably somewhere near one-o-three."

Raul's hand wavered slightly. "I've already sent for one. Is he going to make it?"

Serena's gaze met his. "I'm not sure."

"You're a nurse. You should know."

Her gaze narrowed. "I'm a health care professional, not a miracle worker. And my professional opinion is that if the bleeding doesn't stop, or if his body temperature continues to rise, then yes, he will die."

"He can't," Raul whispered.

"I'll stay with him and do what I can until the doctor arrives."

Raul placed the lamp on the side table and raced out of the room. He needed to make certain Rodrigo had sent for the doctor. He had been called many things, but he was not a murderer. As much as he despised David Cole, he never would have deliberately taken his life. Besides, he needed the man alive.

Serena unwrapped the sheet covering David's body, searching for other wounds. The golden light illuminated a perfectly formed male body that appeared to be at the peak of superior conditioning. There wasn't an ounce of excess flesh or fat on his frame. He was lean and muscular at the same time. There was no doubt that he worked out regularly.

Her professional gaze moved slowly over the matted hair on his chest, his flat belly, and down to his long, muscular legs. Her fingers went to his right ankle. It was swollen twice its normal size, and she hoped it was only severely sprained, not broken.

A flurry of questions swirled in her mind as she retreated to an adjoining bathroom and filled a large ceramic pitcher with cool water. Cradling the pitcher in a matching bowl, she carried them back to the bedroom. She returned to the bathroom a second time and came back with a facecloth and towel. She needed to cleanse the wound and attempt to check the bleeding.

Sitting on the side of the bed, Serena emptied half the pitcher of water into the bowl. Methodically, she wet the cloth, wrang it out, then laid it gently along the cheek of the man lying so still, so motionless, on the bed in her parents' guest bedroom.

She repeated the motion at least a dozen times before most of the blood was washed away. Her eyebrows shifted when she finally surveyed the extent of the wound. Her diagnosis was correct: he would require sutures. The open laceration began at the sphenoid bone and ended mid-cheek; she doubted whether it would heal without leaving a noticeable scar.

David stirred restlessly as he tried surfacing from the heavy darkness holding him prisoner. His tongue felt as if it were too large for his mouth, and the pain in his head tightened like a vise. Had someone put something in his drink?

Opening his mouth several times he tried forming the words, but nothing came out. Was he mute? After several attempts he managed, *"Tengo dolor."*

Serena placed a cool hand on his hot forehead. Even though he wasn't fully conscious he'd spoken Spanish, and she assumed it was his native tongue.

"I know you're in pain," she replied in the same language. "You've hurt your head." Resting the cool cloth over his left eye, she pulled his head to her breasts, cradling him gently.

David mumbled incoherently before he retreated to a place

where there was no pain. He felt himself floating, high above the ground. He floated above treetops, sailing along the wind currents with large, powerful birds.

A sweet, haunting fragrance wafted in his nostrils, and he wondered how was he able to smell flowers so close to heaven. He soared higher and higher, then fell headlong toward the earth in a dizzying tailspin. He opened his mouth to scream. However, nothing came out. The ground rose up quickly to meet him, but instead of crashing he was lifted up again.

This time he felt a pair of comforting arms holding him gently and the voice of an angel telling him that he was going to be all right. She was going to take care of him. Something unknown whispered that he had died and gone to heaven.

Serena realized the man in her arms had quieted, retreating to a world of darkness and forgetfulness once again. She eased his head onto another pillow, noting that the flow of blood had slowed. Covering his body with a sheet, she turned and left the room. She needed to change her clothes before the doctor arrived.

It wasn't until she was in her bedroom that she wondered about the man, wanting to know who he was, what had happened to him so that he'd sustained such a serious injury, and what he was doing at *La Montaña*.

She quickly exchanged her bathrobe and nightgown for a pair of jeans and an oversized T-shirt. At the last minute she brushed and secured her curly hair off her face with an elastic headband, displaying her round face to its most attractive advantage.

It had taken her less than ten minutes to change her clothes, but in that time the doctor had arrived and begun an extensive examination of the injuries of the man in the bed at Interior Minister Raul Cordero-Vega's country residence.

Standing in a far corner of the bedroom next to her father, Serena stared at the incredibly young looking doctor as he checked his patient's vital signs.

"Who is he, Poppa?" she asked Raul quietly.

"Dr. Rivera."

"Not the doctor."

Raul hesitated. He had to tell Serena the truth—or most of it. She would find out eventually. "His name is David Cole. He's an American businessman."

"What is he doing in Costa Rica?"

"He came to meet with me."

Serena shifted a delicately arched eyebrow. "What happened to him?"

"Rodrigo found him in an abandoned van several kilometers from the house. He recognized him and brought him here."

Her next question died on her lips as the doctor stood up and motioned for Raul.

"Señor Vega. I'd like to talk to you." He put up a hand as Serena followed closely behind her father. "Please, Señorita, do not come any closer."

"It's all right, Dr. Rivera. My daughter is a nurse," Raul explained.

Leandro Rivera's eyes widened as he took in the petite figure beside one of Costa Rica's most revered government officials. He knew Vega had a son, but he hadn't known of a daughter.

He smiled easily. "Will you assist me, Señorita Vega?"

"It's Morris, not Vega," she corrected quickly. "And yes, I will assist you."

Raul missed the obvious interest in Leandro Rivera's gaze as the young doctor stared openly at Serena. "How is he, Doctor?"

Leandro jerked his attention back to Raul. "He's suffered a severe concussion. There's been some trauma to the orbit opening and sphenoid bone. His right ankle is also severely bruised. I won't know if there's a break unless it is X-rayed. But it's his head injury that concerns me."

"My daughter said that he's going to need to be sutured."

Leandro nodded. "She's correct. The laceration is too deep to close on its own."

"What are his chances for surviving?"

"I wish I could be more optimistic, Señor Vega, but we'll have to wait."

"How long?" Raul snapped in frustration.

"We'll have to wait to see whether he regains consciousness, and if the medication I give him will counteract the infections in his body. Even if we can break his fever, there still is the risk that he may have sustained some brain damage."

Serena placed a hand on her father's shoulder. "Poppa, Dr. Rivera and I will take over now. Please go and wait in your study for us to do what we have to do here."

Raul stared at Serena, a gamut of emotions crossing his face. It was the second time that night that she'd ordered him about. The tiny girl he had taken into his household and claimed as his own daughter had grown up into a beautiful woman who was still a stranger to him. And it was only now that he realized that he had never taken the time to get to know who Serena Morris actually was. He had called her daughter, yet had never legally adopted her. She continued to carry the name of a man who had not lived long enough to see her birth; a man whose face she only knew through old photographs, while he had bounced her on his knee, sung native Costa Rican songs to her, and nicknamed her *Chica*.

He loved her, but he hadn't given her the attention he had given his son. Gabriel was the fruit of his loins, but Serena was the delight of his heart. She was the joy in his life, because she looked so much like the woman he had fallen in love with at first sight.

He might have temporarily lost his son, but he still had a daughter. A daughter who would come to know the full extent of his love before she returned home to the United States.

"I will wait," he said quietly, then turned and left the room, closing the door behind him.

Dr. Leandro Rivera removed his lightweight linen jacket and rolled back the cuffs of his shirt, his gaze fixed on Serena Morris. He picked up a package of sterile, latex gloves and handed them to her before reaching into his large, black bag for another pair.

"Let's get to work, Señorita Morris."

She smiled at him, delighting him with the soft crinkling of skin around her large, round eyes. "Please call me Serena."

He returned her smile. "Only if you'll call me Leandro."

There was the familiar resounding snap of latex as they pushed their hands and fitted their fingers into the gloves. And, as if they had worked together many times in the past, the doctor and nurse shifted the patient until the light coming from the bedside lamp highlighted the left side of his face.

Serena climbed up on the bed, holding David Cole's head firmly as Leandro prepared to repair his injured face.

CHAPTER 4

Serena silently admired Dr. Leandro Rivera's skill as he deftly closed the deep wound. He covered his handiwork with Steri-Strips and large gauze dressing that covered the entire left side of David Cole's face. Their patient had not stirred throughout the emergency medical procedure, enabling them to work quickly and efficiently. It had been accomplished without a local anaesthetic.

Leandro withdrew several syringes from his bag and handed them to Serena. "I'm going to leave a few vials of antibiotics with you to administer every six hours."

"I'm going to need a stethoscope and a sphygmomanometer," she informed him.

He gave her a questioning look, then glanced at the syringes in her hand. "Your father said that you're a nurse."

She smiled at the tall, good-looking doctor whose delicate features were better suited to a woman. Gleaming black hair covered his well-shaped head, and only a deep wave across the crown kept it from being labeled straight. His slanting, dark eyes and rich, golden complexion boasted a blending of Chinese and of the Ticos, who were identified as direct descendants of Spanish settlers.

"I am a nurse. But not here. I received my formal training in the United States," she explained.

"You are not a Tica?" Leandro questioned, using the self-appointed nickname Costa Ricans called themselves.

"No. I am American. I was born in the States, but I was raised here when my mother married my stepfather."

So, that explained why he hadn't heard that Minister Vega claimed a daughter, Leandro mused. "Do you live in the United States?" he questioned as he prepared a syringe filled with a potent antibiotic.

"I've lived there for the past twelve years."

Concentrating on swabbing an area high on David's bare hip, he continued his questioning. "Do you think you'd ever come back here to live?"

"I don't know," she replied as honestly as she could.

There was a time when she thought about returning to Costa Rica—after her marriage ended less than a year after it began—but she didn't. She hadn't wanted to begin the practice of running away. In the end she'd remained in New York City, where she saw her ex-husband every day until he left the hospital to set up a practice with another doctor.

Leandro injected David with an antibiotic. Turning back to Serena, he flashed a wide grin. "I set up my practice three months ago, and I could use an experienced nurse to assist me."

"I'll keep that in mind."

She did not say that she would never get involved with, work with, or marry another doctor. Being the wife of Dr. Xavier Osbourne for eight months had changed her forever.

"I'll leave my stethoscope and sphygmomanometer for you to monitor his blood pressure, and a digital thermometer. I'll also leave my telephone number. Contact me if his condition worsens before I return tomorrow morning. If he comes to he probably won't feel like eating, but try to get some liquids into him."

Serena nodded. "I'll take good care of him."

Leandro smiled again. "I'm sure you will. You and David Cole are fellow Americans, and I wouldn't want his family to think that he received less than adequate medical treatment while in Costa Rica."

"Why would they think that?"

He stared at her, complete surprise on his face. "You don't know who David Cole is?"

She shook her head, and auburn-tinged curls danced softly around her neck. "No, I don't."

"Then I suggest that you ask your father about him."

She was left to ponder his cryptic statement as he prepared to take his leave. After placing the medical supplies and equipment in a drawer in a highboy, she returned to her bedroom to retrieve her watch. It was nearly midnight, and in another six hours she would have to give her patient another injection.

Serena walked out of her bedroom at the same time her father made his way toward David Cole's. "Poppa." He stopped and turned to face her. "I need to talk to you."

Raul waited for Serena's approach, noting the frown marring her forehead. It was a look he was familiar with. Juanita affected the same expression whenever she was annoyed with something or someone.

"Yes, *Chica.*"

"Just who is David Cole and what is he doing here?"

Raul's mouth tightened noticeably under his trim white mustache. "I thought I answered those questions."

"You only answered part of them. Who are the Coles?" she demanded.

He thought of not answering her, but realized that she would eventually discover that he intended to hold David hostage until Gabriel was released from his U.S. prison.

"The Coles are one of the wealthiest black families in the United States. Their money comes from the exportation of tropical produce and the sale and rental of private villas and vacation resorts throughout Central America and the Caribbean. I was to meet with David to finalize the sale of his family's last Costa Rican holding."

"How was he injured?"

"I don't know," he replied honestly. "You have to ask him when he regains consciousness."

If he regains consciousness, she mused. The fact that he had not awakened when the doctor stitched his face alarmed her, and she wondered if David Cole wouldn't fare better in a hospital, where sophisticated machines could monitor his brain's activity. She made a mental note to speak to Leandro about moving his patient.

"I'm going to sit up with him until Dr. Rivera returns," Serena offered.

Raul laid an outstretched hand on the side of her face. "Aren't you tired from your flight, *Chica?*"

"A little," she confirmed, "but I'm used to functioning on little or no sleep." And she was. She couldn't remember the last time that she had managed to get eight uninterrupted hours of sleep. She worked at a large, urban hospital where cutbacks had caused nurses working double shifts to become the norm rather than the exception.

Raul managed a tired smile. The strain of the past two weeks and now the fact that David Cole appeared more dead than alive had depleted the last of his waning spirit. All he wanted to do was go to sleep and awake to find his son standing at his side and the knowledge that the Coles had completely divested themselves of everything Costa Rican.

"I'm going to sleep in my study. I don't want to disturb your mother." He dropped his hand and motioned with his head toward the bed. "I want you to call me if his condition worsens. As long as he resides under my roof I feel responsible for him."

"Are you going to contact his family?"

"Yes," he replied honestly. He didn't think the Coles would be too pleased to hear his demands. "Good night, *Chica.*"

"Good night, Poppa."

Serena pulled an armchair and matching ottoman close to the bed. Turning off the lamp, she settled down in the chair and raised her bare feet to the ottoman. The fingers of her right hand curled around David Cole's inert left one, and within minutes she joined him in sleep. There was only the whisper of her soft breathing keeping perfect rhythm with that of her patient.

* * *

David stirred restlessly, his eyelids fluttering uncontrollably. The insufferable heat along with the oppressive weight had returned. He couldn't move; he couldn't see or speak. He had not gone to heaven, but Hell!

What had he done to fall from Grace, to spend an eternity in Hell? Had he been too arrogant, too vain? Who had he turned away when they needed his help? What sins had he committed that would not be forgiven?

His head thrashed back and forth on the pillow as pain assaulted the left side of his face. His uninjured eye opened after several attempts, and he encountered a wall of solid blackness. He was in a deep hole in the bowels of the earth, with an unseen raging fire that continually scorched his mind and body.

He heard a long, suffering moan of pain, not realizing that the voice was his own. "Help him, help him," he pleaded over and over. He wanted someone to help the tormented man so he would stop the heartbreaking moaning.

Serena came awake immediately. Moving from the chair to the bed, she sat down next to David and laid her hand on his forehead. The heat under her fingers disturbed her. His fever had not abated. She reached over and turned on the lamp, a soft glow coming from the three-way bulb. Glancing at her watch, she saw that it was only four-ten, and she had to wait another two hours before she administered another dose of the antibiotic.

David's thrashing had twisted the sheet around his waist, exposing his chest and legs. The tightly wrapped bandage on his right foot gleamed like a beacon against his dark, muscular, hairy leg.

He continued his pleading for someone to help the man in pain as Serena inserted the thermometer in his right ear. Within seconds she read the findings. His body's temperature was 102.8.

"I'm going to help you," she replied softly, realizing that he had spoken English instead of Spanish.

David heard the soothing feminine voice, his brow furrowing

in confusion. The voice sounded like that of his oldest brother's wife. Why wasn't Parris Cole with her husband and children? What was she doing in Hell with him?

"Parris…" His voice faded as he floated back to a place where he no longer heard the man's moaning or his sister-in-law talking to him.

Serena filled the large crock pitcher with cold water from the bathroom and emptied it into the matching bowl. Methodically, she dipped a cloth in the water and bathed David's fevered body with the cooling liquid.

She laid the cloth over the right side of his face, waiting until the moisture was absorbed by the heat of his burning flesh. Repeating the motion, she bathed his throat, chest, and torso.

Her touch was professional, although as a woman she could not help but admire the perfection of his conditioned male body. Her fingertips traced the defined muscles over his flat belly and along his thighs and legs. His uninjured foot was narrow and arched, yet large enough to support his impressive bulk. The fact that his hands and feet were professionally groomed was testimony that David Cole was fastidious about his appearance. He had every right to be, she thought, because he truly was a magnificent male. What intrigued her were the calluses on the palms of his hands and fingers. Businessmen usually did not claim callused hands, and she wondered if he perhaps were skilled in the martial arts.

She had noticed that there was no telltale band of lighter flesh around the third finger of his left hand, indicating he hadn't worn a ring on that finger. Something unknown told her, too, that David Cole was not married, and probably would never marry.

Finishing her ministrations, she covered his body once again with the sheet. This time, instead of sitting on the chair she lay down beside him. Turning on her side, she curved an arm over his flat middle and slept until the silvery light of the full moon was overshadowed by the brighter rays of the rising sun.

CHAPTER 5

June 15

David woke up, the haze lifting and his mind clear for the first time in twelve hours. He opened and closed his right eye several times before he was able to focus on the face looming above his. He saw hair—lots of reddish-brown, Chaka Khan type curls.

"Ouch," he gasped, feeling a sharp prick in his buttocks.

"It's over," Serena said, smiling at her patient. "How are you feeling?"

"Like someone kicked my head in." His voice was ragged and sounded unfamiliar to his ears.

Her smile vanished when she wondered if someone had indeed assaulted him. Answers to questions that nagged at her about David Cole would have to wait, because the injuries he had sustained were more critical than any question she had.

She took his temperature, aware that his uninjured eye followed her every move. She had an answer to one of her questions—his eyes were dark—very dark.

"I think you're going to make it, Señor Cole. Your temperature is down a full degree." Sponging his body with the cool water had helped lower his fever.

Leaning over, she curved an arm under his head, lifting it gently while she held a glass with a straw to his parched lips. "It's water," she informed him when he compressed his mouth in a tight line. "You have to take some liquids or else you're going to become dehydrated."

David felt a wave of dizziness and thought he was going to throw up. "I can't," he mumbled, pushing her hand away.

The glass fell to the bed, the water wetting the sheet and pasting it to his groin. The wet fabric clearly outlined the shape of his maleness, and Serena felt a wave of heat steal into her cheeks. She had bathed every inch of his body, seeing him as a male patient; but observing him in the full daylight, awake, she realized she now saw him as a *man*. A very handsome man.

She released his head, a frown forming between her eyes. "I'm going to get another glass of water and you're going to drink it, or else I'll have the doctor hook up an IV for you. The choice is yours."

David's respiration quickened as his head rolled back and forth on the pillow. "I don't like needles," he moaned.

Leaning over his prone figure, she patted his stubbly cheek. "I suppose that means you'll drink from the glass."

"Sí," he answered in Spanish even though she had spoken to him in English.

Serena worked quickly as she refilled the glass, realizing that he was slipping back to a state where he shut out his pain and everything going on around him. She managed to get David to swallow a half dozen sips of water before he retreated to a place of painless comfort.

There was no doubt that Spanish was his first language and English second. She spoke English the first two years of her life. She'd learned Spanish after she and her mother had moved from Columbus, Ohio, to San José, Costa Rica.

He slept soundly as she changed the bedding, rolling him over on his side as she stripped the bed, and put on a set of clean linen. She was breathing heavily when she finished. As a nursing student she had been trained to change a bed without removing the patient, but shifting David Cole was like moving a boulder uphill with a pencil. He was lean, but she estimated his weight to be close to two hundred pounds.

Retreating to her own bathroom to shower and change her clothes, she heard doors on the lower level opening and closing. It was six o'clock and the household was beginning to stir.

She adjusted the water in the shower stall until it was lukewarm, reveling in the sensation of the rejuvenating waters flowing over her body. The healing moisture washed away her fatigue and tension.

Serena lingered in the shower beyond her normally allotted time. If she had been back in the States, she would have showered in three minutes after a strenuous jogging workout in New York City's Central Park before heading off to work.

Shampooing her hair twice, she applied a conditioner/detangler, then lathered her body with a scented bath gel and rinsed her hair and body. The seductive aroma of flowers and musk lingered on her sleek, moist form.

She turned off the water and stepped out of the shower stall. Reaching for a towel, she folded it expertly around her head, turban-style. A second towel blotted the droplets of water from her body as she bent and stretched, using isometric maneuvers.

The image of her ex-husband came to mind, eliciting a smile. The best thing to have come from being married to Xavier was his emphasis on body conditioning. A number one draft pick by the National Football League's New York Giants, Xavier was able to combine his two passions: football and medicine. He attended medical school in the off-season, choosing sports medicine as a specialty.

She met Xavier when he was a resident at the hospital. She had been the head nurse in the operating room, and the attraction between them was spontaneous.

They dated for four months, then married. Serena realized their marriage was in trouble before their honeymoon ended. Xavier had managed to camouflage his explosive displays of jealousy while they had dated, but the second day into their honeymoon he verbally abused a man whom he thought had made a pass at her. The only thing that prevented a violent confrontation was that the man did not understand English. What should have been an exciting and romantic interlude in France became a suffocating prison when she refused to leave their hotel room until the day of their scheduled departure.

Xavier tried curbing his unfounded bouts of jealousy, but it all ended for Serena when he confronted her and the hospital orderly who had walked with her to hail a taxi in a blinding, late spring snowstorm, brandishing a scalpel while threatening to cut the man into tiny pieces.

Her marriage ended that night after she checked into a hotel instead of returning to their apartment. A week later, with two New York City police officers in attendance, she moved her personal belongings out of the spacious Fifth Avenue apartment overlooking Central Park, and six weeks later Xavier was served with certain documents. She hadn't asked him for anything from the union except that he agree to an annulment. He did not contest her demands. And she took her maiden name.

Her exercise regimen increased her stamina, and her jogging endurance resulted in her entering the annual New York City Marathon. It had taken three years, but she now could guarantee that she would cross the finish line with the first fifty entrants. She didn't have the Central Park jogging trails in Limón, but there was always the beach. She decided to wait another day before beginning her jogging regimen. The lingering effects of jet lag continued to disrupt her body's circadian rhythms.

Her motions were mechanical as she smoothed a scented moisturizer over her body, walked into the adjoining bedroom, slipped into a pair of floral print panties, and covered them with a loose, flowing, cotton tank dress. Poppy-red mules matched the airy cotton fabric.

There was a light knock on her bedroom door moments before her mother's head emerged. A bright smile softened the noticeable strain on Juanita's face.

"I knew you'd be up, Sweetheart," she said, walking into the room. "No matter how tired you are, you never can sleep beyond sunrise."

Serena returned the smile. "Good morning, Mother. You look wonderful this morning."

"Makeup does wonders," Juanita replied.

Relieved that her mother had left the sanctuary of her bedroom, she curved an arm around Juanita's slim waist and kissed her cheek. Her clear gaze swept over the older woman's neatly coiffed, short hair and her petite body swathed in a crisp, white linen sheath.

"Makeup cannot improve on perfection."

Juanita's smile was radiant. "You're the best daughter a woman could ever have. *When* I have you," she added.

"Mother, please. Don't start in on me. Not now."

Seeing the anguish on Serena's face, she nodded. "You're right—not now."

Over an early breakfast she'd shared with her husband, after he'd awakened her with the encouraging news of their president's intervention regarding Gabriel, they'd discussed their daughter.

Raul voiced concern that Serena had not let go of the pain from her short-lived marriage, recognizing there was an obvious hardness about her that wasn't there before she married Xavier Osbourne. He'd also revealed that David Cole lay under their roof, recuperating from injuries he had sustained somewhere in Costa Rica.

"I want to tell you that your father and I will be leaving within half an hour," Juanita continued in a soft tone.

"Where are you going?"

"We're flying back to San José. President Montalvo wants to talk to Raul about Gabriel. He's set up a meeting with the American ambassador. Hopefully he can work out a deal where Gabriel will be granted bail, and when he returns to Costa Rica he will be placed under house arrest until his trial."

A powerful relief filled Serena with her mother's statement.

She wanted to see Gabe, hold him close, and reinforce the bond that had developed the moment she held him in her arms twenty-six yeas ago. Closing her eyes, she mumbled a silent prayer.

Seeing the gesture, Juanita smiled, and it was her turn to kiss her daughter's cheek. "I'd better go now. Try to make David Cole as comfortable as possible. Even though he and Raul have never gotten along, I like the young man. The problem may be that they are too much alike to recognize their own negative traits."

Serena pondered her mother's assessment of David Cole after she and Raul left *La Montaña* for the short flight to the capital city. If David and her stepfather shared the most obvious negative trait, then it would have to be arrogance.

She looked in on David and found him asleep and resting comfortably. His skin was noticeably cooler, indicating that the antibiotic had begun working against the infections invading his body. Sighing in relief, she went downstairs to see after her own breakfast.

CHAPTER 6

David woke to the sound of rain tapping against the glass of the French doors. The heat had vanished, along with the oppressive weight, but hunger and thirst had taken their place. The rumblings and contractions gripping his stomach had him wondering when he'd eaten last.

His right hand went to his cheek, fingertips encountering an emerging beard. He jerked his hand away. The stubble on his jaw verified that he hadn't shaved in days. Once he had begun shaving at sixteen, he had never permitted more than a day's growth to cover his cheeks.

Scenes from the wedding flooded his memory. Had he drunk so much that he lay in a drunken stupor for days without getting up to shower and shave?

A frown marred his smooth forehead. He had not gotten drunk. In fact he was very alert and quite sober when he boarded the jet for his flight to San José, Costa Rica! He was not in Florida, but in Costa Rica.

Suddenly he was aware of where he was and what had happened to him. Someone had broken into his hotel room and assaulted him while he was in the shower. Who was it that hit him, and why?

He wasn't given time to ponder the questions. He heard voices—male and female. It was the female's voice that held his rapt attention. He had heard that voice before—but where? It sounded so much like the husky, velvety whisper that belonged to his sister-in-law. He used to tease his oldest brother's wife, telling Parris that she should've been a radio disc jockey because of her hypnotic, X-rated, dulcet tones.

The woman sounded like Parris, but he knew it couldn't be she. This woman spoke Spanish like a native, while Parris had achieved only a perfunctory facility of the language.

Turning his head toward the sound of the voices, David discerned that he had limited use of his vision. Reaching up, he touched the bandage covering the left side of his face. The pressure of his fingers on the area brought on a wave of blinding pain.

The questions tumbled over themselves in his head. Where was he in Costa Rica? How many days and nights had he lost since his arrival? He didn't have to wait for some of the answers.

"*¡Buenos días!,* Señor Cole. I am Dr. Leandro Rivera. How are you feeling this morning?"

David examined the young doctor for a full minute with his uninjured eye before he replied, *"Quiero algo de comer y beber."*

Leandro smiled and placed a slender hand on his patient's forehead. The fact that David Cole was hungry and thirsty was a good sign. There was no doubt that he had not suffered any serious head trauma.

"Señorita Morris will make certain you'll get something to eat and drink, but first I want to check your face."

David could not see the Miss Morris the doctor referred to, but he could sense her presence and smell her perfume. It was a sensual, floral-musk scent. Closing his eyes, he tried remembering where he had detected that scent before.

Sitting down on the chair beside the bed, Leandro pushed his hands into a pair of sterile latex gloves, removed the gauze dressing, and peered closely at the stitches holding the flesh together along the left side of his patient's face. There was only a little redness, but no swelling. He had to smile. Given the conditions, he had done an excellent job of repairing David Cole's face. The wound would heal, leaving a barely noticeable scar— a thin scar that could be completely eradicated by a highly skilled plastic surgeon.

The area over the left eye did not look as good. The eye was still frightfully swollen, and the flesh over the lid claimed vivid hues of red, purple, and black.

Leandro replaced the dressing with smaller butterfly bandages, leaving the left eye uncovered. He would caution Serena not to let David see his face until most of the swelling had gone away. The discoloration would take days, if not more than a week, to fade completely.

He checked the right foot, manipulating the toes and registering David's reaction. He winced slightly, but didn't moan or cry out. Leandro had his answer. The ankle was not broken.

"How's my face?" David asked.

"Healing," Leandro said noncommittally.

"I know it's healing," David retorted. "What I want to know is what did you do to it?"

"I put thirty-six stitches in your face to close a gaping laceration."

David stiffened as if the doctor had struck him when he realized his face would be scarred. Closing his eye, he turned his head, the uninjured side of his face pressed to the pillow.

David Claridge Cole knew himself better than anyone, and his haughty self-image was the result of not only bearing the Cole name, but also of his inheriting the genes of his African-American-Cuban ancestors.

He had entered adolescence with full knowledge that girls were attracted first to his face, then his family's wealth. This all continued into his twenties, once he had made a name for himself as a talented jazz musician. The band had garnered worldwide popularity, while he had personally amassed groupies who waited at stage doors for him in every city Night Mood toured.

So many things had changed since he left the band: he'd become CEO for ColeDiz International Ltd., had a custom-designed, ocean-view house built in Boca Raton, Florida, that he hadn't moved into, and he was in the planning stages of starting up his own recording company. What he had not planned for was marrying. He still had too many projects to realize before he settled down with one woman and fathered children.

"Where am I?" he questioned, his voice muffled against the pillow.

Serena looked at Leandro, who nodded. She stepped over to the bed and touched David's bare shoulder. Shifting, he stared up at her, his eye widening noticeably.

He remembered seeing hair—lots of it—and now he knew who the hair belonged to. Dark curls were secured on the top of the young woman's head, a few wayward ones spilling over her high, smooth forehead.

She was a rich, lush shade of brown spice: cinnamon, nutmeg, ginger, and cloves. And the hypnotic fragrance he had detected earlier came from her. It was a seductive musk with an underlying scent of flowers. Her perfectly rounded face claimed high cheekbones, a short, rounded nose, soft chin, a full, overly ripe mouth that was a deep, rich, powdery cocoa shade, and a pair of large, round eyes that were the clearest brown he had ever seen. There was just a hint of gold in their shimmering depths.

"You're in Limón," she said, speaking English. "My father's driver found you in an abandoned van," she continued in Spanish. "He recognized your face and had you brought here." David nodded slowly, grimacing. Serena was aware of the effort it took for him to move his head.

The voice. The deep, husky voice also belonged to her. She was the angel in his dream. She was the one who held him, comforted him, and offered him succor during his pain and suffering. And the pain was back—with a throbbing vengeance.

"How did you come to be in the van?" Leandro questioned.

"Someone broke into my hotel room and hit me while I was in the shower."

"Why do you think they hit you, Señor Cole?" Leandro continued.

"I...I don't know," he gasped, breathing heavily. The image of the large man towering above him in the shower came back, along with the memory of the blinding, red hot pain. He wondered why he had been assaulted. By whom and for what reason?

Serena felt the muscles in his shoulder tighten under her hand. Without David saying anything she knew he was in pain.

"Why don't you rest, while I get you something to eat and drink?" Her gaze met Leandro's and she motioned for him to follow her.

They stepped outside the bedroom and she rounded on him. "David Cole may be your patient, but he is in my parents' home. My father has assumed responsibility for him. And that means he will monitor any police investigation and *interrogation*."

Leandro stared at her, complete surprise on his face. His expression mirrored Serena's own shock at her reprimand. Never in her nursing career had she ever come to the defense of a patient. Perhaps it had something to do with the setting, and just maybe it had something to do with the patient, but she was totally out of character. Sharing David Cole's bed had also been out of character for her.

What was it about the man that made her go against everything she had been taught as a health care professional? Over the past twelve years she had earned a B.S., R.N. and a Master's in Public Health, and not once had she ever been cited for any professional violation.

What she had to do was acknowledge the reason behind her behavior: fear. Unconsciously she had substituted David Cole for Gabriel Vega. David, in a foreign land and imprisoned by pain, was in a position so like Gabriel's. The only difference was that once David healed he would be free to return home. Her brother, if found guilty of the charges against him, would more than likely forfeit his young life.

They apologized in unison.

"I'm sorry, Leandro."

"Forgive me, Serena."

Serena gave him a warm smile, her lush mouth softening attractively. "I suppose I'm a little overzealous."

He returned her smile. "You have every right to be. And you're right. Your father is paying me to treat Señor Cole, not interrogate him."

She touched the sleeve of his lightweight jacket. "When will you return?"

"I'll be back tonight."

Serena's clear brown eyes were shadowed by sweeping black lashes. "Perhaps we could share dinner," she offered, hoping to make amends for her scathing rebuke.

Leandro nodded. "I would like that. Is eight too late? I have office hours until six."

"Eight is perfect."

She walked Leandro down the staircase and waited until he drove away in his Jeep before she returned to the kitchen to see about getting something for David Cole to eat.

The scent of the woman lingered in the room long after she left, and David drew in a deep breath, savoring the lingering smell of her.

A crooked smile softened his parched lips when he recalled the soft press of a feminine body next to his. He'd awakened briefly during the night to find her beside him and tried reaching out for her, but couldn't. He had been too weak.

Women who shared his bed always shared their bodies with him. But this time it was very different. He found it difficult to move his head or even sit up. He was as weak and helpless as a newborn.

Feeling pressure in the lower part of his body, he knew he had to leave the bed or embarrass himself. Moving slowly, he turned over to his left and half-sat and half-lay on the bed. He reached across his body with his right hand and pulled himself into a sitting position, using the headboard for support. Objects in the room swayed before they righted themselves. He sat on the edge of the bed for a full minute before his feet touched the floor. The sheet fell away from his naked body as he stood up. Without warning, the floor came up to meet him, and seconds before he slipped back into a well of blackness he heard a woman screaming his name.

CHAPTER 7

"David!"

There was no mistaking the hysteria in Serena's voice as she knelt beside him. He lay facedown on the floor, motionless. What she feared most was that he had reopened the gash along his cheek. She managed to roll him over, sighing in relief when she saw that no sign of blood showed through the bandages.

He groaned, then opened his one good eye. Serena's face wavered dizzily before he was able to focus. "I have to go to the bathroom," he explained, his breathing labored.

Slipping an arm under his neck, she cradled his head gently within the crook of her elbow. "I'm going to have to help you whenever you want to get out of bed."

David tried shaking his head, but gave up the effort as a ribbon of pain tightened like a vise over his left eye. "No," he whispered.

"Yes," she countered. "You've suffered a concussion, and it's going to be a while before you'll be able to stand up on your own."

Gritting his teeth, he tried pushing himself up off the floor. "Let me go."

Despite his weakened condition, David Cole was still twice as strong as she was, and Serena couldn't hold him when he turned away and pushed himself to his knees.

"David! David," she repeated. This time his name came out softer, almost pleading. "Let me help you."

He halted, staring at her. There was a silent plea in his gaze that implored her to understand his predicament. It was enough that he was injured, helpless, and naked. But it was an entirely different matter that he needed to relieve himself.

Something in his expression communicated itself to her, and Serena nodded slowly. She understood his embarrassment. "I'm a nurse. This is what I do—every day. You're my patient, David Cole, and I'm going to take care of you whether you like it or no, or whether you're embarrassed because you have to do what every living organism must do to survive." Pausing, she noted resignation in his expression. "Now, are you going to cooperate with me?"

Did he have a choice? The pressure in his lower body was so intense that he doubted whether he could make it to the bathroom before he shamed himself.

He hated the weakness, his helplessness. He had always prided himself on having excellent health, only succumbing to exhaustion after a multi-city tour. But exhaustion was a part of his past once he left the band.

Relenting, he said, "Yes." The single word came out in a lingering sigh.

Serena braced a shoulder under his armpit, supporting his greater weight against her hip, and helped him to his feet. He put one foot in front of the other, taking long strides despite the fact that his knees shook uncontrollably.

"Easy there, Sport," she teased. They made it to the adjoining bath, she helping David over to the commode. Sitting down heavily, he sighed in relief.

Stepping back, Serena smiled down at him. "I'll wait outside for you. Call me when you're finished."

"Thanks." The single word conveyed assuagement and appreciation.

She returned to the bedroom, busying herself smoothing out the sheet and straightening the lightweight blanket on the bed. The rain had stopped and she opened the floor-to-ceiling French doors. The sweet, cloying fragrance of tropical flowers and damp earth was redolent in the humid air. A rising fog hung over the nearby rain forest, turning the landscape a wispy, heather gray.

Ten minutes passed and still David hadn't called out to her. Shrugging a bare shoulder, Serena stood at the open French doors staring out at the land surrounding *La Montaña,* recalling the happy times she had spent there.

Her family moved into the large, beautifully designed house twenty years ago, the day she and Gabe turned ten and six, respectively. The move had been planned to coincide with a most lavish birthday celebration, and never had she felt so grown up as she did that day. The housewarming/birthday gala was never duplicated—not even when she was formally presented to Costa Rican society during her fifteenth year. Her mother had gone along with the Spanish custom of presenting her daughter at fifteen instead of the customary American Sweet Sixteen and coming-out observances.

Gabe, mesmerized by the grandeur of the house and the number of people filling the expansive living room, never spoke more than ten words all that day. After all of the celebrants left he spent the night sobbing uncontrollably. He wanted his old house and old room back.

Serena realized at an early age that her younger brother detested change. He only wanted what appeared to be safe and familiar. Gabe surprised her and his family when he decided that he didn't want to attend a Costa Rican college. He wanted to follow his sister to the United States.

She was elated when Gabe was admitted to a college in South Florida. They were more than thirteen hundred miles apart, but they got to visit each other more often than if he had remained in Costa Rica.

Their roles were reversed once she decided to end her marriage to Xavier. Gabe flew up to New York from Miami and stayed with her until she settled into her new apartment, and she suspected that he had confronted Xavier about his treatment of his sister. Xavier had alluded to it when they met again at her lawyer's office, but when she asked her brother about the incident he refused to discuss it with her.

From the time that he was born she had taken care of and protected Gabriel Diego Vega. However, at twenty-eight she'd let him protect her for the first time.

Serena found it hard to believe that two years had passed so quickly. It was only two years ago that she had become the wife of Dr. Xavier Osbourne. Determination hardened her delicate jaw. Xavier was her past, and she had taken a solemn oath to never marry again.

All thoughts of her brother fled when she glanced down at her watch. David Cole had been alone in the bathroom for almost fifteen minutes. Retracing her steps, she hurried into the bathroom and went completely still. Anger and annoyance pulsed through her as the sound of running water filled the space.

Taking the few remaining steps to the shower stall, she flung open the door. David sat on the floor of the stall, water beating down on his head and rinsing a layer of soap from his large body. She reached over and slapped the lever controlling the flow of water.

David's head came up slowly and he glared at her. "What the hell do you think you're doing?"

Serena swallowed back the angry retort threatening to spill from her constricted throat. "What do you think *you're* doing?"

"Taking a shower," he shot back.

"I said you could relieve yourself, not shower."

"I needed a shower."

Resting both hands on her hips, her gaze narrowed. "What you needed to do was keep those stitches dry for at least forty-eight hours."

"I was beginning to smell."

"Let *me* determine whether you smell, Mr. Cole. And if you do begin to smell, I'll wash you."

Bracing a hand against the tiled wall, David pushed himself to his feet. He rested his forehead against the cool tiles as a wave of dizziness gripped him, while managing to swallow back the bile rising in his throat.

"You will not wash me." His refusal came out haltingly, from between clenched teeth.

Her hand went to his thick wrist and she led him slowly out of the stall. "What are you, David Cole? Stubborn, stupid, or maybe just obsessively vain?"

David leaned heavily against her side when she picked up a thick towel and blotted the water from his body. His gaze was fixed on the profusion of curling hair, neatly pinned up off her long neck. As she leaned closer the soft curls brushed his shoulder, causing him to jerk his arm away.

Her head came up and their gazes met. Even with his limited vision he was astounded by the perfection of the face only inches from his own. Her rich, dark beauty was hypnotic, and he couldn't look away. Silken, black eyebrows arched over her large, round eyes, giving her the look of a startled little girl.

But there was nothing girlish about her body. It was slender as well as lush. The loose-fitting slip dress could not disguise the curve of her full breasts or her rounded hips. From his superior height he could easily see down the bodice of her dress whenever she leaned over, and he felt like a pervert because he liked what he saw. The rich, even layers of browns on her face extended to her shoulders and breasts, reminding him of spun sugar. He didn't know why he thought of her in terms of foods. Perhaps, he mused, because she looked good enough to eat.

"To answer your question, Miss Morris, I am neither of those adjectives. What I am is hungry, thirsty, and in lots of pain. And what I don't like is not being able to take care of myself."

Reaching up, Serena dabbed lightly over the bandages covering his wound, using a corner of the towel. "What you don't have right now is a choice, Mr. Cole. Someone opened your head like a ripe melon, resulting in a severe concussion. You are also running a temperature, which means there is evidence of an infection. You're in my parents' home, where they have assumed responsibility for your safety and recovery. And that means I give the orders and you'll do exactly what you're told to do. Is there anything about what I just said that you don't understand?"

He went completely still, one dark eye focused on her mouth. "Are you in the military?"

His question caught her off guard and she stared back at him, a frown creasing her smooth forehead. "No. Why?"

"Because you give a lot of orders," he shot back.

Her frown disappeared and she gave him a slow, sensual smile. "I only give orders when I have to."

David stared mutely at her smiling face. She'd half-lowered her lids over her hypnotic eyes and stared up at him through her lashes. It was a gesture he'd seen many times when women flirted with him. But this woman was not flirting. What she was doing was ordering him about like a storm trooper.

"Then you must be a supervisor, Miss Morris."

She opened her mouth to come back at him, but didn't. She wasn't going to explain herself. Not to David Cole. He needed her, not the other way around.

Tossing the towel on a chair, she curved an arm around his waist and steered him out of the bathroom. "You're going back to bed and I want you to stay there until I bring you your breakfast. After you eat I'll see if I can't find you something to put on. *La Montaña* is beautiful. However it is hardly the Garden of Eden."

David sat down heavily on the side of the bed, his legs shaking. They weren't shaking because of the weakness wracking his injured body, but because of what Serena had just said.

"*Where* am I?" he whispered.

Serena eased his legs up onto the bed and waited until he lay back against the mound of pillows cradling his shoulders. Pulling the sheet up to his chest, she said, "You're at my parents' house."

"But you said that this is *La Montaña.*"

"It is."

A fist of pain gripped his temples. Clenching his teeth, he closed his eyes. She was lying to him. Her name was Morris, not

Vega. *Raul Cordero-Vega owns La Montaña,* he wanted to shout, but the words never came out. He tried to concentrate on what she'd told him, but his thoughts were a jumble of confusion. She'd said *La Montaña* was her parents' home, and if she wasn't a Vega then what was her connection to the man? Another wave of dizziness accompanied the pain, and within seconds darkness descended and he slipped into a world where there was no pain, no haunting scent of the woman who stood over him.

Serena's fingers grazed David's stubbly cheek before going to his forehead. His brow was moist and clammy. He had over-exerted himself by attempting to shower.

"You're a vain fool, David Cole," she whispered softly. He had lied to her, saying he needed to shower, while the scent of cologne and aftershave still lingered on his large, hard body. The scent of his cologne suited him. It was subtle yet dramatic. It was like its wearer—she knew after less than twelve hours of meeting David Cole for the first time that he was powerful and dramatic.

Despite his physical state, he exuded power and confidence. There was no doubt he was used to giving orders and having those orders followed without question. She recalled some of the rich and powerful people who had been invited to social gatherings at *La Montaña.* They came wearing haute couture and priceless jewels, looking down their noses at the household staff as if they were insects who annoyed them.

A smile softened her lush mouth. Many wealthy people had come to Costa Rica to retire, taking advantage of the weather, Central America's purest democracy and highest standard of living, and the highest degree of economic and social progress. Some came to conduct business because of the nation's political stability, strategic location, infrastructure, inexpensive labor force, and various government incentive programs.

Raul Cordero-Vega, as Minister of the Interior, oversaw the Ministry of Economy, Industry, and Commerce like a despot. The president and his cabinet ministers were aware of her stepfather's zealous nationalistic fervor and did nothing to curtail it. Raul protected Costa Rica for all Ticos.

Serena left David and went downstairs to the kitchen to see if his breakfast was ready. As an American, David Cole was a foreign businessman, and even though Raul had taken David into his home she knew it still did not bode well for the younger man. Like her mother, she had never become involved in Raul's work, but like her mother she knew that he detested all foreign businesses. He referred to them as locusts. They swept through his country, devouring everything in sight before they disappeared like apparitions.

It would be best if David recovered quickly so he could conclude whatever business he had come to Costa Rica to conduct, she mused as she walked into a large kitchen. A large assortment of cooking utensils hung from overhead hooks in the brick wall space.

Luz Maria Hernando smiled and handed Serena a covered tray. "It is ready," she said in accented English. The talented cook took every opportunity she could to use the language. She had come to *La Montaña* a month after it was built as an interim cook and never left. She had secretly asked that Serena teach her to speak English, becoming completely bilingual in the twenty years she lived at the house. She remained in residence at *La Montaña* even when Raul and Juanita returned to San José during the intense summer season. She and Serena were alike because they both loved the heat and the surrounding rain forest.

"Thank you, Doña Maria," Serena said, smiling. She had taken to calling the never-married, middle-aged woman Doña out of respect. At first Luz Maria lectured her sternly, saying she was not worthy of the title Madam, but Serena persisted over the years and Luz Maria accepted the title as well as she accepted accolades for her superior culinary skills.

She had not disclosed the identity of the man sleeping in one of the guest rooms to the cook, telling Luz Maria that one of her father's guests was not feeling well and needed a special diet of soft foods and her special tea, which everyone claimed had magical powers of rejuvenation.

"He will feel much better after he drinks my tea," Luz Maria said in a soft, mysterious tone.

"I have no doubt," Serena agreed. Turning, she walked out of the kitchen with the tray.

Luz Maria never disclosed the ingredients she used to make the tea, but openly promised Serena she would reveal the brew's properties to her when she married and had a child. The older woman said she would pass along her secret recipe because Serena would need it when her children encountered the discomfort and elevated temperatures that usually accompanied teething.

Serena *had* married, but hadn't remained married long enough to plan for children, and her future plans did not include marrying again or having children.

Her footsteps were soft on the carpeted stairway as she made her way up to David Cole's bedroom.

CHAPTER 8

Serena placed the tray on one of the bedside tables, then shook David gently. He didn't stir. It was only after she called his name that he opened his eyes.

Flashing him her sensual smile, she said softly, "It's time for you to eat."

He stared up at her, studying her face as if he had never seen her before. Pushing himself to a sitting position, he ran a hand over his hair. It was still damp from his earlier shower. The sheet had slipped low on his flat belly, and he'd made no attempt to adjust it. When he was fully conscious, his concerns had been where he was and who the woman was who took away his pain and fear and offered him comfort and peace, not his nakedness.

Serena sat down on a chair beside the bed and pulled the sheet up over David's belly. "I'm going to feed you something that is quite similar to oatmeal," she informed him, smiling.

David did not like oatmeal, but he was too hungry to protest. He nodded as she picked up a bowl from the tray. He stiffened noticeably when she spooned a portion of cereal from the bowl and put the spoon to his lips.

"I'll feed myself."

Serena shifted an eyebrow and shook her head. "I don't think so, Mr. Cole. Not the way your hands are shaking."

He looked down at his long, well-groomed fingers, fingers that floated over the keys of a piano and strummed the strings of a guitar with a skill that had elicited chills and tears from those listening to his playing. They were trembling.

"The shaking should go away along with the headache, vertigo, and delirium in a few days." What she didn't tell David was that it would take a lot longer for the bruises over his eye to fade.

Curling his fingers into tight fists, he opened his mouth and closed his eyes, but just as quickly they opened again. The cereal was delicious. It had a sweet, nutty flavor. Within minutes he devoured the cereal.

He was nearly overcome by the warmth and scent of Serena's body as she moved from the chair to sit down on the side of the bed. He wanted to move, yet couldn't. Watching her intently, he saw her reach for a delicate china cup filled with a dark liquid.

"What is that?"

Leaning in closer, her shoulder nearly touching his bare chest, Serena said mysteriously, "A magic brew."

David managed a lopsided, dimpled smile. "Will it turn me into a prince?"

Serena, stunned by the deep dimples in his lean cheeks, held her breath, her gaze fixed on his wide, generous mouth. Even with one eye nearly closed and bruised and one half of his face scarred, David Cole was a beautiful man. His dark eyes, sun-browned, olive skin, and the heavy, silken hair covering his scalp added to his masculine beauty.

"You're already a prince, David Cole," she whispered, verbalizing her thoughts.

His smile vanished as he felt the warmth of her breath on his face. Her round eyes were unblinking, her slender body rigid. It was as if she were waiting—for what he didn't know. He was also waiting, waiting for the spell she had woven to break.

"Frogs don't become princes until they're kissed by a princess," he countered.

She blinked once. "I am not a princess."

Reaching up with his right hand, he smoothed back a curl from her forehead. "Oh, but you are, Miss Morris."

What he did not say was that all of the men in his family thought of beautiful women as royalty. And all of the men in his family had a penchant for beautiful women.

Serena put the cup to his lips, breaking the spell. "Drink."

He took several swallows of Luz Maria's tea, surprised at the flavor. It was unlike any tea he had had before. As a musician he had visited more countries than he could count on both hands and feet, sampling the cuisine in each of them. There were times when he discovered that the most unappetizing looking concoction was the most palatable. The other band members always teased him about experimenting whenever he ordered the unknown, saying he was going to come down with ptomaine or dysentery. Much to their astonishment it never happened, while some of them did succumb to various intestinal maladies.

He took the cup from her hand, holding it tightly between his fingers, and emptied it. He handed it back to her, nothing in his expression revealing what he was feeling at that moment.

"What do they call you?"

Serena thought it odd that he would use that phrase to ask her her name. "Serena," she replied before standing up.

"Any middle name?" She shook her head as she returned the cup to the tray. "Serena is a beautiful name for a princess." Settling down on the pillows cradling his back, he smiled. *And it's the perfect name for someone sent from heaven to give him back his life,* he mused, closing his eyes.

This time when he drifted off to sleep it wasn't to escape from the pain. It was to sleep and heal. The tea had begun to work its magic.

Serena stared at her sleeping patient, a slight smile softening her mouth. "If I'm a princess, then you are a prince, David Cole." Picking up the tray, she left the room. She had to get some clothes for him. Despite the fact that she was used to naked bodies, there was something about David's that bothered her. Not as a nurse, but as a woman.

* * *

Changing quickly from the red dress and mules into a pair of black linen slacks and a white linen, button-front, sleeveless top, she pushed her bare feet into a pair of black, patent leather thong sandals. She wanted to drive into the city and buy something for David to wear before it began raining again. Wherein the rest of Costa Rica experienced two seasons—wet and dry—Limón's Caribbean coastal region was usually wet all the year round. It sometimes experienced less rain in the dry season, which was generally from December to April, when Ticos referred to the dry season as *verano.* The rest of the year was their *invierno,* or winter.

Before she left for her trip she informed Luz Maria that she had invited a guest for dinner. She did not encounter anyone from the permanent household staff as she made her way through a wide hallway running along the rear of the house. However, she did notice several men working diligently on several new trees that had been added to the existing ones surrounding the property.

Other than his family and his country, her stepfather's passion was plants. He was educated as a botanist, and added an enormous greenhouse to *La Montaña* ten years after the house was constructed. It contained every plant, flower, and tree indigenous only to Costa Rica. An aviary was built years later, housing quetzals, macaws, toucans, and tiny pygmy parrots.

Her parents' late-model Mercedes-Benz was not in the four-car garage, and she assumed that Rodrigo had taken it when he drove them to the airport for their flight to San José.

Her first and only car, a bright yellow, 1974 Volkswagen "Bug," was parked in its assigned bay. Raul made certain it was serviced and ready to start up even though it was only driven when she returned to Costa Rica. Gabriel's rugged Jeep was parked in its usual spot, next to a brand new pickup truck. The pickup was used by anyone who needed to navigate the local roads whenever torrential rains made vehicular travel virtually impossible.

The Volkswagen's engine roared to life as soon as she turned the ignition. Shifting into reverse, she backed out of the garage and maneuvered down the paved road leading away from *La Montaña.*

She drove with the windows down, and the muggy stillness descended on her exposed flesh like a heated wet blanket. Dark clouds hovered overhead, foretelling another downpour within the hour. Reaching up, she picked at the damp curls clinging to her moist forehead. For the duration of her stay in Costa Rica she knew she would often have to affect a single braid to keep her hair off her face.

Serena was always astounded by how much the spirit and culture of the Limón region resembled the Caribbean islands. However, Costa Rican history told the story of how the province of Limón had been geographically and culturally isolated for centuries, its Afro-Caribbean population even banned from traveling into the Central Valley until after the 1948 civil war. Communications improved after a major highway was completed in the late eighties, but the region's population was still sparse because of the extreme climatic conditions—constant high humidity and rain interspersed with brilliant sun and clear light.

Tourists found the region fascinating, because it was a naturalist's fantasyland. The whitewater rapids of Río Pacuare, the nesting grounds, marshes and lagoons around Barra del Colorado, Río Estrella, and Manzanillo for turtles and birds, and the string of seductive, white beaches edged with coral reefs all made it a favorite of thousands who came to Costa Rica for sybaritic vacations.

Parking her car in an area close to the *Mercado Municipal,* she continued on foot to the vast, decrepit building whose vendors and merchandise spilled out onto the streets. All around her she heard the familiar, "Wh'appen, Man?" It was the leisurely greeting of Limón's Afro-Caribbeans.

She headed for a vendor's stall that carried men's apparel. It took her an hour to select underwear, T-shirts, shorts, and a pair of large leather thongs. She'd held up each garment, trying to assess if it would fit David, finally deciding to buy several large and extra-large T-shirts, and shorts and underwear with a thirty-six-inch waist. Stacks of jeans caught her attention, but she decided against purchasing a pair because she was unsure of the length. There was no doubt that David Cole was tall, as tall as Raul and Gabe, but he weighed more than the two men.

She planned to return to her car when the items on a vendor's stand caught her attention. It took another quarter of an hour to select a comb, brush, and shaving equipment. A mysterious smile curved her lips when she predicted that David Cole would probably appreciate the grooming supplies more than the clothes.

"Vain peacock," she whispered to herself as she stored her purchases in the back seat of the Volkswagen. A roll of thunder followed by an ear-shattering crash of lightning shook the earth at the moment she slipped behind the wheel. Her return trip to *La Montaña* would have to be navigated in a downpour.

Shoppers scurried as the rain began to fall, seeking shelter. They knew the heavy downpour would end almost as soon as it began. Only a few barefoot children lingered, until their parents shouted at them to come in out of the rain.

Serena shifted gears, squinting through the windshield. The wipers were set to the fastest speed, yet it wasn't fast enough to keep rivulets of water from distorting her view.

Maneuvering over to the side of the paved road, she cut off the engine and waited. Her moist breathing fogged up the windows as heat and moisture filled the small car.

Within fifteen minutes the rain subsided and the sun emerged from behind wispy clouds. The heat intensified quickly with the sun, forcing her to roll down the windows. The small car had become a suffocating tomb.

She downshifted as she made her way up the steep incline to *La Montaña*, maneuvering into her parking space at the garage at the same time Rodrigo emerged from the Mercedes-Benz.

Vertical lines formed between her eyes. She hadn't seen him on the road in front of her.

"*¡Buenas tardes!* Señorita Serena."

"Good afternoon, Rodrigo," she said, giving the man a warm smile. "Have my parents returned?"

Rodrigo shook his head. "No. They are staying in San José for a few days."

Serena stared at the man who had been Raul Vega's driver for nearly twenty years. He was of medium height and alarmingly thin, despite having a voracious appetite. And even though he had recently celebrated his fiftieth birthday his tanned face was smooth, and his straight, black hair claimed no traces of gray.

It was rumored that when he was in his teens he had fallen in love with the daughter of a wealthy landowner. He knew her parents would never consent to their marrying because he was a common laborer. Rodrigo had worked hard, sometimes holding down three jobs, hoping to save enough money to elevate his status, but when the young woman married a wealthy Costa Rican businessman he left San José for Limón, working on a banana plantation for several years.

When one of the plantation workers mentioned that Raul Vega was hiring men to work on the grounds surrounding the large mountaintop house, Rodrigo had left the plantation for *La Montaña*. He secured a position—not to work the land, but as a driver. It was a position he treasured. He was well-paid and had his own living quarters at the beautiful house. There were times when he had nothing to do. However, there were times when he did things that had nothing to do with his skills as an excellent driver. It did not matter, because no one had ever referred to him as a peasant again.

Rodrigo glanced at the packages on the backseat of the Volkswagen. "May I help you with your purchases?"

"Please," Serena replied, pushing her seat forward.

The driver gathered the bags and waited until she closed the door to the car. "Where do you want them?"

"Kindly take them to my bedroom."

She delayed following Rodrigo into the house. She knew she had to check on David, but she also wanted to survey the land surrounding *La Montaña.* She never tired of listening to the raucous cries of the colorful birds, or staring out at the thick, blue haze that always hung over the rain forest. The cloying fragrance of creeping flowers mingling with the smell of damp earth was like the sensuous scent of a priceless perfume. The scene from the mountaintop retreat was breathtaking, and at that moment she wondered why she hadn't returned to Costa Rica to live.

The air was pure, clean, the forest abundant with natural flora and wildlife. The beaches were pristine and the water unpolluted. The country's natural beauty was overwhelming, and its people at peace.

She was now thirty years old and she had lived sixteen of those years in Costa Rica. And over the time she had asked herself that question over and over since she left to live in the United States. The answer was always the same: *Because I am an American.*

The word reminded her of the American convalescing under her parents' roof. Turning, she made her way into the house.

Walking down the hall, she stepped into the guest room and saw David reclining on a chair, eyes closed, his right foot resting on the ottoman. The sheet, draping his body like a toga, floated to the floor in graceful folds. She knocked softly against the open door.

His eyes opened and he glared at her. "Why did you lie to me about my face?"

CHAPTER 9

Serena felt as if the breath had been siphoned from her lungs as she struggled to breathe. It was apparent that he had looked at a mirror.

"I did not lie to you." She struggled to control her temper.

David slowly lowered his right leg, the effort it took to complete the motion clearly marked on his face. That he was in pain was evidenced by his grimace and bared teeth.

"I asked about my face and you said it was healing."

"The doctor said it was healing. And it is."

"What he didn't say was that I would be scarred for life."

Suddenly the strain of what she had undergone for the past two weeks swept over Serena. Hearing of her brother's arrest; listening to the charges leveled against him; hearing the judge deny him bail; seeing him handcuffed and led out of a courtroom; knowing that if a jury found him guilty that he would die in Florida's electric chair.

Gabriel Diego Vega was going to die, while arrogant David Cole was only concerned about a little scar along the side of his face, a scar which probably could be eradicated by cosmetic surgery. Walking over to the bed, she picked up two pillows and launched them at David like guided missiles. One landed on his lap, the other at his feet.

Her mood veered from fear to frustration, and then to full-blown anger. "My brother is going to die, and all you can think about is a little scratch on your face." Swallowing hard, she attempted to blink back tears and failed. They overflowed, staining her cheeks.

"It sickens me to have to look at you." Turning, she raced out of the bedroom, ignoring David as he called out her name.

My brother is going to die. The six words echoed in David's head like the slow pounding sound of a kettle drum. Closing his eyes, he lowered his head, ignoring the band of pain tightening its vise around his temples.

The image he saw behind his lids was that of Serena's face and her tears. He saw the tears *and* her sadness. He was alive, bruised and battered but alive, while her brother was going to die.

When, he asked himself, had he become so selfish? When had he come to think only of David Cole, and no one else but David Cole?

Resting his head against the back of the wing chair, he slowly opened his eyes and stared at the space where Serena had been. He hadn't been that way when he was with Night Mood. He had been a member of a band who thought of themselves as an extended family. They'd traveled, eaten, slept, and rehearsed together. The six men saw more of one another than they did their own biological family members. The six men thought as one, and performed as one unit.

But his own selflessness stopped once he left Night Mood and took over as CEO of ColeDiz. His focus became productivity and profit margins. All he thought about was winning, at any cost.

He remembered a time when he had not wanted anything to do with business. All he'd wanted, knew, and breathed, was music. And as much as he fought the pull, his instincts for business were predetermined. His maternal grandfather, his own father, and his brothers had been, and were, consummate deal makers. A small amount of capital in their hands proliferated like yeast-filled dough.

His first passion had been, and would always be, music, but over the past nine years deal making had become a priority. And with the deal making came a hardness, a self-centered ruthlessness he hadn't realized he possessed—until now.

Serena Morris had taken care of him, while he only cared about himself. He was alive, while her brother was going to die. He could not retract what he'd said, but he could try to make amends.

Using the armrests as support, he pushed to his feet, swaying, then stood upright. He ignored the pain in his head and foot as he gingerly made his way slowly across the room. Stumbling, he gathered the sheet in his right hand and inched his way out of the bedroom and into the hallway. It took Herculean strength for him to turn his head to the right, then the left. His bedroom was at the end of the hallway, so using the wall as his support he turned left. He had to find Serena. He had to apologize. He also needed answers to a few questions. If this was really *La Montaña*, then what was she to Raul Cordero-Vega?

He ignored the wave of heat and then chills which were sweeping over his face and chest. A rush of dizziness caused him to stumble again. Reaching out, he braced a hand against the wall, steadying his progress and slowing his pace.

Moisture beaded his forehead and coated his upper body. Each step he took weakened him, but he would not give in to the relentless pain stealing whatever strength was left in his battered body.

He slowed his halting steps in front of a door. Leaning against its solid surface, he knocked. There was no answer and he tried turning the doorknob. It was locked.

He continued down the wide hallway, his bare feet making no sound on the Moorish style patterned runner. Even though the next room was less than twenty feet away it could have been all of two hundred. Gritting his teeth in frustration, David willed the dizziness to abate. He could abide the pain, but not the dizziness and weakness.

The door to the next room was open; leaning weakly against the door frame, David saw Serena. She stood with her back to the door, staring out the window. She was motionless, her arms wrapped around her body in a protective gesture.

With his uninjured eye he noticed the slender lines of her body in the black slacks. The dark color slimmed her narrow waist and hips. His gaze moved up to her hair, and for the second time since he'd come to Costa Rica he smiled. He liked her hair. Right now it was secured on the top of her head but he wanted to see it down, floating around her face and shoulders in a rich cloud of gold-brown and red curls.

"Lo siento mucho, Serena."

She heard the melodious male voice and spun around. Her gaze widened when she saw David supporting his sagging body against the door. Crossing her bedroom quickly, she wound an arm around his waist, and when he attempted to adjust the sheet it fell to the floor.

Leaning heavily against her smaller frame, David closed his eyes and swallowed back the bile threatening to make him sick. "I'm sorry," he said, repeating his apology in English.

Serena saw the beads of moisture dotting his forehead. Never had she encountered anyone as stubborn as David Cole. *"Usted tiene que guardar cama."*

"I'll go back to bed and stay there," he promised. "It was just that I wanted to apologize to you. And why is your brother going to die?"

Supporting most of his weight on her shoulder, she turned and led him back to his bedroom. "I'd rather not talk about my brother right now. You can apologize after you're better."

"Okay," he conceded, concentrating on putting one foot in front of the other.

They made it back to the bedroom, David falling heavily onto the bed. She lifted his legs and he lay back against the two remaining pillows. Closing his eyes, he successfully swallowed back the bile, berating his foolishness. Serena was right. He had to stay in bed.

He lay motionless as she took his temperature and blood pressure. The sensual scent of her was everywhere—in the air and on his flesh. His head hurt, his face ached, and his right foot throbbed continuously, yet he could not quell the desire he was beginning to feel for the woman taking care of him.

She barked at him like a storm trooper, issuing orders like a drill sergeant, yet he was drawn to her. She was a princess and an angel, one sent from heaven to save his life.

Serena withdrew a sheet from the chest at the foot of the bed and spread it over David's motionless body. His blood pressure was normal, as well as his temperature. A slight smile curved her lips. He was healing.

Placing the back of her hand against his stubbly left cheek, she stared at the perfection of his face. David Cole had every right to be upset. The scar would mar his exquisite masculine beauty.

"Would you like me to shave you?"

David opened his eyes, staring up at her with large eyes that were so black that she couldn't see into their liquid, obsidian depths. The bruise over the left one was now a deep purple instead of its former crimson.

"I'd like that very much."

Serena realized the deep, melodious quality of his voice for the first time. It was a low, rich, soothing baritone. She also recognized the cadence of a U.S. Southern drawl whenever he spoke English.

"I picked up a few things for you to wear. I don't believe it would be in your best interests to continue walking around in the nude." *Not that you don't have a beautiful body, David Cole,* she mused.

He smiled up at her, displaying his enchanting dimples. "How can I thank you?"

Pulling her hand away, Serena cocked her head at an angle and studied his animated features. "Thank me by getting well, David Cole."

"You've got yourself a deal, Serena Morris."

She returned his smile. "I'll be right back."

It took her less than ten minutes to retrieve the clothes she had bought him and to fill the large crock bowl with hot water. Shaving him while he lay in bed presented a problem. It would have been easier if he sat on the armchair. But she did not want to get him out of bed. Her only solution was to straddle his body.

Removing her sandals, she knelt on the side of the bed, then hoisted a leg over his body. David gave her an incredulous look when she supported most of her weight on the heels of her feet as she perched her lithe body over his thighs.

"Can you think of a better way?" she questioned, reaching across his body for a cloth she had placed in the bowl of hot water on the bedside table.

He couldn't answer her, because his body had reacted immediately to the pressure of her buttocks pressed against his groin. The only barriers between them were cotton and linen, and there was no doubt that she felt the rising of his sex under her rear end.

Serena's hands were shaking as she wrang the water out of the facecloth and placed it over the lower half of David's face. What was she doing? She was sitting on a naked man who, although injured, was fully aroused. And there was no doubt that she had aroused him.

She wanted David to close his eyes so he wouldn't see her own reaction to his obvious desire. But he didn't, and seconds later his gaze went from her face to her chest, where her distended nipples were visible through the lacy cups of her bra and the delicate fabric of her linen blouse.

Her gaze widened. "Close your eyes," she ordered in a breathless whisper.

He complied, smiling. "That will be a lot easier to do than getting another part of my body to follow your orders. There are times when *it* has a mind of its own."

Serena felt the heat in her face sweep over all of her body. It settled between her thighs, and it took Herculean will to not respond to the pulsing hardness pressing up against her buttocks.

Shaking a can of shaving cream, she pushed the button, and peaks of cream settled on her fingertips. She marveled that she didn't cut or nick David as she drew the razor expertly over his jaw, circumventing the area over his left cheek where Dr. Rivera stitched the flesh together.

She eased herself off his body, noticing that his arousal had not abated. It was apparent that her patient was a healthy, virile male who would be more than sexually adequate when having to perform.

Sanding at the bedside, she wiped away all traces of shaving cream and applied an astringent to his smooth, brown cheeks.

David opened his eyes for the first time since Serena had ordered that he close them. He realized that she was as affected by his body's reaction as he was by hers. The softness of her flesh, her sensual scent of flowers and musk clinging to her skin, and the firm roundness of her bottom pressing against his sex had him close to exploding. What he did not want to do was embarrass himself by spilling his lust on the bed instead of in her body. His gaze widened in shock. He hadn't known her twenty-four hours and he wanted her! Wanted to be inside her!

Wanting to sleep with Serena Morris went against everything he believed in. He'd never engaged in gratuitous sex! Not ever! Not as a teenage boy nor as a popular musician. Aside from the nickname of Dracula, the members of Night Mood had also called him "The Monk," because he refused to sleep with women when touring.

He had always been careful to not drink too much for fear of losing control and ending up in bed with a woman who would later claim that he was the father of her baby. His retort when the band members teased him was that he wanted no part of a paternity scandal; even more than avoiding any legal entanglements or entrapments, he wanted the choice to be his when he decided to marry and father children.

David did not know why he thought of marriage and children now. Did his thoughts have something to do with Serena Morris? Was it because she had helped save his life that he felt they were connected? That he owed her something? That perhaps he wanted to repay her by offering to share his life with her?

He touched his jaw, savoring the feel of smooth flesh under his fingertips. A slow smile softened his mouth. "You're much better than my barber. Thank you."

Wiping her hands on a towel, Serena returned his smile. "My

barbering skills do not extend to haircuts. Not unless you'd like me to shave your head."

David ran a hand over his close-cut, graying hair. "I don't think so." There had been a time when he wore his shoulder-length hair in a ponytail, and he missed the long hair, black attire, and diamond stud earring from his Night Mood era.

She dropped the razor in the bowl along with the facecloth and towel. Taking a surreptitious glance at her patient, she noticed the expression of satisfaction softening his features.

"I'm going to help you into a pair of boxers. Then I'll see about getting you something to eat," she stated firmly.

He flashed another dimpled smile. "Thank you."

She emptied her purchases on the foot of the bed, picking up a pair of plain white boxers. "I didn't know your size, so I picked up a thirty-six."

Arching a sculpted, black eyebrow, David stared at her. "Excellent guess." He closed his eyes as she drew back the sheet and slipped the underwear over his feet and inched it up his legs. Raising his hips slightly, he facilitated her covering up his nakedness.

The heat in his face had nothing to do with his injury or the extra exertion. For the first time since laying eyes on Serena Morris he was embarrassed. She knew that she aroused him—there had been no way for him to conceal it—and whenever she gazed upon his nude body he knew she was now aware of him not as a patient but as a man.

Opening his eyes, he stared at her staring at his thigh. He knew what had garnered her rapt attention. "It's a bat," he explained.

"I can see that," Serena acknowledged, staring at the distinctive outline of a bat tattooed on the inside of David Cole's upper thigh. "Why a bat?" she questioned, pulling the sheet up and folding it back neatly over his belly.

"I played with a jazz band in my former life. It was called Night Mood. We dressed in black, hung out all night, and slept during the day. I had affected the habit of not going to bed until

I saw the sun break the horizon. The other guys got into the habit of calling me Dracula. When we returned to the States after a two-month tour of Europe we decided to get tattoos. All of the other guys selected cats."

It was her turn to arch her delicate eyebrows. "Why the thigh, David?" The outline of a bat with its wings outstretched was positioned where his member rested against his hard thigh.

"I didn't want it visible so that I'd have to consider having it removed one day."

Serena gave him a skeptical look. "Is that the only reason?"

"Should there be another one?"

"I think so, David Cole. I think you were so vain that you didn't want to mar your body where someone would see it."

"Someone?"

Gathering the bowl and shaving materials, she gave him a sidelong glance. "Women."

"How wrong you are, Serena," he drawled in Spanish. "*Una mujer.* Yes," he confirmed when seeing her expression of surprise. "You are the *only* woman who has seen it."

She went still, staring at him and seeing amusement in his eyes. "Don't tell me you're—"

"I prefer *women,*" he confirmed, interrupting her. "It's just that I don't make it a practice of sleeping with a lot of them."

"That's unusual coming from a musician."

"Former musician."

"Okay," she conceded, "a former musician."

"Knowing this, does that change your impression of me?"

"No. It still doesn't change the fact that you're obsessed with your looks. I don't know if anyone has ever told you, but you're a vain peacock."

Instead of refuting her statement, he laughed, the sound following her out of the room and down the hall.

Serena laughed softly to herself. David Cole was vain. And sexy; sexier than any man she had ever seen in her life. He was what Latin women called *muy guapo.* He was one *fine* man.

CHAPTER 10

David sat up in bed, his back supported by several pillows, while Serena fed him spoonfuls of a flavorful chicken soup with rice and vegetables. He hadn't realized how hungry he was until he began eating. He ate all of the soup and drank half a cup of tea. His lids soon fluttered wildly as he fought against listlessness making it almost impossible to keep his eyes open; within minutes he fell into a deep, comforting sleep.

He never knew when Serena eased the pillows from behind his back and shoulders and placed them under his head. He also was not aware that she leaned over his prone form for several seconds before leaning closer and placing a light kiss on his forehead.

"Sleep well, David," she whispered softly, then walked out of the room.

Serena returned to the kitchen, smiling at Luz Maria. "He ate all of the soup, but only drank half of the tea," she informed the cook.

Luz Maria took the tray from Serena, returning her smile. "That's okay. I made the tea a little stronger this time. He only needed to drink a little bit. Is he complaining about pain?"

"No."

"Good." Her tea, with its natural anesthetizing properties, dulled intense pain almost immediately while causing one to fall into a deep sleep. It contained a popular herb used by Costa Rican natives for many centuries to counter infections that attacked the body.

"Are you ready to eat?"

Serena nodded, sitting down at a massive mahogany table that had been crafted more than a hundred years before. The skilled furniture maker had carved his name and the date on the underside of the table.

She watched Luz Maria as she spooned a portion of soup into a bowl. The talented cook was tiny, barely five-feet in height, and weighed about one hundred pounds, and even though she prepared exquisite meals for her employer and his family she made it a practice not to eat any meat. On occasion she consumed a small amount of chicken. However, she much preferred fish and the vegetables indigenous to the region.

Serena looked forward to eating *casabe, yautía,* and *plátanos* whenever she returned to the Central American country. She liked *plátanos,* or bananas, whether they were green or ripe. Luz Maria placed a bowl of soup on the table, along with a small dish filled with *plátano maduro.* The aroma of the lightly fried, yellow bananas wafted above the other tantalizing smells in the large kitchen.

"Will your papa and mother return in time to share dinner with your guest tonight?" Luz questioned, waiting until after Serena had swallowed several spoonfuls of soup.

"No. It will be Dr. Rivera and myself. My parents are going to stay in San José for a few days. They went to meet with President Montalvo and the ambassador from the United States."

Luz Maria crossed herself, saying a silent prayer. When she heard of Gabriel Vega's arrest she'd begun a daily novena of lighting candles and saying prayers for his return. She could not believe he had killed anyone. She'd watched Gabriel Diego Vega grow up, and everyone who met him was taken with his gentleness and sincerity. She, like Raul Cordero-Vega, believed the people in the United States had falsely accused Gabriel of a crime he did not commit.

Serena saw Luz Maria cross herself, knowing that the older woman had erected a shrine in her bedroom for her brother. Caring for David Cole helped to lessen her own heartache. She did not have to spend all of her waking hours thinking or crying now.

She finished her lunch, thanked Luz Maria, then retreated to her room. She wanted to go for a walk but decided against it. The daytime temperature had gone over the ninety degree mark, making the intense heat dangerous for anyone who remained outdoors longer than necessary.

It was time for *siesta*. She would wait for the early evening to walk down to the river. After her walk she would prepare herself to share dinner with Leandro Rivera.

Removing her sandals, blouse, slacks, and underwear, she pulled a short shift over her head, then lay down on the bed. She stared up at the mosquito netting shrouding the large, four-poster bed. Warm breezes swept into the bedroom and over her exposed limbs from the open French doors leading out to the second-story veranda. Her thoughts strayed to Gabe as she willed herself not to cry. She was unsuccessful. The tears welling up behind her lids overflowed and stained her cheeks. Turning her face into the pillow, she cried silently until spent. Then she fell asleep.

David stared up at Dr. Leandro Rivera as the doctor examined his face. "It's healing nicely, Señor Cole."

"When are you going to remove the stitches?"

Leandro smiled, the skin around his eyes crinkling attractively. "They will dissolve on their own. How's your ankle?"

"I can't put too much pressure on it."

That's because you shouldn't be putting any pressure on it, Serena said silently. She stood at the foot of the bed, watching Leandro take David Cole's blood pressure. Then she saw his obvious expression of relief when he registered David's normal body temperature.

"Señorita Morris will assist you when you get out of bed tomorrow. I've instructed her to have you soak your foot and ankle in cold water to take down some of the swelling."

Turning his head, David looked at Serena. When she entered the room with the doctor he was shocked by the change in her appearance. Her hair was brushed off her face and secured in a tight chignon on the nape of her neck. A light cover of makeup illuminated her large, round eyes and high-lighted the lushness of her full lips. She had even exchanged her perfume for one that reminded him of woodsy spices. A fitted silk sheath in vermillion red matched the vibrant color on her lips. His gaze lingered on her perfectly rounded face, noting that the large pearls in her pierced lobes were compan-ions for a magnificent single strand draped around her long, delicate neck.

She's going out! And he knew without asking that she was going out with Dr. Leandro Rivera. The doctor's tailored dark suit and silk tie were a departure from his usual linen slacks and jacket.

Not knowing why, David felt a surge of jealousy. It wasn't that he was in love with Serena, or even liked her a lot, but what bothered him was that she'd affected him more than any woman he'd ever met. He'd discovered earlier that afternoon that he lacked control over his sexual urges when near her and that she made him think of marrying and fathering children.

"I hope you two have a good time tonight," he said without warning. Leandro smiled, while Serena frowned.

"Thank you," Leandro returned, confirming his suspicions.

"I'll check on you later," Serena said as she turned and walked out of the bedroom. Leandro replaced his instruments in his bag and followed her.

David's gaze followed her retreating figure. He could see the perfection of her strong legs in a pair of red satin, sling-strap heels. She had elected to leave her legs bare, and the smooth brown color shimmered sensually over firm, lean muscle.

And for the second time that day David felt a surge of desire that left him trembling and shaken with an urgency to bury his sex deep within the softness of her enticing body.

Reaching over for the cup of tea on the bedside table, he gulped it quickly, smiling as sleep overtook him so that he did not have to think of Serena Morris or the man who would command her attention for the evening.

* * *

Serena and Leandro walked slowly, side by side, as they made their way along the path leading away from *La Montaña* and toward the Caribbean. He had elected to park his car a quarter of a mile from the house, saying that he needed the additional exercise.

A rising wind swept over her moist face, cooling her bared flesh. She did not know what to expect, but she had not expected her dining partner's wicked sense of humor. They had spent the better part of two hours laughing instead of eating Luz Maria's expertly prepared avocado and mango salad, shredded beef, white rice and black beans, steamed pumpkin, and a chilled dessert made of fresh coconut.

The meal began with her thinking of David Cole's dinner. He'd eaten a bowl of potato soup seasoned with rosemary, tarragon, chives, scallions, and strips of a melted yellow cheese and crispy crumbled bacon. It had pleased her that he ate all that was in the bowl, indicating he was well on the road to recovery. The absence of a fever and his healthy appetite made it a certainty that his period of convalescence would be shorter than she had originally predicted. She knew he was practically pain-free. Luz Maria's magical tea worked as well as Demerol, without any of the addictive properties of some prescribed painkillers.

Leandro caught her hand as he assisted her over the uneven surface of an area of the landscape. Tightening his grip, he smiled down at her upturned face. His four-wheel drive vehicle was parked less than twenty feet away, yet he had not released her fingers.

Rising on tiptoe, Serena pressed her lips to his smooth jaw. "Thank you for coming to dinner."

The skin around his dark, slanting eyes crinkled in an engaging smile. "May I call on you again for dinner?"

"Of course," she replied.

His smile slipped away as he stared down at her. *She's so lovely*, he mused. "What can I offer you to return to Limón and work with me?"

Shaking her head, she forced a smile. "Nothing right now. My life is in the United States."

"Your life or *someone?*"

"My life." There was no mistaking the emphasis on the two words.

Leandro released her hand, leaning over and placing a light kiss an inch from her mouth. "*¡Hasta luego!* Serena."

"¡Buenas noches!"

Turning, she made her way back up the path, not waiting for Leandro to drive away. She felt the heat of his gaze on her back, and she wondered if she had made a mistake to share dinner with the young doctor. She wasn't vain, at least not as vain as David Cole, but she knew that Dr. Leandro Rivera was interested in her the way a man would be interested in a woman. He was a Tico and she was an American, and never had she felt as American as she did at that moment. Perhaps it had something to do with her stepfather's virulent attack on Americans that made her realize that she, like her mother, truly loved the country of their birth. Or maybe it was because of her date with Leandro, a Costa Rican man, that made her aware of how different he was from American men.

She had not dated before she left Costa Rica for the States, so her introduction to the opposite sex was through the men she met in college. The fact that she had spent sixteen of her first eighteen years of life in a Central American country was undetectable once she fully immersed herself in the culture of her biological parents.

Walking into the large house, she smiled. The thick stucco walls kept the heat at bay and permitted the interiors to remain cool despite the intense tropical heat. She made her way up the staircase, feeling the muscles in the back of her legs pulling. It had been a while since she had worn a pair of heels. She could not remember the last time she had put on a dress and heels and gone out dancing.

Not since Xavier, a silent voice whispered to her. Not since she walked away from her ex-husband and her marriage. Her career had become a priority, and dating something she relegated to her past.

Now her priority was her brother. She'd returned to Costa Rica to bond with her family and do what she could to help secure his release from a Florida prison.

She decided to check on David before going to her own bedroom. Leandro had given her specific instructions. He wanted the American businessman ambulatory. It was important that David get out of bed for longer periods of time. He promised to deliver an adjustable cane to facilitate his patient's walking.

Standing at the open doorway she saw that David was not in bed. Walking into the room, she noticed that he sat on the armchair, his injured foot on the footstool.

The large bedroom was semi-dark, the only light coming from the light of a bedside lamp. David appeared to be asleep, eyes closed, his head resting against the high back of the chair.

She moved quietly toward the doorway, stopping when he said, "Do you like him?"

Turning slowly, Serena stared at David staring back at her, registering the deep, melodious sound of his voice for the first time. Whenever he spoke Spanish it sounded as if he were singing a sensual love song. She much preferred to hear him speak Spanish.

"Excuse me?"

"I asked if you like him."

She laughed in a low, throaty chuckle. Folding her hands on her hips, she shook her heard. "Vain and arrogant, too, Mr. Cole?"

A slow smile deepened the dimples in his cheeks. "If you say so, Miss Morris."

"I say so."

Raising a hand, he beckoned to her. "Please come and talk to me."

She did not move. "What do you want to talk about?"

He lowered his hand. "Anything. If I go back to bed I'm going to fall asleep again, and I've slept more in the past two days than I've slept the past month."

Making her way slowly across the bedroom, Serena's eyes sparkled in a friendly smile. "I give you less than a week before you'll be able to go home."

"I have to take care of some business before I return home."

"You'll have to wait for my father to return from San José for that."

David's uninjured eye widened as he felt his pulse quicken. Vertical slashes appeared between his eyes as he stared at Serena standing beside his chair. "Your father?"

Leaning down and gently moving his foot, she sat on the footstool and crossed her outstretched legs at the ankles. "Yes. My father is Raul Cordero-Vega."

He felt as if he had been punched in the gut. His brow furrowed and he wondered if his being at *La Montaña* was a coincidence or was it by design. He knew Vega wanted him in Limón, and for the first time he suspected perhaps Vega was the mastermind behind his assault and abduction. He and Cordero-Vega despised each other, and the woman he was attracted to was the daughter of his nemesis. "But isn't your name Morris?"

"It is. Raul is my stepfather."

David continued to stare at the woman who was the most exotic female he had ever met. The color of her flesh, the blend of her brown and reddish curling hair, and the perfection of her round face and features transfixed him as no other woman had. Her nearness and her fragrant skin heated him until his body reacted violently with a swift rushing desire. He was grateful to be sitting as he placed both hands in his lap.

"How old were you when he married your mother?"

"Two. My father died before I was born."

He examined her closed expression as she stared out the French doors. David did not know how, but he felt what she was feeling, and it was sadness, sadness that was heavy and haunting, knowing all was not right in the Cordero-Vega household. He remembered her tirade about her brother dying.

"Where's your brother, Serena?"

She jumped, startled, even though David's question was spoken softly, caressingly, and what she wanted to do was cry. Gabriel, her brother, the other half of her, was locked away from her. She couldn't hold him or comfort him. Was he treated harshly? Did he get enough to eat? Was he protected from the hardened prisoners who had made incarceration a way of life?

"He's in Florida," she began in a quiet voice.

"Where in Florida?"

Serena did not answer right away as she struggled to bring her fragile emotions under control. "He's in a federal prison," she whispered.

"On what charges?"

Turning her head, she stared up at David. Leaning forward, he stared down at her. David Cole was a stranger, yet she felt as if she had known him for years. Her interaction with him had been impersonal since he had taken refuge in her parents' home, but for some unknown reason she wanted to pour her heart out to him.

Glancing away, she said, "Murder and drug trafficking."

David slumped against the high back of the comfortable armchair. He was a Floridian, and he knew the laws in Florida were harsh and punitive when it came to murder and drugs. Who had her brother been involved with? Was he also an American?

"What happened, Serena?"

She did not answer, could not. Her vocal chords constricted, not permitting her to speak. Closing her eyes, she could see Gabriel's closed expression as he stood in the Florida courtroom while the federal prosecutor read the charges against him.

"He's been charged with smuggling, and killing a DEA agent." Her tone was flat, emotionless. Each time she had to repeat those charges she felt as if someone had pierced her heart with a sharp instrument, allowing the blood to flow unchecked.

"Who was he involved with?"

Her head came up quickly at the same time she rose to her feet. "He wasn't involved with anyone," she snapped angrily. "He went on a sailing trip with a group of college friends. Their boat was intercepted by the Coast Guard and DEA—"

"Was he with Guillermo Barranda?" David interrupted.

She went completely still, her eyes widening in shock. "How did you know that?"

"I'm from Florida," he explained, speaking English for the first time since Serena had come into the bedroom. "The media coverage of the drug bust and the death of a DEA agent was paramount for about a week. The only name I remembered was Guillermo Barranda. The rumor is that his father heads the largest drug cartel in South America." A frown furrowed his forehead. "What was your brother doing with someone like Barranda?"

"They were college roommates."

David grunted, shaking his head. "Someone should've told him to change roommates."

"Since when do you blame children for the sins of their parents?" she shot back angrily.

Her words slapped David as if she had physically struck him. He had no right to judge the younger Barranda. There were enough skeletons in his own family closet to rattle for several generations. There was a time when the Coles were rife with alienation and bitterness for more years than he could count. It was only within the past five years that things had changed and his parents, brothers, and sisters had reconciled with one another.

Lowering his right foot and using the armrests, he pushed to his feet, swaying before he righted himself. "You're right, Serena. *I* of all people should be the last to judge someone else for what his father has done," he replied cryptically.

Standing, she stared at the middle of his hair-matted chest rather than meet his gaze; she had heard rumors about her step-father—nasty rumors about his abuse of the powers of his office—and had always forgiven him because of his passion for the country of his birth. She and her mother had never permitted themselves to become involved with the political machinations that controlled Raul Vega and turned him into a nationalistic zealot.

Nodding, she said, "The adage is true—those who live in glass houses should not throw stones."

He flashed a slow, sensual smile. "Amen."

Serena wound an arm around his waist, feeling the heat from his body seep into her own through the red silk dress. The natural fragrance of his masculine skin was hypnotic and cloying.

They made their way slowly across the room to the bed. David sat down hard, breathing heavily. The effort it had taken for him to get out of bed and make it over the chair had drained his strength. He had been prepared to spend the night on the chair if Serena hadn't returned.

She raised his legs and eased them onto the bed as he lay down. Pulling a sheet up to his waist, she smiled at him. "Dr. Rivera wants you ambulatory. He's sending over a cane to help you keep your balance. We'll start you with taking your meals out of bed. It may take a few days, but as soon as the swelling in your ankle lessens you'll be able to shower by yourself."

This news pleased him. "Thank you."

Serena stared at David. It was the first time since he was brought into *La Montaña* that he'd shown any measure of humility. "You're welcome." Patting his muscled shoulder, she flashed her winning smile. "Sleep well."

David closed his eyes, a smile curving his lips. He still could see Serena, smell her, hear the sound of her throaty voice, and savor the gentle touch of her healing hands. She was his special angel, sent from heaven to give him back his life, and what he wanted to do when he left Costa Rica was take her with him. He never thought that perhaps it was gratitude that drew him to her, because he knew it wasn't. It was something else; something he could not quite identify. Not yet.

CHAPTER 11

June 16

Serena woke as the sun pierced the dark cover of night. Streaks of lavender, mauve, and pale blue had crisscrossed the heavens by the time she had splashed cold water on her face, brushed her teeth, slipped into a sports bra, T-shirt, shorts, and running shoes, and secured her hair atop her head with an elastic headband. The warm rays filtered over her exposed flesh the moment she stepped out onto the veranda. Instinctively she knew she had only another hour before the tropical heat made it virtually impossible for her to jog her daily three miles.

Making her way out of her bedroom, she noticed a black leather garment bag and matching, oversized Pullman outside the door to David's bedroom. She assumed someone had found his luggage and delivered it to *La Montaña*. She would speak to Rodrigo after she returned from her jog.

Rodrigo, along with Luz Maria, was responsible for the day-to-day operation of *La Montaña*. Luz Maria oversaw the kitchen and every aspect of the interior of the large house, while Rodrigo saw to the exterior. He kept the automobiles in working order and made certain the landscaping crew maintained the grounds, greenhouse, and the aviary. He was silent, inconspicuous, and very efficient.

She stretched vigorously, loosening up before she half-walked and half-jogged down the path to the beach. A blue-gray haze hung over the nearby rain forest like a heavy shroud. The raucous sounds of birds filled the air, their differing cries blending like an orchestra warming up before the start of their staged performance.

This was the Costa Rica Serena loved: the heat, the cries of the birds, the clear, blue-green of the Caribbean, the thick, lush world of the rain forest, and the majestic splendor of *La Montaña* rising above the unspoiled perfection of a land not yet defiled by overpopulation or pollution.

Inhaling the cloying fragrance of flowers growing without boundaries, she could understand her stepfather's fervent passion for protecting the land of his birth. It truly was a Garden of Eden. A garden he did not want debauched by the destructive waste that usually accompanied greed and avarice—all in the name of progress.

Dampness lathered her arms and legs long before she reached the beach and began a smooth, rhythmic run along the pristine, white sand. She had run less than a quarter of a mile when she saw tracks and a large turtle that had apparently come ashore to lay and bury hundreds of eggs in the sand before returning to the sea.

The heat from the rising sun was oppressive, stealing precious breath from her lungs, and she knew it would be impossible to run more than a mile before passing out or becoming dehydrated. Stopping, she rested her hands on her hips and inhaled thick, hot air. She had jogged less than half a mile. She did not know how long she would stay in Costa Rica before returning to the States, but she knew that jogging every day was not possible. Her running the marathon was contingent on her logging a minimum of twenty miles a week, and she knew she was going to have to train differently if she were to remain in Costa Rica beyond a month.

Instead of running, she walked back to *La Montaña*. Limón was fully awake with the steady hum of cars and trucks traversing the paved roads as its citizens prepared for a day of work. As she neared the house she saw Rodrigo driving away, and wondered whether he was going to pick up her parents. She had wanted to call her mother, but decided to wait. She was certain that if Juanita had encouraging news she would've called her immediately.

Walking into the coolness of the house, Serena made her way up the back staircase to her bedroom. Glancing at the bags outside David Cole's door, she noticed the quality of the leather and the monogrammed *DCC* emblazoned on gold along the sides of the Pullman and garment bag.

There were so many questions about David that she wanted answered. If his family was as prominent and wealthy as Leandro had hinted, why hadn't she heard of them? And where had he learned to speak flawless Spanish?

She forgot everything about David as she stripped off her clothes and stood under the cool spray of a shower while she washed her hair and her body.

A quarter of an hour later she walked into David's bedroom, hair billowing around her head and face in a sensual cloud of red-brown curls. She had applied an oil-based lotion to the damp strands where they crinkled in soft, loose ringlets.

David turned to stare at Serena the moment he detected the fragrance of her perfume. It wasn't the same as the one she wore the night before. The last time he saw her she was wearing the red silk dress, but this morning she wore a pair of khaki shorts with an oversize T-shirt. Again, he was transfixed by the perfection of her legs.

"Good morning."

They shared a smile. They had spoken in unison.

"Good morning, David."

His smile widened. "Good morning, Serena." Pushing himself up, he supported his upper body on his elbows. "Can you help me to the bathroom?"

She arched an eyebrow, returning his winning smile. "Of course."

Slipping an arm under his knees, she swung his legs around until his feet touched the floor. Moving to his right side, she provided the extra support he needed when he gingerly placed his weight on his injured foot. They made it to the bathroom and she helped him over to the commode.

"I know," he began as she opened her mouth. "I'll call you when I'm finished."

"You learn quickly. I like that," she teased.

I like you, David said silently as he stared at her retreating figure. And he did. He had awakened early and he lay in bed thinking about Serena. She yelled at him and bullied him, and these were traits he did not like in a woman. The women he found himself involved with were typically submissive and compliant. They did not challenge him or issue demands. And he usually told them from the onset that he could not promise more than he was able to give at the time, and most knew he had no intention of marrying or fathering children. Some accepted his stance, while many did not. As a result he had had very few serious relationships that continued beyond two years.

It was said that men usually married women much like their mothers, and David had come to the realization that he was looking for a woman like his mother. Marguerite Cole was quiet and extremely tolerant. She had permitted her much more effusive husband to see to her every need and desire, while she concentrated on nurturing her children and safeguarding her household. Any issues aside from her home and children she left to Samuel Claridge Cole. What he didn't understand was his attraction to Serena, because she was *not* like his mother.

When he had reluctantly left his world of music behind and assumed control of ColeDiz International, Ltd., David found, much to his chagrin, that he took to business like a duck to water. It was less than a year after he'd become CEO that he realized that he was a much more astute businessman than a natural musician. Music was a passion he worked hard at, while business came naturally. What he wanted to do was conclude the sale of the banana plantation and return to the States.

He did not know why, but when he left Costa Rica he did

not want to leave Serena Morris behind. He wanted her to return with him.

She assisted him as he washed his face and brushed his teeth. It frustrated him that he was unable to perform the mundane tasks of maintaining the most basic of hygienic functions without help. His head throbbed painfully as he hobbled back to the bedroom and fell across the bed, wondering how long it would take before the pain vanished, along with the accompanying weakness.

Serena observed David's closed eyes and clenched teeth. He was putting up a brave front while suffering silently in pain. She realized whoever had assaulted him probably intended serious injury, or death. But who, she wondered, wanted him dead? And for what reason?

"I'll bring you something to eat," she informed him softly. Giving him a lingering stare, she turned and walked out of the room.

The dull pain that radiated along the left side of his face would not permit him to nod or speak. He did not want anything to eat. What he wanted was for the pain to go away—for good.

Serena walked through the narrow hallway at the rear of the house that led to the kitchen. Instinctively she utilized the rear of the house to gain access to the kitchen. She realized it was something she and Gabriel did as children on many occasions. When their parents entertained guests in the living room or formal dining room, they had sometimes left their beds and cajoled Luz Maria into giving them samples of the fancy concoctions she had prepared for the elegantly attired visitors.

There were times when she'd spent more time with Luz Maria than she had with her own mother. She loved the fragrant aromas wafting from the large pots on the massive stove and broiling meat in the oven. The cook taught her to bake her own bread, cure meats, and prepare a dish of perfectly steamed white rice whose grains shimmered with the olive oil used during its cooking process.

Built-in shelves along the kitchen walls claimed jars filled with dried herbs and spices grown in *La Montaña*'s greenhouse.

Luz Maria had been given her own section in the structure where she carefully tended the medicinal plants she used to counteract fever, pain, boils, and a plethora of infections and ailments.

Luz Maria Hernando glanced up when Serena walked into the kitchen. Her dark gaze softened as she studied the woman she'd watched flower into a natural beauty. Since she hadn't married or had children, she'd secretly claimed Serena as her own. And the younger woman could have been her daughter because there was a marked resemblance between them: similar coloring and curly hair. At fifty-two, Luz Maria was ten pounds heavier than she had been at twenty-two, yet her body retained a slender firmness that still turned many a male head.

"*¡Buenos días!,* Doña Maria."

"*¡Buenos días!, Princesa.* How is your guest?" she continued in English.

"He's better, but still in some pain."

"A lot of pain?"

Serena shook her head. "I don't think so. I believe it comes and goes."

Luz Maria smiled. "I'll fix him a different tea. It will take away the pain and not make him sleep so much."

Serena watched as the cook walked over to a shelf and selected a jar with a length of yellow yarn tied around its neck. She smiled. Luz Maria had chosen to identify her herbs with colored yarn.

Sitting down on a tall stool near the thick, mahogany table, she studied Luz Maria as she spilled the contents of the jar onto the table and counted out four leaves. Crushing the leaves with her fingertips, she placed them in a small piece of cheesecloth, tied it with a length of thin, white cord, and put the bundle in a large ceramic mug. Ladling hot water from a large, simmering pot on the stove, she poured it over the cheesecloth, permitting the leaves to steep.

"He is young?" Luz Maria asked without taking her gaze from the steaming cup.

Serena smiled, studying the dark head streaked with shimmering strands of silver. "Yes, Doña Maria, he is young."

Luz Maria glanced up, smiling. "He is married?"

"I don't know," she answered truthfully. Seeing the knowing smile curving the cook's mouth, Serena leaned forward, resting her hands on the table. "What aren't you telling me?"

Shifting an eyebrow, Luz Maria stopped smiling, and her expression grew serious. "Do you really want to know, *Chica?*" she questioned, using her stepfather's term of endearment. "Do you really want to know what's in your future?"

There were rumors that Luz Maria Hernando could tell one's future, but Serena had always shied away from such superstition. She felt knowing one's future could not prevent whatever was destined to happen.

Shaking her head, she said, "No."

"I'll respect your wishes, but one thing I'll say is that the young man you're taking care of will be a part of your future."

A rush of blood heated her face. She did not want David Cole in her life. The fact was that she did not want any man in her life—now or in the future.

"What about Gabriel? What is going to happen to him?" Her scathing tone mirrored her fear and frustration for her brother.

Luz Maria's smooth, dusky-brown face creased into a sudden smile. Her novena had been answered. "Gabriel is safe."

"Safe from whom?"

"Safe from himself, and those who seek to take his life."

Slipping off the stool, Serena curved her arms around the older woman, inhaling the differing smells clinging to her body. She savored the fragrance of cloves, mint, and bergamot, while Luz Maria's large, dark eyes narrowed in a smile. The blending of her African, Native Indian, and Spanish blood made for a seductive attractiveness that made Serena wonder why some man hadn't claimed Luz Maria for his wife.

"Thank you, Doña Maria." The woman had never lied to her.

"You want to know about your brother's future, yet you hesitate to know your own."

"Maybe before I leave Costa Rica again I'll ask that you tell me."

"You won't have to ask, *Chica.* I *will* tell you whether you ask me or not, because you will need to know what to do."

Serena pondered her cryptic statement as a chill raced down her spine, causing her to shiver noticeably. *Bruja,* she said to herself. Luz Maria had been called a witch by many of the people connected with *La Montaña,* but it was only now that she was inclined to believe them.

The iciness had not left her limbs even after she'd carried a tray with the tea, a bowl of creamed rice cereal, and a glass of tropical fruit juice to David's bedroom. Luz Maria's prediction that Gabriel's life would not end in a Florida prison cheered her, while the prophecy that her own would be inexorably entwined with David Cole's unnerved her.

There was no doubt that she was attracted to him—only a blind woman would not be—but she wanted that attraction to be a superficial one. He was good-looking. No, she admitted, he was gorgeous. His rich, olive-brown coloring, liberally gray-flecked, black silky hair, delicate features, and dimpled smile were mesmerizing. His tall, muscular body was exquisitely formed, and his deep baritone voice was soft and melodious. The fact that he was wealthy, vain, and arrogant only added to his overall masculine appeal. In his arrogance he was very secure with who he was and what he had become.

She placed the tray on a small, round table next to the armchair, then helped David from the bed over to the chair, noticing that he continued to clench his teeth. It was obvious that his pain had not disappeared completely. After raising his right foot onto the stool, she positioned the tray over his lap.

He fed himself while she changed his bed. She felt his gaze watching her every movement, and wished that she had not worn the shorts. Whenever she turned she saw his one uninjured eye fixed on her legs.

Crossing the room, she stepped out into the hallway and picked up his leather garment bag and Pullman. The leather was soft and supple as heated butter. The bags were well used, yet had retained the distinctive smell of newly tanned hide. Walking slowly under the weight of the bags, she made her way into the bedroom.

David had just drained a large mug filled with a sweet, fragrant tea when he saw Serena laboring under the weight of a garment bag she had slung over her shoulder and another large case she pulled along the floor.

"Let me help you," he offered, putting the tray on the nearby table. He attempted to rise to his feet, then halted. He had put all of his weight on his swollen foot, nearly losing his balance.

"I've got it," she insisted, breathing heavily and dragging the Pullman.

Recognizing his own luggage, David hobbled slowly across the room, favoring his right foot. He knew the weight in the leather pieces, because he'd packed enough clothes for his two-week stay.

All of his suspicions about Vega were now confirmed. He'd thought perhaps someone had assaulted him in a robbery attempt, and if that had been true then he never would've seen his luggage again. Any knowledgeable thief would have sold the two pieces and contents for a tidy sum. Blinding rage surpassed all of the pain torturing his body.

"Put them down, Serena! Now!"

Registering the deep, angry command, she let go of the Pullman and eased the strap of the garment bag off her shoulder. It landed heavily on the floor beside the Pullman. Folding her hands on her hips, she glared up at David as he gingerly made his way over to her. Moisture lathered his face with the effort it took to put one foot in front of the other.

"What are you trying to do?" he questioned. His tone had softened considerably.

Her stance did not change as she stared up at him looming above her.

"Don't ask a dumb question if you don't want a dumb answer," she snapped angrily.

"I wouldn't have to ask if you hadn't shown me what a fool you are to try to move something that weighs more than you do," he countered.

Her gaze widened. "Are you calling me a fool? Maybe I am," she continued, not giving him a chance to come back at her. "I am a fool for taking care of someone who's too stubborn and much too ignorant to acknowledge that I'm only trying to help."

Reaching out, he caught her shoulders and pulled her against his chest. "I'm not calling you a fool. I—"

"Do I have to add liar to the list of your other sterling qualities?" she interrupted.

The warmth, softness, and scent of Serena seeped into David, making him forget who he was, where he was, and the pain wracking his body from head to toe. He held onto her as if she were his lifeline. He wanted and needed her to take away his pain, the yearning surpassing every craving he'd ever known, while defying description.

His outstretched fingers covered more than half her back, and she was certain he felt her slight trembling. Her face was pressed against his shoulder, and as she shifted her head the end of her nose grazed the thick, crisp, curly hair on his broad chest.

He closed his eyes, languishing in her female heat and feeling the white hot pain slipping away. Swaying slightly, he managed to keep his balance.

"Let me go, David." Her voice was muffled in his chest.

Drawing in a deep breath, he let it out slowly. "Not yet."

"Please."

He heard the husky plea, but he would not release her. What he wanted was for her to offer him what all of the women in his past had not been able to do—he wanted Serena to relate to him not because he was David Cole, but because he was a man; a man whose name and family mattered naught to her.

His hold on her slender body eased as he pulled back. The tense silence multiplied and surrounded them with an awareness that had not been apparent before. Without a word of acknowledgement, their roles changed from that of nurse and patient to that of man and woman—male and female.

Serena's arm tightened around his waist, and he leaned docilely into her as she led him back to the bed. She spent the next half-hour bathing and shaving David while he lay motionless, eyes closed. Seeing his nude body did not disturb her as much as Luz Maria's prediction which had caused confusion in her head.

The young man you're taking care of will be a part of your future.

No! a voice in her head screamed. All she wanted was for him to heal, conclude his business with her father, then return to the States.

All she wanted for herself was her brother's freedom.

CHAPTER 12

David spent the morning and early afternoon drifting in and out of a painless sleep, giving Serena the opportunity to unpack his luggage. She hung up eight pairs of lightweight summer slacks, two dozen monogrammed shirts, four jackets, a half-dozen silk ties, six pairs of shoes, and a month's supply of briefs and socks, most bearing the label of Ralph Lauren or Façonnable.

A leather shaving kit contained Façonnable scented soap, deodorant, aftershave balm, and cologne. The masculine, woodsy scent was well-suited to its wearer. A small flannel bag contained a gleaming, sterling silver razor with *DCC* inscribed on its delicately curved handle. She slipped the razor back into its sack, smiling. The disposable razors she'd used to shave him had not even come close to the elegant, engraved shaving instrument.

Emptying the contents of the shaving kit, she discovered an ultra-thin Piaget watch. Examining it closely, she read the back of the timepiece. There was no doubt that the watch's exquisitely thin case in solid eighteen karat gold and black lizard strap cost more than some farm workers earned in a year harvesting crops. There was no question that David Cole spared no expense when selecting his wardrobe and accessories.

Returning to the bed, she stared down at his relaxed face. His bare chest rose and fell gently in sleep. The discoloration over his left eye had changed from an angry purple-red to a shiny, dark blue. Some of the swelling had faded so much that he would soon claim full visibility. The sutures along his cheek held the flesh tightly with no sign of swelling or redness. There was no doubt that his face would be scarred, but she suspected that it would not detract from the natural male beauty which made him devastatingly handsome.

She decided to let him sleep. She needed to contact her parents in San José to find out what progress they'd made in securing the release of her brother.

The phone rang a half dozen times at the Vegas' San José residence before someone picked up the telephone.

"Hola," came a softly modulated female voice.

"Mother?"

"Serena? Have you heard anything?"

"No. That's why I'm calling you."

A soft sigh filtered through the receiver. "Nothing has changed. Raul met with President Montalvo twice, but there's been no word from the American ambassador about a formal discussion. All we can do is pray."

"Doña Maria says Gabe is safe."

There was a moment of silence before Juanita spoke again. "Are you certain she said that?"

"She said 'he's safe from himself and those who seek to take his life.' You know I'm not superstitious, but I believe her, Mother."

"I don't know what to believe anymore. All I want to do is…" Her voice broke, and she was unable to continue.

Serena felt her own eyes fill with tears. "Mother, please—don't." The soft sobbing coming through the wire shattered her control. It pained her to hear her mother's anguish. "Call me when you hear something." She ended the call, hanging up and cutting off the sound of Juanita's weeping.

Blinking back her own tears, she berated herself for telephoning and upsetting her mother. She made a silent promise not to call her parents again. She would wait for them to contact her.

She felt a strange restlessness that wouldn't permit her to lie or sit down. What she wanted was for everything to be a dream, and when she awoke all of the horrors of the past two weeks would disappear like a lingering puff of smoke. Something unknown whispered that she should believe Luz Maria's prediction that Gabe wasn't in any danger, but she would not believe it fully until she touched him without the barriers of shackles or the presence of criminal justice officials.

Her anxiety made her want to jog. However, that was impossible in ninety degree tropical heat. Whenever she ran she gloried in the rush of wind across her face. It made her feel as if she were flying, soaring high above the noisy crowds and burgeoning traffic, and made her free—free from the painful memories of love found and lost.

Love lost. Why was she thinking of Xavier? Was it because of what Luz Maria prophesied about her future being linked with David Cole's?

Why him, when they did not even like each other? Why did she find arrogance and vanity unappealing traits in other men, but not in David?

Walking over to the French doors, she opened them and stepped out onto the second story veranda. The humidity swallowed her whole in a cocoon of weighty, wet warmth. Low-hanging dark clouds indicated an imminent downpour. She sat down on a cushioned bamboo chaise, staring out at the landscape surrounding *La Montaña* and remembering the first time she had stepped out onto the veranda. The view of the mountains, ocean, and the dense growth of the rain forest had made her feel as if she had flown up to heaven, where she looked down and saw all that God had created. A smile had curved her lips and she had whispered, "It is good."

And it was still good. The panoramic vistas had the power to soothe and erase her anxiety. She had waited until four months after her marriage ended to return to Limón, and the moment the small plane touched down at the airport the healing had begun.

Closing her eyes, she listened to cries of the birds calling to one another in the towering trees. The cacophony of sounds was nature's orchestra serenading life. She lost track of time until a rumble of thunder, followed by a driving downpour, forced her off the veranda.

She returned to the bedroom and glanced at a clock on the bedside table. It was only eleven-forty. She had been up for hours, and felt as if she had accomplished nothing. Some of her restlessness was because she truly had nothing to do.

Taking care of David had not taken up much of her time. She changed his bed, gave him his shots, brought him his meals, and assisted with his grooming. Other than that he was now a patient who had required very little attention. She had only to give him injections of antibiotics and check his stitches.

Her role at the hospital, although supervisory, was hectic and demanding. She was responsible for scheduling rotations, supervisory staff meetings, and weekly conferences with hospital administration. There were times when she complained about the responsibility, but she truly loved her profession and marveled at the ongoing successes of modern medicine.

She made her way quietly into David's room. A smile crinkled the skin around her eyes when she saw him leaning against the wrought-iron balustrade, eyes closed. He'd shifted most of his body's weight to his left foot. The now softly falling rain pasted his hair to his scalp and molded his boxers to his hips and thighs. Seeing the moisture bathe his golden-brown body, droplets of water clinging to the hair on his chest, caused a rush of heat to sweep over her body like a backdraft of fire from a launching rocket.

Serena felt like a voyeur, watching numbly as David raised his arms and right foot while slowly turning his face heavenward. He kept the position for a full minute, then lowered his arms, foot, and head. She wondered if he were perhaps meditating, or possibly praying?

Her gaze was fixed on the perfection of his tall, muscled physique, noting the symmetry of his wide shoulders in proportion to his waist and hips. She visually measured the trim lines of his torso's proportion to the length of his legs.

And it was in that minute that she realized that she ached, needing him to physically make her a complete woman.

It had been more than two years since she had lain with a man, and what she had denied, had been denying, was that she missed the intimacy.

She missed the furtive glances, caresses, kisses, missed lying in bed, touching, missed waking in the morning to a warm, hard body next to her own, and she missed the complete possession when she accepted a man into her heart and into her body, when for a short time they would become one and she could claim him as her own.

Moving silently across the space, she stepped out onto the veranda. Ignoring the moisture seeping into her hair and clothing, she stood inches from David, watching the serenity softening his delicate features. He had to know that she was there, but he gave no indication, he did not open his eyes.

Something foreign, unknown, gripped her hand as she touched the center of his chest. The heat from his body almost caused her to pull her fingers away, but she did not.

Drawing even closer, she pressed her chest to his, her arms encircling his waist. She felt a wave of embarrassment heat up her face as he stood rigid, hands at his sides.

"Why don't you come in out of the rain?" she urged softly.

"I love being out in the rain," he countered in the deep melodious tone she had come to savor. "For me it's a renewal, a rebirth."

"A renewal of what?"

Opening his eyes for the first time since Serena touched him, David stared down at her damp, curly hair. He knew the exact moment she had stepped out onto the veranda. He could detect her scented body over the redolent essence of flourishing flowers and fauna surrounding *La Montaña.* He realized he would be able to identify her even if blindfolded. His breathing deepened as he felt the outline of her firm breasts against his bared chest.

"A renewal of life, Serena. Without the rain life would cease to exist. Each time it rains I think of it as a promise that the world and all that is in it will continue until the next time. Unfortunately, most of us take rain and life for granted."

"How true." Her voice was a breathless whisper, lulling and pulling David in. He felt a rush of desire that he wasn't able to control.

The evidence of his desire was apparent. There was no way he could hide his aroused state—not with her body molded to his.

Serena felt his heat melt into her. She wanted him, and it was more than obvious that he wanted her. It had taken only two days for her feelings and her role to change from caretaker to that of caregiver.

She remembered his statement that he had not made it a practice to sleep with a lot of women. That may have been so, but she also instinctively knew that David Cole certainly could attract a woman.

Her own sexual experience was limited. There were usually extended periods of time between her relationships, and if she did enter a relationship it usually was long-term.

Her hands dropped as she attempted to pull away, but David's hands moved quickly up to her shoulders. "Don't leave me—not yet." His gaze dropped to her chest, seeing the outline of her breasts against the damp T-shirt. "I want to hold you."

She felt his hardness pressing against her middle. She did not want him to hold her because she feared her own lack of control. How could she tell a man she'd known for two days that she wanted him to kiss her? That she wanted him to remind her that she was a woman who wanted and needed the intimacy of physical contact.

Flashing a nervous smile, she said, "This is very unethical, David. I'm your nurse."

He smiled his lopsided, dimpled smile. "That's because you've been unethical. Nurses normally would not share a patient's bed, nor do they sit on their patients' laps when shaving them."

Her jaw dropped. She hadn't realized that he was aware that

she had slept next to him his first night at *La Montaña.* "That protocol could not be avoided," she countered.

"And neither can this one." Without giving her a chance to analyze his statement, he slipped his arms down her body, his fingers encircling her waist as he lifted her off her feet until her head was even with his.

Her hands moved up his shoulders, her arms slipping around his neck. Holding tightly to keep her balance, she wasn't given the opportunity to protest as David angled his head until his mouth moved over hers, staking its claim. She felt the demanding pressure of his mouth, savoring the heated contact of flesh meeting flesh.

Then it was over as quickly as it had begun. He lowered her until her sandaled feet touched the solid surface of the veranda floor, unaware of the effort it took for him to maintain his balance while picking her up. If he hadn't used the wrought-iron railing for support, the action would've proved disastrous. If he had fallen forward he would have crushed her. Not only would he have caused further injury to himself, but her as well.

"I'm ready to go in now." His breathing was labored, as if he had run a grueling race. Tasting her mouth confirmed that his body was in concert with what he was beginning to feel for her. It wasn't gratitude for her caring for his injuries, but his wanting her the way a man wanted a woman.

Pulling out of his loose embrace, Serena turned and reentered his bedroom. "Aren't you going to help me?" he called out to her retreating back.

Not turning around, she curled her fingers into tight fists. Her body was going through all of the familiar changes associated with sexual arousal. Her breasts felt hot and heavy and the pulsing center between her thighs made her knees tremble.

"Who helped you get out of bed and walk out there?" Tension hardened her sultry voice. She was angry and annoyed that she had lost herself in the man and in the moment.

The erotic vision of watching him standing in the rain, wearing only a pair of white, cotton boxers lingered in her mind. She could still see the contrast of his rich, brown body against the white fabric, recall the definition in his arms as he'd raised them above his head, and remember the warmth of his body when she'd placed her hand against his chest. The sights were enough to make her lower her guard so much that she would permit her own body to ache for a man.

David stared at her petite figure. There was no doubt that she was angry with him.

And he was surprised at his own reaction to Serena. It wasn't that he was celibate. What he was was *very* controlled. He had gotten used to women coming on to him and learned to counter-act their advances before he entered his twenties. He always wanted to want a woman, not the reverse. He did not want to want Serena Morris, though, but his body would not follow the dictates of his brain.

And he found it ironic that while he lay under Raul Cordero-Vega's roof he coveted the daughter of the man he despised most in the world. How could he tell her that her stepfather ordered his assault? That he was responsible for him being in Limón? That in a fit of rage Vega could possibly threaten to take his life? And why would she believe him—a stranger—if he disclosed his suspicions?

He couldn't tell Serena that it had taken him the better part of a quarter of an hour to make his way out of the bed, to half-limp and half-crawl out to the veranda. He had fallen twice before he was able to support his sagging body against the balustrade.

Serena made it to the door before she realized David hadn't moved. Turning around, she saw in the distance separating them that he held onto the elaborately swirling wrought-iron design. He hadn't moved because he couldn't move.

Retracing her steps quickly, she moved to his side. "Lean on me." The command was soft and comforting. He did lean against her—heavily. Again, it was apparent that he had overexerted himself.

"Not the bed. Please," he added, breathing heavily when she stopped and stared up at him.

"Okay. Then you can sit on the chair." She led him over to the chair where he sat down, his lips drawn back over his teeth. She watched him massage his left temple. "Do you want something for the pain?"

He shook his head slowly. "No. It's not too bad," he lied smoothly. The pain had returned, this time with a blinding fury. It slashed across his left eye, making it difficult for him to focus clearly. Closing his eyes, he willed it gone.

Watching him intently, Serena saw what David would not admit. His rapid breathing and the absence of natural color in his face indicated discomfort—extreme discomfort. Raising his feet to the footstool, she sat down on the floor and cradled his left ankle. Manipulating the foot, she began with his big toe and massaged it with the pads of her thumbs. She listened, rather than saw, as his breathing slowed and the tension in his foot eased. She massaged each toe, feeling the grainy pressure under the flesh give way, then proceeded downward to the ball of the foot, along the arch to the heel.

David opened his eyes when the debilitating pressure over his eye eased. He stared down at Serena massaging his foot. Her dampened hair had begun to curl around her face and shoulders. A few wayward curls fell over her forehead and he yearned to reach over and push them away so they could not obscure the perfection of her features. He wanted to study the shape of her pouting mouth, committing it to memory. Everything about her face was flawlessly young and virginal.

He'd only brushed his mouth over hers and she had not responded, prompting him to believe that perhaps she was quite inexperienced, or might even be a virgin. He wondered how old she could be. Twenty-two? Twenty-three? If she was in her early twenties, then she was too young for him. At thirty-six he wanted a woman secure enough and mature enough to deal with his decision not to commit to a relationship which would eventually end in marriage.

He believed in marriage, respected its sanctity, yet he was not ready for it.

Serena, finished with the left foot, turned her attention to the swollen right one. She repeated the manipulations she'd used on his left foot, exercising a minimum amount of pressure.

"You have magical hands," he said in a quiet tone. "Where did you learn to do this?"

Raising her head, she stared up at him, smiling. "Reflexology? My ex-husband taught me."

He did not know why but a rush of relief settled in his throat, making him momentarily speechless in his surprise. *Ex-husband.* She had been married. She was not a virgin.

"How long have you been divorced?"

"Annulled," she corrected. "It's been two years."

He leaned forward on the chair. "How old were you when you got married? Eighteen or nineteen?"

Serena laughed, the low haunting sound caressing him as if he had reached out and placed her hand over his heart. "I'll accept that as a compliment, but I'm sorry to disappoint you. I was twenty-eight."

His expression stilled, growing serious. "You're thirty?" The question was a statement.

"Yes." The single word lingered like a sigh.

Serena watched David watching her. It was as if he were photographing her with his eyes, seeing her for the very first time. His gaze slid smoothly from her face to her chest before reversing itself. Something foreign, unknown, erupted in the entrancement, and she knew that the man whose foot she cradled so gently saw her in a whole different light.

"How old did you think I was?"

"Early twenties."

"I'd hardly be a nursing supervisor at twenty-three."

"You could be if you graduated from nursing school while still in your teens."

She managed a sultry laugh. "I happen not to be that gifted."

Her smile faded as she studied him studying her. The seconds ticked off until more than a full minute elapsed. "How old are you?" Her husky voice broke the pregnant silence.

"Thirty-six."

She arched a sculpted eyebrow. "You appear older."

He noticed she'd said *appear,* not look. "Perhaps it's the gray hair. Most people in my family gray prematurely."

Serena shook her head. "It's not the gray hair at all. You seem to have a weariness not usually associated with your age. It's as if you're living two lifetimes simultaneously."

A slight smile softened his mouth and deepened the lines at the corners of his large, dark eyes. "How right you are. I'd planned for this business trip to be the last time I'd ever come to this country. I'm here to sell off the last of ColeDiz's Costa Rican investments."

Her gaze widened at this disclosure. "How long do you think that'll take?"

"I've given myself fourteen days. And if it doesn't happen within the two weeks, then I'm going to walk away and leave it unresolved."

A slight frown furrowed her smooth forehead. "But won't you lose a lot of money for your investors?"

His frown matched hers. "There are no investors. ColeDiz is privately and family owned. I'll have to offset the loss by giving up a portion of my personal resources." The banana plantation was worth millions, but he would willingly forfeit the money to rid himself of Raul Cordero-Vega's domination. Vega's claim that the workers at the banana plantation polluted the environment was totally unfounded. All the plastic casings were recycled.

She remembered Leandro saying that the Coles were one of the wealthiest black families in the States, and David had just confirmed that fact.

Releasing his foot, she stood up. "I'm going to change out of these damp clothes, and I'm going to suggest that you also change. I'll check to see whether Dr. Rivera sent over the cane. If he did, then I'll help you walk around before *siesta.*"

She moved over to a chest of drawers and withdrew a pair of shorts she had purchased and another pair of boxers. Retracing her steps, she handed the clothes to David.

He took them, saying, "I think I can dress myself."

She nodded and walked out of the room, closing the door behind her.

CHAPTER 13

David sat staring at the space where Serena had been, his thoughts a tangle of ambivalence, not understanding why his emotions fluctuated from one extreme to the other. He did not know why he felt drawn to Serena when in pain, then indifferent once he was free of pain.

He knew he needed her, but he did not want to want her. But even that was beyond him whenever he stopped seeing her as a nurse and saw her as a woman.

He was shocked when she revealed her age. She looked much younger, but looking back he realized that she exhibited an air of confidence atypical of a woman in her early twenties. And that confidence had not come from her career; it came from living thirty years of life.

Leaning forward and using the armrests, he pushed to his feet. He managed to change his clothes with a minimum of effort. The shorts fit perfectly, even though the style was not one he would have selected. As soon as he was able to put on a shoe he would begin wearing the clothes he'd packed for his trip.

He led off with his right foot, and amazingly it wasn't as painful as it had been. What Serena had called reflexology was miraculous. His entire body felt loose, fully relaxed, and his mind was clear for the first time in days.

Walking slowly across the bedroom and putting most of the pressure on his right heel, David managed to keep his balance. He made it to the door at the same time Serena appeared with an adjustable aluminum cane hanging over her wrist. She had brushed her hair and secured it off her face with an elastic band. A jumble of damp curls floated over the crown of her head, causing the breath to catch in his chest at the innocent sensuality of the provocative disarray. She had exchanged her shorts and shirt for a pale orange cotton dress with narrow straps crisscrossing her shoulders and back. When she shifted slightly he could see that her back was bared to the waist, displaying an inordinate amount of flawless, sable-brown flesh.

He went completely still, unable to move. Desire, hot and rushing, exploded, and he closed his eyes briefly, hoping to shut out the erotic vision of the petite woman standing inches from him.

What was there about Serena Morris that made his body react with such reckless abandonment? He'd seen women much more classically beautiful and voluptuous. The fact that she was shorter than the women he normally found himself attracted to was also puzzling.

Opening his eyes, he stared down at her staring up at him. What he had to admit was that even though Serena appeared young and quite virginal she projected an aura of sensuality that most women could never claim. Her provocative voice, the way she looked up at him through her lashes, and the way she moved were all as measured as a choreographed dance. The entire package screamed silently for him to take her. Take her and enjoy whatever she was willing to offer.

But was she offering? He shook his head. *No.* She'd offered him the knowledge of her profession, and nothing more. It was he who wanted more.

Why now? What could he want from Serena that he hadn't gotten from other women in his past? And why her? Why the daughter of his nemesis?

Arching her sculpted eyebrows, Serena smiled. "Are you ready for your walk around the block?"

Returning her smile, David revealed a mouth filled with large, white, straight teeth. "Lead on, MacDuff."

She handed him the cane, watching as he adjusted its length.

Gripping the rubber-padded handle with his right hand, he took a step, then another. Satisfaction lit up his dark eyes. He extended his left hand, and he was not disappointed when she grasped it.

Serena felt the strength of his long fingers curled around hers. "I think we'll begin with walking the length of the hall. If you get tired let me know, and we'll stop."

Side by side, they made their way out of the bedroom and down the carpeted hallway. David passed the room with the locked door, pausing momentarily. "Whose room is this?"

Serena glanced at the door, then closed her eyes. When she reopened them she saw David staring at her with an expectant look on his face. "It's my brother's."

He nodded, wondering why the Vegas had elected to lock the door. He still maintained a bedroom suite at his parents' West Palm Beach residence, and the door to the suite remained open and available to him whenever he returned.

Thoughts of his own unoccupied Boca Raton house elicited a wry smile. It had taken him two years to locate the architect who could design the house he sought, and another two years from the time the plans were drawn up to the time the towering structure was completed.

His home was configured in three sections—the main house, running vertically from the local road, and two additional "bookend" structures that made up a guest house and a recording studio. The rooms were voluminous, with twenty-foot high ceilings, permitting ample height for the intense Florida heat to rise above the tiled and carpeted floors. The main house contained living and dining rooms, a master bedroom, a smaller bedroom, and the kitchen. Guest bedrooms with private balconies were situated within one of the "bookend" structures, which were fully accessible from the courtyard. A series of French doors displayed a bougainvillea-covered pergola bordering the courtyard.

He thought of the last time he stood in his home, staring out at the swimming pool, noting his approval of the dark finish inside the pool which allowed the water to absorb as much radiant heat as possible during the winter months. What had pleased him most about the structure's overall design was that screens were designed to slide into walls, so that when the house was open, it was truly open.

The only thing that had prevented him from moving in was its lack of furnishings. He was to meet with his oldest brother's wife once he concluded his business with Cordero-Vega to begin the process of selecting furnishings and accessories. The delight in Parris Cole's green-flecked brown eyes was apparent once she strolled through the massive empty spaces. She'd promised to decorate it with furnishings that would make it a designer's showplace worthy of a layout for *Architectural Digest.*

He had waited four years from design to construction, and he was willing to wait another six months to complete decorating its interiors.

"What are the chances of your brother being found not guilty?"

Serena chewed her lower lip before answering. "I don't really know at this point. My father hired one of the best criminal attorneys in Florida, but he wasn't able to persuade the judge to let Gabe out on bail."

David saw the anguish on her lovely face and registered the pain in her words. He had brothers, and he wondered how he would feel if they were to spend days, months, or even years incarcerated.

Tightening his grip on her slender hand, he glanced down at her enchanting profile. "I can't promise you anything, but when I return to Florida I'll see what my father can do. He no longer wheels and deals like he used to, but he still has enough clout to make a telephone call to Florida's inner circle of power brokers."

Stopping, she turned and smiled at David with an open, expectant expression. "You'd do that?"

A smile brought an immediate softening to his battered features. Inclining his head, he said quietly, "Yes, I would."

Rising on tiptoe, she pressed her mouth to his. "Thank you, David."

The warm sweetness of her mouth stoked the smoldering fires burning within him. David was certain that if he had not been holding onto the cane or her fingers, he would have taken Serena in his arms and allowed her to feel the sense of sexual urgency that made him want to take her to his bed.

He did not want to make love to Serena as much as he wanted to copulate. He did not want emotions to enter into the act. What he wanted was for their coming together to be as primitive and unbridled as an act of mating, and once he entered her body he would hold nothing back. There was something about her that touched the most primeval core of his existence, and he wanted to assuage the savage craving by using her body as a receptacle for his seed. The thought that he wanted to use her body for his lust caused him to stumble.

"Why don't we stop and rest?" Serena offered, thinking perhaps that David had tired.

"It's okay. I can make it to the end of the hall." He was breathing heavily, but it wasn't because he had overexerted himself.

Why was he thinking of using her, when he'd never used any woman to slake his sexual frustrations? *I'm losing it,* he berated himself. The last thing he wanted to do was take advantage of Raul Cordero-Vega's daughter while under the man's roof. And if he did, he doubted that he would leave Costa Rica with his head intact.

Continuing down the hall, he noticed an alcove and the door to another room. "What's there?"

"My parents' bedroom."

"How did they meet?"

"His first cousin was my mother's roommate in college."

"Had your mother gone to college in Costa Rica?"

Serena shook her head. "No. Gabriella came to the States to major in English, while my mother majored in Spanish. Both were foreign language majors. My mother came to Costa Rica during a holiday recess and met Raul at a family gathering.

"It was apparent that they were attracted to each other, but Juanita was engaged at the time. Family gossip says that Raul followed her around like a lovesick puppy, telling her that if she broke her engagement he would marry her the following day. Juanita did not break her engagement and married my father Hannibal Morris a month after she graduated college.

"They waited five years before starting a family, because my father wanted to finish medical school. It wasn't until she was twenty-seven that Juanita found herself pregnant. They were overjoyed with the news, but their joy was short-lived. My father died instantly in a head-on accident when a teenage driver lost control of his car during a severe thunderstorm. My mother, who was eight months pregnant, woke up in a hospital's recovery room to find that she had become a mother and a widow.

"She moved in with her parents for a while. Then, when I was six months old, she took Gabriella up on her offer to spend some time with her in San José. She and Raul met again and he pursued her like a man possessed. There were rumors that he took advantage of her grief, but no one would deny that he didn't love her. A year and a half later she agreed to marry him. Juanita presented Raul with his first and only child the day I celebrated my fourth birthday."

"It appears that your stepfather was a patient man."

What he did not say was that Raul Cordero-Vega was also tenacious, stubborn, and obstinate. Each time they met it was he who had compromised, until the last time. But not this time. This time the Interior Minister wouldn't walk away a winner.

"He's not perfect, David. That was something I realized years ago. But he is the only father I have, and I know he loves me as much or more than I love him."

They made it to the top of the staircase, turned, and retraced their steps. The sounds of their feet were muffled in the carpeting which ran the length of the hallway. David's right foot throbbed slightly as he walked into his bedroom and sat down heavily on the side of the bed.

Serena took the cane from him and rested it against the bedside table, where he could reach it if he needed to get out of bed. "Do you want anything to eat or drink?"

He barely moved his head and she knew instinctively that his headache had returned. "No," he managed between clenched teeth. "I just want to rest now."

Swinging his legs into the bed, she covered him with a sheet. She ran her fingers down the left side of his face, noting that the flesh over his cheekbone had tightened considerably. Her fingers moved to his temples and she massaged them gently, releasing his tension. She felt the muscles easing with her tender ministrations.

He stared at her, his gaze as soft and loving as a caress. "Thank you for taking care of me, Miss Serena Morris."

She met his gaze with a gentle one of her own. "You're quite welcome, David C. Cole."

He smiled, his dimples winking at her. "The C stands for Claridge. It's my father's middle name."

"Why don't you try to get some sleep, and when you wake up we'll share lunch and you can tell me all about your family."

His lids fluttered before a sweep of long black lashes lay on his high cheekbones. "You've tucked me in but haven't given me a kiss," he teased.

"Nurses don't kiss their patients."

"You did before."

"When?"

"When I told you that I'd contact my father on your brother's behalf," he reminded her.

Serena felt her face heat up. "That was different. It was a kiss of gratitude."

Rising on an elbow, he reached out his right hand and he held her face gently. "Let me show you how grateful I am that you helped save my life."

Before she was given an opportunity to protest, Serena found herself lying across David's bare chest, her mouth fused to his.

This kiss was nothing like the one they'd shared on the veranda, or the one she had given him in the hallway.

His firm lips moved like watered silk over hers, coaxing her to respond as she felt the blood coursing through her veins and arousing the passion she had locked away when her marriage ended.

She felt the dormant strength in his body as his arms curved possessively around her waist, while his broad shoulders heaved as he breathed in the scent of her bare flesh welded to his. Her breasts grew heavy, the nipples tightening from the shivers of delight igniting between her thighs and journeying upward. She gasped, giving him the advantage he needed, and his tongue slid sinuously between her parted lips.

His heat, the intoxicating smell of his aftershave, and the protective feel of his arms around her pulled Serena into a cocoon of wanting where she forgot everything but the man whose mouth was doing things to her she had not thought possible.

Her hands went to his head, where her fingers played in the short, silky strands lying close to his scalp. Moaning softly, she shifted, feeling his hardness searching against her thighs through layers of cotton.

"Da—vid," she moaned, his name coming out in a long, lingering sigh of complete satisfaction.

"Mi vida, mi alma," he groaned, answering her. And that she was. She had become his life because she had helped give him back his life. And now that he'd kissed her she had become a part of his soul. A soul he did not and could not afford to lose.

Tightening his grip on her slender body, David reversed their positions, devouring her mouth. He pulled back, giving both a chance to catch their breaths before taking her mouth again in a kiss that made her surrender to his unyielding, relentless assault as her tongue met his.

Serena welcomed his weight, throwing her head back and baring her throat. He rained passionate kisses along the column of her neck, moving down to her breasts. One hand searched under the bodice of her dress and closed over a full, firm breast.

Seconds later, his mouth replaced his hand at the same time she arched off the mattress. His teeth closed gently around a turgid nipple. A low, keening sound escaped from her open mouth. Not recognizing the sound as her own, she froze as a rush of moisture bathed the secret place between her legs. Her eyes widened in shock. No! She couldn't! Not with a stranger!

"No, David!" She tried rising, but couldn't because of his greater weight bearing down on her. "Let me go."

Through the thick haze of desire making him a prisoner of his own passions, David heard her desperate cry. Raising his head, he stared down at the fear shimmering with the tears in her large, rounded eyes. What had he done to frighten her? All he did was kiss her.

Cradling her face between his palms, he pressed a kiss on the tip of her nose, then released her and rolled off her body. She slapped his hand away when he attempted to adjust the bodice of her dress.

He stared at her lowered head as she smoothed out the wrinkled fabric after she'd pulled the narrow straps up over her shoulders. "Don't expect me to apologize for kissing you." Her head snapped up at the same time her jaw dropped. "I kissed you because I wanted to," he explained softly. Her expression shifted from one of shock to anger. "If you hadn't wanted it, then you should've said so, and not kissed me back."

Serena scrambled off the bed and glared at him, her hands folded on her hips. "You arrogant son of a—"

"You liked it, Serena," he snapped, cutting off her angry tirade. "Otherwise you wouldn't have had your tongue down my throat."

She went completely still as her mind replayed his accusation. *You liked it.* And she *had* liked it. No, she loved it. The feel of David's hands and mouth had taken her beyond herself. And for the few minutes she lay in his arms she'd forgotten every other man who had ever touched her, wondering what it would be like for him to possess her totally.

Tilting her delicate chin, she stared down her nose at him.

"You're right, David Claridge Cole, I liked it. I liked you kissing and touching me." It was her turn to watch his expression change from cockiness to bewilderment, and she decided to challenge his arrogance. "And I'm willing to bet that you want more than a kiss or a feel." Hooking her thumbs under the straps of her dress, she took a step closer to the bed. "You want all of me, David?" she crooned. "Do you feel up to burning up the sheets? Do you think you can handle me?"

He watched, mouth gaping, as Serena slipped the straps of her dress off her shoulders and gathered the skirt and pulled it above her knees, baring her slim, muscled thighs. Her lids lowered over her eyes, not permitting him to see their clear gold depths.

"Do you mind me being on top?" she questioned, her voice dropping to a lower register where it sounded like a muted horn in a thick fog. "I like submission in *my men* when I make love."

The blood rushed to David's head, tightening the vise of pain around his temples. He wanted the blood in another part of his body so that he could take the seductive witch up on her challenge, but it was not to be. The heat and pain stabbed him behind his left eye, nearly blinding him.

"I can't," he admitted. He shook his head, then chided himself for doing so as the pain intensified. Easing down on the bed, he lay back and placed a muscled forearm over his forehead. "Please go."

Serena pressed her attack. "I'll go, but I want you to remember something, Sport. Don't ever tell me what I want or like. I'm quite capable of verbalizing my wants and my dislikes. If I want you to kiss me or decide I want you in my bed I'll come out and tell you. Do I make myself clear, or do you need the Spanish translation?"

"Lo siento mucho," David apologized, breathing heavily and wishing she would leave him alone.

"So am I," she countered, turning and walking out of the room. And she *was* sorry, sorry that she had permitted him to kiss her, sorry that she enjoyed it so much, and sorry that it reminded her of how sterile her life had become.

CHAPTER 14

Serena spent the afternoon berating herself for her wanton exhibition in David's bedroom. For a brief, crazed moment she had become a *puta,* displaying her wares and offering herself to a man for his sexual pleasure. What had saved her was that he had not been able to follow through with the blatant seduction.

Walking slowly through the greenhouse, she barely noticed the many plants and trees as she recalled David's gasp when she'd bared her thighs. A smile softened and curved her lush mouth when she remembered telling him that she liked being on top. Just for that brief instant she feared that he would faint. It was only after he lay down that she realized that he was in pain.

But something also nagged at her, telling her that David Cole was not a man who would permit a woman to openly challenge him. If he was anything like her father, she knew he would exact punishment at another time, and by his own methods.

Shrugging a slender shoulder, she continued her tour of the enormous, enclosed, glass structure. She and David had not shared lunch because she told Luz Maria to have one of the women assigned to *La Montaña*'s housekeeping staff bring him his lunch. Deciding to forego her own meal, she telephoned Leandro and suggested that he come by after office hours to check on his patient. She wanted him to discharge David so that he could conclude his business matters with her father, then leave Costa Rica. Having him live at *La Montaña* had become too encompassing and distracting.

She stopped at a tree whose bark was covered with a profusion of rare orchids so dark that they appeared black instead of an inky purple. These orchids were only one of Raul Cordero-Vega's many prized hybrids. Raul, a highly educated botanist, had said on occasion that he missed teaching and lecturing. However, he preferred to work for the government, wherein he was responsible for protecting Costa Rica's natural environment for the generations to come after him.

In a corner of the greenhouse was a plot with Luz Maria's herbs. None of them were labeled like her father's, so Serena had no idea what the plants were nor their purposes.

Luz Maria had promised that when she had children she would teach her what commonly grown plants she could use to cure or heal boils, fevers, to counteract the discomfort associated with headaches, menstrual and teething pain, and insect bites, and to slow down the poisonous effects from venomous reptiles or spiders.

Walking the perimeter of the greenhouse, Serena decided it was time for Luz Maria to fulfill her promise now. She had planned to spend three months in Costa Rica, while waiting for an assurance that her brother could be released on bail. She would use the time to her advantage.

She left the greenhouse and spent the remainder of *siesta* in the aviary. Most of the exotic birds were housed in enormous cages, some from floor-to-ceiling, but others were left to fly about with reckless freedom. A brightly colored pygmy parrot lighted on her bare shoulder and pecked at the tiny, gold-hoop earring dangling from her left lobe.

Shooing him away, she watched the antics of the other birds, who had realized a stranger had invaded their habitat. Most fluttered wildly, calling out to one another. The flash of bright color was blinding, ranging from brilliant yellow and vermillion red to seductively deep blues, purple, and black.

La Montaña, the greenhouse, and the connecting aviary represented Raul's material wealth and pride. His wife and his children were his priceless treasures, second only to his love of his country.

* * *

David lay across the bed, staring up at the ceiling. A tiny, dark-skinned woman had brought him his lunch on a tray and he had sent her away, along with the food. His seething anger overrode his need to eat.

He had made a fool of himself, and Serena humiliated him. She had offered him her body and he hadn't accepted what she was so willing to give him. And he wanted her more than he had wanted any woman up to that moment.

It was said that when women became sexual aggressors men usually could not perform because of the reversal of roles; he had become an example when her brazen exhibition stunned and frightened him. He'd found himself inept.

Impotent! How could he be at thirty-six? Sitting up and swinging his legs over the side of the bed, he reached for the cane. Making his way slowly across the bedroom, he opened the French doors and limped out to the veranda. The tropical heat was brutal, sucking the breath from his lungs and making breathing a labored exercise. Squinting against the rays of the brilliant sun, he stared out at the stretch of ocean in the distance. His gaze swung around to the tops of the dense trees shading the cool, dark undergrowth of the jungle. Despite the heat he shivered slightly when he thought of what prowled along the jungle floor. Closing his eyes, he imagined the teeming life inhabiting the rain forest. The cries of the birds, the growls of the jaguars, and the screeches of the monkeys became music, notes strung together to form an exotic rhythmic composition.

For the first time in nine years he heard music in his head. Notes, harmonies, and melodies he wanted to capture before they floated into nothingness. A smile filtered across his face as he opened his eyes. He needed paper. He wanted to write down the hauntingly beautiful sounds reverberating in his mind.

Turning, he limped from the veranda, closed the French doors to keep out the heat, then walked out of his bedroom to Serena's. Her door was slightly ajar, and he heard a man's voice. Listening intently, he realized she had the radio on. He knocked on the door and waited. He knocked again, then pushed it open.

His earlier anxiety quickly vanished. He knew he was not impotent when his body reacted quickly to the sight of Serena coming out of the adjoining bath wearing only a pair of tiny, white-lace, bikini panties.

Serena saw him at the same time he stepped into her bedroom. Startled, she stood still, hands frozen at her sides. Her eyes widened as she watched David staring at her half-naked body. His chest rose and fell heavily in unison with her own trembling breasts.

Somewhere, somehow, she found her voice. "Get out."

Instead of leaving, he turned his back, shutting out the vision of her flawless body. He could still see her perfectly formed, full breasts resting high above her narrow rib cage. The legs he had only glimpsed before were exhibited with slim thighs flowing into strong calves and slender ankles.

"I knocked but didn't get an answer, so I walked in," he said, apologizing.

Serena stared at his broad back as she inched over to a chair and picked up a sleeveless smock dress. He had elected to wear one of the T-shirts she had bought for him.

"What do you want?" she asked, slipping her arms through the sleeves.

"I need paper. Preferably unlined."

"What for?"

"I want to write down some music."

After buttoning the many buttons lining the front of the dress, she walked over to David and stood in front of him. She wanted to scream at him for making her aware of how much she needed him, and for being so damned attractive.

"Before I give you the paper I think we should talk."

Sighing heavily, he nodded. "You're right."

Her gaze moved from his face down to his right hand, which held the cane in a punishing grip. It was apparent that he had shifted most of his weight from his injured foot.

Taking his left hand she led him slowly over to an alcove in the room, where she had set up a sitting area. "Come and sit down."

David eased himself down to a cushioned bamboo rocker, permitting the cane to slide to the sisal area rug covering the terracotta floor. The furnishings in the alcove were delightfully attractive. The orange, black, and yellow print on the cushions and matching tablecloth on a small round table and the carved ebony masks and pieces of sculpture on a bamboo bookcase mirrored the blending of African and Caribbean cultures of Puerto Limón.

Serena claimed a chair facing David. She studied his dark eyes watching her every move as she smoothed out the flowing fabric of her dress. Glancing away, she stared out through the French doors.

"I'd like to apologize for my wanton behavior earlier this afternoon," she began. Her gaze swung back to his. "But I won't retract what I said about letting you know what I like or dislike."

David lowered his head, successfully concealing an emerging smile. The forefinger of his left hand traced the rapidly healing scar over his left cheek. "Did you enjoy kissing me as much as I enjoyed kissing you?" His head came up and she was rewarded with the full force of his dimpled smile.

Her lips twitched as she tried holding back her own smile. "You don't quit, do you, David Cole? Are you ever humble?"

Pursing his mouth as if in deep thought, he shook his head. "Nope."

This response made her laugh, and to her surprise so did David. When she recovered she realized it was the first time she had laughed in weeks.

Pressing his head against the back of the chair, David flashed a sexy, lopsided grin. His bruised eye and scarred cheek made him appear less pretty. The scar marred his face just enough to give him a rugged look.

"How does it look?"

"What?" she questioned, not knowing what he was referring to.

"The scar?"

"I find it kind of sexy."

He arched a sweeping eyebrow. "Sexy? I don't think so."

"All you need is an earring in your ear and you can masquerade as a pirate for Halloween."

He leaned forward. "Give me one of your earrings, and we'll see."

Her hand went to her right ear. "They're pierced."

"So is my left ear."

She stared, wordless. She had shaved and bathed him, and not once had she noticed that his ear was pierced. She removed the earring from her right ear and walked over to where he sat. Leaning over, she inserted the small hoop in his ear.

David closed his eyes, savoring her scent and the warmth of her body. "How does it look?" he queried when she stepped back to survey his ear.

Her smile gave him his answer. "Very sexy."

He returned her smile. "Thank you."

Serena took her seat, shaking her head. "Earrings and tattoos. Have they become the latest accoutrements for an international businessman?"

"You forget that I was a musician first, businessman second."

"Which do you like better?"

"Music, of course. However, it seems as if I have a natural bent for business, while I have to work my butt off to get my music just right."

Crossing her sandaled feet at the ankles, Serena realized she wanted to know more about the man who disturbed her in every way. "Why did you leave the band?"

"My older brother Martin resigned as CEO of ColeDiz to go into politics, and I was next in line so I took over the reins."

"How long ago was this?"

"Nine years."

"Then you were very young."

"Twenty-seven. I was responsible for enterprises in at least a half dozen countries. We own vacation properties in Puerto Rico, St. Thomas, and Aruba, and coffee, sugar, and banana plantations in Belize, Mexico, and Costa Rica. I intend to divest ColeDiz of its only remaining Costa Rican venture."

"What do you plan to do with it?"

"I'll use the proceeds to set up another banana plantation in Belize."

She stared, unblinking, at this disclosure. If he was going to meet with her father, then the sale was not to be a private one. "You intend to sell it to the government?"

He glanced at her from under lowered eyebrows as his expression changed. His mien grew cold, hard, making him look as if he'd been carved out of dark marble, while his blatant masculine beauty faded behind a mask of angry loathing.

A consortium of businessmen had been willing to make an offer for the property until Raul Cordero-Vega intervened. What Vega wanted was for ColeDiz to sell the plantation to the government for half the consortium's agreed upon price. He then planned to sell the plantation to the consortium, yielding a one hundred percent profit for his government's coffers.

"That all depends on your father."

"Why my father?"

"I can't discuss that with you." David did not want to draw Serena into the undeclared war he'd been waging with her stepfather ever since he'd taken over as CEO of ColeDiz International Ltd.

Serena's expression also changed. For the first time she saw David Cole for what he was—a businessman; one who shifted millions, perhaps billions, of dollars from a country or an account as easily as one moved a piece on a chessboard.

She nodded slowly. "I'll respect your decision." Rising to her feet, she said, "I'm going to the kitchen. Would you like me to bring you something?"

"Yes, please. Something to drink."

"Don't run away," she teased, hoping to alleviate the tension that had sprung up between them with the mention of Raul Cordero-Vega's name.

"I wouldn't even if I could."

The instant the statement was out of his mouth David knew that his feelings for Serena were deepening, intensifying. The taste of her honeyed mouth and viewing her naked body were imprinted on his brain for a lifetime. He stared at her staring back at him, and in a breath of a second both knew what the other was thinking and what the other wanted. She had accused him of being arrogant, and he had no intention of changing her assessment of him.

"You have to know that I *want* you, Serena," he said quietly in Spanish. "And it's not for a quick lay," he continued in English. "And don't think I want you out of gratitude for saving my life."

Serena was certain he could hear her heart pounding in her chest as it resounded loudly in her own ears. All she knew about David Cole was that he was wealthy and he had been a musician. And all she could see was that he was gorgeous and arrogantly charming. What she did not want to acknowledge was that he was the most sensual man she had ever encountered. His delicate dark looks, pierced ear, and tattooed, muscled body stimulated her imagination so much that she was certain that sharing a bed with him was certain to become a unique experience.

"I sleep with you, and what am I left with? Memories of a few days or nights of spilled passions, while you go back to Florida and take up where you left off with your wife or your girlfriend. Thanks, but no thanks."

He smiled, shaking his head. "I have no wife or girlfriend."

"Yeah, right. And I'm a prime candidate for a hair transplant."

David's gaze went to the profusion of hair secured at the top of her head. He managed a tight smile. "I may be many things, but a liar is not one of them."

Serena wanted to accept his offer. She wanted to lock her door, then lead David to her bed. She wanted to undress him and undress herself, baring all of her body for his approval. Never had she wanted to lie with a man and offer up all that made her a woman. She wanted and needed to be reminded why she was born female. And if only the situation were different she would willingly do it and not have any regrets.

She did not want them to be in Costa Rica, and she did not want the anguish of her brother's imprisonment casting a pall over the happiness she was certain she would find in David's embrace.

Managing a wry smile, she said quietly, "Perhaps in another time and another place I'd lay with you, but not now."

"You have to know that your stepfather and I don't get along, but that's because we're much too much alike. And like Raul Cordero-Vega, I am also a patient man. I'll wait for you."

"You may have to wait a long time," she whispered.

"I really don't give a damn how long it'll take, Miss Morris." He shrugged a broad shoulder. "I have nothing but time."

Turning on her heel, she stalked out of the room, cursing under her breath. *I don't want him. I don't need him,* she told herself over and over. If she said it enough, she was certain to believe it.

She made it to the kitchen in record time. Luz Maria was nowhere to be seen. Walking over to the refrigerator, she yanked open the massive door. She took out a gallon container filled with fruit juice and placed it on the table. Her sandaled feet slapped angrily on the brick floor as she made her way over to the cabinet housing the glassware.

"He makes you very angry, no?"

Serena swung around at the sound of Luz Maria's voice. "What are you doing, spying on me?" she questioned in rapid Spanish.

Luz Maria folded her arms under her breasts and wagged her head. "There's never a need for me to spy on you, *Chica.* When are you going to believe what I tell you? You and the young man are destined to be together."

"I don't love him, Doña Maria. I don't even like him," she protested.

"Not yet," she predicted. "He's nothing like the other one."

Serena knew who she was referring to. Luz Maria never referred to Xavier by name, saying that he was not worthy of his name coming from her mouth.

Sighing audibly, she let her shoulders slump. "There are very few like Xavier. But why David Cole?" she asked, identifying him to Luz Maria for the first time. "He's—he's so sure of himself. I don't like arrogant men," she continued, trying to rationalize why she should keep David at a distance.

"He's sure of himself because he knows and sees what he wants. He wants you, *Chica,* and he's going to have you. Do not fight what is planned by a power greater than we are."

Throwing up both hands, Serena wondered why she was listening to superstition. *Why?* a silent voice answered. *Because you know she's right. She told you about Xavier, but you refused to listen.* Luz Maria had predicted her failed marriage, saying that she'd had a vision that the altar where she was to stand exchanging vows with Xavier was shrouded in darkness.

She'd married Xavier believing they would remain together forever. But it ended in days, and she ceased being Mrs. Xavier Osbourne eight months after she promised to love him until death parted them, with the annulment, and became Serena Morris again.

She retrieved the glasses and filled them with the juice, feeling Luz Maria watching her. "I don't fight it, then what? I live happily ever after?"

The older woman nodded slowly. "He'll make you happier than you can imagine. He will offer you a life filled with things most women only dream about. He will give you your heart's desire."

"Because he comes from a wealthy family?"

"It's not only money, *Chica.* He will give you children, many beautiful children. He will cherish you the way most people worship precious jewels."

Closing her eyes and shaking her head, Serena breathed heavily through her parted lips. "I can't, Doña Maria."

"Why not?"

"Not while Gabriel is—"

"Forget about your brother," Luz Maria said harshly, forcing Serena to open her eyes and glare at her. "Have you listened to anything I've been saying? Your brother is safe!" The two women stared at each other for a long, suffering moment. "He is safe," she continued, this time her voice soft and comforting. "He will be happy, *Chica*. It is time for you to seek your own happiness."

She did not know why, but she believed Luz Maria. She had quickly analyzed every word and believed. But she had to convince herself that she wanted David enough to share her future with him.

Placing the two glasses on a tray, she smiled at Luz Maria and walked out of the kitchen. She intended to try to see David in a whole new light. She would open her heart and mind to the man who had just promised to wait for her.

CHAPTER 15

Serena delivered the glass of fruit juice, a pad of unlined paper, and a pencil to David. A mysterious smile played about her lush mouth when he thanked her with a smile that made her pulse quicken with its sensuality.

He sipped the juice slowly, watching Serena over the rim of the glass. She reclaimed the chair vacated earlier and picked up a book from the table. Once he'd drained the glass, he gathered the pad and pencil, drawing horizontal lines for treble and bass staffs. Notes appeared on the lines and in spaces in rapid succession as he half-sang and hummed softly under his breath.

The sound of his singing prompted Serena to glance up from her novel. His hand moved rapidly across the pad, drawing more staffs and filling them with notes just as quickly. She was transfixed with his intense concentration. After more than half an hour he put down the pencil and massaged the area over his left eye.

Closing his eyes, David clenched his teeth and prayed that the dull, throbbing pain would disappear so that he could complete the first phase of his music project. When he opened his eyes he found Serena staring at him.

"I think you've overtaxed yourself," she stated, rising fluidly from her chair to settle down on the floor beside him. Peering at the page, she noticed it was filled with a profusion of sharps and flats as well as notes. "It looks very complicated." He had written a musical composition that included parts for piano and guitar, horn and drums.

He stared, complete surprise on his face, his pain temporarily forgotten. "You read music?"

"My mother would be very disappointed if I didn't, after eight years of piano lessons."

Leaning over, David cradled her face between his palms. "You're perfect. We're going to make a wonderful couple. Will you collaborate with me?"

She shook her head. "Surely you jest, David. I'm not an accomplished pianist."

"Let me evaluate how accomplished you are. I assume you have a piano at *La Montaña?*"

"Yes. There's one in the living room."

"Help me downstairs."

"Not today."

Releasing her, he reached down and picked up the cane. "Either you help me or I'm on my own."

Pulling away from him, she rose to her feet. "You're impossible. I've never met a man more stubborn, more vain—"

"And more arrogant than you, David Claridge Cole," he intoned, finishing her statement.

"I don't believe you. Now you're finishing my sentences."

Using the cane for support, he stood up. "Help me, Serena, or you'll be responsible if I fall on my face and—"

"No." She maneuvered close to his right side, then without warning snatched the cane from his loose grip. He nearly lost his balance, but managed to right himself. "I said not today."

David glared down at her from his impressive height, seething. He knew he could easily take the cane from her, but decided it would serve no purpose. He was more than aware that he could not navigate the staircase without her help.

Vertical lines appeared between his dark eyes. "You win." *But only today,* he added silently.

He did not protest when she led him back to his bedroom and settled him into bed. "Stay with me," he whispered when she turned to leave. He patted a space beside him. "Lie down with me."

Her eyes widened noticeably with his unexpected request. "Why?"

"I want to talk."

"Is that all?"

"Yes, that's all. Right now I don't want to be alone."

David felt a lump rise in his throat when Serena turned and walked to the door. He'd verbalized his vulnerability. He did not want to be alone because it reminded him of how alone he had been for the past nine years.

Since he left the band he'd felt adrift, flying from one country to another, sleeping in a different bed every month, and adjusting to different cultures and speech patterns within minutes after the company jet touched down on airport tarmacs.

He always returned home to Florida, reconnecting with his sisters and brothers, their husbands, wives, and children, yet feeling estranged from all of them. Both of his sisters were now grandmothers, while his brothers were fathers with four children between them. He was always "Uncle David" to the many grand- and great-grandchildren belonging to Samuel and Marguerite Cole.

Whenever there was a family gathering he was looked upon as the "loner" because he never brought a woman with him. He had not wanted to send double messages to his family and whomever he was seeing at the time. Introducing a woman to the Cole clan was viewed as an announcement of the imminent exchange of marriage vows.

But did he want to marry? *Yes.* Did he want children? *Yes.* He wanted that, and more. He wanted to marry, and get it right the *first* time, because he had taken a solemn oath that when he married it would be *for life.*

He closed his eyes, sighing audibly. What he wanted to do was wipe his mind blank in the same manner one erased a chalkboard. He could not understand why the urge to marry and have children was now so strong that it taunted him whenever he and Serena were together.

He wanted her. And the want had changed, become an aching need. He needed not just a small part of her, but all of the woman. He heard the soft click of the door as it closed, squeezing his eyelids tightly while welcoming the pain radiating along the left side of his face.

He lay, eyes closed, listening to the sound of his own heart beating loudly in his ears. The ache in his face slipped down to his chest, to his heart, and for the first time in his adult life he wanted to shed tears over a woman. And it was the first time that he hadn't gotten what he wanted from a woman.

He detected her fragrance, then the warmth of her body. David's eyes opened. He smiled and held out his hand. Serena stood next to the bed, smiling down at him. She'd removed her dress and sandals and stood clad only in her panties.

"Would you like me to share your bed?" she asked in the low, husky voice he'd come to adore.

"Por favor." His smile matched the brilliant rays of the tropical sun coming in through the French doors as she placed her hand in his. Pulling her gently down to the bed, David shifted until she lay beside him.

Serena rose slightly and draped herself over his chest, positioning her legs between his outstretched ones. "I told you I like being on top," she whispered in his ear.

He laughed, the sound rumbling deep in his broad chest. "And you also like your men submissive."

"Not too submissive." Angling for a more comfortable position, she rested her head on his shoulder and closed her eyes at the same time his arms tightened around her waist.

There was a comfortable silence, both of them listening to the even, rhythmic sound of their own breathing. Serena's breath caught in her throat when one of David's hands moved down to cradle a hip between his splayed fingers.

"You must think me very brazen to—"

"You're not brazen enough," he countered, interrupting her. "A passive woman is boring—in and out of bed."

"Are you saying that I'm exciting?"

"Just looking at you is exciting, Serena."

Raising her head, she rested her chin on his chest and stared down at him smiling up at her. "Should I take that as a compliment?"

"Sí, mi alma."

"Where did you learn to speak Spanish?"

"My mother taught me."

"With the name Cole?"

"My mother was a Diaz before she married my father. She was born in Cuba, and migrated to the States with her family when in her teens. The Diaz wealth was the result of producing some of the finest cigars to ever come out of Cuba.

"Marguerite Josefina, or M.J., disgraced her very proper family when she became a photographer's model at sixteen. She redeemed herself four years later when she married my father."

"Are you an only child?"

"No." He laughed. "I'm the youngest of five. My mother gave Samuel Claridge Cole two sons and two daughters. My father claims a third son from an illicit affair. It's taken many years, but both my parents have redeemed themselves."

"That's a lot of redemption."

"Fifty years ago having five children was the norm. Having more than three is considered a lot nowadays."

Lowering her chin, Serena pressed her cheek to his shoulder. Why were they talking about children? And why, she thought, was she lying practically naked on this man? Was it because of Luz Maria's prophecy that their destinies were linked?

She knew the answers even before her mind formed the questions. She was in David Cole's bed and in his arms because she had fallen into the sensual trap he had set for her.

It had nothing to do with his looks, his name, or wealth. It was the man. A man whose kisses took her beyond herself, and whose arrogance made her angry enough to lose whatever self-control she had so that she came on to him like a whore offering up her body. She'd shocked him, but he had come back for more. A man who said he wanted her, and had promised to wait for her. But could she afford to take the chance and lose her heart to him? *Sí,* whispered a voice that sounded like Luz Maria's.

Smiling, she rubbed her chin sensuously against his shoulder, the crisp, black hair sprinkled over his chest tickling her nose. She gasped loudly when she felt David's hand slide under the waistband of her lace panties. The heat from his fingers warmed her lower body.

She stiffened once, then relaxed as his fingers traced the outline of her bottom, lingering along the indentation separating the two spheres of firm muscle.

"David!" Serena did not recognize her own voice when his hand moved to capture the heat from her sex hidden under a mound of tight, moist curls.

The fire raging throughout her body swept to his, and David could not stop the lust and his aching need to claim Serena for his own. Every nerve in his body screamed with the fury of a storm battering everything in its wake as he tightened his hold on her body and reversed their positions.

Staring down into her large eyes, he saw the pinpoints of gold darken with her rising passion. He lowered his head and tentatively tasted her mouth with soft, nibbling kisses, while his hands were busy undoing the waistband of his shorts. He shed the shorts and boxers within seconds, but was forced to pull his mouth away when he reached down to pull the T-shirt over his head.

Serena felt his loss when he pulled back, even though his gaze had not strayed from hers. She refused to acknowledge that she was offering her body to a man she'd known less than a week, or that she was going to sleep with a man under her parents' roof for the first time in her life. All she craved was the man looming above her, who with his possession would sweep away the pain and distrust of her short-lived, failed marriage.

Naked and resplendently aroused, David knelt over Serena. A

wolfish, lopsided grin creased his cheeks. Afternoon shadows flooding the room, outlined the perfection of his golden-brown, hard body and glinted off the gold earring hanging from his left lobe.

Holding up her arms, she welcomed him to partake of the feast laid before him. He looped his fingers in the waistband of her panties and pulled them down her hips and legs. His large eyes widened once he gazed upon all of her.

"Me gusta ésta," he whispered, touching one breast. "And I like this one, too," he continued, leaning over and dropping a kiss on the other.

Serena closed her eyes and gave herself over to his slow and tender lovemaking. His mouth charted a path from her mouth to her throat and lower to her aching breasts. Supporting his greater weight on his elbows, he drew one breast into his mouth, biting gently on a swollen nipple.

"You're so beautiful," he whispered over and over, placing moist kisses down the length of her body.

She thought she was going to explode when his hand searched between her thighs and found the distended bud of flesh hidden under the tangled curls. Arching off the bed, she shivered and shuddered violently as his hand closed, holding her tightly.

"David," she moaned when the flame he'd ignited in her threatened to consume her, leaving nothing but minute particles of cinder.

He answered her plea, positioning his sex at her wet, pulsing entrance and pushing gently. His own groan echoed hers as he felt her body opening, stretching to accommodate the length and width of his blood-engorged maleness. It appeared to be minutes, but in actuality it was only seconds before he buried himself up to the root of his manhood.

He fit into her body like a glove a half size too small, and he feared exploding if he attempted to move. Her body was small and tight—inside and out. But he had to move or succumb to the lust and desire merging in a conspiracy to drive him crazy.

Serena alleviated his dilemma when she searched for his mouth and pushed her tongue between his parted lips. Her kiss was nothing like the one they'd shared earlier that morning. Her thrusting tongue unlocked the control he had always maintained when he took a woman to his bed.

Her conditioned body was like the taut skin stretched over a conga, and the rhythms coming from her body were the sounds of primal Africa—wild, unrestrained. He rolled his hips, answering the call of the drums of his ancestors, pounding out a rhythm so ancient that no one knew from whence it had come; their moist bodies writhed in an uncontrollable frenzy. Her body moved in concert with his, arching to meet his powerful thrusts.

Everything faded for Serena—everything except the man lying between her legs and taking her to a place where she soared with the eagles to escape the volcanic eruption spilling lava and incinerating everything in its wake.

Whimpers of ecstasy escaped her when the first ripple of release swept through her. The pressure built steadily as David's hardness swelled until there was no more room for it.

He felt her wet flesh close around him in long, measured, pulsating intervals at the same time that his own passions spiraled beyond his control. "Let it go, Baby," he pleaded hoarsely.

But Serena did not want to let it go. She wanted the fire and passion to last until she burned or drowned in a raging torrent of uncontrollable ecstasy.

"No," she moaned under the unrestrained assault of his powerful thrusting hips.

Holding her head firmly between his hands, David pulled back and drove his swollen flesh into her wet pulsing body, quickening his rhythm until the dam broke for both of them. Burying his face between her scented neck and shoulder, he bellowed his explosive triumph of surrender into the pillow, while Serena sobbed out her shivering delight against his shoulder.

Both lay motionless and breathing heavily, savoring the aftermath of completion. Serena closed her eyes and trailed her fingertips over his damp back.

David's breathing finally slowed and he gathered enough strength to reverse their positions. Pulling her close to his moist body, he reached down and drew the sheet up over Serena and himself. "Let's take our *siesta* now," he whispered against her ear. "We'll talk later."

Nodding, she pressed her bare hips against his groin and smiled. She did not want to talk, because she couldn't talk. Not when she wanted to relive the smoldering passion she'd found in the arms of the man cradling her to his heart.

She drifted off to sleep, and minutes later David found his own solace in a sated sleep reserved for lovers. What he wanted to say to Serena could wait, but he wondered how long he would have to wait to make her his wife.

CHAPTER 16

David woke hours later to find himself alone. The space where Serena had lain was cold even though the scent of her body lingered on the linen and on his body.

Rolling over on his back, he could barely make out the furnishings in the bedroom. Lengthening shadows from the setting sun shrouded everything in an encroaching darkness, and it was obvious that his *siesta* had exceeded the normal two- or three-hour limit.

Stretching like a big cat waking from an afternoon of rest, he smiled, recalling the passion Serena had offered him. What surprised him was that he'd offered all that he had, too, holding nothing back. Once he'd entered her he knew he was lost, lost to the ecstasy she aroused by their just sharing the same space.

Serena had come to his bed, soft and purring, and their brief moment of shared ecstasy would remain with him always. He closed his eyes and relived the feel of her smooth skin, the heat radiating from between her silken thighs, and the exact moment when he touched heaven where his heart opened to the love he had saved for the woman he would share his life and future with.

He could not have imagined when he boarded the jet for this last business trip to Costa Rica that he would also negotiate a deal that would include an affair of the heart—his heart.

An audible rumbling from his stomach reminded him that he hadn't eaten anything since early morning, and he knew he

had to leave the bed where he had placed his invisible claim on
a woman. When he looked at her he saw his unborn children
in her eyes.

Serena hummed to herself as she added a half-dozen *culantro*
leaves to a large pot filled with soup stock. She radiated a glow
that was obvious to all who saw her.

Luz Maria was surprised when she walked into the kitchen and
offered to help her cook. Even though she'd noticed the tiny, dark
red abrasion at the base of the younger woman's throat she did
not say anything. She quickly reminded herself that Serena was
the daughter of her employer. Even though she lectured the
younger woman on occasion, she knew when not to overstep the
invisible boundary set up for employer and employee.

But she did not have to say anything to Serena, because she
knew she had taken her advice and opened her heart to Señor Cole.

Serena added a coarsely chopped onion, green pepper, and two
sweet chili peppers to the pot. "How long will it have to simmer?"

"About an hour and a half," Luz Maria answered.

"Señorita Vega, Dr. Rivera is here."

Serena and Luz Maria turned at the sound of a man's voice.
Rodrigo stood less than five feet away, his dark eyes missing
nothing. Neither woman had detected his approach, and both
were unsettled by his silent stalking.

Serena recovered first. "Thank you, Rodrigo. Please have Dr.
Rivera wait in the *sala.*"

"*Sí,* Señorita.*"

Luz Maria arched an eyebrow at her employer's driver. She
had always considered him a strange man, but something
unknown communicated that he was also a dangerous man. What
it was she had not been able to discern.

After washing her hands in a large, stainless steel sink Serena
dried them, then walked out of the kitchen to the living room. She
had forgotten that she'd summoned Leandro. Her reason for
calling him had changed quickly since she slept with David. A

gentle smile softened her mouth when she thought of their session of passionate lovemaking. That smile was still in place when she entered the living room and saw Leandro rise to his feet.

Extending both hands, she pressed a kiss to his cheek. "*¡Buenas noches! ¿Cómo está,* Leandro?"

"*Cansado.* I'm more than tired," he admitted. "I'm exhausted. I don't think I had a moment to myself from the time the clinic opened this morning. Too many emergencies, including a woman who delivered on my examining table. It was an easy birth, but I would've preferred handling the procedure in the hospital."

"How was the baby?"

He smiled a tired smile. "Beautiful. A big boy. A very *big* boy."

"Momma and baby doing well?"

"Luckily, yes. Enough about my day. How's our patient doing?"

"He appears to be healing quickly. He has headaches, but that's to be expected after a concussion. What's good is that he's ambulatory." She smiled at Leandro. "I will have Luz Maria bring you some refreshments while I check on Señor Cole."

Serena retreated to the kitchen to instruct Luz Maria to bring Leandro a cup of tea that would ease his stress, then she went upstairs to see David.

Leandro's mention of delivering a baby sounded a warning bell in her head. She had slept with David without benefit of contraception. The realization had come to her only after she woke up in his bed hours after they'd made love. She had mentally calculated when she last had her period, and her apprehension increased. She had picked the most fertile time of her cycle to engage in sexual intercourse.

Perhaps, she'd prayed, just perhaps, fate would be on her side. Even though Luz Maria had predicted that she and David Cole would have children, she did not want them now.

Knocking softly on the closed door to David's bedroom, Serena waited, then knocked again. There was no sound of movement behind the closed door. She turned the knob, eased open the door and walked in. Her gaze went to the bed where they'd made love. The twisted sheets were blatant testimony of their passionate encounter.

She walked across the bedroom and toward the adjoining bath, smiling as she considered how quickly her feelings had changed since sharing her body with David Cole. She was certain she wasn't as sexually experienced as David, and of the few men she had slept with none had aroused her to the level of carnality that he had—not even when she'd thought herself in love with Xavier.

Luz Maria's prediction replayed in her mind: *He will offer you a life filled with things most women only dream about.* And she was right. She'd always wanted a satisfying sexual experience with a man. She wanted to be able to lose herself in the man and in the moment without guilt or shame. She always wanted, from the first time she offered her body to a man, to be able to tell him what pleased her and what did not please her. Even though she hadn't verbalized her desires to David, she was certain now that he was worldly enough to accommodate her sexual entreaties without intimidation.

She found David leaning with his back against the shower stall for support while he slowly and methodically dried his body with a thick, thirsty bath sheet.

"Do you need a little assistance?"

His head snapped up at the same time a slow, sexy smile displayed the attractive dimples on his lean cheeks. He hadn't heard Serena come into the bathroom. His gaze lingered on her lush mouth as she moved closer. Her hair, pulled off her face, was pinned in a tight chignon on the nape of her neck, allowing him to view her unobscured features. She had exchanged her dress for a pair of jeans and a blue and white striped cotton camp shirt. The denim fabric hugged her compact body, displaying the indentation of her narrow waist and the womanly flare of her rounded hips.

It was as if he were seeing her for the first time. Her exotic beauty was breathtaking, and he loved listening to her smokey voice. Everything about her evoked music. A bluesy Latin-jazz composition with a subtle, English/Spanish voice-over chorus.

He'd tried analyzing what it was about Serena Morris that made him crave her; why did he feel the urge to write music again, and why had he taken her to his bed when he hadn't known her a week? He'd rationalized it was gratitude, but knew that gratitude usually would not elicit the urge to marry.

He had more than ten days before he concluded his stay in Costa Rica, and he planned that Serena would agree to leave with him when he left for the States. They would fly back to West Palm Beach, Florida, where he would enlist the aid of his family to intervene on her brother's behalf and introduce her to his family as his future wife.

Dropping the towel on the floor, he moved over to a stool and sat down; he selected underwear, a T-shirt, and a pair of shorts from the stack of clothes on a table near the stool. "I think I have everything under control."

Serena realized that he was in control. He was now able to wash and dress himself without her help, and she had no doubt that all David had to do was wait for her father to return from San José before he concluded his business dealings in Costa Rica.

She did not know why, but she did not look forward to his leaving even though she knew he was emphatic about dissolving his family's holdings. Maybe, just maybe, she prayed, something would prevent him from leaving as planned. She hadn't had her fill of him—not yet.

"Dr. Rivera is here to examine you."

David gave her a lingering stare; vertical lines appeared between his eyes. "Where is he?"

"Downstairs. Why?"

"I don't want to compromise your reputation. There is noticeable proof that I wasn't the only one sleeping in my bed. The smell of your perfume is all over the linen, along with other telltale signs that we did more than take *siesta* together."

"Of course," she whispered, feeling the rising heat flare in her face and chest when she remembered what they'd offered each other only hours before.

She had slipped out of his bed while he slept, retreating to her own bathroom, where she washed away the scent of his body and their lovemaking. She returned and found him still asleep, and loathed waking him to change the bed. She felt no shame about sleeping with him, but she did not want to openly advertise their liaison.

"I'll help you down the staircase," she offered, walking over and picking up his cane.

Curving an arm around his waist, she led him slowly out of the bathroom and into the bedroom. Both glanced at the rumpled bedclothes, then at each other. They shared the kind of secret smile usually reserved for lovers only before continuing out to the hallway.

David pushed off the first step, holding the wrought-iron banister tightly and making certain not to put too much pressure on his right foot as he switched the cane to his left hand. Soon he was able to coordinate his movements so that he was able to navigate the stairs unaided. At least he knew he would not require Serena's help if he wanted to leave the boundaries of his bedroom.

The beauty and splendor of *La Montaña* lay before him as he made his way down the curving staircase to the living room. Thick, pale plaster walls provided the perfect backdrop for terra-cotta floors and heavy mahogany furniture in distinctively Spanish style tables and chairs. His gaze lingered on a massive concert piano and several guitar cases resting along a wall in a far corner of the room. Serena had mentioned that she played piano, and he wondered if she also played the guitar.

Leandro Rivera placed a fragile china cup and saucer on a side table and rose to his feet. A wide grin wiped away all traces of fatigue as he visually examined his patient. David Cole's recovery was remarkable.

Only a slight swelling was noticeable over his left eye, while the angry, purple bruise had faded to a shadowy yellow-green. The swelling had diminished in his right foot although he leaned heavily on the cane for additional support. He stared at Serena as she settled David on a straight-back chair. His gaze lingered on her until she walked out of the room, leaving the two of them alone.

"¿*Cómo está,* Señor Cole?"

"Very well, Dr. Rivera."

Leandro picked up his black bag and walked over to David. A noticeable silence filled the room as he checked David's eyes, respiration, and blood pressure. His forefinger traced the healing scar.

"How's the pain?" he questioned, putting away his stethoscope.

"I'm coping."

Leandro shifted an eyebrow. "I can always prescribe something if it becomes unbearable."

David's gaze lingered on Leandro's features. The slight puffiness under his slanting eyes marred his youthful appearance, indicating he hadn't had much sleep.

"I'd rather not take any painkillers."

"What I'll give you is not addictive if you follow the prescribed dosage."

"I'm not concerned about becoming addicted. I've always made it a practice not to take any drugs."

He'd seen drugs destroy the lives of more musicians than he cared to enumerate. Some began taking pills to help them sleep before progressing on to pills to help them wake up. Then there were the recreational drugs—the ones that took away the anxiety so that the fear of performing before a live audience vanished along with inhibitions. Because of the flagrant use of drugs among musicians, the members of Night Mood had taken an oath that any drug abuse was tantamount to expulsion from the band. Not even a single offense was tolerated.

"It's up to you, Señor Cole. But if you change your mind let me know."

"I'd like you to let me know how much I owe you for your services."

Leandro secured the lock on his bag with a loud snap. "That has been taken care of."

"By whom?"

"*El señor* Cordero-Vega."

A shadow of annoyance crossed David's face. He did not want to owe Raul Vega. "How much did he pay you?"

"That I cannot tell you. It is privileged information."

David's temper exploded. "Like hell it is! I'm your patient, not *el señor Cordero-Vega.* Give him back his money. I'll pay for my own medical expenses."

Leandro could not understand what had angered the American. Most people would be more than pleased to know that someone had graciously paid their medical bills. Since he'd opened his clinic some of his patients were unable to pay the fees he charged, and had taken to paying them out over several months, while the brash *Americano* openly insulted Minister Cordero-Vega's selfless generosity.

Grasping his bag tightly, he inclined his head. "There is no need for me to come to see you again unless you request it. Good night, Señor Cole."

David sat rigidly, watching Dr. Leandro Rivera's ramrod-straight back as he crossed the living room, opened the door, and stalked out of the house. He was still in the same position when Serena returned.

Glancing around the room, she said, "Where is Dr. Rivera?"

"He left."

"Without saying goodbye?"

"He said good night."

Folding her hands on her hips, she glared at David. "What did you say to him?"

Closing his eyes and resting his head against the back of the chair, he compressed his lips. "Nothing."

"David!"

He opened his eyes and met Serena's angry expression with one of his own. "All I did was ask him for a bill."

She tapped her foot impatiently. "And—"

"And he told me that your father had paid him."

"So? What's the big deal?"

"The big deal is that I want nothing from your father," he hissed between clenched teeth. *"Nada."*

Her mind reeling in confusion, Serena moved over to the sofa, sat down, and stared at David. There was no mistaking his hostility.

"What's this all about, because it can't be about money."

He shook his head. He could not tell her of the enmity between him and her father. He did not want her to choose between them, because he was certain he would come up the loser.

"You're right. It's not about money. Your father and I have never seen eye-to-eye where it concerns business and..." His words trailed off. He would not tell her that they despised each other.

Studying his impassive expression, she recognized a trait in the man she'd just slept with that was so apparent in her father. They were more alike than dissimilar. "You don't see eye-to-eye because you both want control. It's about power, David." She waved a slender hand. "You men and your asinine *machismo*. When will it ever stop?"

"Don't blame me, Serena."

"I'm not blaming you. My father is not exempt. Both of you are stubborn and hardheaded."

He managed a half-smile. "Don't forget patient." She snorted delicately under her breath while cursing him. "Did you say something, my love?"

"I'm not your love," she retorted, sticking her tongue out at him. Why was it that she couldn't remain angry with him?

"Are you offering me your tongue again, Darling?" he asked, his drawling cadence verifying that he was a product of the American south.

"You're disgusting."

"I'm honest, Serena." Picking up his cane, he pushed to his feet. Limping over to the sofa, he sat down beside her. Leaning closer, he studied her steady gaze. "I want you. Not just your body, but all of you."

Her eyes widened, while she searched his battered face for a sign of deceit. "You want more than I can offer you."

His lids lowered over his near-black eyes. "Are you saying that you can't love me?"

"I tried loving once and it didn't work."

"I'm not your ex-husband," David countered.

"That you aren't."

"Should I take that as a compliment?"

"Take it any way you want. I can't give you what I don't have."

They stared at each other, neither speaking, until they realized they were not alone. Serena turned and found Rodrigo staring at her and David as they sat on the sofa with less than a foot between them.

"*Sí?*" she asked sharply, finding her voice.

"Your father called while you were taking *siesta,*" he said with a knowing grin on his face. He was aware that when her parents called she had slept not in her own bedroom, but in that of the *Americano.* "He and your mother will be flying back tomorrow morning. I will pick them up at the airport at eleven-thirty."

"Thank you, Rodrigo."

"*¡De nada!* Señorita Vega."

Serena waited until Rodrigo left the room before she threw her arms around David's neck. "It worked! It had to, or else they wouldn't be coming back so soon."

Pulling back, he stared at the excitement shining from the depths of her brilliant eyes. "What worked?"

"My brother's coming home."

Her joy overrode her realization that Rodrigo should have given her the message from her parents when he announced Dr. Rivera's arrival. Her happiness was boundless as she permitted David to share the moment as he held her to his heart.

CHAPTER 17

David relished the warmth of Serena's body and her spontaneity. He wanted her again, but needed nourishment first.

"Can you give me the number for the nearest take-out restaurant?" he whispered close to her ear.

Pulling back, she stared up at him. "Luz Maria Hernando's food is better than that of any take-out restaurant in the world." A smile ruffled her mouth. "I take it that you're hungry, Sport?"

"Starved."

"You should be. You sent your lunch back."

"I wasn't hungry."

"It wasn't that at all. You sent it back because you were pouting."

He managed to look insulted. "I don't pout."

"You don't realize you do. When you don't get your way you affect an expression that looks very much like a pout to me."

He gave her a pained expression. "Why are you torturing me, *mi alma?* You know that I'm weak and in pain."

"You weren't so weak during *siesta,*" she teased with a winning smile.

Shrugging his broad shoulders, he waved a hand. "That was different."

Rising to her feet, she crossed her arms under her breasts. "How different?"

He stood up, towering above her. His mood changed and his expression sobered. "That was different because I wanted you so much. And I'll want you even as the breath leaves my body for the last time."

Her pulse quickened, sending a shiver of chills over her flesh. She did not know why, but she felt a wave of fear settle in her chest. David's words echoed Xavier's. Her ex-husband had stated that he loved her so much that he did not want to live without her, and in the end his obsessive behavior was responsible for destroying their marriage.

"Don't want me *that* much, David."

"Don't tell me what to want or feel."

Serena knew he was spoiling for a confrontation, but refused to rise to his bait. The knowledge that her brother was coming home soothed her quick temper.

"Either you can stay here and mouth off, or come and eat."

David clenched his teeth and cursed himself as soon as he did. A wave of pain radiated up the left side of his face. Serena might not share Raul Vega's genes, but she had acquired his quick, biting tongue that stung as sharply as any whip.

"You like your men submissive and I like *mis mujeres* docile."

She arched an eyebrow. "I'm not your woman."

"Yes, you are," he stated confidently. "You just haven't accepted it yet." She spun around on her heel, leaving him to follow.

Everyone was more certain about her future than she was. David wanted all of her, and Luz Maria predicted she would marry him and give him children.

Why was it so difficult for her to accept the inevitable? Was it because of Xavier? Or was it because she did not want to love and lose again?

David limped into the large kitchen behind Serena, returning the warm smile of a petite woman stirring a large pot.

"Doña Maria, this is Señor David Cole. Señor Cole, Doña Luz Maria Hernando."

David took Luz Maria's right hand and placed a kiss on her knuckle. "My extreme pleasure, Doña Maria."

The older woman blushed furiously as she stared at the tall man's bowed, graying, black head. Her vision had manifested itself. She hadn't seen David Cole's face clearly, but she recognized his smile immediately. It was his dimpled smile she had seen in her vision; a smile his children would inherit, along with Serena's eyes.

"*Mucho gusto de conocerlo por la primera vez,* Señor Cole," she returned shyly. What she wanted to say was that she'd already met him several times in her dreams—and it was indeed a pleasure to finally get to meet him in the flesh.

"Señor Cole will no longer take his meals in his bedroom," Serena announced, watching the warm interchange between the cook and her father's guest.

"I'm glad you're feeling better," Luz Maria stated, withdrawing her fingers from David's loose grip.

"Much better. Thanks to your tea and soups."

Luz Maria turned her attention to Serena. "Will you be taking your meals in the dining room?"

"No. We'll eat here in the kitchen. Please sit down," she said to David. "I'll join you in a few minutes."

He nodded and sat down, unaware that Luz Maria watched him as his gaze followed Serena as she left the kitchen, disappearing from his line of vision.

"Tea, Señor Cole?"

His head came around slowly and he stared at Luz Maria as if he had never seen her before. "*Sí,*" he replied absentmindedly.

Serena retreated to David's bedroom and stripped the bed of the soiled linen. She quickly and expertly remade the bed, then dimmed the lamp on the bedside table before drawing the silk-lined, pale drapes over the French doors. She repeated the motions in her own bedroom before she returned to the kitchen.

David's gaze never left Serena's face as he spooned portions of *sancocho*—a flavorful Caribbean stew laden with yellow and white *yautía, ñame,* pumpkin, sweet potatoes, green and ripe plantains, beef, and corn—into his mouth. He ate everything except for the small chunks of meat. The sensitivity in his left cheek would not permit him to chew without experiencing some discomfort.

She speared a slice of ripe plantain, wiggled her eyebrows at him, then popped it into her mouth. His gaze moved slowly down to her mouth, visually tracing the outline of her lips. His smile faded when he recalled the texture and taste of her moist, hot mouth. Within the span of a second he relived the sensual encounter that had left him gasping and dizzy with spent passion. And what he wanted to do was relive that passion with Serena over and over again. He watched her form words, not hearing any of what she was saying.

"Are you all right?"

He nodded, blinking rapidly. "I'm sorry. My mind was else-where. What did you say?"

"I said that if you don't want dessert we can go into the living room, where you can try out the piano."

Wiping his mouth with a napkin, David stood up. He'd reached for his cane and taken several steps before she attempted to rise. She waited, watching intently as he took several steps, then waited for her to precede him.

"What other instruments do you play aside from the piano?" Serena asked once they were seated side by side on the piano bench.

"Guitar and percussion." David rested his fingers reverently on the keys as if he feared contaminating them.

"That explains the calluses on your fingers."

"They come from hours of playing the congas."

Seeing his fingers poised over the keys made her aware of the breadth of his large hands. He struck a chord, the sound resonating melodiously throughout the space. It was apparent that her mother had the piano tuned regularly.

She was mesmerized as he went through a series of scales, his fingers skimming over the keys like a waterfall. Her gaze shifted from his fingers to his face. He'd leaned forward, eyes closed as if he were in a trance, and played everything from Joplin to Handel. When she registered the distinctive notes from Gershwin's *Rhapsody In Blue* she joined him in a duet.

David's piano playing was masterful, and it was the first time since she'd sat down to take lessons that she'd actually enjoyed playing the piano. They shared a wide grin as the last note lingered, then faded into a hushed silence.

Curving an arm around his waist, Serena rested her head against his shoulder. "You're incredible."

The fingers of his right hand encircled her neck. "You're pretty good yourself."

"Not half as good as you are."

"That's only because I have longer fingers."

"Don't be modest, David. It's not becoming."

Lowering his head, he brushed his lips against her ear. "When are you going to change your opinion of me?"

"Never," she whispered. "I've gotten used to your arrogance." *And it wasn't his arrogance she liked. She liked the man.*

"How often do you play?" he questioned, his warm breath sweeping over her bare lobe.

"Not often. But I usually play here at *La Montaña* because I like this piano."

David nodded, his fingers caressing the side of the Steinway. "It should be played every day, because it's truly a magnificent instrument."

"Was your transition from musician to businessman difficult?"

"No," he admitted with a smile. "I had majored in music education and minored in business administration."

"Why business?"

Lowering his eyebrows, he glared. "Because my father deemed it. He expected business to be my major, but after a somewhat passionate altercation we decided to compromise."

A knowing smile trembled over her full lips. "I take it you're used to winning?"

He arched a sweeping eyebrow. "I don't know what it is to lose," he admitted quietly.

She shuddered as if a breath of cold wind had swept over her body. At the same time, a warning voice whispered in her head that David Cole could be a formidable adversary, as was Raul Cordero-Vega. She shook off her uneasiness.

"Did you always want to be a musician?" David did not answer her right away, and she thought perhaps he hadn't heard her question.

"Always." Another hushed silence ensued. "There was a time when my parents thought I was hard of hearing because I didn't respond when they spoke to me. What they didn't know was that instead of hearing people speak I heard music notes, notes in perfect pitch.

"Whenever my older brother and sisters sat down for their lessons I lingered in the room, memorizing every note. A week after my sixth birthday I began my own lessons. Everyone was shocked, including the instructor, when I went through the beginner's book in four weeks."

"Were you a musical prodigy?"

"Oh, no. I was just a possessed pianist who practiced a minimum of three hours each day."

"It paid off, because you play beautifully."

"Will you let me play for you when we return to the States?"

"Where?" she whispered, her husky voice lowering seductively.

"At my home in Boca Raton."

"Will I need a special invitation?"

"Of course not, Serena. My home is yours. You can come to stay—forever, if you so choose."

She slipped off the piano bench and walked over to the floor-to-ceiling windows, her gaze fixed on the all-encompassing darkness punctuated by strategically placed lights illuminating the perimeter of *La Montaña*.

Screams of frustration and fear echoed in her head. Fear that she knew her own destiny, and frustration that Luz Maria's gift had become her curse because she was unable to rally the defenses she needed to stave off David's deliberate seduction.

She found it eerie—no, unnatural—to know that the man sitting at the piano would be the one she would marry even before she was given the chance to fall in love with him.

But could she love him? Could she trust him, or any man, enough to open her heart to love again?

Turning slowly, she met David's gaze as he sat watching, waiting. Her mind told her to resist his pull, but her body refused. If she hadn't lain with him, then she would be able to turn and walk away. Something within her called out to him, and she could not and would not walk away, because she knew he was to be a part of her life. He was her destiny!

David reached down and retrieved the cane resting beside the piano. He managed to find his footing with greater ease than he had since he woke up and found himself at *La Montaña*. What he wanted to do was fling the object across the room and walk unaided. He wanted to sweep Serena up in his arms and climb the staircase to his bedroom for an encore of what they'd shared that afternoon.

He wanted to relive the blinding passion, merging with an uncontrollable lust, that made him fuse his flesh with hers, and his former trepidation about having unprotected sex vanished the moment he filled her body with his seed. In that brief, dizzying moment of lingering lust he wanted Serena Morris as his wife and the mother of his children.

"I'm ready to go back to my room."

Serena nodded, moving quickly to his side. "I thought you would want to try out the guitars before going back upstairs."

"Tomorrow." The single word denoted finality. Tomorrow Raul Cordero-Vega would return to *La Montaña* and tomorrow would be the time for him to reveal his innermost wishes to Serena.

Tomorrow, she repeated to herself, leading David past the living room staircase, along a narrow passage off the kitchen, and through a door that led to the staircase at the rear of the house.

"My brother and I used to sneak in and out of the house using this route."

Following her lead, David trained his gaze on her back. "Were you ever caught?"

She smiled at him over her shoulder. "Once. I stayed out past my curfew and thought I was going to get over when I managed to slip in the back door that Gabe left unlocked for me. What I didn't count on was my father waiting for me in my room. He'd waited so long that he fell asleep on my bed."

David chuckled, remembering his own youthful escapades. "What happened?"

"I undressed in the dark, and when I got into bed I startled him and he swung at me and bloodied my nose. My screams woke up the entire household. Mother thought he'd deliberately hit me, and she let loose with a stream of colorful expletives closely resembling profanity, shocking everyone. Poppa stared at her as if he'd never seen her before, then walked away without saying a word to defend himself.

"They avoided one another for several days before I went to my mother and confessed what had happened. She told me that I had come to her just in time to stop her from leaving her husband. She showed me the tickets she'd purchased. She was going to return to the States, taking us children with her.

"I begged her not to leave, because I realized at that moment I loved my stepfather too much not to have him in my life."

"How was it resolved?"

"I apologized to him, while my mother grounded me for a month. Gabe was given two weeks for being an accomplice."

"How old were you?"

"Sixteen."

Wincing, David thought of how he'd acted out at sixteen. He'd gotten into situations that his parents claimed had turned their hair white.

He chuckled under his breath. "Did you ever break curfew again?"

She shook her head. "No way. Not after seeing my mother go off like that."

They reached the top of the stairs and stood outside the door to his bedroom. The sound of a clock on the drop-leaf table in the hallway chimed the hour. It was ten o'clock, and she couldn't believe that they'd spent more than ninety minutes playing the piano.

For a reason she could not explain, Serena could not look at David. She felt like a breathless girl of eighteen, away from home for the first time. What she felt was similar to what she'd experienced when she went on her first college date. She hadn't known whether to kiss the young man or unlock her door, then close it quickly, before he could kiss her or ask to come in. In the end she'd closed the door.

And that was what she should've done earlier that afternoon. She should've walked out of David Cole's bedroom and shut the door behind her and stayed out. But she hadn't.

She had consciously denied that she felt anything for David— that he was someone whose life she helped save; it was only after she had permitted him to make love to her that she realized that she did feel something, something deep and so profound that she offered more than her body. She had offered up her heart.

"Good night, David." She turned and walked to her bedroom, feeling the heat of his midnight gaze on her back.

David watched her walk away, wanting to go to her, but didn't. He knew she was uneasy about what had passed between them earlier that afternoon, and he wanted to give her time to sort out her emotions.

Sleeping apart would also give him time to assess his own feelings; he had to admit that Serena Morris claimed a part of David Claridge Cole that he hadn't offered any other woman, for it was the first time he'd ever engaged in unprotected sex. He could've stopped to protect her, but a force beyond himself would not permit him to. A force and a power that shattered his rigid self-control.

He stepped into his bedroom and closed the door. Leaving the cane on the doorknob, he moved over to the bed and sat down.

Smothering a groan, he lay across the firm mattress and closed his eyes. He ached from head to foot, but that pain was bearable. He wasn't certain whether he could bear the pain of rejection, though, if Serena decided not to share his future with him.

She helped save my life. She offered me a second chance and I owe her. And because I owe her my life I want to share it with her. His eyes flew open and he stared up at the faint shadows on the ceiling. Owing Serena had nothing to do with falling in love with her. *You love her!* The admission whispered in his head like a song's refrain, and before the sun rose to signal the beginning of another day he believed it.

CHAPTER 18

June 17

Serena woke early the following morning and managed to run two miles returning to *La Montaña* to begin her day. She walked into her bedroom and found David sitting on the rocker in the sitting area. The scent of his aftershave filled the room, and she noticed that he was already groomed and dressed. Instead of the shorts and T-shirt she'd purchased for him he had selected his own shirt and slacks. The swelling had gone down, and he'd slipped on the leather sandals.

He stood up and suddenly the space seemed dwarfed by his impressive height. "Good morning."

Removing the elastic band from her hair, Serena shook out her damp curls, smiling, "Good morning to you, too. How are you feeling?"

His inky-dark gaze moved slowly over her face and body before a slow smile crinkled the skin around his large eyes. "Wonderful."

Her eyebrows arched. "I see you've managed to wash and dress without help."

He held his arms away from his body. "I've given up the cane."

"You'd better not move too quickly, Sport."

His smile widened. "I'll take it slow for a couple of days." He closed the distance between them taking slow, measured steps. He noted her wet tank top and shorts. "Where do you jog?"

"Along the beach."

"How many miles do you do?"

"I was lucky to get in two miles this morning. The heat is too oppressive to try for more."

David stood in front of her, admiring the dewy softness of her moist face. Reaching up he cradled her face between his hands and lowered his head.

She pulled back. "Don't. I'm wet."

He tightened his gentle grip on her delicate face, inhaling the scent of her perfume under the layer of moisture lathering her body. Ignoring her protest, he moved closer and brushed his lips over hers.

Pulling back, he studied her intently before again flashing his winning smile. "I just wanted to give you a proper good morning."

Her fingers curved around his strong wrists. She unconsciously counted the strong, steady, beating pulse. Lowering her gaze, she smiled up at him through her lashes, causing his breathing to falter slightly. "Thank you."

The seductiveness of the gesture jolted David, igniting the all-consuming passion welling within him. He'd awakened unable to believe the emotions assailing him whenever he thought of Serena. The realization that he'd made love to her, and the vivid recollection of her response, left him reeling. He thought his mind had conjured her up. He'd recalled the deep, velvety softness of her skin, the scent of her perfume mingling with the aroma of her body's natural fragrance, the weight and feel of her firm breasts in his hands, and the moist heat of her femininity as it closed around him in a strong, gripping pulsing that threatened to propel him from his bed and into hers.

He'd left the bed, flung open the French doors, and stood on the veranda watching the sun rise, waiting for his traitorous body to return to a state of calmness.

And in the full sunlight he became fully cognizant of the changes within himself. He'd laughed aloud when he realized that a little slip of an American born, Costa Rican bred woman had stolen his heart. He'd traveled the world to the adoring screams of thousands of women, and not once had he taken any of them into his bed or into his heart. It had taken a business trip, his last business trip to Costa Rica, for him to fall and fall hard, and for the daughter of his nemesis.

He'd admitted that he was used to winning, and he was. However, he was prepared to lose the Limón banana plantation if negotiations with Cordero-Vega failed. But he was not prepared to lose Serena. He'd taken a solemn oath that he would not return to Florida without her.

Her lashes swept up, her gaze fusing with his as shivers of an awareness passed between them. It had gone beyond the physical urgency to join her body to his. It was now a realization that their future was inexorably entwined, and Serena knew and accepted the reality that the man holding her to his heart would become her husband and the father of her children.

"Why did you leave him?"

The quiet sound of his questioning voice startled her. She flashed a nervous smile. "How do you know he didn't leave me?" she asked, answering his query with one of her own.

His right eyebrow lifted slightly. "Any man who'd leave you is either insane or a fool."

"He became a fool, so I wasn't given much of a choice."

She related the bizarre changes in her ex-husband's behavior only days into their honeymoon and how he had begun stalking her because he suspected she was involved with other men. Without disclosing Xavier Osbourne's name, she revealed the terms of her annulment and the legal restraints that were imposed to keep him away from her.

"He's never attempted to bother you since the annulment?"

Serena shook her head. "He may have loved me, but he loves practicing medicine more. There was no way he would've jeopardized having his medical license revoked or suspended."

What David did not want was a man from her past threatening their future, or a repeat of the scenario that had kept his older brother and sister-in-law apart for ten years.

A shy smile softened his features. "Do you think you can put up with a scarred, vain, arrogant, frustrated musician-turned-businessman for the next fifty years?"

She felt a spurt of heated blood rush through her veins as she took a breath of astonishment. Luz Maria had predicted it, but a small part of her hadn't believed—until now.

"What are you asking, David Cole?"

His hands moved from her face to her waist, pulling her flush against the solid strength of his body. "I think you know what I'm asking, Señorita Serena Morris."

Her gold-flecked, clear brown eyes locked with his jet-black gaze. "No, I don't," she countered, unwilling to make it easy for him.

A scowl marred his beautiful male face. "Yes, you do."

She would not back down. She couldn't with David, because if she did she would always have to defer to his authoritative personality. He was born into wealth, and was no doubt spoiled. He'd admitted that he was used to winning, and there was no question that he considered her one of his many conquests; she was also aware that she could not escape her destiny, that she would marry him, but she did not want him to think he could negotiate and close the deal on their future within four days of their meeting.

"Tell me," she taunted. "You can say everything else that comes to your mind."

The words lodged in his throat. What was he afraid of? That she would laugh at him? That she would reject his offer? That she would think him foolish because he'd confused gratitude for something more?

Swallowing painfully, he forced a dimpled smile. She returned his smile, and in that instant the vain arrogance she'd accused him of claiming returned.

"I want you to marry me."

Serena's smile faded at the same time her lids fluttered wildly. *He'll make you happier than you can imagine. He will offer you a life filled with things most women only dream about. He will give you your heart's desire.*

Luz Maria's words attacked her at the same time she replayed David's proposal over and over in her head. *I want you to marry me.*

"Why me?" she asked, refusing to relent. What frightened her was that Luz Maria's prophecy had manifested itself within days.

"Why not you?"

Her lids flew up and she glared at him. "I asked the question first."

David shook his head in amazement. "Why are you so stubborn?" he whispered.

"I'm no more stubborn than you are," she retorted.

"We are going to have very willful children," he predicted with a wide grin.

He sobered quickly. "Speaking of children," she said, "what happened yesterday cannot happen again. I'll expect you to protect me whenever we sleep together until—"

"Until what?"

What she was beginning to feel for David was nothing like she'd felt for Xavier. And she'd believed she loved her ex-husband. With David it was confidence, safety, and security. She knew that once joined to him she would be protected. She was also realistic enough to know that their living together would be volatile and passionate—in and out of bed.

"Until we're married," she whispered.

He wanted to shout out his joy. She had accepted his proposal. It was a backhanded acceptance, but that did not matter. What mattered was that she was willing to become a part of his life.

His mint-flavored breath fanned her moist face seconds before his mouth covered hers in a kiss that branded her his possession. Parting her lips, she rose on tiptoe to meet his kiss with her own fiery imprint.

"Why me?" she asked again, between his soft, nibbling kisses.

"Why not you," he mumbled, planting tender kisses at the corners of her mouth. "Because you're the other half of me.

You're what I need to make me whole. You symbolize what I appreciate most about life—rain, music, and the splendor of the rising sun. Your tears are rain, washing away a fear that leaves a comforting peace. Your body throbs with a rhythm that beats in perfect harmony with mine, and your smile reminds me of the rising sun, so that I look forward to sharing everything I have with you.

"What I feel with you I've never felt with any other woman," he continued in the musical Spanish she'd come to love listening to. "You wanted to know about someone else seeing the tattoo." She nodded numbly. "After I got it I felt exposed because of where it is. I did not want to become that vulnerable to a woman. Any woman."

"But I've seen it."

"That should tell you something about the power you hold over me."

"I don't want power, David. I want trust. Without the trust we have nothing."

He froze, his expression impassive. "What about love?"

She blinked once. "That'll come with time."

Nodding, he released her, taking a step backward. "Thank you for accepting me."

She also inclined her head. "Thank you for asking."

Both had retreated behind a facade of formality, where the shock of what they'd agreed to shook them to their very core.

Serena gave him a half-smile. "Now, if you'll excuse me I'd like to take a shower."

David studied the woman who was to become his wife, committing everything about her to memory before he limped past her and out of her bedroom, closing the door softly behind him.

Serena didn't know she'd been holding her breath until she heard the soft click of the lock. "What have I done?" she whispered to the silent space at the same time tears filled her eyes.

Her brother had been charged with drug trafficking and murder, she'd slept with a man she'd known for three days, her parents were expected home within hours, and it was incumbent upon her to inform them that their houseguest had proposed marriage and that she had accepted.

"*Soy loca.*" And she *was* crazy. As crazy as the events going on behind the closed doors at *La Montaña.*

Serena heard the angry sound of her father's voice before stepping into the living room. He was pleading with his wife, who held her head aloft as she climbed the staircase without giving him a backward glance.

"You can't leave me!" Raul shouted to her back.

Juanita stopped, turned and glared down at his angry features. "I'm not leaving you, Raul. I'm going to *my son!*"

"He's also my son."

"What's going on here?" Raul and Juanita froze, their gazes registering the bewilderment on Serena's face. "I thought Gabe was going to be released."

Raul's hands tightened into fists. "He will not be released."

Serena bit down hard on her lower lip. "Why not?" There was no mistaking the tremor in her query.

Raul's angry gaze swept from his daughter to his wife. "Because the U.S. ambassador refuses to get involved."

"That's why I'm leaving," Juanita explained. "My son can't come to me, so I'm going to him." Turning, she continued up the staircase at the same time Raul stalked off to his study.

Serena clapped a hand over her mouth to stifle the screams of frustration threatening to escape. No, no, no! She shook her head, refusing to believe what she'd just heard.

Willing her legs to move, she raced up the staircase and to her mother. The door to the enormous bedroom stood open. As she waited in the doorway watching Juanita Vega rip dresses, blouses, skirts, and slacks from the closet racks, she discerned an emotion in the older woman that she'd seen only once—rage. The other time she'd seen her this enraged was when she thought her husband had hit her daughter and bloodied her nose.

"What happened, Mother?"

Juanita gave her a quick glance before she went back to the closet, withdrawing a large Pullman bag. "I'm going to Florida."

"Without Poppa?"

"*Sí!*"

"Why?"

Juanita's hands stilled as she turned and stared at her daughter. "I don't want him with me. I can't accomplish what I need to accomplish with a foreign-born husband in tow."

"What are you talking about, Mother?"

"I'm still an American, while Raul and Gabriel are foreigners in the States. U.S. officials don't look too kindly on foreigners who commit crimes against their country."

"I'm going back with you."

"You can't. I want you to stay with Raul. I don't want him here alone. As it is, he thinks I'm leaving and never coming back."

"But, Mother—"

"Don't Mother me, Serena! Please, Baby Girl, don't add to the madness affecting this family," she added in a softer tone. "Help me keep *nuestra familia* together."

If her mother wanted her to help keep their family together, then why was she leaving her behind? She'd acknowledged Raul Vega as her father, but the reality was that they shared no blood ties. Juanita and Gabriel were her family.

She did not know how, but she felt her mother's pain, pain that had torn her life and her family asunder. "How long will you be gone?"

Juanita placed a small leather case containing her passport on the bed beside her luggage. "As long as it takes for me to get answers to a few questions, questions that the American ambassador to Costa Rica will not or cannot answer."

"Will you call me?"

Walking over to her daughter, Juanita pulled her close. "I'll try to call every day."

Serena kissed her scented cheek. "Thank you for that." She forced an artificial smile. "Do you need help packing?"

"Yes, Baby."

It took the two women less than half an hour to pack and double check everything Juanita Vega needed to return to the land of her birth.

Juanita made her way to the first floor and informed Rodrigo to take her bags out to the car. She had less than two hours to take the commuter plane out of the Limón airport for a flight back to San José, where she would take a connecting one to Miami, Florida.

Serena waited in the car with Juanita for Rodrigo. The two women were silent, wondering whether Raul would come to see his wife off.

The seconds slipped into minutes. Serena exited the spacious Mercedes-Benz sedan when the front door to *La Montaña* opened and only the driver appeared. She did what she had never done before—she silently cursed Raul Cordero-Vega for his stubborn pride.

Rodrigo took his position behind the wheel, started the engine, and drove off without a backward glance. Serena watched as the car made its way down the curving, winding road, disappearing from view, then turned and walked back to the house.

Raul walked into David Cole's bedroom, slamming the door violently behind him. He struggled to control his temper when the American did not move from his lounging position on the bed.

"I see you've recovered very quickly."

David's impassive expression did not change as he stared out across the room. "I had excellent care," he drawled, his voice a monotone.

As he crossed his arms over his chest Raul's features hardened with a sinister grin. "Lucky for you, Señor Cole, because I need you alive and well. I'd like you to make an international telephone call for me."

David sat up, swinging his bare feet to the floor. "To whom?"

"Your father."

"My father retired from ColeDiz years—"

"This has nothing to do with ColeDiz business," Raul interrupted, his voice escalating with his mounting tension. "This little matter has to do with progeny. A son for a son."

David's forehead furrowed at the cryptic statement. "What the hell are you talking about?"

"I want you to call your father and tell him that if my son is not released from that stinking Florida sewer within the next sixty days he will lose *his* son, body part by body part. I don't care how he does it, but I want my boy out of that hell-hole."

Every nerve within David's body vibrated with a liquid fire that rendered him unable to move, speak. He couldn't believe he was being held hostage for crimes Gabriel Vega had committed more than three thousand miles away from where he stood. A slow smile flitted across his battered face when he realized that Raul Vega was crazy, a madman drunk on his own power.

Resting his hands on his slim hips, he shook his head slowly. "You're sick."

Raul's face darkened with a rush of blood. "And how do you think your father will feel when I amputate your precious fingers and send him one for each day he exceeds my sixty-day deadline?" He noted David's expression of horror. "Fingers, toes, ears. I really don't give a damn, Señor Cole. I'm willing to wager your father will bankrupt ColeDiz to buy and sell the politicians who are responsible for putting my son behind bars if it means getting you back in one piece. And despite your obvious shock, I know you're going to agree to my proposal, because if you don't I'll make certain you'll never father children. Yes!" he ranted as his eyes took on a glazed look. "I'll have you castrated before the sun sets on this very day."

The fingers Vega threatened to amputate curled into tight fists. David longed to wrap his hands around the man's throat and squeeze until he pleaded for him to spare his life. And the truth was he would probably spare the lunatic's life, while Vega would take his as easily as he would swat a bug.

Folding his arms over his chest, he stared down at the floor before his head came up slowly. A hint of a smile touched his mouth. "You really have a lot of confidence in my father."

"What I have is confidence in his name and his money. Enough talk. I'll bring you a telephone and you will make the call. I shouldn't have to warn you that what we've discussed in this room stays between us. Or else—"

"Or else you'll geld me? Or better yet, kill me?" David whispered savagely.

Raul leaned in close to his face. "I won't kill you, but when I'm finished with you you'll pray for me to put you out of your misery."

"*You* would do it? I doubt that, Señor Cordero-Vega. You're too much of a coward, or too smart, to dirty your hands with murder and mutilation."

"That's for me to know and for you to find out. I can reassure you that I'm not a man without scruples. I'm prepared to make your stay bearable. Everything at *La Montaña* is at your disposal. Think of it as your home away from home. The only exception is that you won't be able to leave until I receive confirmation that Gabriel has been released."

"And if he isn't?"

"Then the drama of an eye for an eye and a son for a son will play out until the final curtain."

David thought about his father's failing health. Samuel Cole had suffered a life-threatening stroke four years before, and David was certain he would never survive another if he had to undergo the strain of negotiating for the life of his child.

"I'll make the call. But not to my father."

"If not him, then who?"

"My brother Martin."

Raul's top lip curled under his neatly barbered, gray mustache. "No good. Call your father." Turning, he opened the door, walked out, and returned within minutes with a cordless phone.

David took the instrument, staring at it before dialing the area code for West Palm Beach, Florida. A chill of foreboding numbed him when he heard the break in connection.

"Cole residence," came a familiar female voice.

"Mother, it's David. I have to speak to Dad."

"No 'how are you'?"

"How are you, Mother?" he queried impatiently.

"Well, for an old woman."

"You're not an old woman, and you know it."

"When are you coming home?"

"I don't know. Mother, please put Dad on the phone."

"He's resting."

"Wake him up."

"David—what's wrong?"

"Nothing. I just need to talk to him."

There was a soft sigh before Marguerite Cole spoke again. "I'll get him."

David felt the throbbing pain in his head for the first time in hours. All he'd shared with Serena faded with her stepfather's threat against his life.

"David," came the wavering male voice in his ear.

"Dad, I want you to listen to me and listen good. I need for you to—"

His conversation with Samuel Claridge Cole lasted less than two minutes. He pressed a button and ended the call, then flung the phone across the room, bouncing it off the solid mahogany door before it fell to the floor.

Rage darkened David's eyes, making them appear even blacker, while Raul gave him a satisfied smile. "Very nice, David," he stated quietly, using his given name for the first time.

"I've done your bidding. Now get the hell out of my sight."

Raul bowed slightly from the waist, picked up the telephone, then straightened and walked away, leaving David shaking with a fury that surpassed the pain threatening to bring him to his knees.

His trembling had not subsided when Serena knocked on the door and walked into the room. "Go away," he ordered, unable to look at her.

A frown creased her smooth forehead. "What's wrong?"

"Nothing. I just need to be alone."

She couldn't believe him. He'd asked her to marry him and now he wanted to be alone. "Not a problem, David. You want to be alone? You've got it!" Spinning on her heel, she walked out of the room.

Sinking down to the mattress, he covered his mouth with his hand to keep from blurting out how much he loved and needed her. He lost track of time as he lay on the bed, trying to sort out his exchange with Vega and the telephone call to his father. Vega's threat did not bother him as much as the croaking sounds that his father made when he told him what he needed to do to save his last born.

Then he did what he hadn't done in years—he prayed. He prayed not for his own life, but for that of Samuel Claridge Cole's.

CHAPTER 19

Serena changed her sandals for a pair of running shoes, stopping long enough to inform her father that she was leaving the house.

"Wait, *Chica*." He rose from his chair behind the massive desk in his study. A gentle smile softened the harsh lines in his face. "Perhaps we can talk."

Her gaze swept over the tall, slender, stern man whom she had grown to love despite his gruffness. At sixty-two he was more attractive than he'd been at thirty-two. The weight he'd gained filled out his face, softening the sharp angles of his chin and cheekbones. His hair had grayed, along with his clipped mustache, and the overall effect was one of graceful elegance.

"I'm going for a walk, Poppa."

"Would you like company?"

She wanted to say no, but couldn't. What she wanted was to be alone to sort out what had just occurred between her and David. It was apparent something or someone had upset him; what, she didn't know. But she did not intend to become a scapegoat for his bad moods.

She gave Raul a gentle smile. "Of course."

They left through the rear of the house, waiting for their eyes to adjust to the brilliance of the tropical sun behind the lenses of their sunglasses.

Raul reached for his stepdaughter's hand and held it protectively in his larger one. "Her flight hasn't even left San José, and I already miss her."

Serena registered the fleeting glimpse of weakness in Interior

Minister Raul Cordero-Vega for the first time in her life. She'd wanted to think that Gabriel was his Achilles heel, but he wasn't. It was his wife. Juanita Morris-Vega held the power that could destroy the man so many feared with a single word.

"She'll be back, Poppa."

"I keep telling myself over and over that she'll be back, but something won't let me believe it."

"Who are you afraid for? Yourself or Mother?"

Leading her towards the greenhouse, he wagged his head. "Both of us, *Chica*. If they don't let Gabriel go, then Juanita won't come back. She'll stay with him until—"

"Don't say it, Poppa. Don't bury him."

Dropping her hand, he curved his arm around her shoulders, pulling her close to his side. "You're right."

They wandered through the greenhouse, stopping to examine and inhale the sweetness of the many flowering plants. Serena picked a variety of white and pale pink blooms for the bedrooms and the dinner table, filling a large wicker basket from the dozen or more stacked on a shelf. Before she'd left Costa Rica to attend college, she'd assumed the responsibility of selecting flowers for the house.

It was when they entered the aviary that she decided to bring up the fact that David still resided at *La Montaña*. "When will you conclude your business with David Cole?" she asked quietly.

Raul stopped suddenly, his eyes narrowing suspiciously as he stared at her. "Why? What has he told you?"

She shrugged a slender shoulder and shifted the basket filled with flowers from one hand to the other. "He mentioned that he'd planned to stay two weeks. But with his injuries I just wondered whether you've changed your schedule."

"Nothing has changed. We will discuss the sale of his banana plantation as planned."

What he did not reveal was the price he'd set for David Cole's freedom. A sixth sense also warned him that his daughter's interest in his houseguest was more than that of a nurse for a patient.

"I trust you and *David* are getting along?"

Nodding, she smiled. "Well enough. I find him a little arrogant, but then so are you, Poppa." Much to her surprise Raul threw back his head and laughed. "Well, it's true," she confirmed.

He sobered, his eyebrows lowering. "A successful man must possess a bit of arrogance, while David Cole has amassed a monopoly on it. I much preferred conducting business with his older brother. Martin Cole was quiet, but lethal, whereas David is loud like a clanging bell."

"He is as lethal?"

Raul hesitated, trying to come up with a fitting metaphor for the Cole brothers. "Yes. Martin was like a shark, circling beneath the surface before he struck, while David is a rattlesnake. He sounds a warning, then strikes while he's still rattling."

"Wouldn't you prefer to be warned?"

"Not from someone so young and disrespectful. He wasn't quite thirty when he came to see me for the first time. I rearranged important meetings to accommodate him, and when I would not agree to his demand that I rescind the additional tariff on his banana crop, he walked out of the meeting. It had taken me three weeks to bring all of my ministers together, and we sat like stunned jackasses staring at one another. I swore from that day that David Cole would pay for his impertinence."

A flicker of apprehension coursed through Serena. "Pay how, Poppa?"

"I don't know, *Chica*. But his time is coming."

How could she tell her stepfather that she'd slept with his most combative challenger and planned to marry him? That she would eventually make him a grandfather and that his grandchildren would carry the blood of his archenemy?

She stared at Raul, unable to disclose the secret she held close to her heart. She knew the time would come when she would be forced to choose between the two men in her life, and because she knew her destiny the man whom she called Poppa would be the loser in the undeclared war. She jumped when the sound of thunder shook the earth.

"I'm going back to the house to put the flowers in water."

Leaning over, Raul kissed her cheek. "I'm going to stay here for a while to wait out the storm and talk to my feathered friends."

Serena stared at Raul as he turned to a cage of toucans, and for a brief second she felt like sobbing. Life had thrown Raul Cordero-Vega a cruel curve. He'd temporarily lost his wife and son, leaving him to grieve in silence.

David stood on the veranda, watching Serena and Raul. He noted the tenderness in the older man's touch when he wound an arm around his stepdaughter's shoulders, wondering how one man filled with so much venom could be that gentle. Was it possible that Raul Cordero-Vega was schizophrenic?

Seeing Serena lean against her father while smiling up at him reminded David of his own response to her hypnotic feminine sensuality. They'd argued more than they'd made love, but the one passionate encounter had obliterated all of the acrimony that preceded it. And instead of holding her to his heart he'd sent her away. Her father's unexpected threat swept away the promise of his taking her for his wife, since his existence was now dependent upon her brother's freedom.

He stood motionless, watching the dark clouds roll across the sky, obscuring the brilliance of the tropical sun. He listened for the first rumble of thunder, followed by the distant rustling and screams of jungle wildlife scurrying for shelter.

Closing his eyes, he registered the same ancient rhythms in his head and in his veins that he'd experienced when he entered Serena's body. Why did he connect a tropical thunderstorm, jungle sounds, the pounding rhythms of ancient Africa with making love to her?

What was there about her that reached deep inside of him to make him want her? Just being who she was unlocked his heart and his soul to make him fall in love with a woman for the very first time in his life.

A large drop fell, landing on the tip of his nose. Then another.

The heavens opened up, the rain pouring down on his head and soaking his clothes. It cooled his warm flesh and washed away the madness turning his life upside down.

Closing his eyes and raising his arms, he gloried in the wrath of nature's untamed fury for the span of time it took the rains to sweep over *La Montaña*. It washed away the stench of evil pervading the enormous structure erected on the mountain overlooking the sea and jungle, and it also cleansed him.

His lips mouthed the words that the wind tore from his silent tongue: *"Forgive me, Father, for I have sinned."*

Serena walked into her bedroom, her bare feet making no sound on the cool, wood floor. She'd returned to the house before the storm broke, filling the vases in the dining room and bedrooms with the freshly-cut flowers. After settling a vase on the table in the sitting area, she opened the French doors. The refreshing scent of rain-washed earth filtered through the space. The soil soaked up the moisture like a thirsty sponge, unwilling to give back a drop. Waiting until the downpour subsided, she stepped out onto the veranda, turning her face skyward. The moisture cooled her face and seeped into the light fabric of her sleeveless dress. Her eyes opened, and at the same time she shifted to her left. Then she saw him.

The sight of him on the veranda, arms raised, sucked the breath from her lungs as she inhaled audibly. The vision of his finely woven, white shirt pasted against his chest was more sensual than if he'd stood completely naked. The rich, deep brown of his wet flesh showing through the fabric elicited a familiar throbbing in the lower portion of her body.

David felt, rather than saw, Serena even before he opened his eyes. An invisible force propelled him from where he stood until he was next to her, a secret smile curving his mobile mouth as he registered her delicate beauty. She did not move when he reached out for her. Burying his face in the hair swept atop her head, he pressed his mouth to the fragrant curls.

"Forgive me, *mi amor.* I didn't want to send you away."

Serena fused herself to him, becoming one with him. She wanted to refuse him, reject him, but she couldn't. Her life was entwined with a stranger she'd lain with after three days of their meeting. A stranger whom it was prophesied she would marry. A stranger who would fill her womb with his seed. A sensual, passionate stranger she was falling in love with.

Her trembling fingers feathered over his mouth. "Shh-hhh, David. There's nothing to forgive."

"Yes, there is," he insisted. "I sent you away when all I wanted was to hold you to my heart. Everything was perfect until—" His words trailed off.

"Until what?" Her voice was muffled against the solid heat of his chest.

He couldn't tell her what had transpired between him and her father. She would never believe him. And he did not trust Raul's mental state not to go through with his proposed threats to mutilate him.

"Until I called my father," he began, deciding to tell her half the truth. "He's not doing well."

Pulling back, Serena stared up at his wet face. "What happened?"

"He suffered a stroke four years ago that left him with limited use of his right side and some speech impairment. Extensive therapy restored his speech so that you can understand him, but when I spoke to him this morning his words weren't clear. They came out garbled."

He wanted to say it was because of what he was forced to tell him. That if Samuel Cole didn't use his money and influence to have her brother released from prison he would lose his own son.

Compassion softened her delicate face. "I'm sorry, David. When are you planning to leave?"

His sweeping eyebrows lifted. "Leave?"

She blinked in bewilderment. "Yes. Aren't you going back to Florida to be with him?"

I can't, because your father has made me a prisoner, he replied silently. "No. My family will take care of him. I'll stay and finish what I have to do here." His head came down slowly, and he wasn't disappointed when her lips met his. He drank deeply from her soft, honeyed mouth, and when he pulled back both were breathing heavily. A wild, untamed fire burned in his coal-black eyes, searing her face. "When I leave here, you're coming with me."

Serena felt a surge of elation, followed by a shock of despair. "I can't leave, David."

"Why not?" The two words sounded like a crack of a whip.

"My mother just left for Florida. I promised her that I'd stay with Poppa."

What he wanted to shout at her was that her *Poppa* had threatened his life. That her Poppa had made her an unwilling prisoner so that she had to wait for her mother's return before she could go back to the States.

His lean jaw hardened. "I'll wait for you," he said instead.

Her gaze swept furtively over his face. "It may take a while."

"I have time." What he had was a sixty-day reprieve so that Gabriel Vega could be released from prison. He refused to think beyond the sixty days. Cradling her face between his hands, he brushed his mouth over hers. "Lock your door, but leave your window unlocked. I'll come to you tonight," he whispered.

Serena nodded, pulled out of his embrace, and reentered her bedroom. She glanced briefly at the flowers on the table, a secret smile touching her face. Everything was going to be all right. The voice in her head confirmed that fact.

CHAPTER 20

West Palm Beach, Florida

Martin Cole leaned in closer to hear what his father was saying, his deeply tanned, golden brown face darkening with the rush of blood from the twin emotions of rage and fear. Samuel Cole's garbled telephone message, *David's in trouble,* had sent him racing up from Fort Lauderdale to West Palm Beach, exceeding the state's speed limit by more than twenty miles.

He stared at his father's deeply lined forehead. "Does my mother know about this?"

Samuel raised a partially withered right hand, waving it slowly. "No. I can't tell her," he replied slowly. "I don't want any of the women to know."

Martin nodded, wondering how his mother and sisters would react to the news that David Cole was being held hostage in Costa Rica by a madman. His midnight gaze shifted to the vaulted ceiling of the loggia of his childhood West Palm Beach home. Closing his eyes, he recalled the madness sweeping through the Cole family nine years before. There had been another kidnapping—that of his own daughter.

Ten-year-old Regina Cole had been kidnapped from her grandparents' home by a man who needed the money to pay off his gambling debts. Regina was rescued, unharmed, but not without the lingering effects of a fear of close, dark spaces. For six long, anxious days the child had been locked in a closet. Her captors let her out only to eat and to relieve herself.

What had pained Martin most was that his own father had been indirectly responsible for his daughter's captivity. He'd contracted with a hit man to kill Martin's wife. When his many attempts were thwarted the hit man decided to take the child. What the kidnapper wanted was an exchange: the mother for the daughter.

It had taken years before Martin's heart softened enough to forgive Samuel Cole for his loathsome behavior. An adulterous affair with a young woman more than forty years before had left the elder Cole with enough guilt to swallow him whole, and he'd confused Martin's wife with the woman he'd seduced.

The affair resulted in a son, a son Samuel refused to accept or acknowledge; a son who hated his father as much as his father hated him; a son who finally forgave his father, but only when the older man begged forgiveness as he lay dangerously ill.

It had taken the Cole family forty years to reconcile; forty years to sweep away the remnants of their dirty family secrets, only to be faced with another crisis now. However, this crisis did not start from within. It was from an outsider with a vendetta.

Martin combed his fingers through his steely-gray, curly hair before his gaze shifted to his father's face. The stroke had aged Samuel, making him appear much older than seventy-seven. It had taken the healthy color from his sienna-brown face, the shine from his once-thick white hair, and most of all his vibrant spirit. The bluster that had made Samuel Claridge Cole one of the most feared African-American businessmen was gone. His quick mind, his business acumen, and his uncanny instinct for turning a profit in a failing enterprise had also vanished. He appeared to be a broken man who lived each day to interact with his children, grandchildren, and now great-grandchildren.

However, age was more than kind to Martin Diaz Cole. At forty-nine he was a man in his prime. His tall, large body bore no evidence of softening. Laps in a pool, twice daily, helped him retain the muscle he'd acquired in his mid-twenties. He'd married at thirty-nine, fathered three children, and spent his time managing his own investments with his half brother.

Lacing his fingers together, he smiled at his father. "I'll take over, Dad. I'll call the governor's office and Senator Epstein and Velasquez."

Samuel nodded slowly. "You do that. But there's someone else I want involved."

"Who?"

"Joshua."

A slight frown creased Martin's forehead. "He's retired, Dad. He no longer has security clearance. You can't ask him to leave his family and go back into intelligence again."

Sighing heavily and pressing his head back against the chaise cushion, Samuel closed his eyes. "I'm not asking him to come out of retirement. I just want him to help his brother."

Martin stared at his father, seeing a glimpse of what had made him who he'd been. He recognized the determination of a half-dozen men, and he recognized that Samuel would do anything to protect his family, including going outside of the law.

"I'll call him." Rising to his feet, he leaned over and kissed his father's withered right cheek.

Martin returned to his car without stopping to see his mother. He could not see or talk to Marguerite Cole without lying to her. He'd never lied to her, and he did not want to begin now, not with her youngest child's life at risk.

He picked up a cellular phone and dialed his half-brother's residence in Santa Fe, New Mexico. Drumming his fingers against the steering wheel, he counted off the rings and the seconds.

"Hello," came a deep male voice.

"Josh." There was obvious relief in Martin's voice.

"What's up, Buddy?"

"Can you talk?"

There was a noticeable pause. "What's going on?"

"Can you talk?" Martin repeated.

"Yes. Vanessa and Emily went out about an hour ago. Why?"

"Raul Cordero-Vega is holding David hostage. He won't let

him go until Gabriel Vega is released from prison. His kid is charged with murder and drug trafficking, so we both know there's no way he's getting out."

A long, violent stream of profanity burned the wires as Martin listened to his brother's virulent tirade. "I should've eliminated Vega before I retired. The army traced that cache of weapons stolen from Fort Sam Houston to Vega, but they could never prove it."

"Are you going back in?"

"No. Vanessa threatened to leave me if I came out of retirement." There was another pause. "We can't afford to wait sixty days with this lunatic."

"What do you suggest?"

"Give me time to put something together. I believe it's time Vega and I meet. I'll go as a businessman, even though I'm not certain what I'm going to be selling."

Martin's features softened with his trademark dimpled smile. "Thanks, Josh."

"Remember, Buddy, he's my brother, too."

"I'm going back to Ford Lauderdale. Call me there."

"Do M.J. or the girls know about this?"

"No. Sammy says they don't need to know."

"He's right. I'll be in touch."

Martin heard the dial tone when Joshua ended the connection. He turned on the ignition in his car, his mind filled with details of what lay ahead for the Cole family, and as he left the local road for the highway south he prayed they would be able to rescue David before sixty days elapsed.

CHAPTER 21

Puerto Limón, Costa Rica

David stared at the space where Serena had been. A muscle flicked angrily at his jaw, eliciting a dull throbbing along the left side of his face. He welcomed the pain, as it aroused anger rather than compliance. There was no way he was going to remain at *La Montaña* for sixty days to await his fate, like a calf fattened for slaughter.

He returned to his bedroom, opened the closet, and retrieved his empty garment bag. Running his fingers along a hidden seam, he found the invisible opening and withdrew his passport and a slim billfold filled with credit cards and Costa Rican currency in large denominations. Letting out his breath, he sighed in relief. At least he could leave the country without being detained at customs. He returned the passport and the billfold to their hidden compartment and closed the closet door.

Running a hand over his close-cut hair, he made his way over to the armchair, sat down, and elevated his right foot. Most of the swelling in his toes and instep was gone, leaving only a noticeable puffiness and discoloration around the ankle. It would take a while before he would be able to put full pressure on the foot. He'd managed to walk unaided, but with an obvious limp, and he knew he was going nowhere without being in peak physical condition.

He thought of the U.S. ambassador's reluctance to intervene

in the release of Gabriel Vega. David doubted whether he would be as reluctant to become involved for an American citizen. He had to solicit Raul's aid to contact the ambassador again, this time persuading the man to come to Puerto Limón. It would be ironic if his last trip to Costa Rica would be for the purpose of negotiating on Raul Cordero-Vega's behalf rather than for ColeDiz International Ltd. Both of them would emerge winners. Vega would get his son back and rid himself of the Coles, while David would divest ColeDiz of its remaining Costa Rican enterprise *and* claim a woman and a love that promised forever.

He also mentally catalogued what he would need if he planned to leave *La Montaña* without notifying his host of his departure, refusing to acknowledge his fate if legal arbitration failed.

Serena lay on her bed, recognizing an emotion she hadn't felt in twelve years—a restless waiting.

Then she had been waiting to return to the country of her birth. She had applied to several universities in the States with nursing programs, and within weeks of mailing off the applications she checked the mail daily. It took months before the first response came, and then the others followed in rapid succession. Every school she had applied to had accepted her. Her joy was short-lived when she had to select which school and where. In the end she'd decided on New York. It was close enough for her to see two sets of grandparents in Ohio during the holidays and school recesses.

Peering up at the mosquito netting draped over the four-poster bed, she recalled the joyous occasion when she graduated from nursing school at the top of her class. Her grandparents flew in for the celebration, along with her parents and brother. Gabe fell in love with the land of his mother's and sister's birth, and confided to Serena that he also wanted to attend college in the United States.

Her smile faded when she thought of how her brother's life had been turned upside down. She did not and could not believe

Gabe was involved in drugs or murder. Her very straightlaced brother did not smoke, drink, or swear, and she, too, wondered on occasion why he'd taken up with Guillermo Barranda.

The younger Barranda's reputation of throwing wild parties at his off-campus residence with unlimited supplies of women and liquor was well documented in the Dade County vicinity. Serena had questioned her brother about his intense social activities when she met him in Florida during a three-day holiday weekend. Gabriel confessed that he had fallen in love with a girl who was the sister of a close associate of Barranda. She'd smiled and warned her brother to think with his head and not his heart. Gabe flashed his sensual smile and ducked his head, nodding.

But what was she doing now, if not thinking with her heart and not her head, when it came to David Cole? She had compromised her professional ethics by sleeping with him, because he *was* her patient. Even if David hadn't been her patient, she'd never slept with a man she'd known only three days. Perhaps if Luz Maria hadn't predicted she would marry David, then she would have resisted him.

No, the silent voice crooned in her head. There was no doubt that she'd been attracted to David Cole from the moment she glanced at him; and she could not deny the powerful, invisible force that drew her to him whenever they occupied the same space. Within days the force had pulled her into him, so that she did not know where he began and she ended. In or out of bed, they had become one.

The soft chiming of the telephone interrupted her musings. Reaching over, she picked up the receiver. *"Hola."*

"Hola, Amiga."

"Evelyn!" Serena screamed. "How did you know I was back?"

"I had to hear it secondhand, Miss Morris. And you know I hate secondhand news."

Serena's large eyes sparkled with excitement. "Are you calling from San José?"

"I'm here in Limón at my mother's."

"Give me time to change my clothes and I'll—"

"Stay where you are, *Amiga*. I'm coming to *La Montaña*. I have something to show you. *Adiós*."

Serena heard the sound of the dial tone as her high school friend hung up abruptly. Replacing the receiver on its cradle, she propelled herself off the bed. She met Evelyn Perez when they both were ten, and they had become fast friends. As they approached adolescence they made up stories about finding the perfect man, marrying him, and settling down to have a beautiful home filled with lots of babies.

Evelyn had married her high school sweetheart a month following their graduation, but hadn't had any children.

She combed her hair, securing the curly strands in a single plait, slipped into a sarong style cotton skirt in a vibrant, sungold and black print and a gold tank top. The color emphasized the rich, warm, brown undertones of her flawless complexion.

The black ballet slippers on her feet muffled the sound of her footsteps as she descended the staircase just as the front doorbell chimed melodiously. "I'll get it, Isabel," Serena said to the petite, dark-skinned, silent woman who came to *La Montaña* three times a week to clean and maintain the routines Juanita had set up for the smooth management of her household.

Her delicate jaw dropped when she opened the door and stared at a grinning Evelyn holding a tiny infant in her arms. "You did it!"

Evelyn Perez-Comacho handed Serena her daughter. "Meet Señorita Serena Lupe Consuela Comacho."

Serena's eyes filled with tears, and she blinked them back before they could fall on the sleeping baby girl. "You kept your promise to name your daughter after me."

"I always keep my promises, *Amiga*."

Cradling the child to her breast, Serena stepped aside. "Come in out of the heat."

Evelyn moved past her childhood friend and into the cool magnificence of *La Montaña*. She had always admired the house, even as it was being erected, not realizing she would spend many nights under its roof once she formed a close friendship with Serena Morris.

"Everything about *La Montaña* is still beautiful," Evelyn stated, her dark gaze sweeping around the enormous space before passing to linger on the curving staircase.

Serena nodded in stunned silence. The warmth and slight weight of the child she cradled to her breast garnered all of her attention.

"How old is she?"

"Three months."

Serena glanced briefly at her friend before returning her attention to the baby. "Why didn't you call me to let me know that you were pregnant?"

"It was touch and go at first. I spent the first four months of my pregnancy in bed, because of spotting. As it was, she was six weeks early."

"Come and sit down. We have so much to talk about." She led Evelyn to the area off the living room and both women sat on the love seat. Evelyn placed a large, quilted bag down on a side table.

Serena stared at the sleeping child in her arms, marveling at how much the tiny girl resembled her father. An undertone of deep rose pink shone through the delicate, pale skin covering her dewy, soft face. She removed the tiny, white cotton eyelet hat, smiling at the tufts of black curling hair covering the small, round head.

"She's just like Francisco. You'd think I had nothing to do with helping to create this baby," Evelyn said solemnly.

"She's beautiful, Evelyn." Raising her head, she stared at her friend. Evelyn was beautiful. Tall and slender, she claimed a dark brown coloring that she'd inherited from her Jamaican ancestors, while her thick, jet-black hair was styled to flatter her attractive features. Large dark eyes framed by thick lashes and a full, lush mouth arrested one's attention immediately.

"She's my life. I wanted to conceive for so long that I had just resigned myself that I would never be a mother."

"How is Francisco taking to fatherhood?"

Evelyn's smile was dazzling. "He's a little *loco* about her."

Serena shifted a delicate eyebrow. "Only a little?"

"Okay, a lot crazy. Right now he's in Panama City for the next six weeks with a group of archaeologists who are convening to discuss the artifacts uncovered during a dig along the border with Panama."

"How is he dealing with the separation?"

"Not well. He calls me every night."

Serena smiled. It appeared as if her friends were still very much in love. "Now, tell me. How did you know that I was back?"

"My cousin saw you at the *Mercado Municipal*. When did you get back?"

"Last Wednesday."

Evelyn glanced down at the highly polished parquet floor. "I heard about your brother." Her gaze swept back to meet Serena's. "I know he's innocent."

She nodded, biting down on her lower lip before she forced a smile. "Thanks for the vote of confidence. Let's hope and pray that a Florida jury will find him innocent."

"Anyone who's met Gabriel knows that he's the kindest—"

"It's all right, Evelyn. You don't have to say it." Her expression brightened. "I've been rude. Let me get you something to eat and drink." Leaning over, she handed the sleeping baby back to her mother.

"Is there some place I can lay her? I don't want to get into the habit of holding her while she sleeps. It doesn't take much to spoil her."

Serena rose to her feet and took the quilted bag. "Sure. Bring her upstairs to my bedroom."

The two women took the staircase to the second story bedroom, walking the length of a hallway they'd traversed many times in the past. Evelyn spread a lightweight cotton blanket over the crocheted coverlet on Serena's bed, then gently placed her daughter on the blanket. Placing pillows strategically around the baby to prevent her from rolling off onto the floor, they walked out of the room.

David sat on the armchair, drawing and then erasing pencilled notes as he worked feverishly on a composition for a guitar solo. He wanted to put all of the notes down before he went downstairs to play what he'd composed.

He could discern the distinctive sound of an acoustical guitar playing a classical Spanish flamenco rhythm with a pair of castanets as an accompaniment. He wanted another instrument, but he hadn't decided on which one.

What he needed was a deep, moanful sound—bass violin, organ? *"Cello,"* he whispered. He would use the cello, utilizing half the tempo of the guitar. The cello would represent the low murmur of the wind, the guitar the rustle of leaves before the storm broke, and the castanets the wild, unrestrained tapping of rain against the windows. He wanted to capture in his music the sounds of the exotic, sun-drenched world of the rain forest. And he also wanted to incorporate the peace and tranquility he'd discovered in Serena's arms.

He heard a mournful cry, recognizing it as that of a howler monkey. When he'd first heard the eerie sound he thought it was that of a baby crying.

Forcing his thoughts back to the pad on his lap, he hummed the notes resting on, above, and below the staff of music. The crying began again, this time louder than the first time. He listened intently, sure now the crying came from a human baby. But, he wondered, where was there a baby at *La Montaña?*

He put aside the pad and pencil, rose to his feet, and made his way across the bedroom. The crying grew louder as he neared the door. Moving down the hallway, he stood outside Serena's bedroom. On her bed amid a barricade of pillows lay a tiny baby whose arms and legs flailed wildly. Its face had darkened with a rush of frantic screaming.

"Whoa, Fella," he crooned, limping into the bedroom. "What can be so bad that you have to scream like this?"

He reached down and picked up the fretful infant, cradling it to his chest. The soft, clean smell associated with babies wrang a smile from him. The baby snuggled closer to his warmth and stopped crying. A pair of tiny, round, dark eyes stared up at his larger, darker pair.

"You look as if you've had a lot of experience with babies," said a familiar female voice behind him.

Turning slowly, David smiled at Serena and a woman, he assumed was the child's mother. "I have," he admitted, his gaze fused with Serena's. "I'm uncle to a horde of nieces and nephews. He was crying, so I picked him up," he explained quickly.

"Ella," the women chorused in unison. "She."

David arched his sweeping eyebrows and flashed a sheepish, dimpled grin. "I can't tell one from the other when they're fully clothed," he explained, switching to English.

"You're welcome to change her," Evelyn suggested in Caribbean-accented English.

"No, thank you," he replied, handing the child to its mother.

Serena saw the spark of interest in Evelyn's gaze as her dark eyes swept in a leisurely way over the tall figure of the man who had just comforted her daughter. He'd changed his rain-soaked, cream-colored shirt and slacks for a pair in black linen. The overall effect was powerful, given his dark coloring.

"David Cole, Evelyn Comacho."

Evelyn shifted baby Serena to one arm and extended her free hand. "My pleasure."

He took her hand and brought it to his mouth. "The pleasure is mine," he replied in Spanish. Evelyn blushed and fluttered her lashes. "What is Mistress Comacho's first name?"

"Serena. Yes, she's named for Serena," she explained quickly.

"A beautiful name for an incredibly beautiful child," he countered in a soft voice. He spoke to all in the room, but gazed only at the woman Serena. His midnight gaze was riveted on her face, then moved slowly down her body, leaving a trail of burning longing everywhere it touched.

Serena felt the heat as if he had stoked a gently spreading fire. She forgot that they weren't alone when she permitted him to reach across the invisible space to wrap her in a cocoon of longing. His eyes widened enough for her to see his pupils dilate with the rising passion he was unable to conceal from her. His breathing deepened, his delicate nostrils flaring, while his lips parted.

Evelyn's shocked gaze flitted from her friend to the tall man with the scar running along the left side of his face. He was hypnotically attractive, the scar making his features less delicate while not detracting from what was an obviously beautiful male face. The scar, his black attire, and the small, gold earring in his left ear afforded him the appearance of a modern-day pirate. And there was no doubt that there was something going on between her friend and the man who shifted between fluent English and Spanish with equal facility.

"I'm going downstairs to change the baby," she said in a hushed tone, breaking the munificent silence filling the bedroom.

"And I'm going for a walk," David offered as an excuse to escape Serena. He had to get away from her or else embarrass the both of them in front of her friend.

Serena nodded, unable to force a word from her constricted throat. *How could he?* she raged inwardly. How could he look at her like that in front of a stranger? Only a blind person would miss the silent interchange that had passed between them. What was it about David Cole that made it possible for him to seduce her without saying a word?

She moved to the bed, picked up the baby's bag, and followed Evelyn out of the room, leaving David staring at her back. Just before she reached the top of the staircase, she glanced over her shoulder and found him standing in the hallway, staring.

David had begun what he'd promised to do: wait for her.

CHAPTER 22

Serena met Evelyn in the sitting area where she sat breastfeeding her baby. The two women stared at each other, smiling,

"Are you going to tell me about him, or do I have to pry?"

Serena shrugged a bare shoulder. "There's nothing to tell. He's a business associate of my father. He's staying with us because he had an accident."

"No, *Amiga,* it's not the accident I want to know about. I know what I see."

"And that is?" Serena asked, refusing to make it easy for her friend.

"The fire between you two is…*caliente!*"

"There's no fire, Evelyn."

"The man burns for you. Didn't you feel the heat?"

"Nope."

"*Mentirosa!* Don't you dare lie to me, Girlfriend," Evelyn continued, switching to English.

Serena struggled not to laugh, but couldn't keep the chuckles from escaping when she saw the indignation on Evelyn's face.

"You're right," she admitted softly. "The heat between us is incredible."

She disclosed all that had happened from the moment David Cole lay under her parents' roof, omitting the part where they'd made love. She also told Evelyn of Luz Maria's prediction.

"It's weird, Evelyn. I didn't even want to like him, but meanwhile I find myself believing that I love him."

"What's not to like or even love? The man's absolutely gorgeous."

"It's not his looks," she argued softly. "That's too superficial."

"Whatever it is, don't fight it, *Amiga.*"

They talked for another hour, catching up on what had transpired in their lives since their last meeting; she kissed her friend and tiny namesake, promising she would return the visit before Evelyn returned to San José with her daughter.

Raul Vega emerged from the sanctuary of his study at the same time Serena headed for the stairs, lines of tension ringing his mouth and crisscrossing his forehead.

"Chica."

Stopping, she glanced down at Raul. "Yes, Poppa."

"Let David know that he's expected to take his meal with us at eight."

Noting the strain of his drawn features, she offered a comforting smile. *"Sí,* Poppa." Raul nodded, then turned and reentered his study.

She continued up the staircase, knowing the only time she would see her stepfather would be during dinner. Whenever he was troubled by something he retreated to his study, leaving it only to share the evening meal with his family. She and Gabe had learned early never to enter the room without knocking, or venturing in even when Raul was not in attendance.

She'd tried over and over during her adult years to analyze her relationship with her stepfather, failing to understand his passions. He loved her mother, his children, and his country, but that love was sometimes all-encompassing and suffocating. There were no in-betweens for Raul Cordero-Vega—it was all or nothing. He loved hard and hated even harder.

She was aware of the enmity between the two men in her life, knowing she would have to choose. But she was also confident that Raul would forgive her, because he had become her father and she his daughter.

She walked into David's room and found it empty. Making her

way to the adjoining bathroom, she peered in. It was apparent that he hadn't returned from his walk. The pad she had given him lay on the seat of the armchair, and she moved over to pick it up. Half the pages in the bound pad were filled with pencilled musical notes. He'd composed solos for piano, guitar, sax, and flugelhorn. Along the margins he'd indicated the key and tempo, and a few bore titles: *Book of Secrets. Exotic Pleasures.*

Staring at his latest work-in-progress, she smiled. This composition featured a guitar and cello. A most unusual pairing, but then she had to admit that David was unusual. Instinctively she knew that beneath his tailored clothing and regal bearing was a tempered wildness he'd learned to control with maturity. The pierced ear and tattoo were overt evidence of his atypical behavior for a man born to his station. He'd admitted rebelling against his father's insistence that he join the family business on graduation from college when he pursued a career as a musician. And it was also apparent that he'd substituted Raul Cordero-Vega for his father whenever they met to discuss his family's holdings in Costa Rica. The battle lines were drawn, and neither wanted to concede.

"What do you think of it?"

Serena felt the heat flare in her face at the sound of the deep, musical voice. Turning slowly, she smiled at David. He stood in the doorway, leaning on the cane.

"I'd love to hear it," she replied, her voice lowering seductively.

He limped into the bedroom, stopping less than a foot from her. "I decided not to play what I've written until I finish."

Her gold-brown gaze moved slowly over his face, coming to rest on his mouth. "When do you think you'll finish?"

He returned her enraptured gaze, his lids lowering over his large black eyes. "When I stop hearing the music in my head."

The fire Evelyn had referred to was back—hotter than before. It scorched her face, throat, chest, and lower—to the secret, pulsing area between her thighs. The heat and the throbbing intensified until she doubted whether she could stand unaided.

"Stop that, David," she whispered.

He took a step closer, then another. "Stop what, *mi alma?*"

Her lids fluttered close. "Don't look at me like that."

A half-smile curved his mouth. "Like what?"

Serena's chest rose and fell heavily under her tank top, bringing David's burning gaze to her heaving breasts. "Like I'm—" Her words trailed off. She couldn't say it. She wasn't quite that uninhibited.

His smile widened as he shifted a sweeping, silky black eyebrow. "Like you're something I'd like to eat," he crooned quietly.

Her shuttered eyelids flew open and she stared at him with an expression that mirrored her shock. He'd read her mind. She nodded, numbly, unable to form the words to verify her thoughts.

Reaching out with his free hand, he took the pad from her limp fingers. "Tonight you'll find out just how much I want you."

The heat increased in her face, making it impossible for her to continue to look at him as she turned her back. Was she that open? Were all of her emotions on the surface for him to see? How was it everyone read her so well? Luz Maria, David, and Evelyn.

"I came to tell you that my father expects you to eat dinner with us."

The mention of Raul Vega broke the sensual spell. David's smile faded quickly, a frown taking its place. "At what time has he ordered that I sit at his table?"

Serena spun around, her own passion replaced by annoyance. "Stop it, David. Why must you attack him like this?"

"Because I don't like him, that's why."

"That's not a reason to be deliberately ungracious."

David wanted to shout at her that he wasn't the one who was ungracious. That it was her father who had him assaulted, threatened his life, that before he killed him he would begin a systematic mutilation until he died in agony.

"What do you want from me, Serena? Do you want me to

genuflect and kiss his ring? He's set himself up as a despot. He wants absolute control of everyone and everything. I've taken insults from him that I would've never taken from another man, all in the name of maintaining a professional business decorum with an official of a foreign country. But all of that is going to end because there won't be any negotiations for the sale of the banana plantation."

A sudden chill shook her body. "What are you going to do?" Her voice was a breathless whisper.

He leaned down until his face was inches from hers. "I'm walking away from it. The employees of ColeDiz International Ltd. can take what they want, or leave the bananas to rot where they lay."

She shook her head in disbelief. "No one can touch the plantation unless the government decides to nationalize the property. And that can take months."

His expression was impassive, and that frightened her more than if he'd affected a frown. "I really don't give a damn, because Vega will be left with nothing, and I don't believe the Costa Rican government will want to throw its money away on a worthless piece of property. Your *Poppa* wants to play dirty. What he'll get is someone who's been taught to play dirty by one of the best."

"Who?"

He straightened, recognizing the glimmer of fear in her wide-eyed gaze. "My father."

"If that's the case, then why don't you let our fathers fight this battle?"

David gritted his teeth, welcoming the pain radiating from his temple to his chin. "They are, Serena."

"What are you talking about?"

"Don't ask me. Ask your *Poppa*," he drawled in a nasty, sarcastic tone.

Serena brushed past him as she walked quickly to the door. "You can believe I will."

David flung the pad across the room, wishing he could bellow out his frustration. He was trapped, a prisoner in the home of a man whose daughter he coveted. He couldn't tell her about the betrayal and deadly revenge taking center stage, where a word from her stepfather would shatter their love and the hope of a future together.

His only hope was that his father could survive long enough to secure his freedom. A freedom that would give him back his son as well as claim to another daughter-in-law.

Serena sat opposite David at the dining room table, holding her breath. She'd approached her father after her hostile confrontation with David, but Raul refused to see her. She'd pounded on the locked door until her fist ached, but he hadn't opened the door.

Waiting until Luz Maria brought out all of the dishes, she glared at Raul's expressionless face. "Will you talk to me now, Poppa?"

Raul spread a snowy white napkin over his lap and glared at her. "You know the rules, *Chica*. We do not discuss business at the table."

"If you don't talk to me now, when will you? You owe me that much. Remember, I'm your daughter, not a business associate."

He inclined his gray head. "That is true. You are my daughter." He smiled, softening the hard lines in his face and making her aware of why her mother had married him. Raul Cordero-Vega was still an extremely attractive man at sixty-two.

"But I refuse to discuss business at *my* dinner table," he continued.

"Your table, your house," she ranted, refusing to back down. "When is it ever *our* table, *our* house?"

Raul's fingers tightened around the handle of his knife and fork. "Enough, *Chica*." The two words were spoken quietly, but there was no mistaking the repressed rage in the man staring down at the contents on his plate. His head lifted as his eyes widened.

Something within Serena exploded as she stood up. "No! It is not enough!"

Raul didn't move. "Sit down." When she did not comply, he put down his silverware. The deafening silence swelled as the two men at the table stared at the petite woman who stood facing her stepfather, trembling with defiance.

"Why is it always what *you* want, Poppa?"

"Serena!" Her name exploded from the back of his throat.

David placed both hands on the table and rose to his feet. Rage he did not know he was capable of surfaced, making breathing difficult. "Don't ever raise your voice to her again." His warning, though spoken softly, denoted a threat.

Raul's head jerked around as he glared disbelievingly at the man who challenged him over and over. "You forget your place, Señor Cole. This is between me and my daughter."

"And you forget yours, Señor Vega. In case you haven't noticed, your daughter is an adult. It's time you saw her as one."

"And it is apparent that you've forgotten who you are and where you are, Señor Cole."

"I know exactly who I am. It is you who has forgotten. It is only because I *do* respect *your home* and your daughter that I don't say what I'd like to say."

Raul stood up and threw his napkin down to the table. "I will not take your insults. Not at my own table. Serena, tell Luz Maria to serve me in my study." Pushing back his chair, he stalked out of the dining room, leaving them staring at his back.

Serena's hands were shaking as she covered her face and sank slowly down to her chair. "When will it end?" she whispered, her voice breaking with raw emotion.

David made his way slowly around the table. He resisted the urge to hold her and comfort her. "He's angry and frustrated." He wanted to rationalize her father's pain, but knew Vega's pain had not started with his son's arrest. It'd begun years before, with his obsession to save his country from foreigners.

Her hands came down and she stared up at David, her golden eyes awash with unshed tears. "There are times when I feel that he hates me, David. Why, I don't know."

"He doesn't hate you, *mi amor.* He's angry with himself. And it's up to Raul Cordero-Vega to solve his own problems and come to terms with himself."

"You're wrong. He's always loved my mother and brother. It seems as if he picks and chooses his time to offer me what he's always given them. We can't spend more than three days together before we're at each other's throats. I don't know what's going to happen with my brother, but I swear that when I leave Costa Rica this time only death will bring me back."

She pulled away when David reached out for her and stood up. "Excuse me. I have to tell Luz Maria to bring *my father's* dinner to his study."

David wanted to tell Serena that she did not have to say anything to Luz Maria, that if Raul wanted his dinner served in his study he could tell the cook himself. But the words were lodged in his throat. He'd come to Serena's defense without considering the consequences. It was apparent that she had quarreled with her stepfather many times in the past. She did not need him to fight her battles.

But something would not permit him to sit silent while Raul shouted at her. At that moment he'd wanted to reach across the table and strangle the man, choking off his words and his life's breath. And it was in that instant that he knew he would've willingly given up his life for Serena. He loved her that much.

He waited for her to return from the kitchen. It was only after she reclaimed her chair that he sat down. Both of them ate in complete silence, lost in their private thoughts.

David drank three glasses of a premium red wine while Serena toyed with the stem of her wineglass before she drank one. The wine helped relax him. He soon forgot Vega's virulent exchange with Serena, and he looked forward to taking her into his arms to calm and soothe her fears. He wanted her to know that she didn't have to solicit her stepfather's love, because he loved her. His love was all she would ever need from a man—any man.

CHAPTER 23

Serena retreated to her bedroom after eating dinner, stripped off her clothes, and spent the next hour soaking in the bathtub. The scented candles, perfumed bath oil, and the softly playing, all-music radio station worked their magic as she willed her mind and body to relax.

She forgot the confrontation at the dinner table, the fact that she could not confide in her mother, and even the knowledge that Gabe was locked away in a Florida prison.

She forgot all of the madness affecting her family as the realization that she had fallen in love transported her to a place where she languished in the comforting arms of serenity.

Picking up a bath sponge, she trickled water over her shoulders and down her breasts, her flesh shimmering from the scented oil. It was only when she stood up to step out of the tub that she saw him.

David stood in the shadows of the candle-lit bathroom, watching her. Her breath caught in her chest before it started up again in an erratic rhythm that left her feeling lightheaded.

"How long have you been here?"

Pushing off the wall, David closed the space between them. "Long enough to see everything I like." His hands circled her waist and he effortlessly lifted her from the bathtub. Holding her water-slick body aloft, her feet dangling in the air, he pressed his mouth to hers. He molded her flesh to his, fusing their naked bodies and making them one.

Serena gloried in the feel of the crisp hair on his chest

grazing her sensitive nipples. She curved her arms around his neck and deepened the kiss, her tongue easing slowly, deliberately, into his mouth.

David gasped at the heated invasion of her tongue, opening his mouth wider until she branded him with her soul-searching kiss. He felt her trembling, the quickening of her respiration, and knew her passions were soaring as quickly as his own. He carried her into her own darkened bedroom and placed her on the bed, his body following.

After dinner he'd returned to his bedroom to shave and shower, then come to her, as promised. He'd turned off her bedside lamp and drawn the drapes before he walked silently into her bathroom. He'd stood in a corner, watching her as she lay in the bathtub, eyes closed, listening to the soft music coming from a radio, while ignoring the slight twinge of pain in his right foot. He saw the peace that settled into the features of the woman he'd fallen in love with. She had found solace in a tub filled with scented water, while he needed the scented softness of her body before he found his own peace.

David pulled back to catch his breath before his head dipped again. He drank from her honeyed mouth like a man dying of thirst, and she did quench his thirst, but not the gnawing hunger for the rest of her body.

Serena reveled in the scent of his smooth shaven jaw, the tip of her tongue tracing the length of the healing scar transforming his beautiful male face. Her fingers swept through the short, silken strands covering his well-shaped head before they cupped his ears, then moved still lower to cradle his face between her palms.

"Te amo," she whispered reverently between nibbling kisses. And she did love him. She loved him with a reverent passion that unlocked her heart and soul to offer him all that she possessed.

Her declaration of love battered down the last resistance he'd erected to keep women at a distance. The iron-will control he maintained when taking a woman to his bed fled, leaving him completely vulnerable for the first time in his adult life.

A violent shudder shook his large body when he buried his face in her fragrant, unbound hair. "And I love you," he confessed hoarsely. He repeated it over and over, it becoming a litany. Her slender arms tightened around his neck. Heart to heart, skin to skin, they became one.

"Love me, David." Her husky whisper broke the silence.

He wanted to do more than love her; he wanted to be inside her; he wanted to become one with her.

His lips brushed her lush, soft mouth before he moved lower to taste the silken flesh covering her throat. The soft moans coming from her parted lips impelled him to take her quickly; he ignored the twin emotions of lust and desire becoming one and the same, because he no longer feared not being in control of his passions.

His tongue continued its exploration of her moist body, sweeping over her flat belly. She arched off the mattress at the same time his hot mouth searched and claimed her moist, throbbing femininity. A strangled cry filled the darkened space when he cradled her hips in his hands and lifted her higher. He feasted, his rapacious tongue relentless. Serena could not believe that he'd awakened a dormant carnality that threatened to consume all of her.

He had taken her to such heights that she feared if she didn't jump she would die from the pleasure building in the hidden place where he'd buried his face. His hands shifted from her hips to her thighs, raising her legs until they lay over his shoulders.

Her head thrashed back and forth on the pillow and Serena lost herself in the violent explosion that shook every part of her body. The explosions persisted, one following the other. She opened her mouth to scream out the last cry of ecstasy, only to find her breath captured again by his mouth. David paused to protect her, then entered her pulsing body with a powerful thrust that rekindled her desire all over again. They rode out the violent storm of passion together, losing themselves in a love predestined from the beginning of time.

David strained valiantly to keep from exploding. He wanted

the lustful delirium to continue, but knew it couldn't. He had to release his passion or his heart would explode. Quickening his powerful thrusts, he lowered his head and gave into the eruptions hurtling him toward heaven. The moment before he gave into the force sweeping him beyond himself he surrendered all that he was to the woman who lay beneath him, their hearts beating in unison.

His body shuddered once, twice, and then a third time. He collapsed heavily on Serena's slight frame, laboring to slow his runaway pulse. He did not remember rolling off her and pulling her to lie atop his chest, nor did he remember when they fell asleep.

Streaks of the rising sun had just begun to pierce the cover of the fading nighttime sky when they did wake in each other's arm. Serena felt more relaxed than she had ever been in her life. Moaning sensuously, she rubbed her nose against David's cheek, inhaling the familiar scent of his aftershave.

"Good morning, Lover."

Opening his large eyes, he smiled down at her. "Good morning, Sweetheart. Did you sleep well?"

She stretched, raising a well-shaped leg in the air. "I slept wonderfully."

"I take it you like using me as a mattress," he teased.

"You could've pushed me off if I was too heavy."

David combed his fingers through her curling hair. "You don't weigh enough to be considered too heavy."

"How much do you weigh?"

"An even two hundred," he admitted.

"You don't look as if you weigh that much."

"Muscle weighs a lot more than fat."

Turning over on her side, she faced him, trying to make out his features in the darkened bedroom. The drawn drapes filtered out most of the light from the rising sun.

"How do you keep fit?"

"Swimming."

"How often do you swim?"

"Weather permitting—every day."

"Do you have a pool at your house in Boca Raton?"

"Yes. But I haven't had the chance to swim in it."

"Why not?"

"Because it was just built and I haven't moved in. I'd planned to have my sister-in-law decorate it when I return to the States. But that's going to change now."

"Why?"

He pressed his lips against her hair. "The house will be yours, to decorate in any style you want."

"We'll decide together."

"So, you're going to be a compromising little wife."

"Only this one time, David Claridge Cole."

"What about children?"

"What about them?"

"Do you want any?"

Raising her head, she stared up at him. "I want your babies."

"How many babies do you want?"

"Three."

David laughed softly, pulling her closer to his chest. "I've heard people say baby-making love is very different from regular lovemaking."

"I've never heard that. Besides, I don't believe it."

He shifted his eyebrows. "How would you know if you haven't tried it?"

"I'm not much of a risk-taker, David. Sleeping with you without protection is not something I'm willing to try again."

"How long an engagement do you want?"

"Not long," she confessed, dropping light kisses on his shoulder.

"Good."

"David!" she gasped when his hand eased up between her thighs.

"I need some regular lovemaking, Baby," he crooned against her moist lips.

"I can make it special if you let me get on top."

"Climb on," he urged, settling her body over his. And she did make it special. She took him to heaven with a burning sweetness that shattered him into a million tiny pieces before he lay shaking, spent from the passion she'd aroused in him.

He lingered in her bed until the sun broke the horizon to signal the beginning of another day of his captivity.

Day One had come and gone, and he refused to think of the other fifty-nine that lay ahead.

CHAPTER 24

July 17
West Palm Beach, Florida

Martin Cole, Joshua Kirkland, and Samuel Cole left the large gathering of the Cole family in the dining room, retreating to the library. Children, in-laws, grandchildren, and great-grandchildren had come to the large West Palm Beach mansion to celebrate the seventieth birthday of the family matriarch. Marguerite Josefina Diaz Cole's stunning beauty had not faded with age. Her silver, stylishly coiffed hair framed a smooth, tanned face that claimed a few laugh lines at the corners of her large, dark eyes. She had passed along her delicate features and dimpled smile to several of her offspring, and her superior genes were repeated in several of her grandchildren.

Joshua Kirkland waited for Martin to settle Samuel Cole on a large recliner that had been designed expressly for the elderly man, then sat down opposite his father and brother.

"Everything is set. Vega has agreed to meet with me."

Joshua's penetrating green gaze registered his father's and brother's reaction to his announcement that he was to leave for Costa Rica. Samuel nodded slowly, while Martin smiled.

"Do you think Vega will believe what you're selling?" Martin questioned.

"The man's a botanist," Joshua argued. "I'm told he has a greenhouse filled with several varieties of the tree I'm going to pitch to him. I intend to put his paranoid mind at ease when I tell him that Markham Pharmaceutical will not set up a plant in his country, that our scientists want the bark and needles from the Anneda pine tree." It had taken him a month to set up his cover as a salesman for a pharmaceutical company that was interested in a plant indigenous only to Costa Rica.

"When are you going to bring my boy back?" Samuel asked, his wavering voice breaking with emotion.

Martin reached out and covered his father's hand in a comforting gesture. "Patience, Dad. It's only been thirty days."

"That's thirty days too long," Samuel countered angrily.

Joshua rose to his feet, nodded to Martin, then walked out of the room. He would give his brother time to calm their father's fear that David Cole's life would be forfeited in an act of deadly revenge; legal attempts to solicit support of granting bail for Gabriel Vega had failed. No elected official wanted to take responsibility for securing the release of a murderer and drug trafficker.

Joshua and Samuel Cole had reconciled, both acknowledging the bond which made them father and son. But Joshua was always aware that he would never experience the affinity Martin and David shared with Samuel. However, at forty-three he was mature enough to accept what he could not control. He realized that he had to put the circumstances surrounding his illegitimacy to rest. His wife and daughter had become the most important people in his life.

"How is he taking it?" Joshua asked when Martin met him on the loggia.

Martin slipped his hands into the pockets of his slacks. "Not well. I don't know if he's going to make it."

"It's wearing on all of us. I think it's time we tell the family."

Martin's coal black eyes met his half-brother's pale gaze, a flash of fear sweeping over his deeply tanned face. "We can't."

Folding his arms over his chest, Joshua leaned against a coral column. "I told Vanessa last night. I had to," he continued when Martin stared at him as if he'd never seen him before. "How do

I explain bringing her and Emily to Florida for M.J.'s birthday, and then take off for Costa Rica?"

Covering his face with his hands, Martin shook his head. "Why didn't you tell her that you were going on ColeDiz business?"

"Have you forgotten that Vanessa oversees every investment I've acquired? And nowhere in my portfolio does the name ColeDiz appear." As Samuel Cole's illegitimate son he had not been granted a share in the family business.

Martin lowered his hands. "How did she take the news?"

"Not well at first. It's hell living with a woman who won't respond when you talk to her. It was only when I began packing this morning that she realized that I was going to go through with it."

Martin muttered a savage curse under his breath. He felt so powerless. He had earned the reputation as the consummate risk taker and deal maker, responsible for a billion-dollar family-owned enterprise, yet he could not negotiate for his brother's life.

Combing his fingers through his gray, curly hair, he nodded. "Okay. We tell them."

Joshua smiled and let out his breath. "I'll tell Nancy and Josephine. I'll leave you to tell M.J." He knew it would be easier for him to disclose the news of David's captivity to his half-sisters than to his father's wife.

Martin returned to the dining room, winking at his wife Parris as she sat with their six-year-old daughter on her lap, offering her small portions of cake. Making his way over to her, he hunkered down beside her chair. "I need to talk to you in the library."

Parris Cole's eyes widened slightly. A hint of green sparkled in their clear-brown depths. "What's up?"

"Family business," he whispered.

"What family business, Daddy?" Arianna chimed in her clear, childlike voice.

Running a forefinger down the length of his daughter's nose, he placed a kiss on the tiny tip. She giggled as he pulled her from her mother's lap and handed her to one of his teenage nieces.

"Take care of this chatterbox for me." His sister's daughter tickled Arianna, and the child dissolved into peals of laughter.

Martin walked over to where his mother sat at the head of the table. Cupping her elbow, he helped her to stand. "I have to talk to you in the library."

Her large, dark gaze seemed to race over her son's face. "What's going on?" She arched a sweeping eyebrow when Martin did not respond. "It's about David, isn't it?"

Martin nodded once. "Yes, Mother. It concerns David." He'd told his mother that David couldn't make her birthday celebration because he hadn't concluded his sale of the banana plantation in Costa Rica.

M.J. closed her eyes and placed a slender, manicured hand over her breast. "Is he alive, Martin?"

"Yes, Mother. He's alive."

Pulling herself erect, M.J. tilted her chin and walked out of the dining room. Martin was always amazed at how his mother was able to compose herself so quickly. He had never seen her resort to hysterics during a family crisis. She'd always chosen to grieve in private.

He whispered to his sisters that Joshua wanted to talk to them on the loggia, then informed Vanessa Kirkland that she should join him in the library.

Joshua straightened from his leaning position with Nancy and Josephine's approach. He took their hands and escorted them to several white, twisted rattan chairs with plump coral and white cushions, seating them. Pulling up a chair, he sat down and stared at the expectant expressions on their faces.

Nancy Cole-Thomas, the elder sister, returned her half-brother's stare. "What's going on, Joshua?"

He decided to be direct. He would handle their reactions later.

"David couldn't be here today because he's being held hostage in Costa Rica."

"What!" Nancy screamed.

Josephine's eyes widened in shock. Then she broke down, sobbing uncontrollably. Joshua stood up, pulling Josephine up with him. He held her gently while she sobbed out her grief. When her crying quieted he related the terms of David's release to his sisters.

Josephine glared at her half-brother, anger replacing her anguish. "Why have you waited so long to tell us about this?"

"We had hoped to resolve it before now."

"Resolve it how, Joshua?"

"Using legal means."

"Whose decision was it not to tell us about David?" Josephine continued with her questioning.

"We all agreed."

Josephine arched a sculpted eyebrow. "We?"

"Sammy, Martin, and I."

The women stared at each another. Their father and brothers had decided among themselves not to tell them that their youngest brother had been taken hostage by a deranged foreign official, and threatened with death if his son was not released from a Florida prison.

"How dare you! You had no right to make that decision without consulting us," Josephine said accusingly. "After all, he is our brother."

Joshua stared at her, chilling her with his icy gaze. "As he is also *my* brother."

She nodded, blinking back tears that threatened to flow again. Verbally attacking Joshua would not change things. As a family they needed to pull together, not fight one another. "I'm sorry, Joshua. Forgive me."

He inclined his head, his gaze softening. "This hasn't been easy on any of us."

Nancy wiped away her tears with her fingertips. "What are *you* going to do, Joshua?"

"I'm flying to Costa Rica in the morning."

She rose to her feet and wrapped her arms around her sister and brother. The three stood silently, feeding on each other's strength, then turned and walked back into the large house.

Martin examined the women sitting in the library. They were similar, yet very different. All were tall, slender women who affirmed their own personal strengths, but not without pain and sacrifice.

His wife Parris at forty-one had entered middle-age with a sensuality that left him gasping whenever she offered him her love. Having given him three children, her ripened body was still slim. She'd acquired an abundance of gray hairs in her dark brown, blunt-cut hair that she refused to color. She joked often that she'd earned them.

And she had. A failed first marriage, an abduction and black-mail that separated them for ten years, and subsequent murder attempts had given Parris Simmons-Cole more than her share of pain. But what Martin could not understand was that it was Parris, not he, who offered Samuel Cole forgiveness for what he had done to her and their daughter Regina. She confessed that she had prayed for strength to find the mercy to forgive her father-in-law. She forgave Samuel before he did.

His gaze moved to Vanessa Blanchard-Kirkland. His half-brother's wife was truly Joshua's soulmate. Her gentle love had helped him let go the bitterness he carried for years, and he'd become a loving husband, father, brother, and uncle.

He looked at his father. "David couldn't be here today because he couldn't get out of Costa Rica."

"What do you mean he couldn't get out?" Parris asked.

"He's being held hostage."

There was a chorus of gasps from Parris and M.J. Martin disclosed the telephone call David had made to Samuel with Cordero-Vega's demands. He left nothing out, deciding on complete honesty.

M.J. glanced from her husband to her son. "What are *we* going to do?"

"Joshua's leaving for Costa Rica in the morning," Samuel explained.

All gazes shifted to Vanessa. There was nothing in her expression to indicate the inner turmoil she felt when she realized her husband was going back into the shadowy world of intelligence he'd left behind four years before.

M.J. rose to her feet, throwing her husband an angry glare. "I don't care what you do, but I want my baby back."

Samuel lifted a hand. "M.J.—"

"Dammit! Don't M.J. me, Sammy," she ranted. "Get him back!" Turning on her heel, she stalked out of the library.

Samuel attempted to rise from his chair, but Martin moved quickly and pushed him down. "Let her go."

Shaking his head, Samuel slumped weakly back to the chair. It was all his fault. He was being paid back for his sins. *The sins of the father will fall on the sons.* The words attacked him until he sat sobbing uncontrollably.

Parris and Vanessa left together, leaving Martin to console his father.

Both of them were familiar with waiting—it had happened at another time in their lives, and it was to begin again.

CHAPTER 25

July 18
Puerto Limón, Costa Rica

David sat in Raul Vega's study, staring out the window. The strain of waiting had begun to fray the nerves of both men.

His call to the American embassy in San José was acknowledged, but the ambassador sent his regrets, and there was no way he could tell the ambassador that he was being held hostage with Vega listening on an extension.

Raul tapped a pencil against his forefinger, his dark gaze fixed on David Cole's cheek. His face had healed, the scar only noticeable at close range, and instead of ruining the young peacock's face the scar enhanced it. It made him look dangerously attractive.

Raul knew that the earring he wore in his left lobe was his daughter's. What he had to uncover was their relationship. Whenever he observed them together there was an obvious attraction, but it was coupled with a formality that was unnatural. They would bear watching closely.

"So, your answer is still no."

David affected an expression of indifference. "And will remain no."

"You will lose millions."

"So be it."

Raul's hand came down hard on the top of his desk. "Fool! You risk losing millions—"

"It's *my* millions," David interrupted.

Leaning back against the leather chair, Raul flashed a sinister smile. "I think I can get you to change your mind about selling the plantation."

David ran a hand through his longer wavy hair. "I doubt that."

Lacing his fingers together, the older man met David's steady gaze. "What if I shorten the time for your sentence to thirty days instead of sixty?"

He was past threats and intimidation, knowing that Vega needed him—alive. "You're a day late, because yesterday was thirty days."

"And you have only twenty-nine left before I begin taking you apart."

David stood up. "Save the threats," he sneered. Turning his back, he walked out of the room, closing the door quietly behind him.

Instead of retreating to the sanctuary of his bedroom, he decided to brave the oppressive heat. Opening the door, he stepped out into the sultry afternoon. The beauty of the land surrounding *La Montaña* was breathtaking, and he didn't think he would ever get used to the sun-drenched world where every living organism coexisted in perfect harmony.

The cloying fragrance of tropical flowers growing in wild abandon lingered in his nostrils. Putting one foot firmly in front of the other, he stared down at the flagstone path leading to the enormous greenhouse and connecting aviary. He walked past the structures toward the ocean, ignoring the heat of the sun beating down on his bare head and arms.

He had come to recognize and distinguish a macaw, quetzal, and a three-wattled bellbird after spending hundreds of hours in the aviary. A few of the birds flew over to him whenever he walked in, looking for bits of ripe fruit he usually carried with him.

Walking past an overgrowth of tangled trees, he stepped out into a clearing, stopping short when he saw a man pointing a rifle at him.

"You must not go any farther, Señor Cole."

Nodding, he turned and retraced his steps. It was the third time someone had stopped him from leaving the boundaries of Raul Vega's property. His walks had taken him east, west, and north. The only route he hadn't tried was south. That he would leave for another time.

He returned to the house at the same time Rodrigo maneuvered the Mercedes-Benz up to the garages. The driver alighted and opened the rear door to the spacious sedan. A man's foot touched the concrete, followed by the glimpse of pale, close-cut, silver hair. Then the tall, slim figure emerged. Nothing in David's expression revealed the relief washing over him. He'd come. His brother had come for him.

Joshua's pale eyes, hidden behind the lenses of his sunglasses, missed nothing. He saw David glance at him before he disappeared into the large house situated on a rise above a deep valley. There was a time in his past when David had come to take him home as he lay close to death in a tiny Mexican town. Now he had come for his brother before a madman could follow through on his promises of mutilation and death.

His sharp gaze swept around the land surrounding *La Montaña.* Its location atop the mountain made it almost impenetrable. A sardonic smile touched his mouth. *Almost, but not impossible,* he mused, following the driver's lead into the house.

David lay across his bed, eyes closed, his chest rising and falling in an even rhythm. When he first spied Joshua he thought he had imagined him. He hadn't had any contact with his family, and suspected that their political connections had not met with success; he was fully aware that his father was not above going outside the law to secure his release. And Samuel Cole had sent the best: retired U.S. Colonel Joshua Kirkland, former Associate Coordinating Chief of the Defense Intelligence Agency.

Seeing his half brother summoned a repressed distress that he hadn't wanted to acknowledge: his father's failing health, his mother's anxiety, and his brothers' and sisters' fear that they would lose a sibling. He had come to depend on Serena with a ferocious craving that threatened to break him emotionally. His emotions vacillated between rage and fear; a rage so violent that he considered murdering her father, and a fear that he would lose her—forever.

He shared her bed—every night, returning to his own bed with the rising of the morning sun. Their lovemaking was strong, passionate, and satisfying, but always leaving him wanting more.

He counted off the days, one merging into the other, while he spent the time exploring the property surrounding *La Montaña*, visiting the exotic birds in the aviary, and writing music. It was only at night that he truly came alive, when he lost himself in the scented embrace of the woman he loved more than his own life.

Opening his eyes, he stared up at the whitewashed ceiling. Joshua had come to take him home. He had to let his brother know that he would not leave Costa Rica alone. Serena would go back to Florida with him.

Serena replaced the telephone receiver on its cradle. Her mother's call had elicited an emotion of uncontrollable euphoria. Gabriel had granted his mother an audience.

Juanita laughed and cried at the same time, reporting that her son looked wonderful, he was treated well, he was extremely optimistic, and that he was segregated from the general prison population. She ended the conversation saying that she would remain in Florida until Gabriel's release.

Rushing out of her bedroom, she raced down the back staircase, taking the shorter route to her father's study. The door was ajar, and he stood in the middle of the room, arms folded over his chest. The smile softening his features was radiant. He lowered his arms, extending them, and he wasn't disappointed when she walked into his embrace.

"Oh, Poppa," Serena sighed, curving her arms around her father's waist.

Raul tightened his hold on her tiny body. The strain of side-stepping and tiptoeing around each other for the past month vanished like rain on a heated surface once the sun reemerged.

"It's all right, *Chica,*" he crooned over and over.

Gabriel is safe. Safe from himself and those who seek to take his life. Luz Maria's prediction calmed and soothed her as she stood in the protective arms of her father.

Raul Vega loved her. How could she have thought otherwise? And she loved him as much as she could've loved her biological father.

Pulling back, she smiled up at him. A flicker of amusement lit up his dark eyes when he returned her smile. "I love you, Poppa."

Cradling her face between his hands, he kissed both her cheeks. "Not as much as I love you, Daughter." One hand cupped the back of her head. "I need to ask a favor of you."

Vertical lines appeared between her eyes. "What?"

"Will you act as hostess for me tonight? An American businessman will be staying here for several days, and I'd like to offer him the hospitality we Ticos are known for."

"But—but you don't like foreign businessmen, Poppa."

"It will be different this time."

"Different, how?"

"His factory will remain in the States. We will export what he needs."

Serena nodded. She would agree to anything after the call from her mother. "Yes, Poppa. I will act as your hostess. How many are we serving?"

"There will be just the four of us tonight. And that includes David Cole."

She sighed in relief. Four was a small number compared to the twenty or more she'd seen her mother host in the past. Before she left to live in the United States she'd watched her mother smile, laugh, and chat with a living room filled with people. Juanita had a special gift that made everyone who met her like her on sight. Not only was she stunningly attractive, but she claimed a gentleness that put anyone in her presence immediately at ease.

"When will he arrive?"

"He's already here. Right now he's taking *siesta*."

"Where is he from?"

"New Mexico."

She estimated the time difference between America's southwest and Costa Rica, her mind racing quickly. "I'll tell Luz Maria that we'll eat at six instead of eight. That will allow Mr.—"

"Señor Kirkland."

"Mr. Kirkland," Serena continued smoothly, "to recover from his jet lag more quickly than if we had a late dinner."

"I'll leave everything up to you, *Chica*."

She kissed him again, then turned and walked out of his study, encountering Rodrigo. He inclined his head, then knocked on his employer's door before walking in and closing the door behind them.

David. She wanted to share her good news with him, but they had promised each other that their only direct contact would be when they shared dinner or her bed. She would have to wait for him to come to her tonight before she told him about Gabriel.

Serena checked the dining room table for the second time, making certain all of the silver was free of tarnish, and the crystal goblets free of water spots. She adjusted the table's centerpiece— a magnificent lead crystal vase filled with a profusion of orchids, ranging in colors from the deepest purple to the palest white. The snowy white tablecloth and matching napkins complemented the translucent china ringed in silver.

"The table looks beautiful, and so do you," crooned the last voice she'd heard before she fell asleep at night.

Turning, she smiled up at David. Instead of his usual slacks and shirt, he'd opted to wear an exquisitely tailored, oatmeal-beige suit, a snow white shirt, chocolate brown silk tie, and a pair of imported, brown, slip-on loafers. His graying hair had grown out where he'd brushed it off his high forehead and over his ears. But he hadn't removed the tiny, gold hoop in his left ear.

"Lose the earring," she whispered.

His obsidian gaze raced quickly over her lightly made up face. "No. It stays."

He admired her hair, which was brushed off her face and secured in an elaborate twist on the nape of her neck. A seductive, woodsy fragrance clung to her body under a sleeveless, silk dress in a vibrant orange. The simple, elegant garment cut on a bias skimmed like water over her firm breasts, flat belly, and hips. The hem ended inches about a pair of three-inch, black satin sling-back heels. A generous slit up the front of the dress allowed for a lush view of her strong, bare legs from ankle to knee. Her only jewelry was her single strand of pearls and a pair of matching stud earrings.

The image of her bare legs wrapped around his waist during their passionate bouts of lovemaking caused his stomach muscles to contract. Everything about her, from the orange color on her temptingly curved lips to the matching color on her toes, drew him into a surging vortex of desire that made him want to spend every hour of the day in her arms.

"It doesn't go with the suit."

"It still stays. Speaking of earrings, I owe you a pair."

She flashed him a saucy look. "I'm going to hold you to that."

Rodrigo walked into the dining room, breaking the sensual spell surrounding the secret lovers.

"Señor Cole, may I prepare a drink for you?"

The frown that had settled between David's eyes vanished quickly. "*Sí.* I'd like a Scotch and soda with ice." Of all of Samuel Cole's children he had been the only one who shared his father's penchant for Scotch.

Rodrigo made his way over to a bar and placed a linen napkin over the sleeve of his dark bolero jacket. "Señorita Morris. May I serve you?" he asked, filling a glass with ice from a small refrigerator concealed beneath the massive bar. Tonight his role had changed from driver to bartender.

"I'll have a glass of sherry, please."

Rodrigo quickly and expertly prepared their drinks, and as they stood sipping them Raul Vega and his houseguest walked into the dining room.

She felt a shiver of uneasiness the instant her gaze met and fused with that of the man with the silver hair and deeply tanned face. She missed the expert cut of his dark suit, pristine white shirt, navy blue tie, and black shoes as she felt his pale green, hypnotic gaze trap her within a maelstrom of fear and danger.

Unconsciously, she moved backward, bumping into David. His free hand went to the small of her back until she regained her balance.

David successfully concealed a smile. Serena's reaction to Joshua Kirkland was similar to that of most who met him for the first time. His cold eyes made people feel as if they'd glimpsed their own death. And his brother was deadly when crossed.

Raul placed a hand on Joshua's shoulder, smiling. "Señor Kirkland, I would like to introduce you to my daughter and our hostess for this evening, Señorita Serena Morris. *Chica,* Señor Joshua Kirkland."

Serena extended her right hand, forcing a smile she did not quite feel. "Señor Kirkland."

Joshua took her hand and inclined his head. "My pleasure, Señorita Morris."

An eyebrow shifted at the same time she withdrew her hand from his warm grip. His Spanish was flawless, and she knew that, like David, he'd learned the language as a child.

"You may call me Serena."

Joshua smiled, the gesture transforming his stoic expression and making him an extremely attractive man. "And you may call me Joshua," he teased.

David stepped forward and extended his right hand, preempting Raul from introducing him to Joshua. "David Cole."

Joshua took the proffered hand. "Joshua Kirkland."

His smile froze, masking a cold fury that sucked the breath from his lungs. Nothing in Joshua's expression indicated the rage he felt toward Vega when he saw the scar on his brother's cheek. He wanted to repay Vega for his brutality. He longed to mangle his host's face instead of preparing to sit at his table under the pretense that he would enjoy his food and hospitality.

Raul glanced at Rodrigo, who nodded. "Joshua, may I offer you something from the bar?"

"Scotch, straight up," he replied.

Raul glanced at the bottle of aged Scotch on the highly polished surface of the bar. It appeared that these Americans liked their Scotch. He waited until Rodrigo served Joshua his drink, then took his usual tequila and lime juice.

Raising his glass, he smiled at the others in the room. "Much success for all that we want from this life."

Everyone touched glasses, murmuring their own acknowledgement, while David's gaze never left Serena's face. Joshua watched his brother's reaction to the beautiful, tiny woman in orange silk. Aside from the scar on David's left cheek, he appeared not to have suffered too much at the hands of his captor. He suspected that Raul's daughter had made David's captivity more tolerable.

Serena waited until everyone had finished their predinner drinks, then escorted them to the table. She had instructed Rodrigo to remove a leaf from the table, reducing the seating from its customary twelve. Raul seated her at one end of the table before taking his place at the other end. Joshua and David sat opposite each other.

"Even though I make it a policy not to discuss business at my dinner table," Raul began, his gaze fixed on his daughter's face, "I will make an exception this evening. Joshua will only be with us for a few days, and it's going to take time for him to adjust to our weather and a different time zone."

Joshua smiled a cold smile. "I'm honored and flattered that

you've decided to break a tradition." What he didn't say was that he wanted to break Vega's neck.

Raul waited for Isabel to bring out the first course—a flavorful cold fish soup—then picked up his spoon. Everyone followed suit.

"I wonder if there will be time for me to take a tour of your property, Raul," Joshua stated after he'd swallowed a bite of succulent shrimp. "I didn't get to see much of its magnificence from the car coming in from the airport."

"That can be arranged." There was obvious pride in Raul's voice. "By the way, David Cole is also an American businessman."

Joshua appeared surprised by this disclosure. "How long will you be staying in Costa Rica?" he asked David.

"I can assure you that it'll be more than a few days. *Raul* and I have a few unresolved issues to work through before I go back to Florida. By the way, where are you from?"

"Santa Fe."

David flashed his dimpled smile, shaking his head. "Never been there."

"It's beautiful," Joshua confirmed.

"So is Costa Rica," Raul countered.

Joshua's left hand stilled, and the light from an overhead chandelier glinted off the gold band on his third finger. "That it is. Unpolluted air, clean water—"

"And I intend to make certain it remains that way," Raul interrupted vehemently.

"Which is why I'm here," Joshua said quietly. "As a scientist I recognize the importance of ecological balance."

Raul spooned a portion of soup into his mouth, then touched the edge of his napkin to his lips. "Tell me what you've discovered about the Anneda pine tree."

David listened, smugly amused as Joshua outlined the healing properties found in the needles and bark of the tree. It was apparent that his brother was using the cover of a botanist. The few who knew Joshua well were always astounded by his superior IQ and photographic memory.

Raul, enraptured by what Joshua was telling him, said, "You're saying that the bark and needles contain a very potent bioflavo-noid."

"Proanthocyanidin. It is stronger than any known citrus bio-flavonoid. But when I tested it I discovered that it protected and extended the properties of Vitamin C, which is usually destroyed by oxidation in the body."

"A fascinating discovery," Raul whispered.

"That it is," Joshua agreed. "It is the most fantastic antioxi-dant ever found. It's fifty times more powerful than Vitamin E and twenty times stronger than Vitamin C."

"I, too, find all of this incredible," Serena stated, joining the discussion for the first time. "I'm aware that antioxidants destroy free radicals, which attack cells and destroy many of them, even altering DNA and making it impossible for cells to reproduce themselves. You claim you can get this miraculous antioxidant from the Anneda tree. Wouldn't you endanger these valuable trees by stripping their bark and needles?"

Joshua arched a pale eyebrow, turning his attention to Serena. A background check on Raul Cordero-Vega had revealed that Serena Morris wasn't his biological daughter, but she could've been, with her line of questioning. She sounded like Vega did when he ranted that he wanted to save Costa Rica for the Ticos at any cost.

"Not necessarily," he replied in a soft, quiet tone. "My research team is currently working on a renewable plant source of this pro-anthocyanidin, so we won't endanger the supply of trees."

Raul winked at Serena. She'd voiced his very concern. He shifted his attention to Joshua. "We will talk tomorrow about your research study. Eat, drink, then rest. I'm certain you're still fatigued from your journey."

"*¡Mil gracias!*" Joshua said, offering a smile. He had given himself three days to confirm that David was still alive, survey Vega's property, then formulate a plan to get his brother out of Costa Rica.

CHAPTER 26

Serena lay in the warmth of David's embrace, savoring the unyielding strength of his hard body. "Do you think my father's softening?" Her sultry voice was a whisper in the stillness of the darkened room.

"What about?"

"Americans."

David chuckled, placing his arm over her back. "I doubt that, Darling."

"You have to admit that he was rather charming tonight."

His grip tightened on her waist, shifting her body effortlessly until she lay on his chest. "You were charming, brilliant, and very, very beautiful. I can't wait for you to host our dinner parties."

Angling for a more comfortable position, she settled her legs between his and laid her cheek against his shoulder. "Neither can I."

His left hand played in the curls she'd unpinned from the elaborate chignon just before slipping into bed. "There are so many things I can't wait for: marrying you and seeing your belly swell with our unborn children. I want our home filled with love and lots of noise. The noisier the better."

"I want to be able to go to bed with you and wake up with you by my side, David," she confessed. "I'm tired of the deception."

"It will end soon."

Nodding, she rubbed her nose against the crisp hair covering his broad chest. She prayed it would end soon, because she was unsure how long she could continue to hide her feelings for the man holding her to his heart.

Turning her head slightly, she kissed his chest, moving down his body until her hot mouth seared his flat belly and still lower. David threw a muscled arm over his head, swallowing back the groans threatening to erupt from the back of this throat.

Serena had offered her body, holding nothing back, but this time she offered more. She was selfless as she worshipped him, taking him into her mouth with a claim that made him surrender all he had, all that he was to her.

It took Herculean strength for him to sit up, reach down, and pull her up to his chest. Within the span of several seconds he reversed their positions, slipped on protection, and entered her, both of them gasping from the force of his penetration. He took her hard and fast, and when they returned from their erotic trip to heaven, both were breathing and sobbing with emotion wrung from their souls.

"This can't continue," David rasped, pulling her closer to his damp body. "Not like this."

"I know," she confirmed, willing the tears staining her cheeks to stop. But they continued until she cried herself to sleep. She never knew when David left her bed six hours before sunrise.

Opening the French doors to her bedroom, he stepped out into the heavy tropical heat, then closed the doors behind him. He stood on the veranda, staring out into pitch blackness, swearing silently that he would not sleep with her again until they were back on American soil. Their desperate game of deception had changed him, and instead of feeling joy after making love he felt guilty, guilty for sneaking into her bedroom each night, and guilty for pretending he felt nothing for her in the presence of others when all he wanted was to hold her and kiss her until she was breathless.

He walked the short distance to his own bedroom, slipped in through the partially open French doors. He hadn't taken more than two steps when light flooded the room and Raul rose from the chair where he'd sat waiting for him.

There was no mistaking his rage as a cold, loathing smile twisted his lips. "I bring you into my home and you disgrace me by using my daughter."

David's temper rose quickly, matching Vega's. "I haven't used her."

"What do you call it? You treat her like a *puta*. You have your way with her, then you leave her after you've spilled your lust. You've made her your whore!" he shouted in English.

David lunged at him at the same time Raul brought up his right hand, striking him across the left cheek with a riding crop. The blinding pain caused him to stumble backward, but he righted himself and lunged at Vega again.

This time he found his target. His long fingers curved around his nemesis's neck, tightening and cutting off precious air to his lungs and brain. "I love her!" he shouted, punctuating each word as he shook Vega, his head rolling around on his shoulders as if he were a rag doll.

Through the red haze of rage, he heard a solid click, then a familiar voice saying, "Let him go, Señor Cole."

David looked up into the large, round bores of a double-barreled shotgun. A deranged smile curled Rodrigo's lips as he wiggled his eyebrows in an unconscious agitated gesture. Rodrigo might have just pleaded for him to release his boss, but something in the emaciated man's eyes said *don't.*

Closing his eyes briefly, David felt his anger ebbing. For a moment he'd been ready to take a life and give up his own at the same time. His hands fell away and Vega slumped to the floor, gasping and wheezing.

Rodrigo lowered his weapon. He stared down at his employer, uncertain whether Señor Vega would want him to help him. He decided against it as Raul rose to his feet on wobbly knees.

"You're a dead man, David Cole," he whispered, holding a hand to his injured throat.

"So are you," David countered. He bent over and picked up the riding crop. What he wanted to do was flail the skin off the older man, but threw it at him instead. "The next time you take a whip to me, be prepared to kill me, *Señor Vega.*"

He watched the two men leave his bedroom, then collapsed across the bed. Fire radiated along the left side of his face when he pressed the rapidly swelling flesh with his fingertips. They came away with only a trace of blood, but he knew without looking in a mirror that Vega had reinjured his cheek.

Serena slept late the following morning, and it wasn't until she heard a knock on her door that she woke up. Pulling the sheet up over her naked breasts, she pushed an abundance of unruly curls up off her forehead.

"Come in." The door opened and her father stalked in, his mouth set in a hard, tight line. She smiled at him. "Good morning, Poppa."

He did not respond as he sat on a chair in her sitting room. The silence was deafening. She stared at him while he looked out the French doors.

"You've disgraced this house," he whispered, breaking the silence.

Her eyes widened. "What are you talking about?"

"I bring *him* into my house and he takes you like a *puta* under my very roof."

Serena scrambled from the bed, tucking the sheet around her body. "How *dare* you call me a whore!"

Raul sprang to his feet. "What else are you?" He wanted to scream at her, but his injured vocal cords throbbed painfully. "How could you let him use you in such a manner?"

"He didn't use me. I love him, Poppa. And when I return to the United States I'm going to marry him."

"No, *Chica,*" he said, shaking his head. "That cannot happen, because in less than a month he will be dead. Your lover has a death sentence hanging over his head." He gave her an evil smile when her eyes filled with tears. "Did you think he was waiting for you, so the two of you could leave *La Montaña* together?"

Watching the play of emotions cross her face, he knew that was what she'd thought. "I'm sorry to disappoint you, but the truth is he hasn't left *La Montaña* because he *can't*. And if he tries to escape I'll have him shot on sight."

He took a half-dozen steps, bringing them face-to-face. "Don't try to leave, *Chica,* because you'll never make it through customs. I've taken the liberty of holding on to your passport for safekeeping."

Serena clapped her free hand over her mouth to keep from slapping her stepfather's face. She turned her back instead, and waited for him to leave her bedroom. As soon as the door closed, she walked over and locked it.

What happened next was a blur, because she didn't remember taking a shower or dressing. What she did remember was flinging open her door and pounding on David's, screaming his name at the top of her lungs.

When he finally did unlock the door, she took one look at his face and crumbled to the floor in a dead faint.

David scooped her limp body up in his arms and carried her down the rear staircase to the kitchen. Her head hung loosely over his arm, eliciting a rush of fear when he could not detect her breathing.

Luz Maria rushed toward him. "Put her on the table," she ordered. He stood helplessly by, watching the cook as she placed a cool cloth on Serena's forehead. She stirred and let out an audible sigh.

Blinking furiously, she stared up at the ceiling. "What happened?"

"You fainted."

She turned her head to the right, her round eyes widening and filling with fear when she saw the angry welt running across David's left cheekbone. "David." His name came out in a weak mewling.

"I'm all right, *mi amor.*"

Reaching out, she caught his wrist. "Did he do that to you?"

"It was an accident," he lied smoothly. Curving an arm around her waist, he helped her to sit up.

"Drink this," Luz Maria suggested, handing her a cup of tea. "It should help settle your stomach."

Serena's hands shook slightly as she grasped the cup. She took several swallows, then handed the cup back to Luz Maria. "I've had enough."

Luz Maria shook her head. "You need it, and so will the baby."

"What baby?" Serena and David asked in unison.

Luz Maria stared at David, then Serena. "Why do you think you fainted?"

It was Serena's turn to stare at David as she mentally calculated when she'd last had her period. "Oh, no," she whispered with the realization that she hadn't had a menstrual flow since she left the States. It had been the last week in May, and it was now the middle of July.

Her gaze was frantic. When had it happened? After the first time she and David had been very careful... The first time! The first time they slept together he'd gotten her pregnant.

"David..."

"It's okay, Darling," he crooned, rubbing her back in a comforting gesture.

She pressed her face against his arm, shaking her head. "He told me everything. He said you're a prisoner, and that he's going to kill you."

David's hand halted. "When?"

"He came to my room this morning. He—"

"Don't," he said, cutting her off. "We're going to make it through this."

"How can you say that?" She replayed Raul's threats, the fearful image of David lying shot flooding her mind.

Cradling her face in his hands, David flashed his dimpled smile. "Do you trust me, Darling?" She nodded. "Then let me handle everything."

What he had to do was find Joshua. Whatever his brother planned to do, he had to do it quickly.

Things had changed: Vega was aware that they'd been sleeping together. There was the possibility that Serena was carrying his child. And there was no doubt that the stress of not getting his son back had forced Vega to panic.

David left Serena with Luz Maria as he returned to the main part of the house, hoping he would meet up with Joshua. He had to find a way to communicate the sudden change in his hostage situation.

He found Joshua and Vega in the greenhouse. They were examining the pine needles of a tree when he approached them. Joshua noticed him before Vega did. He went completely still, his eyes turning pale until they appeared virtually transparent. David shook his head, the motion barely noticeable. He folded his hands together, then opened them like a book. Just before Vega turned he put up two fingers.

"What do you want?" Vega snapped before he could catch himself. He didn't want Joshua Kirkland to suspect that things were not well between him and his fellow American.

"I'm sorry to interrupt you—"

"But you are interrupting me, Señor Cole," he said facetiously.

Joshua held up his left hand. "Raul, you and I have time. Take care of whatever you need to do with David. I'm going to take that walk I've been promising myself before it gets too hot." He gave Vega a feigned smile. "I'm overwhelmed with the magnificence of everything I've seen thus far."

David offered Joshua his right hand. "If I don't get to see you before you leave, have a safe trip back home."

Nodding, Joshua took the proffered hand. "Same with you. If you get the opportunity to come to the southwest I'd like for us to get together. I have a close friend who lives in Las Cruces. He's south of where I live, but we get together every once in a while and go hunting."

"What does he do?" David questioned, stalling for time.

"He breeds horses. The name is Sterling. He's easy to find. Ask anyone in Las Cruces where his ranch is, and they'll give you directions."

"I'll keep that in mind if I'm in the neighborhood."

"In fact, I'm supposed to meet with him next week. If you're back by that time and have nothing on your calendar, drop by."

David nodded. Joshua had given him what he needed to know. He would return to Costa Rica in a week, and he wouldn't come alone.

Raul waited impatiently while the two Americans concluded their inane conversation. He walked back to the house, David following. He didn't know why, but he felt a shiver of icy fear snake up his spine. He'd turned his back on David Cole, and only hours ago the man had his hands around his neck. If Rodrigo hadn't been there he was certain David would've strangled him. *No,* he thought. It would be the last time he would ever show David his back.

The two men walked into the study, Raul closing the door. He rounded on David. "What was so important that you had to interrupt me?"

"I'm willing to negotiate the sale of the plantation."

Raul stared, complete surprise on his face. But the surprise was momentary. "Why now?"

"Why not? I want to get my affairs in order before I die."

"You won't die if my son is released on or before the designated date."

David crossed his arms over his chest in a gesture of defiance. "I'm not willing to wait that long."

"It is not possible. I have business to conclude with Mr. Kirkland."

"What you have to discuss with Mr. Kirkland is conjecture. Maybe you'll let him have your trees, or maybe you won't. The banana plantation is a reality—several million realities."

Raul's mind began working overtime. He could get two for the price of one. He would secure the plantation outright, without the government having to wait to nationalize it, and he could keep David Cole as a hostage beyond the sixty-day limit if necessary.

If he wanted to he could keep David in Puerto Limón for an eternity. David couldn't walk off the property because of the armed guards watching the perimeter, and he couldn't make any outside telephone calls without his being aware of it.

He had come to accept the younger man's quick temper and arrogance, but David had compounded it by sleeping with his daughter. That he could not and would not ever accept.

"We'll talk."

David hid a smile. "When?"

"After the *siesta*. But first I must offer my regrets to Mr. Kirkland. He and I will have to reschedule our very interesting deliberations." He massaged his tender throat. "Perhaps he will want to remain at *La Montaña* until you and I conclude our business."

I doubt that. David mused. Offering a slight bow, he turned and walked out of the room. He had redirected Raul's focus to ColeDiz. It would give Joshua the time he needed to return to the States to plan his return trip *and* rescue mission.

CHAPTER 27

July 21
Las Cruces, New Mexico

Joshua sat in the pickup truck beside Matthew Sterling as Matt drove out of the parking area at the Las Cruces airport.

"When was the last time you got any sleep?" Matt asked, the slow drawl of east Texas evident in his speech.

"I don't remember," Joshua admitted. "And I don't think I'm going to get any until this madness is over."

Matt's gold-green gaze was fixed on the road ahead of him. Joshua had called him, saying that he needed his *assistance*. And he knew exactly what he meant. However, it had been four years since they both retired from the shadowy, gray world of undercover intelligence. He had been an independent operative, while Joshua was a key player in U.S. military intelligence.

"Are you going back in?"

"No, Matt. This is personal."

Pushing back the front of his wide-brimmed straw hat with his thumb, Matt threw Joshua a quick look. "Who?"

"My brother David."

Shifting into a higher gear, Matt increased his speed, the pickup eating up the dusty road. "Tell me about it."

Joshua did, leaving nothing out. He related the details of the telephone call, his trip to Costa Rica, and evidence of David's injuries.

"I'm going to take perverse pleasure in gutting Vega," he stated quietly.

"Forget about gutting him. Leave the knives to me. Guns are more your specialty."

Joshua wanted to smile, but couldn't. He hadn't slept in nearly seventy-two hours. He'd left Costa Rica after a day and a half, enraged. He'd left his younger brother with a madman whose intent was to destroy David's face before he executed him.

"Why don't you catch a few winks? Whatever we need to plan can't be done with you falling on your face."

Closing his eyes, Joshua mumbled a low thanks, and willed his mind blank. He slept, but violent dreams disturbed him as he stirred restlessly. He saw Vega's face with a gaping mouth but no words came from it. Then he heard a baby crying, but couldn't see the baby. The nightmares continued in vivid color before they finally faded, leaving him in peace.

Matt curved an arm around his wife's waist. He saw the terror in her eyes. "It's all right, *Preciosa*."

Eve Sterling shook her head. Her dark eyes filled up with unshed tears and she bit down hard on her lower lip to keep it from trembling. "It's not all right, Mateo. I could lose you."

He knew she was frightened. Eve only called him Mateo when she was frightened or angry. He still found it hard to believe that his marriage of convenience had become a marriage for life. He'd married Eve Blackwell under the guise that he would look for her abducted son in Mexico, but during the charade he'd fallen madly in love with her. They had gotten her son back, and given three-year-old Christopher Delgado a sister a year later.

"I'll be back, Eve. I'm too ornery for anything to happen to me."

"If you're coming back, then why are you sending me and the children to Florida?"

"Joshua and I have made arrangements to fly into Florida. We'll spend a few days there before we come back. It will give you and Vanessa a chance to see each other."

"Don't try to placate me, Matthew Sterling. Vanessa and I got together last—"

Her words were cut off when he covered her mouth with his, robbing her of her breath. "They're announcing your flight. Come, I'll see you to the gate."

Matt leaned down and swung his three-year-old daughter up in his arms. Her hazel eyes were a stunning contrast in her gold-brown face framed by fat, black curls that bounced over her forehead.

"How big is Daddy's big girl?"

Sara Sterling raised her chubby arms upward. "This big, Daddy."

He waited until they reached the gate, then handed his daughter to her mother. Turning, he held out a callused hand to his stepson. "Shake or a hug?" he asked Christopher Delgado.

Christopher shrugged his narrow shoulders. "Anything."

Matt solved his indecision when he swung the seven-year-old up in his strong arms. "Let's do the guy hug."

Chris pounded his broad back, while Matt's large hand thumped his son's lightly. "Take care of your mother and sister for me."

"Sure thing, Daddy." Chris had started out calling Matt Papa, but changed quickly once his sister started calling him Daddy.

He lowered the boy to the floor. He gave his family a final, lingering look before turning to walk out of the terminal to the parking lot. Slipping into the rental car beside Joshua, he met the pale gaze of the man sitting behind the wheel.

Letting out his breath slowly, he said softly, "Let's rock and roll."

CHAPTER 28

July 28
Puerto Limón, Costa Rica

Luz Maria's prediction that Serena would bear David Cole's child was confirmed.

Dr. Leandro Rivera displayed a tender smile. "Congratulations. You're at least six weeks along," he said, stripping off his latex gloves. "How have you been feeling?"

"Tired."

"That's natural. I'll let you get dressed, then we'll talk."

She waited for Leandro to leave before she attempted to sit up. What was there to talk about? She was pregnant and David Cole was the father of the tiny life growing in her womb.

Meanwhile her stepfather had retreated into a state of madness. She did not know who he was anymore. He locked himself in his study, refusing to come out, except to eat. He threatened to kill David immediately if she mentioned anything to her mother when she called. Serena discovered that he taped every call—incoming and outgoing—so she couldn't lie and say she hadn't said anything to Juanita even if she wanted to.

David continued to come to her room, but not to sleep. They lay together, talking about everything except the madness tearing their world apart until she fell asleep. He left then, using the door instead of the veranda. Their love and what they'd shared was no longer a secret.

She buttoned her blouse and tucked it in the waistband of her slacks before pushing her feet into a pair of sandals. Her limbs felt leaden as she made her way slowly out of the examining room to Leandro's office.

He rose to his feet when she walked in. Taking her elbow, he escorted her to a large, comfortable chair. "Did you drive here alone?"

"No. Rodrigo brought me." Even though Raul had taken her passport, he still did not trust her to go out alone.

"Lucky for you."

She yawned, covering her mouth with her hand. "I can't keep my eyes open."

Leandro sat down behind his desk. "I suggest that you take a lot of little *siestas.*"

She yawned again. "I'll try."

"Don't try, Serena. Do it. That's an order."

Staring at the young doctor, she gave him a tired smile. "Yes, Doctor."

He was Dr. Rivera when he lectured her sternly about what she could do and not do. Then he became her friend Leandro when he said that if she needed his help—for any reason—she could call on him.

She left his office with samples of vitamin supplements, and prescriptions for more. She waited in the car while Rodrigo filled the prescriptions. The wait afforded her the opportunity to sleep, and when the Mercedes sedan stopped at *La Montaña* she arrived refreshed.

David was waiting in the living room when she walked in. She saw the tension ringing his generous mouth and detected a throbbing muscle in his lean jaw. The angry welt over his cheekbone had taken a week to fade without leaving further permanent scarring to the area.

He stood up and crossed the room to meet her. "How are you?"

"Very pregnant."

Closing his eyes, he let out his breath in a slow, audible sigh. Nodding, he opened his eyes and smiled down at her. "Congratulations."

Serena placed her hand over his heart. The heat from his body was stifling. "Congratulations to you, too."

He covered her hand with his, smiling the smile she'd come to love. "Come upstairs with me. I have something to show you."

Hand in hand they climbed the staircase to the upper level. Their footsteps were muffled in the runner along the hallway. It seemed like years rather than weeks when they had walked the hallway for the first time. It was a time when David promised Serena that he would solicit his father's help for her brother's release. It was also the first day that she'd kissed him—really kissed him.

It was also the first time later that afternoon that they lay together and shared a love that had deepened despite the betrayal and deadly revenge that threatened their lives and, now, that of their unborn child.

David pulled Serena into his bedroom and closed the door. Leading her to the armchair where he'd sat waiting for his face and foot to heal, writing pages of music, and watching and waiting for the sun to rise, he eased her down to the plump cushion. Sitting down on the footstool, he pointed to an envelope on the nearby table.

"Pick it up, Darling."

Serena felt the heat of David's gaze on her face when she picked up the white, business-size envelope. Sliding her finger under the flap, she opened it and withdrew a single sheet of paper. Her head came up slowly and she stared numbly at the man sitting at her feet.

"What does this mean?"

"It means that I've sold the plantation and the proceeds will be deposited in a bank in Florida in your name."

Clamping a hand over her mouth, Serena shook her head. "No," she mumbled through her fingers.

David grasped her shoulders, holding her captive. "Yes. I have to take care of you and the baby."

"And what about you? Do you think I want to have this baby by myself?"

"If something should happen to me you'll—"

"I'll what, David!" she screamed at him. "I'll go on living and pretending that you never existed? That having more money than I could hope to spend will take the place of having a father for my child?"

"Serena," he crooned softly, hoping to calm her.

"Don't Serena me, David Cole!" She crumbled the paper and threw it at him. It hit his shoulder and fell to the floor. "How can you give up like that?"

"I'm not giving up. What I'm doing is securing your future."

"Without you, I have no future." Closing her eyes, she squeezed back angry tears.

Pulling her from the chair, David settled her over his lap. He buried his face between her neck and shoulder, inhaling her scented flesh. "And without you I'm nothing."

"We have to get away. We have to escape from this hell."

Cradling a hand under her chin, he raised her face to his. "We will, *mi amor.* Have patience."

"I'm sorry. I don't have your patience."

His mouth brushed over hers. "Yes, you do."

Serena reveled in the feel of his moist lips, caressing and healing. She opened her mouth, allowing him free rein as he kissed her with a passion she'd almost forgotten.

His kiss deepened until she found herself writhing with a heated desire that matched the drums pounding out the sensual rhythms of ancient Africa.

David carried her to the bed, leaving her to lock the door, the French doors, and draw the drapes. Then he returned to the bed. He undressed her, then himself. His midnight gaze swept leisurely over the tiny, compact body that carried the fruit of their love before he came into her outstretched arms.

Parting her thighs with his knee, he pushed into her hot, moist, throbbing flesh, sighing as she closed around his swollen flesh, welcoming him home.

Their lovemaking was slow, gentle, and healing. It was only when he touched heaven and floated back to earth that David realized that he hadn't kept his secret promise not to make love to her again until they were on American soil.

A part of him wanted to believe he was going home, and a part said that he'd never go home. Joshua left Costa Rica a week ago, and hadn't returned. It was now the eighth day, and he did not want to believe that he had abandoned him.

Joshua thanked Rodrigo when he opened the door of the spacious sedan. He glanced up at the lines of the beautifully designed house Raul Vega called *La Montaña,* frowning. Behind its magnificent facade was a man who had lost touch with reality. A man who'd used his political office as a ploy to abuse and control. A man who was ruthless and cavalier in his disregard for other human beings. Shifting a pale eyebrow, Joshua followed the driver into the coolness of the house. The abuse and power would end in another twelve hours.

Joshua was shown to the spacious room he'd occupied during his first trip to *La Montaña.* It was on the first level at the rear of the house.

"Tell Señor Vega that I would like to take my *siesta* early. I will meet with him for the evening meal."

Rodrigo inclined his head. "*Sí,* Señor Kirkland. I'll let him know your wishes."

Joshua swung his single piece of luggage to the bench at the foot of the massive four-poster bed. He had traveled light because he did not intend to spend the night.

He took off his clothes, placed them neatly on the bench, then lay on the bed and slept.

CHAPTER 29

Raul's mood was ebullient when he emerged from his study to share dinner with the returning Joshua Kirkland. Things had gone quite well during the week Joshua had returned to the States. David Cole had sold his banana plantation, and now he was ready to negotiate with Markham Pharmaceutical for his prized Anneda pine trees.

He walked into the dining room, his smile widening when he spied his daughter talking to Joshua. It was the first glimpse of animation she'd exhibited in more than a week. It was unfortunate that Joshua Kirkland was a married man, because he appeared better suited to Serena than David Cole. Shaking his head, he dismissed David from his mind.

"Joshua," he exclaimed, offering his hand in greeting. "Welcome back to *La Montaña*."

"*¡Mil gracias!* Raul," Joshua returned, giving the man a warm smile. His penetrating gaze searched for his brother. He'd thought he would be joining them for dinner.

"Something to drink?"

"I'll wait for dinner."

Raul dropped an arm over his shoulder. "How was your flight?"

"Excellent."

"I hope you'll be able to spend more time with us this trip."

Joshua stared at Raul, chilling him with his icy gaze. "I left my ticket open. I'll stay as long as it'll take me to conclude my business. Providing my visa doesn't expire."

He removed his arm. "Don't worry about your visa. I'll have someone take care of that."

"Gracias," Joshua said softly. He waited until Serena took her place at one end of the table, then sat down on the chair he'd occupied during his last visit.

Raul signaled to Isabel, and she rolled the cart in bearing the evening's first course.

Joshua stared at the empty chair opposite him. He hadn't realized how hard and fast his heart was pounding until he clenched his hands under the table. Where was his brother?

"Has David Cole returned home?"

Raul stared at Serena instead of Joshua. "Yes, he has. He left Costa Rica three days ago.

Joshua stared at his place setting rather than look at Raul Vega. *Stinking, filthy liar,* he ranted inwardly. Within seconds he'd composed himself. "I'd hoped to see him again."

"Perhaps you will if he comes to visit New Mexico."

"Yes, perhaps."

The dinner continued with little or no conversation. Serena ate as if she were in a trance, not tasting any of what she'd swallowed. It was only when Rodrigo entered the room to whisper to Raul that he had an important telephone call and he left the room did she speak.

"He's lying. David's still here," she whispered.

"Where is he?"

"Upstairs."

Raul came back into the room, a deep frown settled into his forehead. "I'm sorry, Joshua. I must offer my apologies again. I just received a call from my president. I must return to San José immediately."

Pushing back his chair, Joshua stood up. "No need to apologize."

"I'm not certain how long I'll be away. But it shouldn't be long because the government is on holiday during July and August."

Joshua stood up. "I'll wait, Raul. Remember, I need your approval for the exportation of this drug."

"*¡Mil gracias!*" He stared at Serena, then turned on his heel and rushed out of the room.

She watched Joshua staring at her stepfather's departing figure. "Sit down, Mr. Kirkland, and finish your dinner. Luz Maria has outdone herself tonight."

Joshua took his seat, his jaw tightening. He'd wanted Raul in attendance when he rescued David, but Matt disagreed, saying they were going to Costa Rica to bring his brother home, not torture his captor.

The two people ate in silence, neither wishing to intrude on the other's thoughts. Joshua finished first, refusing dessert.

"I'm going for a walk before I retire for the night," he informed Serena.

She gave him a polite smile. "Good night."

"Good night," he returned softly.

She sat at the table, watching Isabel clear the table. Then she made her way to the kitchen. She found Luz Maria sitting at the table writing furiously and pushing sheets of paper into an envelope.

"What are you writing?" she asked, sitting down beside her.

"The recipes of my teas. You will need them."

Placing an arm around the older woman's back, she laid her head on her shoulder. "It's late, Doña Maria. You've prepared a wonderful dinner, and it's time you went to bed."

"I will go to bed when I finish this last one."

"Why the rush?"

"You will need it tonight."

"Why tonight?"

Luz Maria stopped writing, her eyes filling with tears. "I will not see you after tonight. Not for a long while."

"Stop that." Serena's voice broke with emotion. "I'm going to be here for a while."

"No, *Chica*. You will leave here. You must." She scribbled another two lines, then pushed the sheet of paper into the envelope with a stack of others. "Here. I have written down everything."

Serena stared at the envelope as if it were a snake. David had given her an envelope the day before. Its contents had changed her life, and she knew the contents of Luz Maria's would also change her life.

She took it, blinking back tears. "Thank you."

Luz Maria smiled a sad smile. "Thank you for being the daughter I never had."

Serena stood up and fled the kitchen as fat, hot tears rolled down her face. She hated herself for crying, but somehow crying came so easily now that she was pregnant.

She made it to the sanctuary of her room, closed the door, and fell across the bed—fully clothed.

A large, dark shape moved silently along the veranda. The man found the room he sought, then forced the lock to the French doors. They opened easily, quietly. He spotted his target. David Cole lay on the bed, asleep. He smiled. At least he didn't have to wait for him to get dressed.

Clapping a hand over his mouth, he pulled him up as if he weighed two pounds instead of two hundred. "Don't move, David. It's me, Matt. I'm going to take my hand away slowly. What I want you to do is take only what you need and what you can carry with you. Don't bother with a passport. I have one for you. I'll give you a minute. *Comprende,* Friend?"

David nodded, trying to slow down his runaway heart. How did Matt Sterling get into the room without making a sound? Moving quickly, he headed for the door.

"Where are you going?"

Matt's voice stopped him. "I have to bring Serena."

"Serena?"

The door opened and Joshua stepped into the room. There was enough light from a half moon to make out his dark clothing. "What the hell is going on here? We have to leave—now!"

"Who is Serena?" Matt whispered.

"The girl." Joshua groaned.

"We can't take her. We don't have enough room in the chopper," Matt argued softly.

"You can't leave her." There was no mistaking the panic in David's voice. "She's pregnant." There was a stunned silence. "She's carrying my baby."

Joshua whispered a vulgar curse about what David had found time to do while in captivity.

"We've got less than fifteen minutes," Matt warned, glancing at the glowing numbers on his watch.

"Take the girl," Joshua ordered. "I'll come later."

"No!" David's voice echoed loudly in the dark.

"Get him the hell out of here," Joshua ordered Matt. He turned and disappeared, silent as a whisper lingering on a breath of wind.

Matt grabbed David and pulled him to the veranda. He showed him a cord attached to a grappling hook. "Lower yourself to the ground and wait for me."

David obeyed, sliding down the nylon cable until his feet touched solid ground. He refused to think of how Matt Sterling had made it past the armed men guarding the property. Glancing up, he waited for Serena. His heart raced wildly when he saw Matt lead her to the area of the veranda where he'd climbed down. She couldn't climb down by herself. What if she fell?

His fears were allayed when he saw her clinging to Matt's back as he made his way down the rope with the agility of a mountain goat.

Serena clutched Luz Maria's recipes to her chest, her eyes wide with fright. She wasn't given much time to react when Matt swung her over his shoulder in a fireman's carry and raced across the lawn. David followed, listening for footsteps that would signal that one of the guards had spotted them.

Matt led them to an area that had been cleared for the planting of trees, where a helicopter sat, its blades whirring in preparation for a liftoff.

Serena was settled on one of the rear seats. Matt motioned for

David to sit beside her. Then he hopped in beside the pilot moments before it rose horizontally above the ground.

David cradled Serena at his side, trying to calm her quaking. "It's okay," he crooned over and over until she stopped shaking long enough to realize what had just happened.

"David." She sighed.

"I'll explain everything later."

Serena lost track of time once they transferred from the helicopter to the sleek confines of a private jet. She slept, clutching her chest, as David held her gently.

It was over. He was free. She was free. Both were free to live and share a love that promised forever.

The ColeDiz jet touched down at a private airfield in West Palm Beach. The three passengers deplaned, and an hour later found themselves speeding away from the airport in a car that was parked in a lot awaiting their arrival.

David and Serena dozed while Matt sat watching the attractive couple. He nodded his approval. They would make beautiful babies.

The driver maneuvered into the curving driveway leading to a mansion overlooking a lake. A small crowd had gathered in the bright early morning sun. Matt stepped out first, a grin creasing his sun-browned face.

Eve rushed into his arms, holding tightly to his neck. "Welcome home, my love."

"Glad to be back, *Preciosa.*"

Martin walked slowly toward the car, the tiny lines at the corners of his eyes fanning out when he saw his brother. David had changed. There was a lot more gray in his longer hair. The sun glinted off the gold earring in his left ear. And in that instant he knew David the businessman was gone forever, replaced by David the musician.

Holding out his arms, he embraced his youngest brother roughly, kissing both cheeks. Pulling back, he surveyed his face, examining the scar.

"You were always a little too pretty for your own good."

David laughed, patting his older brother's back. "Jealous, brother?"

"I don't think so, brother." His obsidian gaze noted the tiny woman standing behind David. "Who have you brought home?"

David reached out and pulled Serena in front of him. "Serena Morris, my future wife and the mother of my children."

Leaning down, Martin kissed her cheek. "Welcome to the family."

She lost track of names and faces as she was kissed and hugged by people who fussed over her as if she were an ancient relic.

She noticed one woman standing off by herself, staring out at the car that had backed out of the driveway.

"Where's Joshua?" Vanessa Kirkland questioned.

David walked over to his sister-in-law and folded her to his chest. "We left him behind, Vanessa."

"No!" she screamed hysterically, pulling away from him. She continued to scream as everyone stared at her, shocked.

Three-year-old Emily Kirkland's chin quivered when she heard her mother screaming. "Mommie. I want my Mommie."

Matt Sterling swept Vanessa up in his arms before she collapsed to the ground and carried her into the house.

Martin turned to his wife. "Call a doctor. She has to be sedated before she upsets all of the children."

Serena pressed closer to David, her questioning gaze meeting his. "Who is Joshua to you?"

"He's my brother." Her round eyes widened until he could see into their clear-gold depths. "He'll be back. And when he does, then we can plan our wedding."

Everyone turned to walk into the house, their joy temporarily dampened by the knowledge that Joshua hadn't returned with the others.

David kissed Serena, then went upstairs to see his mother and father. He would reunite with them before introducing Samuel and M.J. to their latest daughter-in-law. He would wait until later to tell everyone that he was to become a father.

EPILOGUE

Serena stared at her reflection in the mirror. She could not believe the vision that stared back at her.

Turning, she smiled at her mother. "I think this is the happiest day of my life."

Juanita returned her smile. "Wait until you give birth. That will be the happiest day."

Cradling her slightly rounded belly, Serena closed her eyes. She was beginning the third month of her first trimester, and it was only the second day that she hadn't experienced a bout of nausea. It was as if the baby decided to cooperate for her mother's wedding.

Joshua returned from Costa Rica two days after she, David, and Matt returned. Vanessa Kirkland had alternated between fits of tears and rage when she told him that if he ever left for another mission she would divorce him.

She'd met her future mother- and father-in-law as well as her brothers- and sisters-in-law. She lost track of all of the names of their children and grandchildren, deciding it would be years before she would call them by their correct names.

Gabriel was released from prison in a special plea bargain. Guillermo Barranda's father offered to turn himself over to the American authorities in exchange for his son and his son's friend.

It was only after Gabriel was safely back in Costa Rica that he told his mother that the U.S. Government had approached him to help them force the elder Barranda from his Colombian sanctuary. The drugs were smuggled onto the boat without Guillermo's knowledge, and the death of the DEA agent was also staged. Juanita got her son back, the U.S. imprisoned the Western Hemisphere's most powerful drug lord, and Raul Vega was asked by his government to resign his position as Interior Minister.

Raul had become a recluse. He sent his love and his regrets, refusing to attend her wedding. Serena was relieved, because she knew it would take a long time, perhaps even a lifetime, for her to forgive him for the pain he'd caused her and David.

Sara Sterling and Emily Kirkland skipped into the room, giggling excitedly. Both girls were dressed in pale pink with garlands of tiny pink rosebuds entwined in their dark, curling hair.

"My princesses are here." Serena smiled at the grinning little girls.

"Are you ready to get married now?" asked Emily.

Serena noted the child's exquisite, delicate beauty. She was her mother's child, with the exception of her eyes. They were green—a darker green than her father's—but they had the same penetrating stare, and that sometimes seemed too wise for a child.

Parris rushed into the room, stopping short when she saw the bride. "You look beautiful, Serena." She wore a simple, pale pink, silk gown with long sleeves and a rounded neckline. She had opted for a garland of flowers in lieu of a veil.

"David says it's bad luck to see the bride before the ceremony, so he gave me these to give to you."

Serena took the small box and opened it. A pair of brilliant diamond studs lay on a bed of white velvet.

Parris peered at David's gift, wincing. She estimated each stone was at least two carats. "They're breathtaking."

"Help me put them in, Parris."

Juanita glanced at her watch. They were late. "It's not good to keep the groom waiting."

"He'll wait, Mother. He's confessed to being a patient man."

"I know you're not talking about David Claridge Cole," Parris sputtered. "He's the most impatient man I've ever met."

Serena shrugged. "Well, that's what he told me."

"Cole men will tell you anything until they hook you."

"But is it worth it, Girlfriend?"

"Hell, yeah."

"Oo-oo," Emily said, putting a hand over her tiny mouth. "You said a bad word, Auntie Parris."

"Let's go, ladies," Parris said, shooing the little girls from the room. "Take your places. We have a wedding to go to."

Juanita stood up and extended her hand to her daughter. "I've been waiting a long time to give you away to a man who will love you forever."

"I've been waiting, too, Mother."

Serena stood beside David in the coolness of the loggia at the West Palm Beach house where he'd grown up, exchanging vows. He'd elected not to cut his hair, replaced her gold hoop with a small diamond stud, and transferred his shares in ColeDiz International Ltd. to Joshua. He was in the preliminary stages of starting up his own recording company—Serenity Records—but most of all he looked forward to beginning his life anew with a woman who was sent from heaven to show him how to love.

They exchanged rings and kisses, then turned to receive the good wishes of everyone who'd come to celebrate another generation of Coles who dared to risk everything for love.

"Uncle David!"

He glanced up to find his niece rushing into the loggia. He'd sent Regina Cole an invitation, but she'd called to say that she hadn't completed her latest film, and that she would not be able to attend his wedding.

She had blossomed into an incredible woman, her beauty eliciting gasps when her image filled the screen. Her first role at seventeen had garnered her an Academy Award nomination, and now at nineteen she was one of the most sought after actresses in the film industry.

Holding out his arms, he folded her against his body. "I'm glad you could make it."

"You know I wouldn't have missed this for all of the money in Tinseltown. I still can't believe you married. Not Mr. Player, Player."

"Shh-hhh," he whispered, placing a finger over his mouth. The bright Florida sunlight glinted off a band of diamonds on her left hand. "What's this?" he questioned, raising her hand.

"A wedding band," she replied, flashing her trademark dimpled smile.

"I can see that. But who did you marry?"

Regina turned and pointed to an elderly man standing a few feet away. "Him."

"What!" The word exploded from David's mouth before he had a chance to censor himself. He recognized the man immediately. He was the award-winning director Oscar Spencer. He was well-known, and he was fifty years older than David's nineteen-year-old niece.

Martin Cole turned slowly, unable to believe his ears. His oldest daughter married—and to a man older than he was. "The S.O.B. is old enough to be her grandfather."

"Careful, Buddy," Joshua said, his eyes narrowing. "Let me handle this."

"No, let me," Matt Sterling interrupted. "I'm not her father or her uncle. I'll cut him up in so many little pieces that they'll have to blot him up to find his DNA."

Parris clutched her chest, hoping to slow down her heart. Quickly regaining her composure, she extended her arms to her daughter. "Darling. Why didn't you tell us you were getting married?"

"I wanted to surprise everyone. You are surprised, aren't you, Mommy?"

"Yes, I am," she replied slowly. "Very surprised." She waved to her husband. "Martin, come meet your daughter's husband."

"Careful, brother," David whispered as Martin stalked past him.

Everyone held their breath as Martin Cole extended his hand to his daughter's husband. He slapped the older man on the back, knocking the breath out of him.

"Welcome to the family."

Oscar Spencer's dark eyes brightened in the network of lines crisscrossing his face. "Thank you for accepting me."

"I told you the Coles were extraordinary," David whispered to Serena.

She nodded, touching her belly, knowing that the child she carried beneath her heart would also be extraordinary.

Rising on tiptoe, she kissed her new husband, then whispered what she wanted him to do to her later—much later.

HARVEST MOON

CHAPTER 1

Mexico City, Mexico—August seventeenth...

Oscar Clayborne Spencer died today at the age of seventy-seven after a decade-long bout with lung cancer.

The multiple award-winning film director, who won an Academy Award for his last film, Silent Witness, *also earned more than a dozen awards from the Cannes, Venice, and Sundance Film Festivals during his illustrious thirty-five-year movie career.*

Spencer is survived by his wife, Regina Spencer, and son, Dr. Aaron Spencer, of Bahia, Brazil.

Funeral arrangements will be private.

Regina Cole-Spencer's left hand trembled noticeably as she reached for the telephone on her bedside table. She loathed having to make the call. It would have been easier if she had called Aaron when his father was first diagnosed with the illness that had laid claim to his life second by second, minute by minute, and day by day for a decade.

Her fingers curved around the receiver. She knew the telephone number without glancing at the yellowing, frayed business card lying atop the highly waxed surface of the table; she had picked up the receiver and dialed the South American country's international code more than a dozen times over the past week, only to replace it in its cradle before the impending connection. But this time the call would be completed.

Oscar had issued an explicit order for her not to contact Aaron until after his death. Now was that time.

Her husband died quietly in his sleep, slipping away from their life together and into the next with the aid of the potent narcotic the doctor prescribed to make Oscar's pain more tolerable toward the end.

Pressing the buttons, she punched in the numbers and then closed her eyes and listened to the sound of the steady, measured ringing.

"*Olà. São Tomé Instituto de Médico Pesquisa.*"

Regina heard the feminine voice speaking Portuguese, and was instantly reminded that Brazil was the only South American country whose official language was not Spanish.

"*Hola,*" she responded in Spanish, a language she had learned from her Cuban-born grandmother and had perfected since living in Mexico for nearly a decade. "I would like to speak to Dr. Aaron Spencer."

"*Lo siento,*" the receptionist replied in the same language, "Dr. Spencer is not scheduled to work at the institute today."

There was a long silence. It was obvious the receptionist wasn't going to be forthcoming with any information regarding Oscar's son's whereabouts.

"It is imperative that I reach him. This is a family emergency," Regina added.

"I can page him and have him return your call."

She let out an audible sigh. "Thank you." She gave the woman her name and the telephone number to her house in a remote town nearly a hundred miles south of Mexico City, and hung up.

Rising from a tapestry-covered armchair, she walked over to the French doors and stared out at the lush property surrounding *El Cielo*. An expression of profound sadness settled into her delicate features as she opened the doors. The cloudless summer sky made the Sierra Madre Del Sur mountain range seem close enough for her to reach out and touch. She had lost count of how often she had awakened to stare at the jagged peaks blending with the sky. The first time she stood on the veranda staring down at the valley she had felt as if she had come to heaven. The mountain peaks had appeared to pierce the verdant, rolling hills of the valley to rise heavenward like spires on a Gothic cathedral, prompting her to call the property *El Cielo.* It had become heaven and a safe haven for her, as it was to become a final resting place for Oscar Spencer.

For eight years she did not have to concern herself about whether someone recognized her as Regina Cole, the actress who at seventeen had been nominated as Best Actress in her first film. No one had ever stared at her or whispered behind their fingers whenever she and Oscar dined out or shopped in town. They were allowed their privacy as private citizens, to share their lives uncensored as a married couple.

The telephone chimed softly, and she returned to the bedroom to answer the call. *"Hola."*

"This is Dr. Spencer," came a deep, powerful voice speaking fluent Spanish.

Regina inhaled, then let out her breath slowly. "Dr. Spencer," she continued, switching to English, "I'm Regina Spencer. I called you because I want to inform you that your father passed away earlier today." Her eyes filled with tears. "He did not suffer."

There was an interminable silence before Aaron Spencer spoke again. "What was the cause of death?"

"Lung cancer." Tears she had kept at bay now overflowed and stained her cheeks.

"When was he diagnosed with cancer?"

"His doctor discovered it ten years ago."

"Ten years! You waited ten years, and for my father to die, to call me, Miss—"

"I was just following his wishes, Dr. Spencer," she countered, interrupting him. "He forbade me to call you until after he'd died." She felt a rush of heat suffuse her face. He had no right to yell at her, and he had no right to accuse her of something he knew nothing about.

"What do you mean, he forbade you? Just who the hell are you, anyway?"

Her fingers tightened on the receiver. "I *was* your father's wife."

A soft curse came through the wire as Aaron Spencer mumbled angrily under his breath. "And now you're his widow." He had not bothered to hide his sarcasm. "Have you made funeral arrangements?"

Sitting down on the armchair, Regina pressed her back against the cushion, closing her eyes. She hadn't realized how tired she was, or how great a strain she had been under for more years than she could count.

"No, I haven't. I waited because I wanted to call you. If you intend to come to Mexico, then I'll hold off until you arrive. If not, then I'll proceed with my original plans."

"Don't do anything until I get there."

Nodding, she opened her eyes. "When shall I expect you?"

"I'll try to be there sometime tomorrow. Give me the address where you're staying."

She blotted her cheeks with the back of her right hand as she gave her late husband's son the directions to the sprawling property she had occupied with Oscar since they fled Southern California.

He repeated the information she had given him, and without offering the ubiquitous "goodbye" or "have a safe flight" she hung up.

All she had shared with Oscar swept over her as she left the chair and lay down on the large bed where she had slept alone since becoming Regina Spencer. She thought she had prepared herself for this moment. She had thought she would welcome the time when Oscar would slip away from her to a place where he would never feel pain, or see the sadness she valiantly tried to conceal from him.

She'd thought she had a lot of time to get used to the day when she would eventually become a widow, but she was wrong. She was wrong, because when she married a man fifty years her senior she never thought she would come to love him as much as she did.

Aaron Spencer sat in the dark long after he'd called a carrier which would take him from Salvador to Mexico, numbed by the news that his father was dead. It had been twelve years since he last saw or had spoken to Oscar, and despite their estrangement he had never envisioned him not being alive.

There had been one time when he picked up the telephone to call Oscar and set things right between them, but it had been too late. His father's telephone had been disconnected, and the recorded message indicated no forwarding number.

The anger he had carried for years diminished with time, but the pain hadn't. And now, with Oscar's death, there would never be peace between them. He could have forgiven Oscar for anything, but not for marrying the only woman he had ever loved.

A heavy sadness descended upon him like a leaden blanket, and he was swallowed up in a morass of despondency. He sat motionless in the sanctuary of his study, staring into nothingness, until a light knock on the door pulled him from his self-pitying reverie.

"Yes."

"Senhor Spencer, Miss Elena is here to see you."

Aaron scowled, squeezing his eyes tightly. He should've told his housekeeper that he wouldn't be receiving guests.

"Tell her I can't see her now."

There was a whisper of soft feminine voices, then a rapid tapping on the solid mahogany door. "Aaron. Please open the door."

He groaned audibly. At any other time he would've opened the door for Elena Carvalho, but not now. He wanted to be alone, alone to reexamine his life over the past twelve years.

"I'll call you, Elena."

"When, Aaron?" came the soft, pleading voice on the other side of the door.

"Tomorrow."

There was a pregnant silence before Elena spoke again. *"Boa noite,* Aaron."

"Boa noite."

He counted off the seconds until he heard movement in the alcove outside his study, indicating Elena Carvalho had left, then he let out his breath. He lost track of time before he left the chair to lie down on a chaise, sleeping fitfully until he rose to prepare himself to leave Salvador for his flight to Mexico City.

CHAPTER 2

"*Señora Spencer. El abogado està aquí.*"

Regina Cole-Spencer registered her housekeeper's softly modulated voice. She did not know how long she had stood at the window, staring at the undulating landscape.

"Thank you, Rosa. Please send him in."

The solid oaken door closed quietly, only to open again within minutes. Ernesto Morales stepped into the large, richly appointed room, waiting until his vision adjusted to the dimly lit space. All of the drapes had been drawn across the expanse of one wall except for six inches, and it was at these six inches that Regina Spencer stood at the wall-to-wall window, peering through sand-beige silk at the verdant property she had owned with her late husband.

His admiring gaze swept over the tall, slender figure of the young widow clad in a pair of black linen slacks with a matching, short-sleeved blouse. Her trademark waist-length, curly, black hair was secured in a chignon on the nape of her long neck. A slight smile touched Ernesto's mouth. Even in mourning she was beautiful and very elegant.

When word had reached him that Oscar Spencer had finally succumbed to the disease laying waste to his frail body, he had experienced an uncharacteristic emotion of forgiveness. Now, with Oscar Spencer's death, he no longer had to experience guilt about coveting the man's young wife.

"*¡Buenas tardes!* Señora Spencer."

Turning slowly, Regina stared across the room at her late husband's attorney. She smiled at him—a sad smile.

"*¡Buenas tardes!* Thank you for coming so quickly."

Ernesto crossed the room, his footsteps silent on the priceless handwoven rug. "I came as soon as I could. I was scheduled to appear in court this morning, and unfortunately I couldn't postpone it."

He stood inches from her, his dark gaze measuring the undisguised pain in her large eyes, the tension ringing her full, generous mouth, and the resignation in her stance that indicated she had done all she could do for Oscar Spencer, that she had honored her marriage vow to love him in sickness and in health. And now her husband was dead, but she was alive—alive and breathtakingly beautiful at twenty-seven.

His hands went to her shoulders, tightening, as he lowered his head and placed a kiss on both cheeks. "*Lo siento mucho,* Regina."

"*Gracias,* Ernesto," she returned, lapsing easily into Spanish. She wondered how many more times she would have to hear the *I'm sorry* phrase before she left Mexico to return to the States. As soon as the doctor confirmed Oscar's passing, the household staff had come to her, one by one, offering their condolences. And now it would be Oscar's business associates.

"Please sit down. Can I have Rosa bring you something to drink?"

Ernesto waved a hand. "No, thank you." He waited for Regina to sit before he took a comfortable armchair near hers, staring intently at her as she closed her eyes and pressed her head against the cushioned back.

"I've placed a call to Aaron Spencer to let him know about his father." She opened her eyes and met Ernesto's steady gaze.

"What did he say?"

"He said he'll arrive here today." She smiled again, this time indicating a weighted fatigue. "Oscar gave me my instructions, and I've followed them. What did he tell you?"

Ernesto nodded slowly. It was apparent Regina had known her late husband very well. Even on his deathbed Oscar Spencer continued to direct. He had given him specific instructions as to how he wanted his estate divided.

"You'll have to wait for Dr. Spencer's arrival before I make the conditions of the will known. I can assure you that you will be adequately provided for."

Sitting up straighter, Regina glared at the attorney. "You think I married Oscar for his money?"

"No! Oh no," he apologized. "I happen to know that you've never needed your husband's money."

Visibly relaxing, she nodded, her frown disappearing as quickly as it had appeared. Ernesto was right. She did not need Oscar's money, or for that matter any man's. She was a Cole, and the name symbolized wealth and prestige, not only in the United States but throughout the Caribbean and in many Latin American countries.

Ernesto also relaxed. He had made a grievous *faux pas*. If he hoped to court the young widow, he was not beginning well. Like many others who met Regina Spencer for the first time, he had found it hard to believe she had married a man whose age eclipsed hers by fifty years, but during the years he had observed them together he realized she truly did love him. There also were times when he thought her youth, beauty, and repressed passion had been wasted on the elderly man.

How many times had he fantasized running his fingers through her long, curly hair? Feasting on her perfectly formed, full, lush mouth? Caressing her slim curves and full breasts? Too many for him to count.

"I'd like to ask you a question," he began slowly, softly. "And if you choose not to answer it, I will respect your decision." She inclined her head. "I've been your husband's attorney since he moved from California to Mexico, and we've discussed many things. Many, many personal things. But not once did he ever disclose why you married him."

A slight frown marred Regina's high, smooth forehead. Ernesto was asking what so many had asked over the years. Her answer was always the same.

"My reason for marrying Oscar will remain my secret."

What she did not tell him or the others was that she and Oscar had promised each other that only their families would know the real reason behind their union.

It was Ernesto's turn to incline his head. His gaze shifted, lingering on the length of Regina's long, graceful neck. It was only the second time he had seen her with her hair pinned up off her neck. A secret smile touched his spare lips. He would wait for what he thought would be an appropriate time for her to mourn. Then he would make his intentions known to the very young and very beautiful widow. He was confident that she would not reject his subtle advances. After all, he was Ernesto Morales de Villarosa, and he could trace his family's ancestry to the period of the Spanish grandees who had settled Mexico in the early sixteenth century.

A swollen silence filled the room as the brilliant summer sun began its slow descent behind the nearby mountains. Regina leaned over and turned on a lamp on the table between the armchairs, flooding the space with soft golden light.

Ernesto stood up and reached across the distance separating him from Regina. He grasped her hand, pulling her gently to her feet. "I must be going. I've promised my mother I would share dinner with her."

Tilting her chin, she smiled at him. "Are you certain I can't have Rosa bring you something to drink?"

Squeezing her fingers, he returned her smile. "Maybe another time. Perhaps, after everything is settled, I hope you will allow me to…" He stopped, struggling to rephrase his statement.

Her smile faded as she tried meeting his furtive gaze. "To what?"

He registered the coldness in the two words. Had he moved too quickly? "I hope you'll allow me to handle your legal affairs," he continued, lying smoothly.

"Of course, Ernesto. I see no reason to change legal counsel at this time."

He offered a mock bow. "*Gracias. ¡Buenas noches!* Regina."

"*¡Buenas noches!* I'll see you to the door."

She led the way down a carpeted hallway to the entry, feeling the warmth of Ernesto's steady gaze on her back. She knew the attorney was interested in her, and had been for a long time.

Oscar had retained him to settle his estate, and she would concede to her late husband's wishes, but what Ernesto Morales did not know was that—if Oscar had willed her the house and its contents—she planned to dispose of everything as quickly as possible before she returned to Florida. She had been away from her family and the country of her birth for too long, and she found it hard to believe that it had been eight years since she had called the United States home.

She and Ernesto stood at a set of massive, ornately carved mahogany doors, staring at each other. She offered her right hand and he took it gently and placed a kiss on a knuckle.

"I'll call you to let you know the time for the service," she reminded him.

He nodded, released her hand, opened the door, and walked out of the large house and through the courtyard of the magnificent structure built on a hill overlooking a picturesque valley. He glanced over his shoulder just before he turned in the direction of the garages and saw that Regina hadn't moved. She stood in the doorway, a slim, shadowy figure against the rapidly waning daylight.

Regina was in the same position when she heard the sound of Ernesto's car drive away and the arrival of another. Straightening from her leaning position, she recognized the car as a taxi. She saw the driver stop, exit the vehicle, and come around to open the rear door for his passenger. Not realizing she had been holding her breath, she let it out slowly when she saw the figure of a tall man emerge from the backseat.

Even in the encroaching darkness there was something about the man that reminded her of Oscar, and without seeing his face she knew the passenger was Dr. Aaron Spencer.

Reaching into the pocket of his suit trousers, Aaron withdrew a money clip, peeled off several bills, and handed them to the driver. He then waited for his luggage to be unloaded from the trunk. It was only after he had hoisted a garment bag over his shoulder at the same time the driver picked up two carry-on bags and set them down in the entryway of the house that he noticed the door stood open and a woman stood at the entrance awaiting his arrival.

He counted the steps which brought him face-to-face with a young woman dressed entirely in black. His large, dark, slanting eyes widened in shock. *She couldn't be!* He shook his head. This woman couldn't be Regina Spencer. There was no way she could be his stepmother!

Regina took several steps backward and opened the door wider to permit Aaron Spencer to enter. "Please come in, Dr. Spencer."

The instant she opened her mouth she confirmed what Aaron did not want to accept. The deep husky sound of her sensual voice had resounded in his head hours after he'd hung up from her call. He had sat in his study, staring into darkness, and re-calling her statement: *Dr. Spencer, I'm Regina Spencer. I called you because I want to inform you that your father passed away earlier today. He did not suffer.*

After hearing her statement he had wanted to cry, but did not—because he could not. He could not because he had spent twelve years hating the man who had given him life.

He walked into the opulently decorated entryway, then turned and looked down at the woman who had been his father's wife. He visually examined her, complete surprise freezing his expres-sion. Not only was she very young, she was also stunningly beautiful. He did not notice the slight puffiness under her large, dark eyes which indicated she had not gotten enough sleep. All he saw was the delicacy of her features, the lushness of her per-fectly formed mouth, the flawlessness of her brown skin, and the soft curves of her womanly body.

She extended her hand. "I'm Regina."

Lowering the garment bag to the floor beside the matching leather carry-ons, he took the proffered hand. He inclined his head, his gaze fixed on her mouth. "I'm sorry we have to meet under these circumstances."

Regina felt a tingle of awareness when her hand was swallowed up by Aaron's much larger one. "Yes. It is unfortunate." She withdrew her fingers, still feeling the warmth of his flesh lingering on her palm.

Aaron Spencer had inherited his father's height and lean face, but that was where the similarities ended. His features were nothing like Oscar's. Her gaze caught and held his as she silently admired the exotic slant of his eyes. His nose was bold, almost aquiline, and his mouth was strongly masculine with firm upper and lower lips.

She watched him watching her, a knowing smile flashing the dimples in her cheeks. He was intrigued. It was obvious he hadn't expected his stepmother to be younger than he was. He gave her a lazy smile, and his lips parted to reveal a set of perfect white teeth.

Regina felt her pulse quicken and she glanced around his shoulder at her housekeeper, who had approached silently. "I'll have someone show you to your room. Rosa, please see Dr. Spencer to the guest room in the east wing."

Rosa nodded, smiling. "*Sí,* Señora Spencer."

She watched Aaron pick up his luggage and follow Rosa through the entryway to a flight of curving stairs leading to the upper level. Even after he'd disappeared from sight she was able to recall the width of his broad shoulders under his expertly tailored suit jacket. And in one glance she had taken in his close-cropped, gray-flecked black hair, the richness of his sun-browned dark skin, and the masculine sensuality he wore as proudly as a badge of honor.

She realized Aaron Spencer wasn't as handsome as he was sensually attractive. Even his voice was erotic—deep, powerful and seductive.

What she did not want to acknowledge was that she was attracted to the son of her late husband.

A man who was her stepson!

Aaron stood in the middle of the bedroom where he would reside during his stay in Mexico, staring at the queen-size bed's wrought-iron headboard. Twin emotions of rage and sorrow assaulted him as his hands curled into tight fists. He had flown thousands of miles and across several time zones to attend the funeral of a man whom he had symbolically buried years before—a man he hadn't seen or spoken to in twelve years. Just this once he wanted Oscar alive, so he could damn him for destroying the love and trust between them, and for not permitting him to trust a woman.

Closing his eyes, he relived the scene which had haunted him for years—the one where Sharon had come to him, her eyes awash with tears, when she told him she couldn't marry him because she was going to marry his father.

She had waited exactly one week following his graduation from medical school to disclose her intentions. She returned the engagement ring he had given her for her birthday, then stood up and walked out of his life and into his father's. He did not attend their wedding, telling himself that he did not have a father.

But he did have a father—a man whom he despised. But Oscar Spencer had spent the last ten years of his life dying from a disease that had ravaged his body; a disease that left him racked with pain and suffering; a man whose last days on earth he could have helped make comfortable because of his medical training.

Slipping out of his jacket, Aaron placed it over the back of a plush armchair. He hadn't spoken to Oscar, and his father had forbade anyone linked to him to contact his last surviving relative. A wry smile tugged at a corner of his mouth. Whatever Oscar's reason for not contacting him no longer mattered.

"And that suits me just fine," he whispered between clenched teeth. *Now, we're even,* he added silently.

It took an hour for him to put away his clothes, shave, shower, and change into a pair of black slacks, an oatmeal-hued, short-sleeved silk shirt, and a pair of black, Italian-made loafers. He dimmed a lamp on one of the bedside tables, closed the door to the bedroom, and made his way down the hallway to the staircase leading to the main level.

It was apparent his father hadn't spared any expense when he purchased and furnished the sprawling house for his young wife. Priceless, colorful handwoven rugs covered wood floors, and the tapestries covering the seat and back cushions of various chairs, chaises, and settees were exquisite. Walking into the living room, he ran his fingers over a side table boasting a marble inlaid surface. The dark-green, gold-veined marble was the perfect complement for the surrounding gleaming oak.

His footsteps were silent on a sand and ocher blend print rug as he moved over to a hand-carved, Mexican stone fireplace. He stared at a pair of massive, gilded candlesticks flanking an ornate ormolu clock resting atop the mantel. The candlesticks and clock were a bit too fancy for his more Spartan taste.

His gaze shifted upward and he stared into the mirror hanging above the mantel, seeing the reflection of his stepmother standing under the arched entrance to the living room. He went completely still, wondering how long had she been there.

His pulse quickened as he noted the ethereal slimness of her body in a black, floor-length slip dress and the cloud of ebony curls falling over her bare shoulders and down her back.

Turning slowly, he watched her walk into the room, seemingly floating toward him and closing the distance between them within seconds. An unfamiliar tightening in his groin caused him to gasp, and his eyes seemed to darken with an emotion he knew was lust. His body's violent reaction had betrayed him. It had been a long time—in fact years—since the mere sight of a woman had aroused him physically. He prided himself on his iron-willed control. Women who set out to seduce him always failed in their attempts to get him to commit to a future with them.

Regina was different, because she was seducing him unknow-ingly. She stood two feet away, golden light from an overhead chandelier shimmering on her exposed, velvety flesh. Trans-fixed, he inhaled the hauntingly clean smell of her body. The scent was reminiscent of the lingering fragrance of a refreshing rain shower. His penetrating gaze searched her face, lingering on her lips. She had not applied any makeup except to outline her lush mouth in a vermilion-red.

Perfect, he mused. *Incredibly perfect.* It was no wonder his father had been drawn to her. Regina Spencer was a temptress—a modern-day Delilah. What man could resist her once she set out to lure him into her beguiling web?

Arching a sculpted eyebrow, he wondered if she was aware of her seductive powers. If she was, he pitied the hapless man who would become her next victim. There was one thing for certain—he would not be the one.

She managed a forced smile, offering him an enchanting display of matching dimples in her silken cheeks. "I don't know whether you're hungry, but I had the cook prepare a simple repast. We'll dine on the patio," she said, not giving him time to accept or decline her invitation.

Turning gracefully, she walked out of the living room, leaving him to follow. He followed numbly, staring at the wealth of curling black hair falling to her narrow waist.

Regina led him outdoors to a patio overlooking the lighted courtyard. A small, round table had been set for two. A dozen blackened antique iron lanterns, suspended from stanchions, bathed the space in a warm yellow glow. She extended her left hand, and the light caught the circle of diamonds on her third finger.

"Please be seated."

He did not sit, but walked around the table and pulled out a chair for her. "Thank you," she murmured softly, permitting him to seat her.

Aaron lingered over her head, feasting on the soft swell of her breasts rising above the dress's décolletage and the sensual fragrance of her body before he reluctantly rounded the table and sat down opposite her.

She removed the cover of a soup bowl, watching Aaron follow suit. It was only a week ago that she had shared her last supper with Oscar. There were days when he hadn't been able to tolerate eating solid food, but he awoke one morning complaining that he was hungry. They'd shared breakfast in his bedroom, and an early supper on the patio. Oscar was more animated than he had been in weeks. They'd laughed and danced together, humming to their own music before he returned to bed, complaining of fatigue. That night was the last time his feet would ever touch a solid surface.

Aaron spooned the rich, flavorful fish soup into his mouth, watching his stepmother closely. She ate as if in a trance, and he knew she went through the motions because it was necessary to sustain her life. Laying aside his spoon, he reached over and picked up a bottle of chilled white wine.

"Regina?" Her head came up quickly. "May I serve you some wine?"

"No, thank you." Her husky voice had dropped an octave, and he was enthralled with its cloaking pitch. "I don't drink." She picked up a goblet with mineral water and took a sip.

Tilting his head at an angle, he narrowed his gaze. "Are you recovering?"

She laughed softly, the sound floating up in the warm, summer night air. "No. I just have no tolerance for anything alcoholic."

"How does it affect you?"

"Migraine."

He nodded. "That's enough reason not to drink."

They ate in silence, both content to listen to the strumming of a flamenco guitar. After twenty minutes a woman joined the guitarist, her clear, lilting voice lifting in song and sending chills throughout Aaron's body. He had forgotten why he'd flown from Brazil to Mexico. He wanted the reason to be different from the fact that he would bury his father without having cleared his conscience, to let Oscar Spencer know how deeply he had hurt him. And if he had to sit across from Regina, he didn't want it to be because she was his stepmother. He didn't want to be reminded that she had and still belonged to his father—a man he had not forgiven for his deceit, not even in death.

He finished the fish entrée, dabbing his lips with a cloth napkin while watching his stepmother. There was a weariness about her that should not have been apparent with someone her age. And he wondered about that. She said his father had been ill for ten years, which meant she probably had been in her early twenties when she and Oscar had become involved with each other.

How could she? he mused. How could she sleep with a man old enough to be her father, possibly her grandfather? What was there about Oscar Spencer that young women could not resist? Had Oscar seduced her, or had Regina seduced him? There were a lot of questions he needed answers to with regard to Oscar and Regina's marriage, but he decided they could wait.

"Where did my father die?"

She went completely still. It was the first time Aaron had mentioned Oscar, and she had to remind herself the reason she was meeting with Aaron Spencer was because Oscar had died.

"He was at home. He did not want to die in a hospital."

"You said he did not suffer."

She shook her head. "No. His doctor made certain he wasn't in any pain toward the end." Aaron sat motionless, staring at her, his expression impassive. Her gaze narrowed. "Do you think I would've permitted my husband to suffer more than was necessary, Dr. Spencer?"

"Aaron," he chided in a deep, quiet tone. "I'd prefer that you call me by my name."

"Then Aaron it is."

Placing his elbows on the table, he rested his chin on a clenched fist. "Did my father give you any specific instructions on how he wanted to be buried?"

"You didn't answer my question, Aaron."

"And you didn't answer mine, *Regina.*"

The strain of caring for a sick husband for the past eight years suddenly overwhelmed her, and she wanted to scream at Aaron Spencer that he had no right to question her role as wife and caretaker. Closing her eyes, she filled her lungs with deep drafts of nighttime mountain air. All she wanted was for it to be over; she wanted to bury Oscar and leave Mexico—forever.

Opening her eyes, she glared at him. "He'd talked about being cremated. Then said he'd allow me to make that decision."

Vertical lines appeared between Aaron's eyes. "Have you considered cremating him?"

"No."

He nodded, seemingly letting out his breath in relief. "Where do you intend to bury him?"

"I thought I'd leave that up to you."

"I won't make that decision. You're his wife."

"And you're his son," she retorted. "You and Oscar share bloodlines. Don't you have a family plot somewhere?"

Raising his chin, he averted his gaze. "No. My mother was buried in Chicago, her parents in South Carolina, and her only sibling in Bahia."

"How about Oscar's family?"

"He was an only child. He has a few distant cousins, but he lost contact with them years ago."

Running a hand through her hair, Regina pushed a wealth of curls off her forehead. "Then we'll bury him here at *El Cielo.* He will be closer—to…heaven."

Her voice quivered as she struggled to regain control of her fragile emotions. She would not permit anyone to see her cry. She would do what she had been doing for years—she would grieve in private.

Rising to her feet, she placed her napkin beside a plate of untouched salad. Aaron also stood up. "I'm sorry, Aaron, but I must retire. Please stay and finish your meal."

She took a step, but he reached out, his fingers snaking around her wrist and halting her departure. "There's one thing I *need* to know," he said in a dangerously soft voice.

For the second time since she had come face-to-face with Aaron Spencer, Regina registered the fiery brand of his touch. "What is that?"

"Did you love my father when you married him?"

She flinched, then squared her shoulders. He was just like all the rest. Everyone thought she had married Oscar for his fame, or for his money. Her head came around slowly as she tilted her chin to stare up at the man standing inches from her.

"I did not love him when I married him," she answered as honestly as she could. "But I did fall in love with him before he died. And I made certain to tell him I loved him—every day. Is there anything else you *need* to know?"

Aaron released her wrist, his gaze boring into hers. "That's enough, for *now.*"

"Goodnight, Dr. Spencer," she said softly, her eyes narrowing.

He opened his mouth to reprimand her about using his professional title, but swallowed back the words. At that moment he felt vulnerable because Regina Spencer disturbed him, disturbed him in ways that aroused old fears and uncertainties. He watched her until she disappeared into the house.

He would stay and bury his father, then leave Mexico and not look back. His life and his future were in Brazil, and that future did not include interacting with Oscar Spencer's widow.

CHAPTER 3

Regina returned to her bedroom and changed out of the dress and into a pair of cotton eyelet pajamas. She much preferred sleeping nude, but had acquired the habit of wearing pajamas to bed because she had never known when she would be summoned to Oscar's bedroom and she hadn't wanted to waste time getting dressed.

Walking over to the French doors, she opened them and stepped out onto the second-story veranda. The calming silence of the Mexican night swallowed her whole, filling her with a peace she had not felt in years. The past ten years had changed her into someone who had become a stranger—even to herself.

She had missed a lot of milestones a woman her age should have experienced: dating, traveling with her girlfriends, and attending parties. She had missed seeing her brother and sister grow into adolescence, and she felt detached from her parents, grandparents, aunts, uncles, and her many cousins.

She met Oscar Spencer at seventeen, married him at nineteen, and he left her widowed at twenty-seven. She had given him a total of ten years of her young life, and she wondered about the next ten. For the first time in her life she was alone—alone to make decisions that would not include anyone but herself.

A soft chiming shattered her musings. Leaving the veranda, she returned to the bedroom to answer the telephone. *"Hola,"* she said softly.

"Cupcake."

A bright smile softened her delicate features. "Daddy!"

Minutes after her husband died, she had called her parents and left a message with their housekeeper. The woman informed her that her family had gone up to West Palm Beach for a few days.

"We just got back and heard the news. How are you, Baby?"

"I'm fine, Daddy."

"Hold on a minute, Cupcake. I can't talk to you and your mother at the same time."

Regina sank down to the bed and pulled her knees to her chest. Hearing her father's voice reminded her of what was waiting for her once she tied up all of the loose ends of her life in Mexico; she never realized how much she missed her family until she heard their voices or they left after a visit. They had always come to see her in Mexico, because most times Oscar was too weak to travel more than a few miles from home.

Martin Cole's soft, Southern drawl came through the wire again. "Your mother says you should expect us within two days."

"No, Daddy, don't. I don't want you to come."

"Why not? I'm not going to let you go through this by yourself. Hasn't Oscar Spencer taken enough from you?"

Biting down hard on her lower lip, she chose her words carefully. Her father still hadn't forgiven her for marrying Oscar, and whenever he came to visit her and Oscar, it had been obvious he afforded the older man a modicum of respect because of his age, not because he was her husband. Oscar had been twenty years her father's senior.

"I'm not alone, Daddy. Oscar's son is here. And after we bury him and settle the estate, then I'm coming home."

There was a noticeable silence before Martin responded. "Are you coming home to visit?"

Her smile returned. "No. I'm coming back to stay."

"I like the sound of that. Are you certain you don't want your mother or me to come? She can come without me."

"I want to handle this myself. I'll keep in touch, and let you know when to expect me."

"Okay, Baby. Let me put your mother on before she has a fit."

Regina spent the next quarter of an hour talking to her mother. She laughed, the low, seductive sound of her voice filling the room when Parris Cole confided that seventeen-year-old Tyler Cole had shown a marked interested in a girl at his school.

"I can't believe it," she chuckled. "My little brother in love."

"I wouldn't call it love," Parris countered. "But I must say that he's quite infatuated with her."

"Is she at least a nice girl, Mommy?"

"She's lovely, but as quiet and shy as he is."

Wincing, Regina shook her head. "Do they talk?"

"He spends hours on his phone with her."

"I guess that means that they talk. How's Ari?"

She missed her brother, but missed her sister more. They were thirteen years apart, and she did not know why but she felt more like Arianna's mother than her older sister. Arianna called her every week to talk, and she usually wound up giving Ari advice about everything from interacting with her parents to dealing with the erratic behavior of her peers.

Parris offered an update on Arianna's latest escapades. She ended the call with a promise that she would contact all of the Coles for a family reunion once she confirmed a date for her return.

"As I told Daddy, I'm not certain how long it will be before Oscar's estate is settled, but I'm hoping to be back within a month."

"Today is August eighteenth. Which means we can expect you the middle of September," Parris stated firmly.

"Let's say October first."

"I can't wait, Angel. I don't think you realize how much I've missed you."

"I know, Mommy, because I've missed you more than I want to admit. But you know I had to fulfill my marriage vows."

"And you did. Now it's time for you to live."

What she wanted to tell her mother was that she had been living, that marrying Oscar had been her choice, and that she had loved him as much as Parris loved Martin. She had given Oscar Spencer eight years, eight years she did not regret.

She rang off, replaced the receiver in its cradle, then lay across the bed. Closing her eyes, smiling, she remembered the night the Academy of Motion Picture Arts and Sciences honored Oscar with his namesake for his directorial effort for *Silent Witness*.

She had crawled into bed with him and held him while he shed shameless tears of joy. She had not shared his joy, because she blamed the Academy for waiting until the brilliant director was sixty-seven, ill, and at the end of his career, to honor him. It was at that moment that she swore she would never make another film, but Oscar had persuaded her to accept one more—one more before she left the business for good. And his prediction had come true when he said he doubted whether she would complete more than three films.

Now, opening her eyes, she leaned over and turned a switch on the bedside lamp, leaving one bulb lit in the crystal base. There was enough light for her to see the familiar objects in the room. Pulling a sheet up over her body, she closed her eyes and slept a dreamless sleep.

Regina overslept for the first time in years. The sun was up, the household stirring, while Aaron waited for her on the patio. He'd declined Rosa's offer of breakfast, preferring to wait for her. He wanted to conclude the arrangements for his father's funeral, then confirm his return trip to Brazil.

He had slept fitfully, his mind filled with painful and agonizing memories—memories of pain, rage, and guilt. His father had wanted to explain his decision to marry Sharon, but he wouldn't listen. He had turned his back on his father, knowing no amount of rationalizing could counter his deception.

His dark gaze was fixed on a small green lizard that had attached itself to the sand-colored wall. The tiny reptile was joined by another, and the two lizards regarded each other for a full minute before one scampered away.

He detected Regina's approach seconds before he saw her. The familiar fragrance of her perfume wafted in the warm morning air, filling his sensitive nostrils. Rising to his feet, he stood, turned, and stared numbly as she crossed the patio. His respiration quickened. She was awesome, more shockingly beautiful than he remembered.

She was elegantly attired in a black business suit with a slim skirt ending several inches above her knees. A fitted, hip-length jacket claimed a single button, calling attention to her tiny waist. A pair of black, patent leather pumps and a single strand of large, magnificent cultured pearls with matching earrings completed her attractive presentation.

Extending her right hand, Regina gave Aaron a bright smile. "I'm sorry to have kept you waiting."

The wait was worth it, he mused. "It's all right. My body's circadian rhythms still have not adjusted to your time zone." Ignoring her proffered hand, he leaned over and kissed her cheek. "Good morning."

Her eyes widened, and she pulled back. "Good morning," she mumbled softly.

Aaron moved over to the table under the shade of a brightly colored umbrella, and pulled out a chair. She thanked him while allowing him to seat her. He circled the table and sat opposite her. What he had not been able to observe the night before was ardently displayed in the full sunlight.

She had brushed her hair off her face and secured it in a simple twist at the back of her head. Sleep had erased the slight puffiness under her eyes, and they gleamed like polished onyx. His mesmerized gaze catalogued the sweep of her naturally arching eyebrows, the delicate symmetry of her features, and the stubborn set of her rounded chin. Her face was slender, with cheekbones set high enough for her to be thought of as exotic.

Her gaze locked with his as each engaged in a silent examination of the other. She studied his face, feature by feature, wondering if he, too, had disapproved of his father marrying someone as young as she was.

"How old were you when you married Oscar?" he questioned softly, verbalizing her musings.

She arched an eyebrow. "Nineteen."

He recoiled as if she had struck him. "And how long were you married?"

"Eight years."

He frowned. "He was fifty years older than you." He made it sound like an accusation instead of a fact.

Tilting her head, she stared down her nose at him. "Fifty years older than me, and twenty years older than my father."

He couldn't believe it. *She's only twenty-seven.* He knew she was young, but he had hoped that she was at least in her thirties. He was thirty-seven—ten years older. That meant she was practically still a child when she married Oscar. At least Sharon had been twenty-four, and a woman—a very experienced woman.

"Did your father object to you marrying a man so much older than you?"

"He couldn't object. He didn't know I was married until a week after Oscar and I had exchanged vows."

"He disapproved?"

She shrugged a shoulder. "I'm not one to seek approval from anyone—especially my parents."

Sitting up straighter, Aaron draped an arm over the back of his chair. He was intrigued with Regina Spencer, intrigued enough to want to know more about the woman who had seduced Oscar and had gotten him to marry her. And he did not want to deceive himself because he knew his father, regardless of his age, was a suitable catch for any woman. Not only had Oscar been considerate, gentle, and brilliantly creative, but he also had been a very wealthy man.

There was no doubt Regina had married Oscar for his money. Why else would a nineteen-year-old girl marry an old, terminally ill man?

Whatever his suspicions, he knew they would be revealed at

the reading of Oscar's will. Only time would tell why she had married his father. She had admitted that she did not love Oscar when she married him, so it had to be for money.

Regina glanced at the watch on her wrist. "We're scheduled to meet with the funeral director at eleven-thirty."

Aaron looked at his own watch. It was after eight-thirty. "How long should it take us to get there?"

"We *should* make it within two hours, but one can never tell with the city traffic." That meant they had to eat breakfast, then leave within half an hour. And as if on cue, Rosa appeared, pushing a serving cart filled with juice, fresh fruit, freshly baked bread, and a steaming pot of strong, fragrant Mexican coffee.

Rosa placed the dishes on the table, then poured coffee into translucent china cups painted with delicate blue flowers. "Will there be anything else, Señora?"

"Tell Jaime to have the car ready for nine-fifteen. Dr. Spencer and I will be going to the city."

"*Sí,* Señora."

Aaron waited until the housekeeper walked away, then turned his attention to Regina, studying her with a curious intensity. Everything about her indicated she had been spoiled and pampered. She issued orders to others as if she had been doing it for years. The night before she hadn't waited for him to acknowledge whether he had wanted to eat when she said, *We'll dine on the patio.* She had turned her back and walked away, expecting him to follow her. What surprised him was that he had—he'd followed her like someone in a trance.

And he had also spent a restless night dreaming—dreaming of the rare occasions when he shared more than two months in a given year with Oscar Spencer, and dreaming about the woman who had offered his father companionship during the last eight years of his life. And it was now—in the full sunlight—that he knew he wanted to know everything about Regina.

Buttering a slice of bread still warm from the oven, he said, "Where are you from?"

Regina, caught off guard by the questions, nearly spilled the cream she poured into her coffee cup. "Florida."

He arched a questioning eyebrow. "You don't sound as if you're from the South."

She took a sip of the rich, strong brew. It was perfect. She had grown to love coffee and everything about it: taste, smell, and its soothing properties.

Placing her cup on its saucer, she met Aaron's questioning gaze. "I was born in New York, and spent the first nine and a half years of my life there. Then I moved to Florida. How about yourself?"

"My father didn't tell you about me?"

She shook her head. "Your father did not discuss his past with me. I knew he'd been married twice before he married me, and that he had a son from his first marriage."

A muscle flicked noticeably in Aaron's left cheek, and at the same time his mouth tightened into a thinning line. It was apparent Oscar hadn't told her the reason for their estrangement.

"I find that odd," he remarked in a quiet tone.

"Odd? Why?"

"Because a husband and wife should not have secrets between them."

Sitting up straighter, Regina leaned forward. "Is there something Oscar should've told me about why he did not want me to contact you until after his death?"

"What you're asking me is something you should've questioned your late husband about."

"I did." The two words exploded from her mouth.

His eyes widened when he registered her rising temper. A rush of color suffused her clear, gold-brown skin, and her breasts rose and fell heavily under the lightweight fabric of her suit jacket.

Spreading his hand out, palms upward, he drawled, "And?"

"And he wouldn't tell me."

Placing his hands on the table, Aaron leaned forward, a feral grin curving his strong, attractive mouth. "And neither will I."

Regina recoiled as if he had slapped her and slumped back against the cushioned softness of her chair. Whatever it was that kept father and son alienated would remain untold. Oscar had carried the secret to his grave, and no doubt Aaron would do the same.

It no longer mattered to her. She planned to begin her life anew, and her future would not include either of the Spencer men. She would always love Oscar and carry his memory within her heart, but that was what he would be become—a memory— while Dr. Aaron Spencer would return to Brazil and his research projects, which had become his lifelong obsession.

She would return to Fort Lauderdale, Florida, reconnect with her family, then put into motion what she wanted to do with the rest of her life.

Picking up her cup, she flashed Aaron a dazzling dimpled smile. Surprisingly, he returned it with a bright one of his own.

He took a sip of coffee, rolling it around on his tongue before letting it slide down the back of his throat. It was excellent. In fact, the quality was far superior to the beans grown on his coffee plantation.

"Did you learn Spanish after you moved here?" he queried, still wanting to know more about his enticing dining partner.

"No. My grandmother taught me."

"Cuban?"

"How did you know?"

"Lucky guess." What he didn't say was that the largest con-centration of Spanish-speaking people in Florida were of Cuban ancestry.

"How about you, Aaron? Why do you prefer to call Brazil home?"

He hesitated, savoring the soft, husky sound of his name rolling off her tongue. It was the first time she had said his name without his prompting her. Whenever she addressed him as Dr. Spencer he felt her sarcasm.

"My research."

"Is that the only reason? Couldn't you do your research in the States?"

"I could, but there's no way I could manage my coffee plantation from thousands of miles away."

What he did not say was that living in Brazil was far enough away from the States so that he wouldn't have to hear or read about Oscar Spencer, though the news of his winning the coveted Academy Award for his last film had reached him when he sat down to view the evening news ten years ago. The moment he'd heard his father's name mentioned, he turned off the television. The pain of Oscar and Sharon's deception still had not faded, after two years.

"Why don't you hire an overseer to manage your plantation?"

"I have one."

A slight frown wrinkled her smooth forehead. "I don't see the correlation." Her family's business conglomerate, ColeDiz International Ltd., owned coffee plantations in Belize, Puerto Rico, and Jamaica, yet her father or uncles were never directly responsible for planting or harvesting the crop.

Aaron smiled a full smile, the gesture transforming his face and causing Regina to catch her breath. His eyes tilted higher in an upward slant, and his full upper lip flattened against the ridge of his teeth, offering her a glimpse of their perfection. Her gaze moved slowly from his mouth to his eyes as they appeared to wink at her. She found his smile so infectious that she returned it with a dimpled one of her own.

"At the risk of sounding like an elitist, do you actually think I went to medical school to labor in the fields?"

Her smiled faded. He was laughing at her. Did he think she was totally ignorant? She struggled to control her quick temper.

"Save your sarcasm, Dr. Spencer, because I'm not in the mood for it right now."

He sobered quickly. "I wasn't laughing at you, nor did I mean to insult your intelligence."

"Tell me, Aaron, what exactly do you mean?"

He now understood why Oscar had been drawn to the young woman sitting opposite him. Beneath her overt beauty it was apparent that Regina Spencer's mien was that of entitlement. She was spoiled, as well as demanding. She'd met Oscar, wanted him for whatever her personal reasons, then claimed him as her husband.

And he knew he had to be careful—very, very careful—not to fall into the same trap. He'd been in Mexico less than twenty-four hours, and in that time all of his thoughts were filled with the image of the woman with whom he was sharing breakfast. He usually did not explain his work or himself to any woman, yet he found himself wanting to with Regina.

"Hospitals in South America were recruiting American-trained doctors, and I signed up to do my pediatric internship and residency in Brazil."

Regina paused, a spoon filled with fruit poised in midair. "Why Brazil, and not one of the other countries?"

"I had lived half my life in Brazil. After my mother died in childbirth, my father agreed to share responsibility for my up-bringing with her twin sister. My very proper schoolteacher aunt had declared openly that she would never marry. She quickly changed her mind after going to Brazil on vacation, where she fell in love with a man who was a coffee grower. She married him after a whirlwind courtship, then worked out an arrangement with Oscar in which I would spend the school year in Brazil and the remaining time in the States.

"Her husband died during my second year in medical school, leaving my aunt heir to a small but very profitable plantation in Bahia. She was a woman who never wanted to learn anything about coffee except how to brew it, but when she found herself totally ignorant about the product which afforded her her income she quickly changed her mind. Within a year she became an authority on every phase, from growing the plant to harvesting it. So when I was offered the chance to return to Brazil to be close to her, I accepted it."

Regina was fascinated by his story. "Does she still run the plantation?"

Aaron wagged his head slowly. "No. She died three years ago."

"I'm sorry, Aaron." The three words came out of their own volition, those words she had heard people offer her so often since she had become a widow.

He pulled his lower lip between his teeth, staring directly at her. "I miss her, Regina. I miss her more than I can verbalize. She may have been my aunt, but she became more than that. She was my mother."

Reaching across the table, Regina covered his larger hand with her slender fingers. For the first time she noticed the difference in their coloring. Both were brown—hers a gold, his a rich, warm sienna. His fingers were long, his hand well-formed—the hands of a healer whose touch made her aware of her dormant sexuality for the first time in her life. And what she did not want to admit was that his touch was also that of a seducer.

His free hand closed over hers. "I decided to live in Bahia after I completed my residency. I became interested in microbiology, and joined a research institute that relies solely on the government and private donors for funding. I now head that institute. I'm also its largest benefactor. Every penny of profit I squeeze from the plantation I put into the institute."

His fingers tightened on hers. "I will not leave my research, nor will I ever leave my plantation. Not for anyone or for anything."

But you have left it, Aaron, she wanted to remind him. He'd left it so he could pay his last respects to his father.

"Now I understand," she replied quietly.

He released her fingers, then picked up his coffee cup. He took a sip, savoring its rich taste on his tongue. His gaze met his step-mother's over the rim, and he registered a curiosity that hadn't been there before. It was apparent she was as intrigued about him as he was about her, but he knew whatever he felt or was beginning to feel for his father's widow would never manifest itself.

As soon as Oscar was buried, he would take his leave. Oscar was his past, and Regina Spencer was certain to become his past, too.

They finished their breakfast in silence. Half an hour later both were seated on the rear seat of a late model BMW sedan as the driver maneuvered expertly down the winding narrow roads toward the bustling, smog-filled, overcrowded streets of Mexico City.

CHAPTER 4

Aaron stared out the side window rather than glance down at the length of Regina's long, shapely legs in the sheer black hose. He realized she was tall, and the black patent leather pumps added another three inches to her already impressive height, putting her over the six-foot mark. It was apparent she was secure with herself—quite secure, very beautiful, and now no doubt an extremely wealthy young widow.

"The funeral service will be private," Regina stated, her low, husky voice breaking the comfortable silence. Not turning his head, he nodded. "Oscar wanted it that way," she continued. "He made all of the arrangements a month ago. He wrote his obituary, eulogy, and updated his will."

Shaking his head, Aaron mumbled a colorful expletive under his breath. "I thought he would've changed, but it's obvious he was controlling up until the end."

Regina bristled at his sarcasm. "It was his life, and he had every right to control it."

This time he turned and glared at her. "And everyone else's around him."

"He wasn't that way with me," she said in defense of her dead husband, but the instant the words were out of her mouth she knew it was only a half-truth. Oscar's decision to marry her had come with a stipulation: that she attend college after she completed her second and final film. She agreed, and when they relocated to Mexico she enrolled in the *Universidad* with a major in landscape architecture.

His grim expressions fading, Aaron gave her a tentative smile. "Then he was *very* different with you."

There was no mistaking the softer quality of his voice. Oscar had agreed to share custody of his son with his sister-in-law, but had issued his demands once she decided to move to Brazil: Aaron would live in Brazil during the school year, but return to the States for every school recess; he would attend an American college and—when he considered a career in medicine—an American medical school.

It wasn't until he returned to the United States to attend college and medical school that he came to know the man he called Dad. He wasn't a man to whom he felt close enough to confide his secrets. He was Oscar Spencer, the brilliant movie director; the man whose word was the final one on a movie set; the man whose acting techniques were followed and executed by actors earning millions of dollars a film; the man whose methods were taught in many drama schools all over the world.

Shifting his expressive eyebrows, he offered Regina a warm, open smile for the first time since their meeting. It was apparent she had not known her husband *that* well.

"How did you meet Oscar?"

It was her turn to gaze out the window. "I met him on a movie set."

His body stiffened in shock. "You worked in film?"

She nodded. "Yes. I was an actress. Oscar directed me in my first film. His genius secured me an Academy Award nomination, and of course his own award."

Slumping back against the leather seat, Aaron felt as if someone had put their fingers around his throat, closing, squeezing, and not permitting him to draw a normal breath. *She was also an actress!* Like the first two women Oscar Spencer had married, Regina had also been an actress. What was it about these women that his father had not been able to resist?

He also had to ask himself why he, too, was drawn to actresses. His own mother had been one. Then he had fallen in love

with Sharon, who had been a drama major. And now there was
Regina Spencer—his father's widow, and now his stepmother.

What he was forced to admit to himself was that he *was* attracted to Regina. It just wasn't her beauty. Only a blind man
would not see her most obvious appealing characteristic—her
face—but it was the total package: her voice, body, and most of
all the controlled sensuality she probably wasn't aware she possessed. It was apparent her youth and her sensuality had prompted
Oscar to offer marriage, while it was evident that greed and
cunning made Regina accept his proposal.

Like father, like son? No, he prayed silently. He had wanted
a lot of things in his life, but he never wanted to be Oscar Clayborne Spencer.

Aaron sat on a straight-back chair beside Regina, listening to
the funeral director. His father had delineated every phase of his
funeral, including specific instructions for a graveside, closed-
casket service only. There was not to be a wake.

He waited for the conclusion of the arrangements, then asked,
"May I see my father's body?"

The solemn-looking director glanced at Regina. She lowered
her lashes, signaling her approval. "*Sí,* Dr. Spencer," he replied,
rising to his feet. "Excuse me, Señora."

She nodded, acknowledging their departure. She did not know
why, but Aaron's request to see his father's body surprised her.
Not once since his arrival had he exhibited any emotion which
had indicated sorrow or grief. She thought perhaps because he
was a doctor—who was familiar with death and dying—that he
had become an expert in concealing his feelings. It was either
that, or his and Oscar's alienation had vanquished any or all love
between father and son.

She could not imagine not having her father in her life, even
though she had spent the first nine years not knowing who he was.
Closing her eyes tightly, she mentally dismissed the repugnant
family secrets that had forced her twenty-two-year-old pregnant

mother to flee Florida and hide from Martin Cole for a decade. If Martin hadn't gotten his half brother to find her mother, her existence would have mirrored Aaron's—not knowing where her father resided or whether he was dead or alive.

She shook her head, not opening her eyes. That was not what she wanted for herself, and, if she ever remarried, for her children.

"Are you all right, Señora Spencer? Perhaps you would like me to get you something to drink?"

Regina opened her eyes, realizing the funeral director had returned. His expression mirrored his concern. Offering him a gentle smile, she said, "No, *gracias,* Señor Padilla. I'm fine."

And she was. She and Aaron had finalized the arrangements for the graveside service, and within another three days the earth would claim Oscar's body as it had every existing organism since the beginning of creation.

Aaron walked into the small, air-cooled antechamber and stared at his father's cadaver. The sight of the emaciated form numbed him as he stood motionless, holding his breath. The man lying on a table bore no resemblance to the one he remembered. The Oscar Spencer he knew was tall, proud, elegant, not withered with age and disease. The angular face—which had been a collage of African and Native-American features that had afforded him a refined handsomeness both men and women had found attractive—was now a shrunken death mask.

Scathing, acerbic words he had rehearsed for years died on his tongue, and the longer his gaze lingered on his father's body the more he knew he had made the most grievous mistake of his life. He should not have permitted a woman to come between them. It should not have mattered that he loved Sharon enough to offer marriage. She should have become the recipient of his venomous fury, not Oscar.

They had been father and son—bound by blood. And there had been no doubt that his father had loved him, loved him more than he deserved to be loved.

Turning on his heel, he walked out of the room, closing the door behind him. He delayed returning to the director's office, pressed his back to a wall, and struggled for control of his fragile emotions. Covering his face with both hands, he mumbled a prayer of forgiveness.

"I'm sorry, Dad. I am so sorry, Father." His voice seemed to rumble in his chest, the very sound of it knifing his heart and leaving him to hemorrhage unchecked. Why hadn't he followed through after the telephone call? Why hadn't he hired someone to find his father? The whys attacked him relentlessly as he stood in the shadows, wanting to bellow out his pain and frustration.

His mother had given up her life giving birth to him, and his father had wasted away slowly in a foreign country without the flesh of his flesh at his side. Pushing himself away from the wall, he retraced his steps and made his way back to the director's office.

His tortured gaze impaled Regina as she rose to her feet at his return. He didn't know why, but he wanted to blame her—blame her for not contacting him sooner. What had she been trying to prove by playing the dutiful little wife and *obeying* her husband's demands? As he moved closer to her something unknown communicated that Regina was anything but a docile or submissive woman.

He stood over her, his eyes conveying the fury warring within him. "I'm finished here."

She tilted her chin and shifted an arching eyebrow. "So am I." Taking purposeful steps, she walked out of the office, her head held high and her back ramrod straight.

Aaron found himself doing what he had done the night of his arrival—following her lead. He wondered whether she had been the one doing the leading in her marriage. Had she talked Oscar into not contacting him until after his death? Had she feared that his reconciling with his father would leave her with a smaller portion of her husband's estate?

Quickening his stride, he caught up with her as she pushed open the door and walked out onto the sidewalk, his fingers tightening around her upper arm. She lost her footing, falling back against his chest. His free arm curved around her waist, pressing her hips to his middle until she regained her balance.

Turning in his embrace, she stared up at him, her breasts heaving in a measured rising and falling rhythm. The restless energy of Mexico City's populace crowding the wide avenues, the raucous sounds of honking car horns, and the incessant babble of spoken Spanish along with native Indian dialects faded as Aaron lost himself in the fragrant softness of Regina's curving body.

He noted the obsidian darkness of her large eyes for the first time, eyes so black no light would ever penetrate their midnight depths. His gaze lingered leisurely on her lush, succulent mouth—a mouth that begged to be kissed.

The conflicting emotions of anguish and defeat that had assailed him when he saw Oscar's body hadn't faded, and he wanted to ravage Regina's mouth until she pleaded with him to stop. He wanted to punish her, make her feel pain, and in doing so hopefully eradicate his own. Her eyes filled with tears, turning them into gems of polished onyx as she struggled valiantly to keep them from overflowing and embarrassing her.

Aaron held her to his heart, feeling her warmth, the fragility of her slender body, the sweetness clinging to her flesh, and registering the shudders she was helpless to control. Tightening his hold on her waist, he molded her length to his, burying his face against her silken neck.

"I just want it over, Aaron," she sobbed softly.

Inhaling deeply, he enjoyed all that made Regina Spencer who she was. Holding her and reveling in her sensual femininity made him realize that he did not think of her as the woman who had married his father, or as his stepmother.

She was a temptress who managed to lure him into her web of seduction without saying a word, and he was more like Oscar Spencer than he wanted to admit, because, like his father, he was trapped in a spell from which he did not want to escape. He had known her less than twenty-four hours, yet he wanted to know her in every way possible. She was a woman of mystery, and he wanted to peel away the layers under the overt beauty, to discover the real person who appeared secure and mature beyond her years.

"It will be over—soon," he crooned in a deep, comforting voice.

Nodding, she touched her fingertips to her eyes. "I want to go home."

He led her around the building and to the parking lot. Their driver stood beside the car, holding open the rear door. Aaron helped her in, then slid onto the seat beside her. She sat, back pressed to the seat, eyes closed. Reaching over, he took her hand in his, holding it protectively. Her fingers stiffened momentarily, then relaxed in his grip.

She opened her eyes and smiled at him through a shimmer of sparkling tears. "I'm sorry I fell apart back there."

He returned her smile with a wink. "You're entitled. I know it hasn't been easy for you."

"What I had to go through was nothing. It was Oscar who suffered—"

"You don't have to talk about it," he interrupted.

"Yes, I do. I promised Oscar I would tell you."

Vertical lines appeared between his eyes. "Tell me what?"

She pulled her hand away from his. "Everything. I met Oscar for the first time when I was seventeen…."

CHAPTER 5

Ten years ago

A black, stately Mercedes-Benz sedan maneuvered silently up to a set of iron gates rising upward to twelve feet. A man, standing more than half that height, appeared seemingly from nowhere and tapped on the tinted glass on the driver's side of the vehicle. The chauffeur pushed a button, lowering the window, and extended a printed invitation.

The guard's sharp gaze swept over the square of vellum, then shifted as he tried catching a glimpse of the woman sitting on the rear seat. His gaze did not falter at the same time he raised a small, palm-size cellular phone to his ear.

"Cole," he said quietly into the receiver. The gates opened and the Mercedes-Benz eased forward up an ascending, curvilinear driveway.

Regina Cole stared out the window, noting a series of gardens, a guest house, and a tennis court. The driveway ended at a *porte cochere.* Beyond were two more welcoming areas: a covered courtyard with scrolled gates, and an open courtyard with statuary and more gardens. She knew every inch of the house. Designed with the features of a Tuscany villa, it fused the grandeur and comfort afforded a man of Harold Jordan's station.

She had come to the sprawling mansion six months ago, spending a week under twenty-foot high ceilings and lazing around the Olympic-size swimming pool with the Pacific Ocean as the backdrop. Harold Jordan had summoned her and award-winning director Oscar Spencer to his home to discuss the film he decided to finance—a discussion which lasted only an hour.

Harold had invited her back more than half a dozen times during the filming of the virtually unknown artistic masterpiece, *Silent Witness,* but she had deftly sidestepped each request with a preconceived, rehearsed declination. There was something about the thrice-married producer which made it impossible for her to relax in his presence. At forty-nine, he was thirty-two years her senior. However, their age difference had not stopped him from pursuing her with the craftiness of Machiavelli.

This evening was different. Harold had summoned everyone who had had anything to do with the production of *Silent Witness* to his home to celebrate the film's eleven Academy Award nominations. She still had five months before she turned eighteen, yet she had garnered a Best Actress nomination for her first film.

The news had numbed her for hours. Then she had picked up the telephone in the sparsely furnished Los Angeles apartment she shared with another actress and called her parents in Florida. Hearing their drawling Southern cadence reminded her of how far she was from home, and despite her joy she felt more alone than she had ever been in her young life. She had wanted her parents and the other members of her family present when she shared her jubilation, not strangers; she needed people around her whom she loved, and who made her feel safe.

And there were times when she did not feel safe, despite sharing the apartment with another young woman and hiring drivers to take her everywhere. Years of therapy helped her cope with her fears, but hadn't eradicated them entirely. It was only on the set, in character, that she was no longer Regina Cole, but whoever her character was. It was then she no longer feared close, dark spaces. It was then she could breathe without a suffocating darkness crushing her body and her mind. And it was then that she could look out at the audience and smile, because she was completely free of the demons who attacked swiftly, silently, and without warning.

The car stopped at the entrance to the Jordan residence and a white-jacketed valet opened the rear door. The young man extended a tanned hand and Regina laid her slender fingers on his palm. His gaze widened appreciably as she placed one black, silk-shod, sling strap-sandaled foot on the terra-cotta path, then the other. Smooth, incredibly long legs were displayed under a body-hugging black dress in a stretch knit with a wide neckline and cap sleeves.

His mouth went suddenly dry as he pulled her gently to her to feet, she meeting his gaze. He was an even six-foot in height, and Regina Cole's head was level with his. A warm wind blew in from the ocean, lifting her waist-length curly hair. Turning her face into the breeze, she smiled. His smiled matched hers. She was even more beautiful in person.

Tucking her hand in the crook of his arm, he led her toward the glass-paned mahogany doors. "This way, Miss Cole."

Regina's trademark dimpled smile faded the moment she spied Harold Jordan standing in the entry waiting for her arrival. He was as casually dressed as she was. He had selected a pair of black linen slacks and a white raw silk shirt with a Mandarin collar piped in black.

He extended both hands, his fingers encircling her tiny waist. "My queen," he crooned, pulling her to his slim, hard body.

Tilting her head, she avoided his wet kiss and it landed on her chin. "Good evening, Mr. Jordan."

The warmth of his gaze grew cold, his eyes resembling pale-blue topaz. They were a startling contrast in a face deeply tanned by the brilliant, Southern California sun.

"How many times must I remind you to call me Harold?" His reprimand, although spoken softly, was cutting.

Forcing a smile, she said, "You're old enough to be my father." He flinched as if she had struck him. "And because you are, I can't address you by your name."

"You can't, or you won't?"

Her smile faded. "I cannot."

Harold Jordan's patience had been worn thin with his continued attempts to seduce the very beautiful and very talented young
woman who managed to occupy his every waking moment. If
she had not been the daughter of a wealthy man she would've
shared his bed as soon as she hit the streets of Hollywood.

But Regina Cole wasn't a starving actress waiting tables or
auditioning on a casting director's couch to land a role. She had
arrived in Los Angeles trained by the best drama coach her
father's money could procure, and the training paid off. She had
been nominated for Best Actress amid a field of veterans for her
first film.

It wasn't just her acting talent which had drawn him to her, but
the total package. She was the antithesis of the flaxen California
blond. Her jet-black hair flowed to her waist in loose, shiny curls,
a perfect foil for golden-brown skin further darkened by the hot
sun.

The moment he stared at her black-and-white head shot he had
been transfixed by the perfection of her delicate features. The
large dark eyes, staring out at him from the photograph, along
with her straight nose and lush, full mouth, had held him spell-
bound until she walked into his office. She'd smiled at him, displaying a set of deep dimples and greeted him in a low, smoky
voice which belied her youth. He'd stared, temporarily paralyzed, and a slight arching of one sweeping eyebrow let him
know she was aware that he was not unaffected by her startling
natural beauty.

He did not remember his interview with her until after she'd
left his office. All he recalled was her height, the sensually
haunting fragrance of her scented body, the boyish slimness of
her hips, and the firm, fullness of her thrusting breasts.

Regina Cole had successfully parried his advances, but this
night he would not be denied. Having her share his bed would make
the eleven nominations for *Silent Witness* pale by comparison.

Grasping her hand, he led her through an arched hallway off
the opulently furnished living room and out to the patio. A state-

of-the-art sound and lighting system filled the area around the pool with music and flattering lights. The glow of the setting sun bathed every light surface in a fiery orange.

Harold gave her a warm smile. "May I get you something from the bar?"

"Club soda, please."

His hand moved up her back, his fingers catching in the wealth of hair floating over her shoulders like curling black ribbon. "Can't I interest you in something stronger? I can assure you you won't be carded tonight."

"Club soda with a twist of lime."

He stared at her, a polite smile in place. "Even if you were old enough to drink what would be your preference?"

"Club soda," she insisted stubbornly. She had experimented with drinking with her friends during her sixteenth birthday celebration, and she woke with a severe migraine the following day. The episode was enough for her to never drink alcohol again. Along with her mother's voice, she had also inherited Parris Simmons-Cole's intolerance for most alcoholic beverages.

"Then it's one club soda with a twist for the pretty lady," Harold whispered close to her ear.

Regina watched him make his way to the bar before turning and searching the crowd for her mentor. She saw Oscar Spencer as he listened intently to one of the film's supporting actresses; the skimpily attired woman gestured wildly, the many bracelets on her wrists sliding noisily up and down her bare, tanned, well-toned arms.

Resting her hands on her hips, Regina smiled at the bored expression on Oscar's face. She found him to be the most patient man she'd ever had the pleasure of knowing. And if it hadn't been for his genius, she knew, her performance would never have been good enough to earn an award nomination.

"Congratulations, beautiful," whispered an assistant director as he walked past her in his quest to find some much needed liquid refreshment.

She flashed her celebrated smile. "Thank you, Neil."

Oscar turned in her direction, nodding his acknowledgement. She beckoned with her forefinger and he excused himself from the chatting, clinging actress. He wove his way through the swelling throng, reaching her at the same time Harold arrived with her drink.

The producer handed her a goblet filled with a clear, chilled, carbonated liquid with a sliver of green. "A club soda with a twist."

Regina took the glass, giving him the smile he had come to expect from her. "Thank you."

Harold nodded, dropping an arm over Oscar's shoulder. "Have your feet touched the ground yet?"

Shaking his head, Oscar offered a shy smile. "Actually, they've never left the ground."

Regina slipped the cool, refreshing drink, peering over the rim at the director. She knew he was apprehensive about celebrating his nomination prematurely. It had taken him more than thirty years to prove his genius in an industry that had employed its own efficient strategy of excluding people of color from the major studios. But Oscar had quietly made a name for himself, directing low-budget independent projects.

Then, at sixty-six, he did what he had never done before—he made the rounds of the studios to finance a script sent him by a recent graduate of an avant-garde film school. His instincts told him he had a winner, and he was right—once he finally convinced Harold Jordan to underwrite the cost of the project.

She had answered the casting call along with hundreds of others, knowing she was born to play the role of a young woman who, while on vacation in Mexico, falls in love with a priest who is living a double life. Like Oscar, she knew her instincts were correct once she received the call from her agent telling her she had gotten the part.

Her parents had flown out to the West Coast with her younger brother and sister to congratulate her on winning her first starring role, but she knew the reunion was more of a reconciliation than a celebration. Martin and Parris Cole had indulged what they had thought was her fleeting passion for acting, hoping and praying it would wane with maturity.

However, it did not wane, but intensified, and a week after she graduated from high school she packed her bags and left Fort Lauderdale, Florida, for Los Angeles, California.

She checked into a hotel, then called her parents to give them her address. Within twenty-four hours her father had set up an account in her name at a major California bank, permitting her to withdraw enough monies each month to maintain the lifestyle she'd had in Florida. And two weeks after her arrival she found a comfortable, two-bedroom apartment in an upscale L.A. neighborhood. She lived alone for a month before she offered her spare bedroom to another actress who had just separated from her boyfriend.

She had now been a Californian for nine months, and during that time she had made one film and had not gone out on one date. It wasn't as if she hadn't been asked out by men of varying ages, but it was her own age which kept her away from the clubs and the private parties. She was old enough to drive, yet still not old enough to vote, smoke, or drink. And the realization was sobering, because legally she was not an adult.

Harold removed his arm from Oscar's shoulder, his pale, penetrating gaze never straying from Regina's face. "Do you think we have a chance at the triple crown—Best Picture, Director, and Actress?"

She took another sip of her drink. "I'm not so certain the Academy will want to give me a Best Actress award, given my age and inexperience."

Oscar's dark brown eyes narrowed in concentration. "Your age and the fact that *Silent Witness* is your first film should have nothing to do with it."

She shifted her expressive eyebrows. "Must I remind you of politics, my friend?"

The director shook his head. He had been involved in the film industry longer than his talented protégée had been alive, and had known firsthand how politics had played havoc with his own directorial tenure. He'd won numerous awards at the Cannes, Venice, and Sundance Film Festivals, but never his namesake— the coveted, gold-plated statuette.

He was now sixty-seven, and he knew he did not have many more years in the film industry. He had planned for *Silent Witness* to be his last project, but changed his mind after working with Regina Cole. At first he thought her garnering the lead for *Silent* was a fluke. However, he had quickly changed his mind after working with her.

He found her intelligent, extremely talented, and uncannily perceptive. She usually knew what he wanted even before he outlined what he required of her. Watching her transform herself into a character usually sent chills through his body. She always sat apart from the others on the set, meditating. Once the signal was given for her to take her place for a scene, the transformation was complete. She was no longer Regina Cole, but her character.

He wanted to direct her once more before he officially retired. He wanted and needed to know if the magic was still there, if they could become a winning combination for the second time.

Harold excused himself, walking away and leaving Regina alone with Oscar. She took another sip of her drink, then lowered the glass and smiled at the tall, spare, elegant black man. Oscar Spencer was old enough to be her grandfather. In fact he was twenty years older than her forty-seven-year-old father, but somehow she did not regard him as a father figure. She saw him as a protector. Quietly, surreptitiously, he had shielded her from the obvious and lecherous advances of some of the men on the movie set.

When she was first introduced to Oscar she had found herself staring mutely at the man whose quiet voice and gentle manner put her immediately at ease. After working with him she realized he never had to raise his voice to issue an order. A withering glance and a noticeable tightening of his moustached mouth usually indicated his displeasure, and no one appeared willing to challenge his authority on the set.

Oscar's private life had remained that—private—though the tabloids did uncover that he had been twice married, both times to actresses. His first wife died in childbirth, giving him his only child, a son. The second divorced him within the first year of their marriage, citing irreconcilable differences.

She noticed that women of all ages were drawn to him, but at sixty-seven he did not seem the least bit interested in initiating an ongoing relationship. She had shared an occasional dinner with him, but only at his home. He always sent a driver to pick her up from her apartment, and after they shared a meal and several hours of intelligent conversation, the driver drove her back home.

Taking another sip of the club soda, she noticed an unnaturally bitter taste on her tongue. A slight frown marred her smooth forehead. Perhaps the sliver of lime had given the liquid an acrid flavor.

"Is there something wrong with your drink?" Oscar questioned, seeing her frown of distaste.

She shrugged a slender shoulder, taking another swallow. "I don't know. It was fine when I first tasted it, but now it seems so bitter." Her words came out slurred, in a singsong fashion. She blinked furiously, eyelids fluttering rapidly as she tried focusing. Why was the room spinning? And why couldn't she see Oscar's face clearly?

Oscar's graying eyebrows met in a frown when he noticed her dilated pupils. Reaching out, he pried the glass from her hand and poured the contents into a large planter.

"Let's get out of here," he ordered quietly. Curving an arm around her waist, he led her across the patio and around the rear of the house to an area where several dozen cars were parked.

Supporting Regina's sagging body, he made his way over to a middle-aged man who jumped up from a chair at his approach. "Preston, please tell my driver to bring my car around."

"Yes, sir." He raced away to do the director's bidding.

Regina felt her knees buckle as her head rolled limply on her neck. "Oscar." Her voice was barely a whisper. "I think I'm going to be sick."

Pulling a handkerchief from the breast pocket of his jacket, he held it close to her mouth. "Let it come up and you'll feel better."

She did not want to throw up—not in public. Then, whatever she had eaten or drunk refused to stay down. "No," she moaned, pushing his hand away and swallowing back the rush of nausea.

Oscar solved her dilemma when he held her jaw firmly and thrust a finger down her throat. Within seconds she purged the contents of her stomach onto the octagonal-shaped flagstones. Her eyes filled with tears, which streamed down her cheeks. Her throat burned, her stomach muscles ached from the violent contractions, and she couldn't keep her knees from shaking.

"It's all right, Regina. You're going to be all right," he crooned over and over, wiping her mouth with the handkerchief.

The odor of undigested food was revolting, and Regina thought she was going to be sick all over again. What was wrong with her? What had she eaten or drunk to make her throw up?

The caretaker returned with the driver and stepped out of Oscar's car. His eyes widened when he noticed the splatter on the flagstones. Wrinkling his nose, he cursed to himself. He hated the superficial, self-centered people who attended Harold Jordan's parties. They always drank too much and wound up throwing up, and he always had to clean up after them. There were times when he let them lay in their own filth, while calling them pigs, and they were—overpaid, plastic pigs who wallowed in slop but were able to clean themselves up and then flash their perfect smiles to their adoring fans, who worshiped them as if they were royalty.

The chauffeur alighted and opened the back door. Oscar settled Regina onto the backseat of the car, then reached into a pocket of his slacks. He withdrew a large bill and handed it to Preston. "Here's a little something for having to clean it up."

The caretaker pocketed the money, smiling. "Thanks, Mr. Spencer."

Oscar managed a smile he did not quite feel and slipped onto the backseat beside Regina. He pulled her limp body close to his side, struggling to control his temper. What he wanted to do at that moment was return to the house and put his hands around Harold Jordan's throat and squeeze the life out of his body. He stared at the driver's broad shoulders instead.

Not turning around, the driver asked, "Where to, Mr. Spencer?"

"Take me home." The three words were quiet—quiet and lethal.

CHAPTER 6

Regina drifted in and out of sleep, succumbing to the smooth motion of the car rolling over the hills and through the canyons of Los Angeles. She remembered someone picking her up and carrying her from the car, but not much else.

She was totally unaware that Oscar Spencer's housekeeper had undressed her and covered her nude body with a freshly laundered pajama shirt belonging to her employer. She slept throughout the night as Oscar sat at her bedside watching her sleep. It wasn't until the following morning that she awoke—disoriented, wondering why she wasn't in her own bed at her own apartment.

She lay in bed, trying to remember what had happened the night before. Pushing a wealth of ebony curls off her forehead, she sighed audibly. She had gotten sick at Harold Jordan's house. Oscar had compounded her dizziness and nausea by forcing her to regurgitate.

Oscar! Sitting up quickly, she realized she was at Oscar's house. She swung her legs over the side of the bed and managed to make it to the adjoining bathroom; she washed her face and rinsed her mouth with a cool, mint mouthwash, then searched the spacious, Spanish-style residence for its owner. Within minutes she found him in his study. He sat at his desk, his back to the door, talking on the telephone.

"You stinking son of a bitch!" he ranted through clenched teeth. "You know damn well what you did. You drugged her, Jordan! Don't lie to me. All I have to do is have a doctor pump her stomach and have a lab analyze the contents. Don't tell me what I won't do. It's over. I'll make certain you'll never get near her ever again. Don't threaten me, you perverted cretin. One call to the police and you'll be wearing a pair of bracelets that will require a key to remove." He slammed down the receiver, his shoulders heaving.

Regina's legs felt like blocks of ice. She hadn't gotten sick because she had eaten something that hadn't agreed with her. Harold Jordan had drugged her, and she did not have to guess why. He wanted her—in his bed. And because she hadn't come to him willingly he had taken the initiative of putting something in her drink.

"Oscar."

He swiveled the chair at the sound of her husky voice. Her hair spilled over her forehead and shoulders in a cloud of curling, raven spirals. The hem of his nightshirt ended above her knees, allowing for a generous view of her long, shapely legs.

Forcing a smile, he rose to his feet and closed the distance between them. He was impeccably dressed in a pair of dark linen slacks and a matching raw silk, long-sleeved shirt.

"Good morning. How are you feeling?"

Her large, dark gaze was fixed on his mouth. "Well, considering I was drugged."

He shifted a thick gray eyebrow, nodding slowly. "I suppose you overheard my conversation?"

Her expression was impassive. "I heard enough. How did you know he drugged me?"

"It's not the first time a woman has gotten *sick* at one of Harold Jordan's parties."

Closing her eyes, she wagged her head from side to side. "But why me, Oscar? I've seen Harold Jordan with enough women whom I assume are sleeping with him."

He moved closer, cradling her slender face between his hands. "Don't ask me why, Regina. All you have to do is look in the mirror. You're a stunning young woman. And there will be a lot of Harold Jordans who will want you to share their beds."

"But some of these women were very beautiful," she insisted.

Oscar held her tortured gaze. "You are young. Very, very young. And there are some older men who like young girls."

Hot, fat tears squeezed from under her eyelids and made their way down her cheeks. "When I sleep with a man I want that to be my decision. And only when I am ready."

Kissing her on both cheeks, he pulled her closer. "There is a lot of ugliness beneath Tinseltown's glitter and glamour, ugliness someone your age should not have to encounter. You should've been told that before you left home."

Opening her eyes, she stared up at him. "I heard it, Oscar. I heard it all, and still I *had* to come."

A wry smile curved his mouth under his clipped moustache. "You've heard it, yet you still had to come. The bright lights had your name on them, and they were calling you. You have it all, Regina Cole, yet you had to come. You have a perfect face, a perfect body, and an acting ability which rivals Katherine Hepburn's and Bette Davis's and you had to come to see if you could make it. Instead of you having to fend off Harold Jordan's advances, you should be in a college lecture hall taking notes."

She smiled through her tears. "You sound like my father."

"That's because I'm old enough to be your father." He returned her smile, wiping away her tears with his fingers. "In fact, I'm old enough to be your grandfather. And if I *were* your father, I'd cut you off without a penny and force you to come back home."

She took in a quick breath of astonishment. "Daddy would never do that to me."

Oscar's smile widened. "Of course he wouldn't. That's because you're his precious little princess." His expression sobered. "If you were my daughter I doubt whether I'd be able to do it, either."

Her expression matched his, giving her the appearance of being much older than seventeen. "My parents weren't thrilled that I decided to pursue an acting career instead of going to college. But there was nothing they could do about it once I graduated from high school."

"But you graduated two months shy of your seventeenth birthday. Legally you are still a minor and their responsibility."

"That's true. We had round-the-clock marathon discussions, and in the end they gave in. Both knew that I had to fulfill my dream or I would spend the rest of my life floundering while trying to find myself."

"They are truly exceptional parents, Regina. I still don't think I would've let my seventeen-year-old daughter leave home for a movie career."

"That's because you don't have a daughter, Mr. Spencer. I bet you wouldn't have raised the roof if your son left home at seventeen."

He shrugged a shoulder, the gesture both masculine and elegant. "Boys are different."

"And you're a sexist," she teased, offering him a warm smile.

"I suppose I am. I must remind you that I'm a product of my generation. We raised our sons and protected our daughters. And because I don't have a daughter, as of right now I'm unofficially adopting you. I'll make certain what Harold Jordan did to you will never happen again."

Combing her fingers through her hair, Regina pushed it off her forehead, her gaze never straying from the older man's face. "You think I need another father?"

"No. What you do need is someone to look out for you until you're able to protect yourself, or until you come to your senses and return to Florida."

She stared up at him from under her lashes, her delicate jaw tightening with a surge of determination. "I'm not leaving. A thousand Harold Jordans will not force me to walk away from my acting career until I'm ready to leave."

"And you're going to leave, Regina Cole," Oscar predicted sagely. "I doubt if you'll complete more than three films."

She felt a shiver of apprehension snake its way up her spine. "Why would you say that?"

"Wisdom and instinct, my child. And I'm going to live long enough to tell you I told you so."

Regina did not want him to be right. She did not want the heated, verbal confrontations with her parents, the thousands of hours she spent with drama coaches while sacrificing the time she should have spent with her friends and family members, to be negated.

Oscar Spencer was wrong. She would not walk away from her acting career. Not until she tired of it. And she hoped she wouldn't tire of it until she was an old, old woman.

Oscar Spencer kept his promise. He became her surrogate father and protector. Regina continued to rent and share her apartment with the other actress. However, in the coming weeks she found herself spending more and more time at the director's house. They established a habit of sharing dinner—every night. There were times when he sent her home with his driver, but many more when she slept over in the bedroom where she had spent the night following her drugging episode at Harold Jordan's house.

She hadn't heard from or seen Harold since that night, but realized that in less than a week she would be forced to come face-to-face with the man who had maliciously and methodically planned to rape her. She would attend the Academy Awards ceremony with Oscar, but regardless of the outcome she had made a decision not to attend any of the post-awards parties.

She sat at the table in the dining area at her apartment, studying the script her agent had delivered to her the day before. Vertical lines appeared between her eyes as she shook her head. It had taken only one reading for her to reach a decision. She could not consider the leading role.

The soft chiming of the telephone startled her, and she reached for the cordless phone lying inches away on the table. Pressing a button, she said softly, "Hello."

"How do you like it?"

She recognized her agent's gravelly voice immediately. "I like it, but I can't consider it."

"Why?"

"You know I won't take my clothes off."

A long, lingering sigh of frustration came through the receiver. "Regina—Baby Doll—don't do this to me. You know you're perfect for the part."

Her frown deepened. "Simon, don't fight with me. You know I don't do nude scenes."

"You're a big girl now, Baby Doll. By the time filming begins you'll be eighteen and—"

"It wouldn't matter whether I was eighteen or eighty," she interrupted. "I'm not going to do nude scenes."

Simon Garwood smothered a savage curse under his breath. "What do you want me to do?"

"Tell them to take out the nude scenes and I'll consider it."

"What if I tell them to use a body double?"

Regina heard a distinctive beep come through the wire. "Hold on, Simon. I have another call."

As soon as she depressed the button she heard the excited babble of raised male and female voices. "Hello?"

"Oh, my goodness—"

Her pulse quickened as she heard Oscar's housekeeper's trembling voice. "What's the matter, Miss Brock?"

"Mr. Spencer just took sick. The emergency medical people are here and…"

Closing her eyes, she tightened her grip on the telephone. "Is he alive?"

"I think so. But he's so still."

Even though she was sitting, Regina felt her knees shaking uncontrollably. "Where are they taking him?"

Sobbing, Miss Brock gave her the information, and a minute later she told Simon she would get back to him, then called the car service to pick her up.

She did not remember changing into a pair of faded jeans, oversized T-shirt, and a pair of running shoes. At the last moment she braided her flowing hair into a single plait and covered it with a navy-blue baseball cap. It was only when she was seated in the back of the late model Ford sedan that she pulled a pair of sunglasses from her purse and slipped them on. When she strode through the doors of the small, private Los Angeles hospital she was unrecognizable as the actress who had been nominated for her role in *Silent Witness*.

She asked the clerk at the admitting desk for Oscar Spencer's condition, lying smoothly when she introduced herself as his granddaughter. The clerk told her she had to wait until the admitting doctor completed his examination.

Regina lost track of time as she sat waiting on a nearby chair. She alternated staring at a clock and counting off the minutes with pacing. Two hours had passed before a middle-aged doctor approached her. His somber expression told her what she loathed hearing.

He extended his hand. "I'm Dr. Rutherford."

Rising to her feet, she shook the proffered hand. "Regina Simmons." She had decided to use her mother's maiden name. "How's my grandfather?"

The doctor pointed to the chair she had just vacated. "I think you'd better sit down, Miss Simmons." She complied, and he sat down beside her. "Your grandfather's condition is grave."

Her eyes widened behind the dark lenses. "How grave?"

"A CAT scan detected a large mass on his right lung. We're going to need you to sign some papers so we can remove it."

Closing her eyes, she swayed slightly as she bit down hard on her lower lip. How could she sign? She wasn't a relative. And besides, she was only seventeen. What did she know about giving permission for an operation?

Oscar had a son. A son who was a doctor. A son who hadn't seen or spoken to his father in more than two years. She studied the doctor's angular, patrician face. The green scrubs were not flattering to his sallow complexion.

"If...if he doesn't have the operation..." She couldn't continue.

"Without the operation I doubt whether he'll survive the year if the tumor spreads to the other lung."

"And with it?"

"We won't know if the mass is benign until it's biopsied. If it isn't, then the worse case scenario will be that he'll probably have to undergo radiation or chemotherapy to save the other lung, or keep the cancer from spreading. These procedures could possibly prolong his life by several years."

A wry smile curved her mouth. Oscar Spencer had promised to protect her, while the responsibility for his very existence was suddenly thrust upon her because she had elected to masquerade as his granddaughter.

She did not have a choice. That was taken out of her hands the moment he led her out of Harold Jordan's house.

"Where do I sign?" she asked in a firm voice.

The doctor patted her hand in a comforting gesture. "You've made the right decision, Miss Simmons. The clerk in the admitting office will have everything ready for you."

After signing the necessary documents for Oscar's surgery Regina lost track of time. She waited in a small, sunny room filled with large potted plants and colorful prints on the cool, beige walls. She made three trips to the hospital's coffee shop, each time purchasing large containers of the strong brew.

Becoming a Californian had changed her. She now drank coffee though she had never consumed it before, while eating less meat and more vegetables. She wasn't quite a vegetarian, but there were weeks when she did not eat fish, chicken, pork, or beef. The result was a loss of nearly ten pounds; ten pounds she could not afford to lose. Standing five-ten in her bare feet, she now tipped the scales at one hundred twelve pounds.

When her parents had come to Los Angeles to see her they hadn't been able to hide their shock at her weight loss. Her father promptly made a reservation at a restaurant and ordered every high calorie selection on the menu. Meanwhile, her mother had stared at her with tear-filled eyes before asking whether she was feeling well. She had spent more than two hours reassuring them she felt wonderful and that she was healthy. The elder Coles' fears were allayed once they saw her image on the screen. Their daughter was sensually entrancing.

She thought of her parents, brother, and sister as she sat sipping coffee, realizing how much she missed them. She missed five-year-old Arianna following her around and imitating her every motion, and seven-year-old Tyler. Her brother was quiet, reflective, appearing mature beyond his young years. He rarely smiled, and if he did it was a shy, attractive one. Everyone teased him and called him "old man." Tyler did not seem to mind. He existed in his own private world, daydreaming and keeping his fantasies to himself.

Sighing heavily, she closed her eyes, willing back tears. In a moment of melancholy she realized she was homesick. She wanted to go home—back to Florida. She was only seventeen, and Harold Jordan's drugging attempt and planned rape had compounded earlier childhood fears.

Her eyes opened and she stared at the highly waxed black and white vinyl floor tiles, a slight smile curving her mouth. As soon as Oscar recovered from his surgical procedure she would return home for an extended visit. The upcoming film her agent wanted her to accept would wait, wait until she was ready to step onto a movie set and in front of a camera again.

CHAPTER 7

Present day

Regina stared at Aaron, who stared back at her in obvious astonishment. "I wanted so much to go home. But…"

"Did you ever return to Florida?" he questioned after her words trailed off into a prolonged silence.

"It was another two years before I was able to go home. Meanwhile, I'd moved into your father's house, even though he had a twenty-four-hour private duty nurse. His moods vacillated from highs to lows. *Silent Witness* won seven Academy Awards, taking Best Picture and Director. Oscar had finally earned his namesake, but his depression continued."

"You did not win for best actress?" he queried.

"No, and I hadn't expected to. I made one more film before I left the business completely."

"Why?"

"Because Oscar was dying. The cancer returned, and this time he lost the lung. I completed the second film, and we flew to Vegas and married. And when I returned to Florida it was as Oscar's wife." Her slender fingers curled into tight fists.

"My family was shocked. My father in particular was very angry, because I'd married a man who was so old. They didn't know that Oscar was terminally ill. The mass the doctors removed from his lung had been filled with malignant cells. He spent more than six months undergoing chemotherapy, which weakened him so much that he couldn't get out of bed for days at a time.

"We arrived in Florida in time to attend my uncle's wedding, spent a week at my parents' home, then returned to California to close up the house. We left the States for Mexico to avoid the photographers and reporters who had gotten word that we had married, and rented a small house near Acapulco. I thought living near the ocean would lift Oscar's spirits, but it didn't. Six months later we purchased *El Cielo*."

Her eyes filling with tears, she tried blinking them back. "He loved living at *El Cielo*. Every morning he would get up and make his way over to the window and stare out at the mountains. He'd shake his head and smile, saying he loved the higher elevation because he felt closer to heaven. It took Oscar almost ten years to die. His will to live was so strong that it confounded every doctor who treated him." She smiled through her tears. "He always protected me, even though I couldn't protect him."

."He was ill, Regina," Aaron countered. "Terminally ill. There was nothing you or anyone else could do to change the manner in which he died."

She bowed her head and bit down hard on her lower lip. "I refused to let him suffer. I made certain he was never in pain toward the end."

A suffocating silence ensued, Regina and Aaron lost in their private musings. She was relieved that she had finally unburdened herself. She had told her parents she married Oscar because he was sick, yet had never disclosed the details of her near-rape at the hands of Harold Jordan. That was a secret she had carried for ten years—until now.

Aaron swallowed several times before he could bring himself to speak. "Words cannot convey my gratitude. You truly were an extraordinary wife."

What he could not say was that it should have been him, not Regina Spencer, who should have taken Oscar to the hospital for his chemotherapy. He should have given his father the injections of morphine whenever the pain had become unbearable. And he should have been the one who sat at Oscar's bedside, holding his hand when he drew his last breath. He should have been there for his father at the beginning and at the end of his illness, but he wasn't because of his so-called wounded male pride—a pride that had kept him from a father whom he knew loved him with his last breath.

"I did nothing extraordinary," Regina stated softly. "I did what I did because I promised Oscar I would take care of him."

"And I thought you'd married him for his money." Aaron could not help verbalizing what he had rationalized the moment he laid eyes on his father's widow.

Her body stiffened in shock. She knew he had been stunned by her youth, but she did not think he would be like the others who thought she had married Oscar for his money.

"Do you actually believe that?" she whispered. She could not disguise her annoyance as the query flowed tremulously from her lips.

Shrugging a broad shoulder in a manner that reminded her of Oscar's elegant body language, Aaron ran a hand over his face, nodding. "I'm ashamed to admit I did," he confessed. "When I first saw you that's what came to mind. Why else would a woman marry a man old enough to be her grandfather, if not for material gain?"

"Maybe other women, but not Regina Cole," she stated arrogantly.

A frown furrowed his high, smooth forehead. "Cole?"

"Yes, Cole," she confirmed, smiling.

Aaron studied her intently for a moment, his eyes narrowing in concentration. "Are you related to the ColeDiz Coles?"

He might have lived most of his life in Brazil, yet he had always kept abreast of the American business market. His diligence paid off, because three U.S. pharmaceutical companies had agreed to underwrite the cost of several of his research projects for five consecutive years. He remembered ColeDiz because

Black Enterprise and *Forbes* had listed the company as one of the wealthiest in the United States.

Regina watched Aaron with smug delight. He was no different than the others, whose expressions had given them away whenever Oscar introduced her as his wife. Some of them thought, and many had whispered, that Oscar was her *sugar daddy,* and she was only waiting for him to die so she could inherit his money. Oscar Spencer had earned less money than his comparable contemporaries, and three-fourths of his wealth had come from astute investments.

"Yes." The single word was a soft, husky whisper.

"Ouch," he gasped, grimacing. He saw the slight smile tugging at the corners of her lush mouth, and let out his breath slowly. "I'm truly sorry, Regina. Can you forgive me for being a narrow-minded fool?"

"There's nothing to forgive. And I've never apologized for marrying your father—not to anyone. I was the one who proposed to him."

Aaron placed a forefinger alongside his lean jaw. "That really must have shocked Dad."

"Believe it or not, he was speechless. He refused to give me an answer until I threatened to move out and leave him with the live-in nurse, whom he had come to despise. He fired her once, but I rehired her as she was walking out the door."

"Why?"

"Because she was the only one who would put up with his mood swings. There were days when his food ended up on the floor or on the walls."

"And you were the only other person who would put up with him."

Regina heard a measure of gentleness in his voice for the first time. "I was Oscar's wife, and the nurse was a trained professional. I paid her well to take care of her patient."

"She stayed because you paid her. But what about you, Regina? You didn't have to stay. And most of all, you didn't have to marry him."

She had asked herself the same questions over and over, but was never able to come up with a plausible answer. Was it gratitude because Oscar had saved her from becoming a rape victim? Or was it because of her own fears—fears that returned and attacked whenever she found herself alone? Living with Oscar and taking care of him had not permitted her time to think about the six days of terror which she would carry with her to her grave.

There were times when she had thought of returning to her acting career, but she dismissed the notion as soon as it came to mind. She had been away too long, and the lure of the bright lights had lost their appeal. She would follow through with her plan to return to Florida and start over.

"I stayed because I loved him."

Aaron shifted his attention to the passing landscape, Regina's statement reverberating in his head. *I stayed because I loved him.* Sharon had said almost the same thing: *I can't marry you because I'm in love with your father. Try to understand that I can't leave him.*

He had not understood—not at the time, because he had felt betrayed by the two people he loved most in the world. But Sharon and Oscar were his past, and it was time he began anew.

He was thirty-seven, in excellent health, all of the institute's research grants had been renewed for another year, and his coffee plantation was thriving. It was the first time in a long time he looked forward to reaping a bountiful harvest.

His father's death reminded him of his own mortality, and he realized it was time he existed for more than his research. Oscar had his movies, but he also had taken time to marry and beget a child to carry on his name and bloodline.

Aaron wondered how he had become so obsessed with his work that he had neglected himself, as well as ignored his own need to share his existence. When had he become so selfish that he had not permitted a woman into his heart and into his life? How had he survived the past twelve years, interacting with women only when he sought physical release?

There had been one exception. He had had a fleeting liaison with a woman two years ago, but decided to end it when she broached the subject of marriage.

Closing his eyes, he tried conjuring up Natalia Estevào's face and failed. What he did see was the hauntingly delicate face belonging to Regina Cole-Spencer. He opened his eyes and turned around to look directly at her. As he studied her with a curious intensity, his gaze seemed to undress her as she observed him through lowered lashes.

His strong, masculine mouth curved into a sensual smile, and she returned it with one of her own. He was transfixed with the dimples in her velvety cheeks as they winked back at him. Reaching over, he held her hand, squeezing her fingers gently and not letting go until the driver stopped the car in the courtyard of the house built on a hill overlooking a picturesque valley.

He and Regina were connected by a bond, and the bond was Oscar Spencer. She had taken on the role as his father's helpmate and comforter, and for that he was grateful. Eternally grateful.

Their smiles were still in place when he helped her from the car. She squinted against the blinding, brilliant rays of the blazing summer sun. Mexico was experiencing one of its hottest summers in decades. Even in the mountain region the daytime temperatures peaked in the nineties.

"I'm going to take *siesta* in my garden," she informed Aaron in the low, smoky tone he had come to listen for whenever she opened her mouth. "Feel free to take advantage of anything at the house. I'll let the household staff know that they're to take care of your requests. If there is something they can't provide for you, just let me know."

The front door opened at their approach and Rose greeted Regina in rapid Spanish, exclaiming excitedly about *el abogado* and *una carta*.

She smiled at her efficient housekeeper. The petite, forty-something woman had never cut her hair and a single, black, silky plait hung past her knees. "Dr. Spencer and I will see

Señor Morales in the solarium. We will also need some liquid refreshment."

Aaron waited until Rosa left before he turned to Regina. His gaze raced quickly over her face. "Are you having a legal problem?"

A slight frown formed between her eyes. "I don't know. I suppose we'll find out once we talk to Ernesto Morales. Oscar retained him to oversee his legal matters."

She led the way down a long, narrow corridor that opened out to an expansive hallway laid out in the shape of a cross, with arched passages leading in four different directions. Turning in a northerly direction, they walked into a large, cool room filled with rattan furniture and massive potted plants. Thick, pale plaster walls kept the heat of the sun from penetrating the space, making it a cool place to sit and enjoy the beauty of the surrounding foliage, outdoor garden, and the towering peaks of the nearby mountain range. Decorative wrought-iron grillwork on arched windows brought to mind a Moorish, rather than a Spanish, influence.

Aaron walked over to an antique armoire rising more than ten feet in height above the brick floor, running his fingers along the smooth surface of the nearly black wood. He did not have long to admire the quiet magnificence of the space when a slender man entered the room, cradling a leather portfolio under one arm. The lawyer's eyes caught fire as they caressed Regina's face and body. He watched Ernesto Morales lean over and place a kiss much too close to her smiling lips. It was more than apparent that the man was attracted to his father's young widow.

"*¡Buenas tardes!* Regina," Ernesto whispered in her ear.

Her smile widened. "*¡Buenas tardes!* Ernesto. I'd like you to meet Oscar's son, Dr. Aaron Spencer."

Ernesto jumped back as if someone had seared his flesh with a white-hot branding iron. Turning slowly, he widened his gaze as Aaron moved from the shadows and into the middle of the room. He drew himself up straighter, knowing he could never match the height of the tall American looming above him. Oscar Spencer had been tall, at six-two, but Aaron Spencer eclipsed his father's height by at least another two inches.

Extending his hand, Ernesto inclined his head slightly. "Señor Spencer. Ernesto Morales. I'm sorry we have to meet under these circumstances. However, I must say that your father was truly a great man."

Aaron shook his hand. "Aaron, please. And I'd like to thank you for handling my father's estate."

Regina waited until the introductions were concluded, then extended a hand toward a cushioned sofa. "Gentlemen, please be seated."

Both men waited until she was settled on a matching loveseat before they sat down. She turned her attention to Ernesto. He was fashionably attired in a melon-green linen suit which flattered his dark hair and suntanned face. She had always found him attractive in a delicate sort of manner. He was of medium height, slender, and his features were too fragile for a man. They would have been better suited on a woman.

Her gaze shifted to Aaron, widening appreciably. She much preferred his strongly defined masculine face and body, and his deep, powerful voice. If she had to choose between the two men, there would be no doubt that Aaron would be her choice. He hadn't just sat on the sofa, but had draped his tall body on the cushions while crossing one leg over the opposite knee. There was something about the manner in which he sat that reminded her of her own father.

"Ernesto, Rosa mentioned something about a letter."

The lawyer blinked slowly as if coming out of a trance, then unsnapped the lock on his leather case and withdrew a single sheet of paper from an envelope.

"Oscar Spencer gave me specific instructions as to how he wanted me to handle his estate. I was not to open this envelope until forty-eight hours after his death." He stared at Aaron before shifting his gaze to Regina. "I cannot reveal the terms of the will until ten days following his burial."

"Why the delay?" she queried.

"*Lo siento,* Regina," he replied. "I'm only following your husband's wishes."

She, too, was sorry. That meant her life was on hold for the next two weeks. As it was, she had to wait three days to bury Oscar, then wait another ten. It was as if she were in suspended animation. There was no going back and no forward movement.

She glanced over at Aaron, who hadn't taken his gaze off her from the moment he sat down. "How soon do you have to return to Brazil?"

He blinked once. "I have an open reservation for my return flight. I'll stay as long as it will take for *you* to conclude everything here."

What he did not say was that he would remain in Mexico as long as it took for him to shield Regina from men like Ernesto Morales, who looked at his father's widow as if she were a sacrificial lamb offering herself up for his personal agenda. Oscar might not have been able to protect her, but as long as she remained in Mexico *he* would. He owed her that much.

Rosa entered the room, carrying a tray with a carafe and three glasses. She quickly and expertly filled the glasses with a frothy fruit drink, handing one to Regina. Within a minute the men were served, and then the silent, efficient housekeeper walked out.

Ernesto, not bothering to taste his drink, placed his glass on the tray beside the carafe. He gave Aaron a sidelong glance. "There's no need for you to stay away from your research, Dr. Spencer. As Regina's legal counsel I will make certain to safeguard her interests."

Turning his head slowly, Aaron glared at Ernesto. "I have no doubt about that, Señor Morales. But because Regina is *mi familia* it has become my responsibility to protect her."

A rush of color darkened the lawyer's face with his increasing annoyance. "Do you think Señora Spencer needs protecting?"

Aaron arched an expressive eyebrow. "Not now. But there may come a time when she will."

Regina stirred uneasily on the loveseat. The two men were discussing her as if she were not in the room. She decided to change the subject, because there was one thing she did not need at this juncture in her life, and that was protection from either of them.

"Ernesto, you should know that the service has been scheduled for Friday morning at ten o'clock. It will be held here at *El Cielo.*"

He nodded, vertical slashes appearing between his eyes. "I'll be here. If the funeral is Friday, then the reading of the will shall take place on Monday, September first, at eleven o'clock in my office." Rising to his feet, he forced a false smile. "Please excuse me, but I must get back to my office."

Aaron rose with him, extending his hand, but Ernesto busied himself with his case, pretending not to see it. "I'll have Rosa show me out," he mumbled angrily under his breath.

Waiting until Ernesto left the room, Regina stood up. "What was that all about?" she shouted at Aaron.

Slipping his hands into the pockets of his suit trousers, he closed the distance between them until they stood only inches apart. He was close enough to feel the moist heat of her breath on his throat.

"Don't tell me you didn't know what was going on?"

Running a manicured hand over her neatly coiffed hair, she closed her eyes, then opened them. "No. All I know is that you insulted him."

Leaning down from his superior height, Aaron flashed a feral grin. "The man could've called you with the same information he felt compelled to deliver in person. Can't you tell that the man has the *hots* for you?"

Regina stared at his mouth, then laughed, the sound bubbling up from her silken throat like warm honey. "You're imagining things."

She knew Ernesto was attracted to her, but it wasn't something she would admit to Aaron—not when she was no better than Ernesto. She was equally attracted to her stepson.

"And you're in denial, Mrs. Spencer. Do you ever look in the mirror? You have to know that you're a beautiful woman. I don't blame the little man for salivating. What annoys the hell out of me is that he can't wait until his client is six feet under before he—"

"You've said enough, Aaron," she warned quietly, cutting him off.

His jaw tightened in frustration. She was wrong. He hadn't said enough. What he wanted to tell her was that she was the first woman in a long time who made him physically aware that he was a male—a male who desired a female for more than a slaking of his sexual urges. He longed to tell her that she had unknowingly rekindled a fire he thought long dead—that she was a woman who made him examine himself and acknowledge his weaknesses and shortcomings, a woman he needed to repay for her selflessness. She had sacrificed ten years of her life to care for his father.

His head jerked up and he stared at the wall behind her. "Forgive me. I was out of line."

"Don't apologize to me. It was Ernesto you insulted."

Aaron's expression darkened with an unreadable emotion. "Ernesto got what he deserved. I will not apologize to him."

Regina's fingers curled into tight fists. "I will not have you insult my guests in my home."

Removing his hands from his trousers, he brought them up and cupped her face between his palms. "I'm sorry you feel that way, but I will not apologize to your *abogado*." Leaning over, he pressed his lips to her forehead. "I'm going to take *siesta* now. I'll see you later, Stepmother." He released her and strolled out of the solarium, leaving her with her mouth gaping.

"Don't you dare call me that!" she shouted at his broad-shouldered back.

The deep, rumbling sound of his laughter floated back to her, then faded with his departure. Regina folded her arms around her body in a protective gesture and floated down to the loveseat. A mysterious smile flitted across her full mouth. Aaron Spencer bore no facial resemblance to his father, but he truly was his father's son, willful and stubborn.

He had accused Ernesto of having the *hots* for her, but what Aaron did not know was each and every time he touched her she melted like a pat of butter on a heated surface.

Closing her eyes, she prayed the two weeks would pass quickly. Aaron was never to know how much he affected her— how, from the moment they met her whole being seemed to be filled with a waiting, a waiting to experience what it was to be born female.

CHAPTER 8

Aaron spent his *siesta* pacing the floor of his bedroom. When he tired of staring at the same objects, he opened the French doors and stepped out onto the veranda. He stared at the mountains until the heat finally drove him back inside, where he changed from the dress shirt and slacks to a pair of walking shorts, a T-shirt, and running shoes.

The inactivity was beginning to play on his nerves. His normal day usually began at sunrise, when he drove down to the coffee fields to meet with his foreman. Three days of the week were committed to seeing patients at Salvador's municipal hospital, and the other three were spent at the research institute.

He returned to the veranda and strolled leisurely down its length. He turned a corner, then stopped. Moving to the wrought-iron railing, he leaned over, his gaze narrowing when he saw Regina talking to a man. She pointed to a profusion of ivy climbing over a pergola.

Aaron smiled when he noticed she had changed from her suit into a pair of white cotton, straight-leg slacks, a sleeveless, white shirt, and a pair of black ballet slippers. A curling ponytail was secured at the nape of her neck with a large, shiny hairclip.

She gestured, her delicate fingers caressing the leaves of the white blooms interspersed with the ivy. She took a few steps, the man following her lead and listening intently as she pointed to differing flowers and shrubs.

Reluctantly pulling his gaze away from Regina, he surveyed the exquisite beauty of the mountaintop garden. He recognized a large stone sundial, several statues, solid slabs of stone steps leading over a rise, and the reflection of the sun's rays on a shimmering pond. The lushness of the land reminded him of Bahia.

He had retained his American citizenship, yet he could not understand why he felt more at home in Bahia than he did in any place he had ever visited or lived. Maybe it was his African ancestors who called out to him in Bahia, the most African part of Brazil, that quieted his restlessness. Or perhaps he thought of it as safe haven—a place where he could hide, and divorce himself from everything that had to do with his past. But the hiding was over. He had been forced to confront his past, because he had returned to North America to bury his father.

Regina went down on one knee, extracting a clump of weeds growing too close to the rocks surrounding the man-made fishpond. The fish darted in and out of the plants growing in the cool, clean water, some of them floating to the surface when she sprinkled a handful of dehydrated fish food mix into the pond. One large carp pushed a smaller one away from the floating particles, his gaping mouth swallowing up the food as if it were a shovel.

"That's no fair," Regina said, laughing softly under her breath. "Let the little guy get some."

"That's the way of the world. The big get better, and the small stay the same," rumbled a deep voice above her.

Startled, she fell back and stared up at Aaron standing over her. He had been so quiet that she hadn't heard his approach.

"The next time you sneak up on me, try to make some noise. You nearly gave me a heart attack."

Instead of helping her regain her footing, he sat down beside her, his large body shielding hers from the direct heat of the sun. Reaching over, he placed two fingers on the pulse in her neck, counting the beats of her rapidly pumping heart.

He removed his hand. Smiling, he said, "You'll survive."

Bracing her elbows on the damp earth, she closed her eyes. "Just barely."

He gave her a questioning look. "If you want me to perform CPR, then you'll have to lie back down."

Her lids flew up, her gaze fixed on his mouth. If he had to perform CPR on her, he would have to place his mouth over hers.

"No," she replied in a breathless whisper.

His eyes were dark, unfathomable, as they moved slowly over her face, down to her heaving breasts under the cotton fabric, then back to her mouth. "Are you sure?"

She nodded, her head bobbing up and down like a buoy on the water. "I'm sure."

She jerked her head as his right hand came up and touched her hair. "Don't move, Regina. You have a few weeds in your hair."

The moment he touched her, she froze. Aaron Spencer was too close, his body too large, and he was much too warm. She suffered his touch as he methodically picked every particle of dirt and grass from her hair. Running his fingers over the antique silver hairclip, he examined it. Then without warning, he released the clasp, freeing her hair until it spilled over her back.

He ignored her gasp of surprise, turning the exquisite piece of jewelry over on his palm. "What are these stones?"

Regina was certain he could hear her heart pumping when she sat up and folded her knees under her body. "The blue ones are sapphires and the white ones are—"

"Diamonds," he said, finishing her statement. She nodded, grasping her hair and braiding it into a fat plait. "White gold?" he questioned.

"No. It's platinum."

He examined the Art Deco piece more closely. "It looks like a family heirloom."

"It is. It was my grandfather's gift to my grandmother for their first wedding anniversary. I'm the only one of her granddaughters who still has long hair, so she gave it to me when I got married."

"Hold still and I'll put it back." Aaron lifted Regina effortlessly until she sat between his outstretched legs. Then he undid the braid and secured her hair within the hairclip.

She suffered his closeness, the press of his hard chest against her back, the sensual scent of his cologne, and his fingers combing the tangle of curls until they hung loosely down her back.

Chuckling softly, she glanced at him over her shoulder. "You missed your calling. You should've been a hairstylist."

He leaned forward, his rumbling laughter floating seductively over her. "Didn't you know that I was multitalented?"

"No." She giggled. "What other talents are you hiding?"

"I cook."

She affected an expression of surprise. "No."

He nodded, smiling down at her. "Very, very well."

"What else?"

"I'm an excellent horseman. How about you, Regina?"

She tingled when he said her name. His voice had lowered, and it sounded like a caress. His nearness was overwhelming, and she did not know how, but she felt the movement of his breathing keeping rhythm with her own.

"I act, and I dabble a little in dirt."

Aaron curved a thick, muscular arm under her breasts, pulling her closer to his body. "What do you mean by dabble?"

"I design gardens."

His arm tightened before relaxing. "Look at me, Regina." Half-turning in his embrace, she stared up at him over her shoulder. "Did you design this garden?"

Her heart was thundering uncontrollably, and she knew he had to feel it. Every muscle in his chest and abdomen was molded to her back, bringing a wave of moisture that settled between her breasts.

"Yes, I did."

His expression was one of disbelief. "But you said you were an actress."

"You asked me how I met Oscar, and I told you I met him as

an actress. What I did not tell you was that I attended college and earned a degree in landscape architecture."

"When did you find time to attend classes if you were caring for my father?"

"Each semester I scheduled classes around his doctor visits and therapy sessions. It took me nearly eight years to complete a six-year degree program."

Aaron's gaze swept over the lush beauty of the garden, which had an exquisitely simple planting scheme of timeless romance and classical landscape design.

"How many gardens have you designed?"

"Just this one."

"It is truly a masterpiece."

A feeling of confidence swept over her at the same time an expression of satisfaction showed in her eyes. "Thank you."

Tightening his grip on her waist, he lifted her again until she sat beside him. He curved an arm around her waist, pulling her close. She felt the heat of his bare thigh through the cotton fabric covering hers, and for a brief moment she lost herself in his protective masculinity. She rested her cheek against his shoulder as if it were a gesture she had made before.

Even when Oscar led her out of Harold Jordan's house she hadn't felt as protected as she did now. She wasn't certain when it had occurred, but within the span of time Aaron curved an arm around her body she had unconsciously looked to him to protect her. Perhaps it was what he had said to Ernesto about her being his family, and therefore his responsibility.

She had put up a brave front for ten years, and she was tired of being a martyr. She had loved Oscar, but becoming his wife had exacted more than she expected once she gave him all of herself, leaving no reserve whenever she found herself bogged down in a tormented helplessness once his condition worsened. She'd ached with anguish and loneliness, refusing to cry because she did not want Oscar to know that she had weakened. Her mantra had become "stay strong and smile through all of the adversity." What she hadn't expected was for him to survive ten years. Each time he lived to celebrate another birthday she had weakened and aged with him.

But now she could lift her face to the sun and dance in the rain. She could laugh and cry without having to censure herself. And she could look forward to falling in love again, and to experiencing her sexuality for the first time.

Lowering his head, Aaron touched his mouth to her hair, reveling in the soft curls caressing his lips. "Are you sure you want to leave all of this?"

Sighing audibly, she nodded. "I'm sure, Aaron. More sure than I've ever been in my life."

And she was.

What she wasn't sure about was her intensifying feelings for the man holding her close to his heart.

"What about Oscar?"

"What about him?"

"You're going to leave him—"

"I'm burying him here because he loved it here," she countered, interrupting Aaron. "I didn't say I'd never come back. I just need to get away for a while."

"I'd like to offer you a deal."

"What kind of a deal?"

"I'd like to buy this property from you."

Pulling back, she stared up at him. "Why?"

He swallowed painfully, trying to form the words stuck in his throat. "I shut my father out of my life for twelve years, and I'm not very proud of that. I don't want strangers to trample over his final resting place. I know that may sound silly, but…" His words trailed off.

"It's not silly," Regina countered. "I can't promise anything until after the reading of the will. But if I'm left the property, then you won't have to buy it, because I'll give it to you as a gift."

Aaron curved a hand around her neck, then lowered his head. "Thank you," he whispered before his lips brushed against hers.

A brief shiver of awareness rippled through her body as Regina stiffened momentarily. She savored the feel of his firm lips on hers, the contact leaving her mouth burning with a lingering fire.

The kiss ended seconds after it began, and she wanted it to continue. She wanted to lose herself in the mastery of his mouth, and more. But common sense reared its head, reminding her of who she was and who Aaron Spencer was.

What was wrong with her? She was sitting in her garden, kissing a man who was the son of the man who lay on a table in a funeral home in Mexico City. Her husband wasn't even buried, and she was lusting after his son.

Pulling out of his loose embrace, she stood up and walked back to the house, her face aflame with shame when she realized what she wanted to share with him, because she had spent more years than she could remember denying her femininity.

Quickening her stride, she mumbled a fervent prayer. She wanted Aaron Spencer gone. His presence and his masculinity were constant reminders that at twenty-seven she was still a virgin.

Regina sat in her sitting room, watching intermittent drops of rain slide down the windows. In less than half an hour the graveside ceremony would begin. Earlier that morning the heavens had opened up to shed their own tears for Oscar Clayborne Spencer. It had rained heavily for an hour, then stopped, and now a watery sun broke through the heavy dark clouds to dry the earth.

The gravediggers had come the day before and dug a grave within the perimeter of the garden. Oscar's final resting place would be surrounded by a five-foot stone wall covered with a profusion of bougainvillea and Cherokee roses.

She closed her eyes. *I'm ready,* she told herself. She was ready to close a chapter on a part of her life, and hopefully she would never have to reopen it.

Opening her eyes, she glanced across the room to find Aaron standing in the doorway to her bedroom, arms folded over his chest, waiting for her. An expertly tailored black suit, startling white shirt, and a black silk tie caressed his tall, muscular body as if each item had been created expressly for him.

"Please come in." Her voice was low and cloaking in its timbre as she gestured to a chair facing her own.

Aaron walked into the bedroom, successfully curbing the urge to examine the space where Regina had sought solace since his arrival. After their encounter in the garden he'd seen very little of her, except at the evening meal. It was as if she had revealed too much of herself, and had elected to hide to fortify herself for the next phase of her life: burying her husband.

Undoing a button on his double-breasted jacket, he sat down opposite her and draped one leg over the other. "How are you holding up?"

Regina tilted her chin and stared up at the ceiling. "Well enough, I suppose."

Leaning forward, he reached out and captured her hands between his. They were trembling, and icy cold. "I can ask your doctor to give you something to calm you down."

She gave him a direct look, her eyes widening. "I'm okay."

As he lowered his head and his voice, Aaron's gaze narrowed. "Are you certain?"

She let out her breath slowly. "Quite certain." She glanced at the watch showing beneath the French cuff of his shirt. "I think we should go down now."

Nodding, he stood up, pulling her up with him. He curved an arm around her waist and led her out of the bedroom and down the staircase to the lower level.

Regina knew she had lied to Aaron. She wasn't all right, and she needed something to stop the trembling which had begun when she awoke earlier that morning. But she was too much of a coward to request a sedative.

She paused before walking out of the house, picking up a black raffia and silk hat with a wide, turned-up brim and matching, satin, grosgrain ribbon circling the crown from a small, round table and placing it on her head. Her dress was a simple black silk sleeveless sheath, and her only accessories were pearl earrings and a matching, single strand floating from her long neck.

Nodding to Aaron, she placed her hand in the bend of his elbow and permitted him to lead her to the tent where rows of chairs were set up for the attendees.

She recognized the doctors and nurses who were responsible for Oscar's medical care, all of *El Cielo*'s household staff, Ernesto Morales, and Pablo Vasques, the artist whose works Oscar had collected since they attended a showing in Mexico City the first year they moved to *El Cielo.*

The priest, who had heard Oscar's last confession before he administered the last rites, moved into position behind the dovegray casket, which rested on a device which would finally lower it into the damp, dark earth.

Regina heard the softly spoken words of the priest as he began the funeral mass, silently mouthing the prayers and the responses. A warm breeze filtered over the assembled, bringing with it a sweet, lush, redolent fragrance of fresh flowers. Leaning heavily against Aaron's solid shoulder, she cried softly, holding the handkerchief he had given her over her mouth.

Aaron closed his eyes, willing his own tears not to fall. He had to be strong, strong for Regina. Curving an arm around her tiny waist, he held her until her sobbing subsided. He was amazed at the gamut of emotions her sobbing wrang from him as he vowed silently that he would take care of her. When he returned to Brazil he would take her with him.

The mass ended, and Regina and Aaron thanked the priest for what he had offered Oscar before and after his death. Then they extended an invitation to all to stay for a light repast before they returned to their homes and places of business.

CHAPTER 9

Regina felt a restlessness akin to an itch she could not scratch. It had been five days since the funeral, and with the advent of each new day she felt as if she had been confined to a prison without bars.

"Why, Oscar?" she whispered angrily at the brightening sky as she stood at the open French doors. Why was he testing her by making her a prisoner? What had he hoped to prove by mandating that she remain in Mexico an additional ten days? She thought about calling her father and requesting that he send the ColeDiz corporate jet to pick her up and fly her to Florida for a few days, but quickly changed her mind after she realized that if she left Mexico she would not return—not for a long time. She had to think of the people she employed at *El Cielo,* who would now have to seek other employment. She had to see to their immediate needs before her final departure.

A sharp knocking on the bedroom door shook her from her reverie. Crossing the room, she opened the door to find Aaron standing on the other side. The sun wasn't up, yet he was dressed for the day. Her gaze moved slowly over his stark white T-shirt, body-hugging jeans, and work boots.

Folding his arms over his chest, he regarded her delightfully disheveled beauty. Her damp hair curled over her forehead in provocative disarray. She wore a pale blue camp shirt with a pair of faded, laundered jeans that flaunted the curves of her womanly body.

"Good morning," he drawled softly, winking at the surprised

expression on her face. "I decided to take a walk this morning, and wondered if you would like to accompany me."

She knew what he was up to. "I am not depressed."

He arched an eyebrow. "I didn't say you were. I'm just inviting you to come for a walk with me before we share breakfast."

"I'm also not hungry."

His arms came down as he glared at her. "What do you want to do, Regina? Join Oscar? You're not eating, and—"

"How do you know I'm not eating?" she countered.

"Because Rosa says you barely touch what she puts on your tray. You've locked yourself away in this room for the past five days—"

"Mind your own business, Aaron Spencer!" she screamed at him. She didn't need him spying on her. All she had was another five days. Then she would be free.

He took a step, bringing him close enough for her to feel the warmth of his moist breath on her face. "Oh, you think you aren't my business, Mrs. Spencer? You became my business the moment you called me to tell me my father had died," he continued without waiting for her reply. "And you are my business because you married my father."

"A father you turned your back on," she said accusingly, her temper rising quickly to match his.

A tense silence filled the room as Aaron breathed in shallow, quick gasps, successfully curbing his runaway temper before he said something he would live to regret. The nostrils of his nose flared as he compressed his lips tightly.

"Do not speak of something you know nothing about," he warned in a dangerously soft voice.

"Then why don't you enlighten me?" There was no mistaking the challenge as she folded her hands on her narrow hips.

Aaron glanced over her head, staring at the open French doors. "I can't tell you about it. Not now."

"When?" The single word was soft, coaxing.

His gaze shifted, lingering on her seductive mouth. "Before I return to Brazil I will reveal why I hadn't seen or spoken to my father in twelve years. Now, will you walk with me?"

She had to smile. "You'll say anything to get me out of this room, won't you?"

"Almost anything," he admitted truthfully, "except lie to you. And there is one thing you should know about me, Regina, and that is I will *never* lie to you."

She studied his face, noticing the softening of his lean jaw. There was a lethal calmness in his expressive eyes as he regarded her. "Or I to you, Aaron."

The tension vibrating around Aaron vanished, replaced by a warm, peaceful feeling which made him want to reach out and hold her close to his heart. He hadn't lied when he told her he wanted her to walk with him, even though he would have been content to just sit beside her. After burying Oscar she had retreated to her bedroom, locking herself away from the world. The few times he had knocked on her door she had refused him entry, claiming she was tired.

After the second day Rosa approached him, reporting that Señora Spencer was still not eating the food she prepared for her. He reassured the housekeeper that Señora Spencer was grieving and that she would eat when she became hungry. And she did eat. Most times she picked at the food, taking small portions, but it was enough to keep her alive.

"I'll wait for you in the courtyard." Turning on his heel, he walked out of her bedroom and down the hallway.

It was Regina's turn to watch him walk away, leaving her to follow, and it was another ten minutes before she made her way to the courtyard. She had brushed her damp hair and secured it with an elastic band at the back of her head.

She saw him leaning against a stone fountain with his arms crossed over his chest and his legs crossed at the ankles. The rising sun turned him into a living, breathing statue of burnished gold. The power of his upper body was clearly displayed under the jeans and T-shirt, and she tried to imagine him taking care of patients, and failed. She wasn't sure what she expected a doctor to look like, but it certainly wasn't the way Aaron Spencer looked.

"Where do you plan to walk to?"

His head came around slowly as he lowered his chin and smiled at her. "Not far," he said mysteriously, reaching for her hand. "Maybe we'll go as far as the road, then come back."

"It's over a mile to the road."

He gave her a questioning look. "Is that too far for you?"

"No."

And it wasn't. There had been days when she walked every acre of the land surrounding *El Cielo.* Those were the days when Oscar slept for hours after the doctor administered the drugs which took away his pain.

They walked in silence for over an hour, enjoying the dawning of a new day as birds called out to one another while hopping and flying nimbly from branch to branch.

"Come this way," she urged, leading Aaron up a hill. They climbed the rise, stood on its summit, and gazed down at the verdant valley below them.

Shaking his head, Aaron stared at the natural beauty of the panoramic landscape unfolding before his eyes. "It's incredible."

Regina extended her left hand, the rays of the sun glinting off the precious stones encircling her finger. "Look, Aaron. There's a golden eagle."

He squinted, staring at the large bird soaring with the wind currents. "Are eagles usually this far south?"

"Yes. They're more common in the Rocky Mountains, but we see them here because they build their nests along the Sierra Madre Occidental and Del Sur mountain ranges."

"There's another one."

She nodded. "That's the male."

"He looks smaller than the female."

"That's because he is. I don't know why, but the females are slightly larger than the males," Regina explained.

Aaron stared at the magnificent birds as they dropped several hundred feet without flapping their enormous wings. "They probably have a nest hidden away somewhere close by."

"They do. I observed them for weeks, bringing back pieces of leaves and twigs for a nest. Then they disappeared. When I saw the female again she was bringing back food in her beak, and I assumed it was for her babies. Weather permitting, I used to come up here every day and watch for them. Then one day I saw the babies leave the nest. They weren't quite as magnificent looking as their parents, but they were a sight to behold."

She and Aaron watched the eagles until they disappeared in their mountaintop retreat, then turned and retraced their steps. "I have a confession to make," she said softly as they neared *El Cielo*.

Aaron gave her a sidelong glance. "What's that?"

"I'm hungry."

Lowering his head, he hid a smile. They had walked for nearly ninety minutes, and there was no doubt she had burned calories she could not afford to lose. She was slimmer now than when he first met her.

Releasing her hand, he said, "Race you to the kitchen."

Regina was one step behind him as she sprinted toward the house. They reached the front door at the same time, Aaron stepping aside to let her enter.

He bowed from the waist. "After you, *Princesa*."

Affecting a haughty pose, she strolled into the house, glancing back over her shoulder at his smiling face. He was good for her, but she wasn't going to tell him that. It would remain her secret.

Rosa smiled when she saw the couple walk into the kitchen. "Your breakfast is ready."

Regina returned her smile, heading for the small bath off the kitchen. "I'd like to eat in the kitchen this morning instead of on the patio."

"*Sí*, Señora."

Rosa set the large table in the corner of the kitchen while

Aaron waited for Regina to wash her hands before following suit. He crowded into the small space as she dried her hands, his large body pressing intimately against hers.

"Stop, Aaron," she whispered harshly at the same time she tried concealing her anxiety with a nervous smile.

He pressed closer. "You're taking too long."

"Let me out first."

Ignoring her demand, he reached around her waist, turned on the faucets, and washed his hands with her anchored between the sink and his body. She stared at the corded muscles in his wrists and forearms. The heat in her face increased until she found it difficult to draw a normal breath.

"Aaron!"

"*¿Sí, Princesa?*" he whispered, his lips grazing her ear.

Closing her eyes, Regina breathed in and out through her mouth. "What do you think you're doing?"

"I'm washing my hands before I sit down to eat." His voice was deep, even. Reaching for the towel she clutched to her chest in a deathlike grip, he pulled it gently from her stiff fingers and dried his hands.

Regina turned slowly to face Aaron. The very air in the small space was energized as an invisible thread of awareness began to form between them. Her gaze was fixed on his face when she saw his gaze slip down to her chest, where the outline of her distended nipples were clearly visible through the sheer fabric covering her bra under the cotton T-shirt.

It did not matter that they shared the same last name. It did not matter that she had married his father, or that she was his stepmother, either, when Aaron leaned down and pressed a kiss along the column of her slender, scented throat.

"Let's eat before I start something I can't finish," he whispered savagely.

Her fingers caught and tightened on the front of his T-shirt, holding him fast. "Start what?"

His eyes widened as he stared at her. "You don't want to know."

"Yes, I do, Aaron. I do want to know."

What she wanted to tell him was that he couldn't tease her and then end it when he felt his control slipping, that he had lit a fire within her, reminding her that she was a woman who had yet to experience what it was to be born female, that he was the first man who made her conscious of her repressed sexuality.

Shaking his head, he said, "No."

Regina tightened her grip on the cotton fabric. "If you can't explain yourself, then stop playing games, Aaron. Remember, I had to grow up faster than most girls, and I was not given the opportunity to perfect techniques for teasing boys."

She released his shirt, pushed past him, stalked into the kitchen, and somehow still managed to give Rosa a warm smile. *"Mil graçias, Rosa."*

"De nada, Señora Spencer."

Sitting down at the table, she had spooned small portions of fluffy scrambled eggs, potatoes with peppers, and sliced *chorizo* onto her plate, and had filled her cup with steaming coffee by the time Aaron made his way to the table to join her.

Aaron's expression was a mask of stone as he glared across the table. She was a fine one to talk. Just being who she was, just looking like she did, was a tease. *She* was the tease—an unsuspecting, innocent one.

He was the one who slept restlessly, his dreams plagued with the image of her incredible face. Even in his sleep her sensual, velvet voice whispered in his head. And whenever he closed his eyes he could detect her presence as the haunting fragrance of her perfume wafted in his sensitive nostrils.

She had accused him of playing a game, but what he was beginning to feel for Regina Spencer was not a part of any game. The simple truth was that he wanted her. Not just her body, but all of her!

He poured coffee into his cup, added a teaspoon of milk, took a sip, then lowered it slowly. Placing an elbow on the table, he rested his chin on his fist, his gaze never straying from Regina's face.

"I don't play games," he said so softly she had to strain to catch the words. "What I do play is for keeps."

She arched an eyebrow, her fork poised in midair. She was aware that Aaron still smarted from her verbal spanking, and knew he wouldn't be content to let her get away with it.

"I'm impressed," she countered facetiously.

"You should be."

Regina felt a sense of foreboding sweep over her when she registered the three words. Even though Aaron's mouth had curved with a smile, his gaze held no humor. It was flat and cold, narrowing until his eyes resembled slits.

"Are you threatening me, Aaron?"

His expression did not change. "No. I just want to remind you that I stopped being a boy a long time ago, which means I don't remember how to play, as you put it, *games.*"

She searched for a hidden meaning behind his words. The silence grew more tense with each passing second as they stared at each other. Her fingers curled tightly, leaving half-moon impressions on her palms.

She knew without a doubt that she was attracted to him, and now and only now did she realize Aaron was equally intrigued. She was conscious of his virile appeal and knew that many of his mannerisms reminded her of Oscar, even though he looked nothing like his father. He claimed the same quiet magnetism of Oscar, yet there was more, much more, that drew her to him. She grew more uncomfortable as his gaze was riveted on her face before moving slowly over her upper body.

Her eyes narrowed, holding his steady gaze. "What is it you want from me, other than *El Cielo?*"

He leaned forward and lowered his voice. "I'm very surprised that you have to ask me that. You should know."

Regina went completely still as she stared wordlessly at him. An oddly primitive warning shouted at her that she wasn't quite ready to offer herself to a man—especially Aaron Spencer. She had been on a roller-coaster ride for the past ten years, and even though she had finally gotten off she still hadn't fully recovered from the harrowing emotional experience.

Swallowing several times to relieve the dryness in her throat, she said softly, "Why don't you tell me *exactly* what it is you want from me?"

His gaze softened as he flashed her a sensual smile. Reaching across the table, he captured her fingers and held them firmly within his warm grasp. How could he tell her that he was no different than his father, because he, too, could not resist her, that he wanted her in his life?

"I want to protect you, Regina," he stated instead. "And to do that I need you to come back to Brazil with me. I know I'll never be able to repay you for what you've been to my father, but I hope to be able to offer you a little of what you've had to sacrifice over the years. Spending some time with me in Bahia will give you the opportunity to relax and see another part of the world. I'll rearrange my work schedule at the institute and show you a Brazil that is a primordial, tropical paradise."

A nervous laugh escaped her parted lips at the same time she slumped back against her chair in relief. Luckily, he did not want to sleep with her.

"I can't go back with you now."

"Why?"

"Because I have to go home. I've been away too long. I'll be all right once I'm with my family."

"When do you think you can come?" There was no mistaking the disappointment in his voice.

"I don't know. I need time to get used to living on American soil once again."

He released her fingers. "Whenever you decide to visit, I just want you to know the invitation will always be open to you. You don't have to call me in advance. Just come down."

"Thank you." Her soft tone matched her smile.

He shrugged his broad shoulders, the gesture so elegant that Regina had found herself watching for it. She wondered how a man as tall and muscular as Dr. Aaron Spencer could appear so masculine and graceful at the same time.

She sipped her coffee, listening intently as Aaron told her of a Brazil she had never learned about in her geography classes. He related the mad passion of Carnival to the enormity of the dark Amazon. He told her of the vast size of a country encompassing nearly half of South America, whose population was clustered around the Atlantic coast, leaving much of the country and the massive Amazon Basin scarcely populated and inaccessible.

Regina and Aaron talked for hours, unaware of the tightening bond in which they were unable to know where one began and the other ended.

CHAPTER 10

Regina and Aaron stared at Ernesto Morales, both astounded by the contents of Oscar Clayborne Spencer's will. It was a simply worded document, but its stipulations were shocking: she was awarded the house and all of its contents, but she was restricted from selling *El Cielo* and the surrounding property for twenty years; the fourteen paintings by Pablo Vasques, appraised at over a million dollars, were also left to her, but were not to be sold during her lifetime; the three people who made up the live-in domestic staff would continued to reside at *El Cielo,* maintaining its upkeep while earning their full annual wages for the twenty years; cash, stocks, and bonds worth more than one million, eight hundred-fifty thousand dollars would be used to set up a medical foundation in the names of Oscar and Arlene Spencer at the *São Tomé Instituto de Médico Pesquisa* in Bahia, Brazil. The funds would be disbursed over a ten-year period with Regina Cole-Spencer as the foundation's sole administrator.

It had taken Ernesto less than three minutes to confirm that Oscar was still controlling; he had become the master puppeteer, pulling the strings and manipulating lives from his grave.

Regina rose to her feet, the two men also rising. Leaning across the table, she extended her hand to Ernesto. "Thank you for everything."

He grasped her slender fingers, coming around to stand next to her. "It's been my extreme pleasure. If you need legal advice setting up the foundation I'll be available for you."

She smiled. "Thank you for the offer, but I'll have someone at my father's company do it. ColeDiz accountants are experts in setting up tax-exempt, not-for-profit foundations."

Aaron moved closer to Regina, curving his left arm around her waist, while offering Ernesto his right hand. "I want to thank you for the trust my father placed in you."

Shaking the proffered hand, Ernesto seemed genuinely surprised by Aaron's approval. "It's been my honor to have known a man such as your father." He turned his attention to Regina. "I will need your power of attorney if you want me to manage the payment of wages for your employees."

"Thank you again, but I'll continue to pay them."

He successfully concealed his disappointment behind a polite smile. Now that he had revealed the contents of Oscar Spencer's will, there was no reason for his widow to continue their association. He did not blame Regina as much as he blamed Aaron Spencer. He did not know why, but since the man's arrival he had felt as if he had waged an undeclared war with the younger Spencer. Within a span of days Aaron had appointed himself as his stepmother's protector. Who did he expect to protect her from? Certainly not Ernest Morales de Villarosa.

Regina picked up her handbag. "I will be in touch with you before I leave Mexico."

Ernesto flinched noticeably as his face paled under his deep tan. "You are *leaving* Mexico?" There was no mistaking his surprise.

She nodded. "I'm going home to see my family."

"When—when will you return?"

"I honestly don't know."

His dark eyes showed disbelief and confusion. Regina Spencer's decision to leave Mexico had turned his world upside down. "Please keep in touch."

"I will," she whispered softly.

Turning, she walked out of the attorney's office, Aaron following closely behind her. He held her arm and escorted her to the parking lot. It wasn't until they were seated in the rear of the car and their driver had maneuvered out of the lot that they stared at each other; both had elected to conceal their emotions behind a mask of indifference. Oscar Spencer had skillfully bound them together.

Regina Cole-Spencer would become a part of Dr. Oscar Spencer's future, and he hers.

The return trip to *El Cielo* was accomplished in complete silence as she seethed inwardly, wanting to resurrect Oscar so she could scream at him for being a Machiavellian miscreant. She couldn't sell *El Cielo,* she couldn't sell the paintings—whose strange and macabre images disturbed her rather than soothed—and she would be responsible for disbursing and approving funding for a foundation named for Aaron Spencer's late parents.

She wanted to design gardens, not become a foundation administrator. *Damn you, Oscar,* she cursed silently. Damn him for forcing her to become involved with Aaron, because it had only taken two weeks for her to realize that her feelings for her stepson went beyond logic and reason. As she lay in bed before the sun rose to signal the beginning of another day, she knew she could not ignore the truth: she wanted to lie with Aaron; she wanted her first sexual encounter to be with him.

The driver pulled into the courtyard at *El Cielo,* and she did not wait for him or Aaron to help her from the car as she stepped out and made her way to the garden. Ignoring the blinding rays of the intense sun, she sat on the low stone bench facing Oscar's gravesite.

"You had to do it," she whispered angrily. *You just had to force us to be together, didn't you?* she continued in a virulent, silent tirade.

Squeezing her eyes tightly shut, she tried to fathom why Oscar would draw up a will with so many restrictions. Why had he made it so complicated, when their marriage hadn't been?

She shuddered, opening her eyes; she detected someone standing behind her. Without turning around she knew it was the man whose presence had disturbed her the moment he stepped from the taxi and onto the property of *El Cielo.*

Patting the space beside her, she said, "What do you think, Aaron?"

He sat, stretching his long legs out in front of him. His gaze was fixed on the headstone, which had been placed on the grave a week ago. "Oscar was a class act up until the very end. He didn't have to leave me anything."

Regina smiled. As annoyed as she was with Oscar, she had to agree with his son. "He left it to your research institute."

"It's the same thing. He knew how much medical research means to me. That's all I ever talked about when I was in medical school."

"If you liked research so much, why didn't you specialize in microbiology instead of pediatrics?"

He turned and smiled at her. "At the time I loved pediatrics more."

Who or what do you love more now, Aaron? she mused, watching a tiny lizard making its way over the cool, pale pink marble marking Oscar Clayborne Spencer's final resting place. His father had left him a considerable amount of money to continue his research projects, and she wondered if he would relax enough to make time for something or someone else in his life.

"We've made a breakthrough in predicting cerebral palsy in newborns," he continued, the pride in his voice clearly evident. "A team of neurologists at the institute detected that high levels of key markers in the blood of newborns may predict who will go on to develop cerebral palsy, a motor disability that affects a half million Americans."

"What is the cause of the disease?"

"We're not certain of the cause. There have been theories that cerebral palsy is linked to maternal or fetal infections during pregnancy, but there's no proof of this."

Nodding, she smiled. "You're very lucky, Aaron. You've executed a marriage of pediatrics and medical research with wonderful results."

"We have a long way to go before we can prove our theory."

"One of these days I'll read about you accepting your Nobel Prize for Medicine, and I'll tell everyone that I know that doctor."

He concealed a smile. "It's not about prizes or awards. It's about making human life worth living."

For the first time she saw Aaron Spencer as the healer he had been trained to be. It was the first time he had broached the subject of his research.

"I'll arrange for the transfer of *El Cielo* to you as—"

"Don't bother," he interrupted. "You can't sell the property for twenty years, so let it remain as it is. As long as you own it I know I'll always be able to come back here."

"Twenty years sounds like a long time."

"It is, and then it isn't." And it wasn't. The twelve years he had been estranged from his father seemed more like three. He still could recall everything about his last volatile encounter with Oscar as if it had been two weeks ago.

Regina stared at his impassive expression. "When do you plan to leave for Brazil?"

He turned his head slowly and stared at her, his gaze cataloging and committing to memory the exquisite features of her incredibly beautiful face. "I'll wait for you."

"It may take me a month before I finalize everything."

He shrugged a broad shoulder. "It doesn't matter. I'll still wait."

"But what about your research, your plantation?"

"They will be there when I get back."

She twisted the circle of flawless diamonds around the third finger on her left hand in a nervous gesture. "But you told me that you would not leave your research or your plantation. Not for anyone or for anything."

Aaron crossed his arms over his chest, resting the forefinger of his right hand alongside his jaw, his eyes narrowing as he quickly read the letters carved into the marble headstone. "That was then, Regina." His voice was low, rumbling sensuously in his chest.

"And now?"

Her pulse was racing so uncontrollably that she doubted whether she could stand if called upon to do so. She knew what Aaron was going to say before the words left his lips.

"Now there's you."

Closing her eyes, she bit down hard on her lower lip. "What about me?" She jumped, startled, when his fingers curved around the slim column of her neck.

He leaned closer, their shoulders touching. "I have to take care of you."

"I don't need your protection. I don't need any man's protection. Not anymore."

Placing a finger under her chin, he raised her face to his. The bright sunlight illuminated the liberal sprinkling of gray in his close-cropped hair, and she wondered what he would look like if he allowed his hair to grow. Had he cut it short to conceal the fact that he was graying prematurely? It would not have mattered to her, because all of the men in her family were mixed gray before their fortieth birthdays—her father, uncles, and male cousins.

His lids lowered over his expressive slanting eyes as he flashed the sensual smile that always sent shivers racing up and down her spine. "What if I tell you that I *want* to take care of you?"

Her eyes widened. "Why?"

The sound of her husky voice floated around Aaron like a cloaking fog, drawing him under and seducing him with its hypnotic timbre. How could he tell her that what he was beginning to feel for her was so different and foreign that it frightened him? That he did not know what drew him to her as if he had been caught in a spell from which there was no escape—a spell he did not want to escape?

"I don't know," he replied truthfully.

Reaching for his hand, she laced her slender fingers between his. "Everything will fall into place in its own time," she predicted sagely.

Will it? he wanted to ask her. *Will you come to love me as much I think I love you at this time?*

The realization that he was falling in love with his father's widow was not as traumatic as it had been when he first recognized the emotions which had not permitted him to feel completely at ease in Regina Cole-Spencer's presence.

He found her more secure at twenty-seven than most older women he had been involved with. She also challenged him in a way he had never permitted a woman to challenge him.

He also realized that he was more like Oscar Spencer than he wanted to admit, because he, too, wanted Regina Cole for himself. Oscar had appointed himself her protector to keep her from the clutches of a perverted movie producer, while he wanted to protect her from anything seen or unseen which would cause her harm. And to do that he would have to marry her.

He would remain in Mexico with her, hoping it would give him the time he needed to help her grieve, heal, and then love again.

"I want you to understand something, Aaron."

"What is it?"

"I'm going to leave *El Cielo*," she predicted quietly, "and when I do everything I will have shared with you *here* will end."

He successfully concealed a smile. She had challenged him again, and this time he would accept the challenge.

"Point taken," he replied in a dangerously soft tone.

Pulling her hand from his, she stood up and walked out of the garden and back to the house. She did not tell Aaron that she had grown to depend on him more than she had thought she would, that she hadn't wanted him to return to Brazil because then she would be alone—left to the demons who attacked relentlessly while she woke up screaming for someone to rescue her.

He had offered to remain in Mexico with her until she verified a date for her return to the United States. She would take the time given them, then walk away from Aaron Spencer and not look back.

* * *

Regina sat on a chair in the sitting room of her bedroom, staring out at the mountains as she spoke to her father. "I know he left me with a lot of responsibility, but I can handle it."

"Have your lawyer fax me all of the particulars and I'll have Philip Trent set up everything for the foundation." The soft-spoken, efficient attorney who had headed ColeDiz's legal department for the past twenty years had been responsible for filing the legal documents changing Regina's name from Simmons to Cole.

"I also need another favor, Daddy."

"What else, Cupcake?"

"I have fourteen paintings I want shipped to the States."

"What are they appraised at?"

"In excess of a million." Martin whistled softly under his breath. "I hate them," she said. The lifeless looking subjects and dark colors depressed her.

"Why did you buy them?"

"I didn't. They were Oscar's."

"Why don't you sell them?"

"I can't. Not as long as I'm alive."

There was a swollen silence before Martin Cole's soft, drawling Southern cadence came through the wire again. "Oscar Spencer is lucky he's dead, or I would break his neck. What the hell kind of life did you have with him where—"

"I don't want to talk about it," Regina snapped angrily, interrupting her father. "He's dead, Daddy. Let him rest in peace."

"I'll send a courier to pick them up, and I'll have them stored for you. What else do you need?"

There was no mistaking her father's annoyance when his tone changed. His voice was softer, more controlled.

"I need you to set up a payroll and a household account for *El Cielo.* Oscar made provisions for the permanent live-in staff for the next twenty years."

"That was very generous of him."

"I agree." This time there was no evidence of facetiousness in her father's voice. "How long do you project all of this will take?"

"Hold on while I talk to Philip."

Regina ran a hand through the hair she had unpinned from its elaborate chignon. Twisting a black curl around her finger, she examined it; she realized her hair was too long. Unbound, it reached her waist, and the only styles she affected were a single braid, ponytail, or a chignon. The long, curly hair and her dimpled smile had become her trademarks when she was an actress, but that phase of her life had been over for years.

A few times she had thought she would return to the stage, but changed her mind. Now she loved the entire process of designing gardens, from drawing up the plans to seeing the blooming plants harmonizing with the surrounding landscape.

"Cupcake?"

The endearment wrung a smile from her. Her father had not let go of his childhood nickname for her. "Yes, Daddy."

"Philip projects it should take about three weeks, give or take a few days."

She glanced down at the open desk diary on the round rattan table. "If that's the case, then expect me back around the first of October."

"I'll tell Philip to make this a priority."

"Thanks, Daddy. I don't know what I'd do without you."

"I want you to promise me one thing."

"What's that?"

"When you come back this time you'll stay for a while. I'm getting too old to fly around the world searching for my first-born." She laughed, the low, husky sound reminding Martin of his wife's voice.

"You're not old, Daddy. You're only fifty-seven. Wait until you're eighty-five, like Grandpa. Then you can say you're old."

"Your grandfather has been asking for you."

"You tell him that I'll be home soon."

"You know your mother is planning a big party for you."

"I figured she would. I'm looking forward to seeing everyone again. Daddy, I love you."

"And I love you," Martin stated quietly.

"I'll see you."

She hung up, then closed her eyes. Everything was falling into place, and she looked forward to returning to her family with the same obsession which had made her leave Florida for Los Angeles two months before her seventeenth birthday. It had taken ten years, but she had finally come full circle.

CHAPTER 11

Regina met with the gardener, chauffeur, and housekeeper, informing them that they would be guaranteed a place to live while collecting salaries if they maintained a residence at *El Cielo* for the next twenty years. All were too stunned with their former employer's offer to say anything as they stared at her with gazes filled with shock and gratitude.

"I'm going to hire someone to oversee the property," she continued. "He will be responsible for repairs and the general upkeep of *El Cielo*."

"Are you going away, Señora?" Rosa questioned, taking furtive glances at the others.

"*Sí*, Rosa."

"Will you be back, Señora?" Rosa had appointed herself spokesperson for the group.

"*Sí*," Regina repeated. "I will be back, and so will Dr. Spencer. We may not come back at the same time, but I promise you both of us will return here many, many times." This seemed to satisfy the housekeeper, and her lips parted in a warm smile. "Rosa, I'd like to talk to you," she continued at the same time the gardener and driver walked out of the kitchen, patting each other on the back.

"Señora?"

Her dark gaze met the equally dark one of Rosa Galan. "You can take the rest of the day off."

"But, Señora, who will prepare dinner for you and Dr. Spencer?"

"I will."

"*Sí*, Señora."

It was not the first time she had taken over the cooking duties. Regina shared her father's love of cooking, but hadn't indulged herself with concocting new and exotic dishes. She had spent so much time looking after Oscar, and whenever she cooked for him most times his sensitive stomach would not tolerate anything but soft, bland food.

Once she returned to the States she would look for an apartment, decorate it, then plan her career as a landscape architect. Florida would be an ideal location because of its abundant sunshine and tropical conditions.

Aaron changed his clothes, made two calls to Bahia, then went in search of Regina. *Siesta* had ended, and he knew he would find her in one of two places: the garden, or her bedroom. He knocked on her door and encountered silence. He waited and knocked again. It was apparent she wasn't in her bedroom.

His footfalls were silent as he descended the staircase and went to the garden. He asked the gardener if he had seen Señora Spencer. The man informed him that he had left her in the kitchen with Rosa.

Returning to the coolness of the house, he found her alone in the kitchen. Standing in the entrance to the large, modern, functional space, he leaned against a wall, crossed his arms over his chest, and stared at her.

He thought she looked younger today than at any time since he had met her. She had pulled her hair back and braided it in a single plait, securing the curling end with a red elastic band. Wisps of black curling hair fell over her forehead and ears. She had also changed from her tailored dress into a pair of well-worn jeans, a navy-blue T-shirt, and black ballet slippers. Her overall appearance was one of unabashed feminine innocence.

She hadn't noticed him watching her as she busied herself sectioning a chicken on a cutting board. She wielded a cleaver with consummate skill, which verified that she was more than comfortable with the inside of a kitchen.

"What's for dinner?"

Regina dropped the cleaver, it falling with a dull thud onto the cutting board. A slight frown marred her smooth forehead. "Stop creeping up on me," she gasped, wanting to scream at Aaron, but couldn't, not when her heart was pounding like a rapid-firing piston.

He closed the space between them with long, fluid strides and grasped her wrist between his fingers, monitoring her pulse. "I really did frighten you, didn't I?"

"Yes." She stared at his throat rather than meet his gaze.

His brow furrowed in a frown. "What makes you frighten so easily?"

She snatched her hand from his loose grip. "Nothing. It's just that I didn't expect to see you standing there, that's all."

"What do you want me to do?"

"Whistle. Sing. Just make some noise."

His frown deepened. She was afraid of something, and he knew he wasn't the cause. "How's your blood pressure?"

"It's normal. Why?"

"I don't want you stroking out on me."

She gave him a saucy smile. "I can reassure you that I won't have a stroke or a heart attack."

He returned her smile. "Good. And I promise I'll whistle before I come up on you again." Moving closer, his chest only inches from her back, he examined the different foodstuffs on the counter. "It's been a long time since I've had gumbo."

Regina suffered his closeness as she pretended indifference to his presence. She wanted to flee the kitchen and hide behind the door to her bedroom. It wasn't that she wanted to hide from Aaron so much as that she needed to hide from herself, and the feelings he aroused in her.

"Do you mind if I help?"

"Not at all," she said a little too quickly, realizing she would agree to anything to make him move away from her. Then she remembered his admission that he was a very good cook.

"I'll take care of the chicken while you slice the peppers and the okra," he said.

"Okay."

Aaron washed the chicken, patted it dry, then tossed the pieces in a large plastic bag filled with flour seasoned with salt and pepper. He preheated the oven, added butter and vegetable oil to a Dutch oven, and placed the chicken in the pot, then into the oven to brown.

"How spicy do you like your food?" he questioned as he picked up several CDs from a countertop next to a compact disc stereo system.

She glanced at him over her shoulder. "I don't mind if my food bites back."

"All right," he drawled, grinning broadly. "So, the girl likes it hot and spicy."

"If the truth be known, I like it *real* hot *and* spicy."

He gave her body a raking gaze, then slipped six CDs onto the carousel. "Like your music?" She gave him a lingering stare. "I doubt very much if my father listened to the Barrio Boyz, Babyface, India, Jon Secada, Marc Antony, or DLG."

"He liked Babyface and Jon Secada."

Picking up a case for DLG—Dark Latin Groove—he read the selections aloud. "*La Quiero A Morir.* That's heavy, Regina. Dying for love. Dad was more comfortable with Frank Sinatra, Nat Cole, and Sarah Vaughan."

She sucked her teeth at the same time she continued to trim the okra. "Don't be so cynical, Aaron. One of these days love is going to jump up and bite you on your behind so hard you won't have time to holler."

"You think so?" he questioned, stalking her and reminding her of a large cat.

Holding a small paring knife in front of her, she warned softly, "Stay away from me, Aaron."

"Put that thing away." Before she could inhale, he caught her wrist and took the knife from her loose grip. "I didn't being my medical bag, so let's try to act civil." Pulling her up close to his body, he swung her around in tempo with the pulsating Latin rhythm. "Dance with me," he urged when she went stiff in his arms. He tightened his grip on her waist, molding her to the length of him until they were fused from shoulders to knees. "It's been a long time since I've danced with a woman."

Curling her arms around his neck, Regina relaxed, closed her eyes, and inhaled the hauntingly sensual scent of his natural body fragrance mingling with his cologne.

"What's the matter, Aaron? You don't get out much?"

He laughed, the sound rumbling like thunder in his broad chest. "Apparently not enough. I'm usually invited to a lot of parties during the Christmas season, but I manage to make it to only one or two."

Pulling back, she smiled up at him staring down at her. "What about Carnival?"

He shifted his eyebrows. "I stay away from Carnival."

"Why?"

"It's become a little too boisterous for me." He swung her around, his hips moving sensuously against hers as he kept pace with the throbbing rhythm.

She nodded, concentrating on the intricate dance steps Aaron executed. He had failed to mention that he was also an excellent dancer. She followed his every move. The selection ended but he did not release her, and she did not want him to.

Dancing with Aaron reminded her of what she had missed. She had never been given the opportunity to date, dance, or flirt with a man. He was offering her that, and more. She registered the changes within her whenever he tightened his grip on her waist, making her aware of how different their bodies were. She successfully swallowed back a moan when she felt his rising hardness press against her middle, bringing with it a heaviness in her breasts she was unable to control. She was certain he was cognizant of the changes at the same time his breathing deepened.

Then, without warning, he went completely still, and she was certain she would have fallen if he hadn't been holding her and possibly injured herself.

His hands moved from her waist to cradle her face. She tried escaping him, but he tightened his hold. "Don't," he whispered, his moist breath caressing her mouth. "Please don't move."

Closing her eyes against his intense stare, she realized she couldn't move. She couldn't escape him even if she wanted to. It was too late. Aaron Spencer had become the itch she couldn't scratch. Within two weeks he had become a part of her existence, and try as she could, she could not remember when he had not been at *El Cielo*.

She looked for him when she woke up, and before she retired for bed. They had taken to sharing all of their meals and walks together, and many times *siestas* in the garden. And there were occasions when they were content to sit beside each other without initiating conversation.

She knew he was going to kiss her, and she was helpless to stop him. It wouldn't be the first time a man kissed her, but it would be the first time she would not have to take her cue from a director.

Aaron stared at Regina as if seeing her for the first time. He hadn't realized the length of the lashes brushing the tops of her high cheekbones, the smooth, velvety texture of her skin, and the narrowness of her delicate nose. His hand splayed over her cheek, his fingers entwining in the curls framing her face. His head came down slowly, inch by inch, until his mouth hovered over hers, capturing her breath as she exhaled.

Angling for a better position, he slanted his mouth over hers, increasing the pressure until her lips parted slightly. That was what he needed to stake his claim, his tongue meeting hers in a heated joining which raced through his body like the rush of molten lava.

He tasted her mouth tentatively, kissing every inch of it. Then, with a rush of uncontrollable desire, he devoured its sweetness like a child who had been deprived of candy for years.

Regina moved closer, shocked at her own eager response to the feel of his lips on hers as she returned his kiss with a reckless abandon she hadn't known she possessed.

He drew back to catch his breath and she collapsed against his chest, her fingers tangling in the fabric of his shirt. Not only had he heated her blood, but his repressed passion had scorched her soul.

"Please, let me go, Aaron." Her velvet voice came out in a breathless whisper.

Burying his face in her hair, he shook his head. "I don't want to—but I will." Releasing her, he stepped back, staring at her staring back at him. Passion had dilated her pupils, while her breasts rose and fell over her narrow rib cage.

"Aaron—"

"It's all right, *Princesa,*" he crooned, interrupting her with a knowing smile. "If you don't want me to kiss you again I won't."

Her lids fluttered in confusion. "I didn't say I didn't want you to kiss me."

Crossing his arms over his chest, his gaze narrowed. "Then what is it?"

"I want you to check on the chicken. I can't abide burnt food." He stared at her, complete surprise freezing his features. "If you're not going to help me, then get out of my kitchen," she challenged, pushing him aside to open the oven door.

He laughed, the sound exploding from his throat, as he watched her turn over pieces of chicken with a long-handled fork. His hungry gaze devoured her slim body in the revealing jeans, his laughter fading when she turned and glared at him.

"What's so funny?"

He sobered. "How can you turn your emotions on and off like a faucet? You kiss me passionately, and then in the same breath you talk about checking on the chicken."

"I can kiss you passionately because I've been trained to turn on the passion. You keep forgetting that I was an actress."

His eyes widened, anger glimmering in their dark depths. "Are you saying that what we've just shared was an *act?*"

Rising on tiptoe, she pressed her mouth to his. "That's for me to know, and for you to find out."

His arm snaked out and held her fast. "Don't play with me, Regina."

Leaning closer, she bared her straight, white teeth. "Or you'll do what, Aaron?" Their gazes fused, locking in a battle of wills where neither wanted to concede. *"¿Qué?"* she spat out.

She was asking him what he was going to do, and he couldn't come up with an answer. *"Nada,"* he replied in the same language. If she continued to tease him there was absolutely nothing he could or would do. He would take everything she threw at him until he won. And he would not stop until she was his wife.

Regina sat on the patio with Aaron, enjoying the warmth of the late summer night. It had cooled down considerably, and she lay on a chaise, staring up at the starlit sky.

Dinner had been a success, the gumbo flavorful and spicy from the piquant chili powder. She had prepared a side dish of savory white rice, with an accompanying avocado and orange salad, and baked a small loaf of Rosa's homemade bread. Her beverage was iced tea, while Aaron had opted for a frozen citrus fruit drink.

"How about a walk?" he asked lazily, his voice floating above as he stood over her.

Extending her hand, she permitted him to pull her to her feet. "I ate too much."

"You don't eat enough."

"I do eat," she protested.

"Not enough," he argued softly.

"Do I look anorexic to you?"

"No." And she didn't. Her height and narrow hips made her appear much slimmer than she actually was. He glanced down at her sandals. "Do you want to go into the house and change your shoes?"

She smiled up at him through her lashes. "Where are you taking me?"

He shrugged a shoulder. "Nowhere in particular."

"I'll keep the sandals on."

After cooking, both had retreated to their bedrooms, where they showered and changed. Aaron had exchanged his jeans and T-shirt for a pair of khakis, a matching shirt, and a pair of woven leather loafers, while she opted for a red silk shell, matching slim skirt, and leather sandals.

Aaron was transfixed by the rich color contrasting with her golden-brown flesh. Of all of the colors he had seen her wear, he preferred her in red.

Taking her hand, he led her down the patio, across the courtyard, and toward the garden. A half-moon lit up the clear sky, providing a modicum of light along with the lanterns strung around the perimeter of the courtyard and along the path leading to the garden.

The brush of flying insects on their exposed flesh, the sounds of scurrying night creatures, and the cloying fragrance of blooming flowers hung heavily in the air, and the more they ventured into the garden the closer Regina pressed against Aaron's body. He felt the slight trembling of her hand as they left the light behind and were swallowed up by a blanketing darkness.

"What is it?" he whispered at the same time she turned and clutched at his clothes in a desperate clawing that quickened his pulse.

"Take me back," she gasped frantically, hyperventilating.

"Where, *Princesa?*"

"Back to the light!"

Her trembling increased until she shook uncontrollably. Bending slightly, he swept her up effortlessly in his arms and retraced their steps, not stopping until he mounted the staircase and placed her on the large bed in his bedroom.

Turning on a bedside lamp, he sat down beside her, counting

the beats of her runaway pulse. It was as fast as if she had run a grueling race. Leaving the bed, he walked into the adjoining bathroom and returned within minutes with a cool cloth, placing it over her moist forehead.

Tears leaked from under her eyelids as she cried silently, praying for the demons to flee and leave her in peace. Even after seventeen years they refused to relinquish their hold on her mind.

Running his fingertips over her moist cheeks, Aaron leaned down and pressed a healing kiss on her mouth. "It's all right, *Princesa.* I'm here for you," he crooned, hoping to calm her.

"They won't leave me in peace," she cried, burying her face against his strong throat. "After so many years they still come back to haunt me."

"Tell me about it, Baby."

Opening her eyes, she stared up at his dark, handsome face through her tears. Would he understand? Would he laugh at her for something she should have gotten over years ago?

"I'm afraid of the dark," she whispered.

He gave her a tender smile, nodding. "Go on, Baby," he urged in a quiet tone.

"It happened a week before I turned ten."

"Go on, Baby," he repeated when she hesitated.

"I was kidnapped."

Lowering his head, Aaron pressed his lips to the side of her scented neck, cursing to himself. Didn't her family know how to protect their children? Why weren't they aware that their children were the most vulnerable when it came to kidnapping and extortion?

"Can you tell me about it?"

She nodded, savoring his warmth, strength, and protection.

CHAPTER 12

"My parents left me with my grandparents in West Palm Beach for a few days so I could visit my cousins, who lived in Palm Beach. My aunt Nancy asked me to sleep over at her house, but I decided to stay with my grandmother and grandfather because one of their pedigreed cocker spaniels had delivered a litter of puppies. I remembering sitting on a stool in a gardening shed watching them, but I can't remember any of what happened next."

"You don't know who abducted you?"

She shook her head. "No. The only thing I remembered was waking up in a locked closet and pounding on the door until my hands were swollen. And when I pleaded to be let out to use the bathroom, I was gagged and blindfolded. Someone watched me whenever I had to relieve myself to make certain I would not remove the blindfold."

"Was it a man or a woman?"

Her face burned in remembrance. "It was always a man. Each time I was let out of the closet to eat or use the bathroom I was blindfolded."

"How did you manage to see to eat?"

"I didn't. They bound my hands behind my back and fed me."

Aaron's shock turned to a white-hot fury as he listened to the horror no one—especially a nine-year-old child—should have had to endure.

"How long were you held captive?"

Sighing heavily, she mumbled, "Six days."

Shifting, he eased her over his body, his arms tightening protectively around her waist. "What happened after that?" His voice was soft, coaxing.

"My uncle and his friend found me. They made it seem as if it had been a game where they had to rescue me, and somehow I managed to repress the entire incident until I returned to Florida."

"Where did you go after the abduction?"

"Ocho Rios, Jamaica. My mother and I lived with my uncle for six months before we moved back to Florida with my father."

"Why did you move back?"

"My mother was pregnant, and she was experiencing complications, so my father moved us back to the States."

Running his hand over her hair, Aaron closed his eyes. She had relaxed so that her slow, even breathing was a soft whisper under his ear. He had wanted Regina in his arms and in his bed, but he hadn't wanted his role to be that of comforter.

"Is there anything else you want to tell me?"

"I used to wake up screaming, and it would take hours before the household would settle down after each episode. I stopped visiting my cousins because I didn't want them to know that I was afraid to sleep without a light on in the room. My parents sent me to a psychiatrist, who prescribed a very mild tranquilizer to help me sleep."

"I don't advocate medicating children."

"My father shares a similar belief. He took me to a prominent child psychologist who helped me work through most of my anxiety. I joined the drama club when I entered junior high school and found a way to escape completely. On stage and in character I did not have to be Regina Cole, but could be anyone I chose to be."

"Are you saying that acting became a form of therapy for you?"

"It *was* my therapy. As Regina I was always looking over my shoulder, wondering who was following me. But on stage I was

Hamlet's Ophelia or Othello's Desdemona, with nothing to fear except the audience's reaction to my performance."

Sighing, she closed her eyes, feeling safer than she ever had in her life. She'd relived the entire ordeal in her head, and she was no longer afraid to allow the images to surface. They came back, rushing through her mind like frames of film—the suffocating darkness, the blind humiliation of someone watching her relieve herself, and the macabre laugh whenever the food shoved into her mouth dribbled down her chin onto her soiled clothing. She had slept in the small, dark space with only the smell of her unwashed body to remind her that she still lived.

"You're safe now, *Princesa.*"

Smiling, she nodded against his chest. "I know, Aaron."

They lay together, their breathing deepening until they fell asleep, entwined in each other's arms.

Regina woke up in complete darkness, her heart racing. She was wrong. The demons hadn't left. They had vanished when she related her abduction and captivity to Aaron, but once the lights were extinguished they'd come back like a silent, creeping fog blanketing her sanity. The humming began, low and seductive until it grew louder and louder, becoming hysterical screams which sounded like someone being tortured.

"Help her," she pleaded as tears flooded her eyes and stained her cheeks. "Oh, please help her. Don't leave her to die in there."

Aaron came awake immediately. He sat up, reaching out for Regina, who thrashed wildly on the bed. Holding her firmly against his body, he pressed his mouth to her ear.

"They're gone, Regina," he crooned. "They can't hurt you."

"They—they're still here." She sobbed uncontrollably. "They want to kill me."

Stroking her hair, he shook his head. "No, Baby. They can't get you because I won't let them. Didn't I promise to protect you?"

Regina heard the man's deep, soothing voice and the demons fled, leaving her in peace. The voice sounded familiar. At first she thought it was her father's, but it did not have the soft, drawling cadence that identified Martin Cole was from the southern region of the United States. This voice was more nasal, claiming a midwest twang. As a drama student she had studied accents and regional dialects, and there was a time when she could identify the country or region of anyone who opened their mouths to speak.

She inhaled deeply, identifying the now familiar cologne worn by Aaron Spencer. Then she remembered. She was in Aaron's bedroom, and in his bed.

"Aaron." His name came out in a long, shuddering whisper.

"I'm here," he whispered. "I'm here for you."

"Turn on the light."

He continued stroking her hair, his hand moving over the curls spiraling around his fingers. "No, Baby."

Her breathing quickened. "Please." She managed to swallow a sob.

"Nothing's going to happen to you in the dark."

"Take me back to my room." There was no mistaking her rising anxiety as her trembling voice broke.

"No. You're going to spend the night with me, and when the sun comes up you'll realize—"

"Take me back now!" she shouted, interrupting him.

Aaron tightened his hold on her waist as she tried escaping his grip. "No, Regina."

Her right hand came up, but he was too quick for her. His fingers caught her wrist, holding her with a minimal of effort. "Don't fight with me," he warned between clenched teeth. "I promised you I would take care of you, and I will," he continued, this time in a softer voice. "I won't let anyone or anything hurt you." He felt some of the rigidness leave her limbs. "My father protected you and, like him, I'll also protect you. You trusted Oscar, didn't you?"

Biting down on her lower lip, she nodded. After a pause, she said, "Yes."

"I'm his son, *Princesa*. Blood of his blood and flesh of his flesh. And I've taken an oath that I will protect you the same way he did when he was alive. If I never ask anything of you, I'm going to ask that you trust me."

Regina half-listened to Aaron as she struggled with the lingering vestiges of her fear. How could she vanquish seventeen years of fear in one night? Could she actually trust Aaron to protect her from her unseen enemies? He could not spend the rest of his life looking after her. He had promised to remain in Mexico with her until she left for the States, but had he hoped he could help eradicate the fears she had carried for more than half her life in less than a month? What did he intend to do—sleep with her every night?

She could demand that he let her return to her bedroom, but something told her Aaron Spencer would not relent. He was determined to force her to remain in his bed, and in the darkened bedroom.

Going completely pliant in his arms, she curved her body into his. "I'll try."

He let out an audible sigh. "Thank you."

They lay together, monitoring each other's heat and respiration. Aaron had removed only his shoes, but Regina felt every muscle of his body as if he were completely nude. Lying in his embrace made her aware of the solid hardness of his chest and thighs, the power in his upper arms, and the unleashed strength in his large hands.

What was she doing? She was sharing a bed with a man whom she desired from the moment she saw him. There was something so subtly virile about Aaron Spencer that the times she caught herself staring at him she found it difficult to draw a normal breath.

Whenever he caught her staring, he did not look away but returned it boldly with one of his own. She had come to look for the intensity in his dark, deep-set, slanting eyes, wondering what was he thinking. And she did wonder if he knew how much she wanted him, and that the wanting was of a physical nature.

Resting her head on his thick shoulder, she closed her eyes. The demons had finally left her, and in their place was a deep, silent longing to know what it was that made her crave the man holding her to his heart.

Her breathing deepened in a slow, measured rhythm, belaying the rush of desire racing headlong throughout her body as the realization washed over her again that she wanted Aaron to make love to her. She wanted him to introduce her to a world of passion she had never known.

She had never known or glimpsed passion—not even when her two movie roles called for on-screen lovemaking with handsome and very popular male co-stars.

Turning to her right, she pressed a light kiss at the side of his strong mouth, eliciting a slight intake of breath from him. "Thank you for being here for me."

Aaron smiled, lowering his head until his lips were inches from hers. "You're very welcome," he murmured seconds before his mouth closed over hers.

What had begun as a gentle brushing of lips deepened until Aaron moved over her body, pressing her down to the mattress so that there was a sweet, deep intimacy to their kiss.

He felt the blood pool in his groin, and knew he was lost. The desire he had fought from the instant he saw Regina Cole-Spencer exploded uncontrollably until he was shaking from the passion, struggling not to erupt and embarrass himself. He did not want to pour out his passions on the bed, but inside of the woman writhing under him.

Pulling back, he buried his face in her unbound hair, which spread out on the pillow in a cascade of black, silken curls. *"Princesa,"* he groaned as if in pain.

"Aaron?" She answered his groan with her own moan.

"I don't want to take advantage of you. Tell me now if you want to take this further."

Her breath was coming faster. "And if I say I don't?"

"Then I'll stop."

A haze of passion swept over Regina, her mind reeling in confusion. Her body wanted Aaron, needed him, while she knew it was wrong to remain in his arms and in his bed. Could she sleep with him in the dark and not experience guilt in the full sunlight? Could she successfully affect indifference after sleeping with him when it came time for her to leave Mexico? What was it about Aaron Spencer that made her so wanton and so reckless? She knew the answers to all of her questions would come from offering herself to him.

Aaron did not want to stop. He wanted to take off her clothes, then his own, and feast on her body like a man dying of hunger and thirst. Making love to her would right all of the wrongs, heal all of the wounds, reconcile his past with his present.

She's your father's widow, a silent voice reminded him. She might be Oscar's widow, but Regina Spencer was the woman he had fallen in love with—the woman who had bewitched him, the woman who challenged him to his face, and still he wanted and desired her, the woman who warned him that whatever they might share in Mexico would become a part of their past and remain their past.

He cradled her face gently between his large hands. "What is it going to be?" he whispered against her parted lips. "Yes or no?"

Regina closed her eyes, knowing he couldn't see her expression in the darkness. The heat flooding her breasts increased, sweeping down and settling between her thighs while bringing a fiery heat that made it impossible for her to remain motionless. At the same time, she felt Aaron's surging hardness throbbing against her thighs. It was too late. Too late for her retreat. It was too late for both of them.

"Yes!" she gasped.

She wasn't certain of what was happening as everything fused into a slow-moving act which made her feel as if she were an observer instead of a participant.

Aaron left the bed and removed his clothes, she listening to the whisper of fabric grazing his skin as he took off his shirt, slacks, and briefs. He returned to the bed, the heat of his muscled physique enveloping her when he relieved her of the dress and the delicate scrap of silk concealing her virginal body.

She hadn't realized that she had been holding her breath until after he had pulled her into a tender embrace where her nakedness touched his, making her aware of how different their bodies were.

"Aaron?" Her voice was soft, tentative.

"Yes, *Princesa?*"

Swallowing several times to relieve the sudden dryness in her throat, she wondered how was she going to tell him that it was her first time, that she had never shared her body with a man.

"You're going to have to help me with this." Her fingers were splayed over his chest. "You're going to have to show me how to please you."

He pressed a kiss to her forehead, smiling. "You don't have to do anything. You please me because I'm here with you. You please me just by existing."

That was not what she meant, but he did not give her the opportunity to explain herself when he took possession of her mouth in a slow, drugging kiss that elicited a rush of moisture between her thighs. She squeezed them together to stop the pulsing, but to no avail. His mouth moved lower, to her breasts, and she was lost, lost in a maelstrom of desire which set her aflame with a surge of desire that shattered her dammed-up sexuality.

Regina had tried many times to imagine a man actually making love to her, and failed miserably. When she had executed her love scenes in *Silent Witness,* Oscar had outlined explicitly what he wanted from her and her co-star. She had enacted the scenes like the professional she had been trained to be, but she had felt none of the responses Aaron now wrung from her.

The heat from his mouth swept from her own mouth to her core. Waves of passion shook her until she could not stop her legs from shaking. He suckled her breasts, worshiping them, and the moans she sought to suppress escaped her parted lips.

His tongue circled her nipples, leaving them hard, erect, and throbbing. His teeth tightened on the turgid tips, and she felt a violent spasm grip her womb.

Her fingers were entwined in the cotton sheets, tightening and ripping them from their fastenings at the same time she arched up off the mattress.

"Aaron!" His name exploded from her mouth as he inched down her body, holding her hips to still their thrashing. Shame replaced her passion when she realized where he had buried his face. "Stop! Please!"

But he did not stop. His hot breath seared the tangled curls between her thighs and she went limp, unable to protest or think of anything except the pleasure her lover offered her. She registered a series of breathless sighs, not realizing they were her own moans of physical satisfaction. Eyes closed, head thrown back, lips parted, back arched, she reveled in the sensations that took her beyond herself.

Then it began, rippling little tremors increasing and shaking her uncontrollably and becoming more volatile when it sought a route of escape.

Aaron heard her breath come in long, surrendering moans, and he moved quickly up her trembling limbs and eased his sex into her body. He was met with a resistance he hadn't expected. Gritting his teeth, he feared spilling his passion onto the sheets. He drew back, and with a strong, sure thrust of his hips buried his hardness in the hot, moist, tight flesh pulsing around his own.

Regina caught and held her breath, feeling if she had been impaled on a red-hot piece of steel when Aaron penetrated her virginal flesh, but the burning subsided the moment he began moving in a slow, measured rhythm, quickly renewing her passion.

Her arms curved around his waist as rivulets of moisture bathed his back and dotted her hands. She could not think of anything or anyone except the hard body atop hers as their bodies found and set a rhythm where they were in perfect harmony with each other.

Reaching down, Aaron cupped her hips in his hands, lifting her higher and permitting deeper penetration; he quickened his movements. Regina assisted him, increasing her own pleasure as she wound her legs around his waist.

Aaron's heat, hardness, and carnal sensuality had awakened the dormant sexuality of her body, and she responded to the seduction of his passion as hers rose higher and higher until it exploded in an awesome, vibrating liquid fire that scorched her mind and left her convulsing in ecstasy.

She hadn't quite returned from her own free-fall flight when she heard Aaron's groan of satisfaction against her ear as he quickened his movements and then collapsed heavily on her sated form. There was only the sound of their labored breathing in the stillness of the bedroom as they lay motionless, savoring the aftermath of a shared, sweet fulfillment.

He reversed their positions, bringing her with him until she lay sprawled over his body, her legs resting between his. "Did I hurt you, *Princesa?*"

"No," she drawled, placing tiny kisses on his throat and over his shoulder. There had been pain, but it was offset by the pleasure he had offered her.

"I hadn't expected you to be so small," he murmured in the cloud of curly hair flowing over his face. "I—"

She stopped his words when she placed her fingertips over his lips. "I'm all right, Aaron."

His right hand moved over her bare hip, caressing the silken flesh. She had no idea how sensuous her voice sounded in the dark. He drew in a deep breath, luxuriating in the intoxicating fragrance of her perfume mingling with the lingering scent of their lovemaking.

He could not believe the passion she had aroused in him; if possible, he had wanted to make love to her all through the night. Inhaling her scent, tasting her flesh, caressing her silken body, had tested the limits of his control. He smiled, knowing there was the possibility that he would make love to her many more times before they left Mexico. He did not want to think about her leaving, even though she had promised to come to Bahia.

If she did not come to him, then he would come for her. Now that Regina Cole-Spencer had become a part of his existence, he had no intention of letting her walk out of his life.

CHAPTER 13

Regina turned over, encountering an immovable bulk, and woke up. Realization dawned as she stared up at Aaron staring down at her. A gentle smile softened her lush mouth.

"¡Buenos dias!" she whispered shyly.

Slanting eyes crinkling attractively, he returned her smile. *"Bom dia,"* he replied in Portuguese. Shifting to his side, he placed an arm over her flat middle, pulling her closer. "How do you feel?" he continued in English.

She shrugged a slender shoulder. "Okay."

He arched a sweeping eyebrow. "Just okay?"

"Yes. Why?"

His expression sobered as he glared at her. "Why didn't you tell me you were a virgin?"

When he awoke earlier that morning he had noticed the dark-red stains on the sheet. He had felt as if someone had punched him in his gut once he realized the woman sharing his bed had given him the most precious gift any woman could offer a man. His eyes clung to hers, analyzing her reaction to his accusation. He should not have been surprised when she did not flinch or glance away.

"I tried to tell you," she argued softly.

He frowned. "You didn't try hard enough."

"But I did. I asked for your help."

"Asking for help is not the same as saying that you'd never slept with a man." She lowered her gaze and stared at his smooth, bare chest. "You were married for eight years, *Princesa.*"

"Oscar and I never shared a bed. Our marriage was in name only."

Anchoring his hand under her chin, he raised her face to his. "Why couldn't you have told me that?"

A slight frown furrowed her smooth forehead. "I told you everything I wanted you to know. What did or did not occur between Oscar and me in the bedroom was of too personal a nature to discuss with anyone. Even you."

"You're right—as usual," he conceded.

Curving her arms around his neck, she pressed her breasts against the solid wall of his broad chest, smiling when he gasped audibly.

"I'm going back to my bedroom to shower," she said quietly. "I'll see you later."

Aaron wanted to beg her to stay, stay with him until thirst, hunger, or the need to relieve himself drove him from her scented arms, but didn't. He knew it would be several days before they would make love again. He would wait for her tender flesh to heal before losing himself once again in the passion she evoked just by them sharing the same space.

Three weeks sped by as quickly as in a blink of the eye for Regina.

She and Aaron waited two nights after their initial passionate joining before sharing a bed again, while at the same time dreading the moment when they would be forced to part.

The courier her father had promised to send arrived in Mexico and escorted the fourteen paintings back to the States for safekeeping within days of their telephone conversation; the documents setting up the accounts for the Oscar and Arlene Spencer Foundation for Medical Research and *El Cielo*'s employees were finalized; all of her valuables and personal heirloom pieces were packed and shipped to her parents' home to await her arrival.

She spent her last night in Mexico in her garden, sitting on the stone bench facing Oscar's grave. Closing her eyes, she fought back tears. She was leaving her husband, not knowing when or if she would ever return.

"I'm leaving tomorrow morning, Oscar," she whispered. "I'm finally going home." Biting down on her lower lip, she forced a trembling smile. *I love you,* she added silently. She loved him, and she also had fallen in love with his son, and she was mature enough to realize her love for Aaron had nothing to do with their sexual encounters.

The days and nights when they did not make love offered her a modicum of objectivity. She craved his passion, that she would not deny, but she also treasured his companionship. But even more than passion or companionship, it was his protection she desired. She was able to sleep alongside him in an unlit room without waking up drenched in sweat or with tortured screams exploding from the back of her throat. The few times she whimpered in her sleep, he woke her with a gentle caress and whispered soothing, gentle words to reassure her that she had nothing to fear.

She would leave Mexico in the morning, reunite with her family, remain in Florida through the end of the year, and then perhaps take Aaron up on his offer to visit with him in Brazil.

Aaron stood on the second-story veranda outside his bedroom, staring down at the slender figure sitting by his father's grave. It was a sight he had grown accustomed to since he had come to *El Cielo,* and it was a sight that wrang a gamut of emotions from him. It saddened him to know he would never see, touch, or speak to Oscar again. The sight also rankled him, because for the second time in his life a woman he had fallen in love with also loved his father.

He lost track of time as he rested his arms on the wrought-iron railing, reliving the events of the past month. The past five weeks had changed him. Since he had become involved with the *São Tomé Instituto de Médico Pesquisa* he had never been away from his research for more than three weeks. Since becoming the director he had found himself traveling throughout the world at least twice each year to attend medical symposiums to share the institute's theories with others in his field of study. Medical research had been his passion for more than twelve years—until now.

Now his passion was Regina Spencer.

Regina said her final goodbye to Oscar and returned to the house to prepare for her last night on Mexican soil. The household was quiet, and all of the permanent household staff conspicuously absent. They had said their final farewells after the evening meal. The driver was scheduled to drive her and Aaron to the airport in Mexico City. He would board an early morning flight for Salvador, Brazil, while she awaited the arrival of the ColeDiz Gulfstream jet from the West Palm Beach airport.

Her footsteps were slow and sure as she climbed the staircase. She felt a heaviness in her chest which would not permit her to breathe normally. Swallowing back a wave of anxiety, she drew herself up straighter and visually examined everything around her, committing it to memory.

She would miss *El Cielo,* her garden, and the employees who had become her extended family. She refused to think of missing Aaron, because she had become too dependent on him. They had agreed not to spend their last night together.

Pushing open the door to her bedroom, she walked in and stopped abruptly as Aaron rose from the chair beside her bed. Her eyes widened when she saw an emotion in his dark gaze that was indefinable.

"What are you doing here?" Her voice was a low, breathless whisper. "We agreed not to see each other until—"

"*You* agreed," he interrupted, visibly annoyed that he had gone along with her plea. "Do you think it would make it any easier to say goodbye at the airport?"

"Yes, Aaron, it would." She threw up her hands in a gesture signaling hopelessness. "Why do you think I suggested it?"

His gaze narrowed as he moved towards her with the slow,

stalking walk she had come to love. There were so many things about Aaron that she loved that she had lost count.

Reaching for her, he held her upper arms and pulled her to his chest. "I think you suggested it because you want to avoid what is going to happen right now."

She tilted her chin, giving him a direct stare. "And that is?"

"Not wanting to hear the truth."

"And what is the truth, Aaron?"

He studied her thoughtfully, his eyes betraying his innermost feelings and telling her what she knew before he uttered the words. "I love you."

Closing her eyes, she swayed slightly at the same time he tightened his grip. "Don't."

"Don't what? Don't love you? I'm sorry, *Princesa,* but I can't turn my feelings on and off the way you're able to."

She opened her eyes and glared at him. "Go away! Please," she continued in a softer tone.

He shook his head slowly. "No, Regina. Any other time I would oblige you, but not tonight."

Pulling out of his loose grip, she turned and walked out of the bedroom. She hadn't gone more than ten feet when he caught up with her.

"Why are you running away?"

She turned to face him. "I'm not running away. I just need to be alone."

The flash of anger in his dark eyes vanished, replaced by a tenderness that twisted her insides into knots. He loved her, while she was too much of a coward to let him know that she loved him.

She laid her hand alongside his jaw, feeling the throbbing muscles under her fingertips. "I'll come to you later."

Grasping her hand, he brought it to his lips and kissed each finger, his gaze never leaving hers. Bending over, he brushed his lips over hers. "I'll be waiting."

He released her hand, turning and walking down the hallway in the direction of his bedroom.

* * *

Aaron lay on the bed, arms folded under his head. He hadn't turned on the lamp because the eerie, silvered light of a full moon lit up the bedroom. He had told Regina he would wait for her, and now he had lost track of time, and still she had not come.

Closing his eyes, he felt a lump form in his throat. He had told her he loved her, and she recoiled as if he had struck her. *Fool!* He had been a fool to let her know how he felt. What was the matter with him when it came to affairs of the heart? Why was it he couldn't select a woman who would love him as much as he loved her? The whys attacked him relentlessly until he relaxed enough to fall asleep.

Within seconds something shook him into awareness. He detected the familiar, rain-washed fragrance, then the silken touch of her body as she moved beside him on the bed. Regina had come to him, as promised. She would spend the night with him.

"Please love me, Aaron." Her husky plea broke the pregnant silence.

And he would love her. He would make their last night together special. Moving over her naked form and supporting his greater weight on his arms, he cradled her face between his hands.

"This is not goodbye," he crooned seconds before he covered her mouth in a hungry, soul-searching kiss that indicated they would not be satisfied with a prolonged session of foreplay.

Aaron was relentless when he branded her throat, breasts, and her inner thighs with a passion which would linger in her memory during their separation. His rapacious mouth charted a path from her lips to her feet. Just when she recovered from one shock, she was assailed with another.

Her soft moans of pleasure escalated into long, surrendering groans, with a rising heat rippling under her skin. Her whole being was flooded with a desire that sucked her into an abyss of abandoned ecstasy.

She reached for him, hoping to capture the source which would end her erotic torment. She wanted his hardness in her; she needed him to relieve the burning ache which threatened to shatter her into pieces so that she would never be whole again.

Aaron felt her fingers close around his engorged sex, and groaned aloud. Pulling away from her, he picked up the packet on the bedside table. Making certain to protect her, he eased himself into her wet, hot body.

It became a battle of wills, neither willing to succumb to the explosive passion sweeping them beyond themselves. Tightening his grip on her waist, he reversed their positions, hoping to prolong his ecstasy. But it was not to be. The caress of her distended nipples on his chest, and the vision of her perfectly formed breasts in the full moonlight weakened his resolve, and he surrendered to the explosive passions sweeping him to a place where he had never been.

The triumphant growl of fulfillment floating up from Aaron's throat sent a shiver of chills down Regina's spine, and within seconds she, too, gave in to the hot tide of passion buffeting her up, down, and around until she collapsed on his body, weeping uncontrollably.

He reversed their positions again, withdrawing from her trembling body. Gathering her to his chest, he held her until her sobs subsided, then buried his face in her hair. A pain he had never known assailed him when he realized he had deluded himself. He could not leave her; he would not leave her.

Aaron woke up two hours before dawn reaching for Regina, but encountered an empty space where she had been. Sitting up, he reached for the lamp. Light flooded the room, revealing an envelope on the pillow where her head had lain only hours before. His hand was steady when he picked up the envelope and withdrew its contents. A check for his research institute was nestled between the folds of a single sheet of pale-blue parchment stationery.

He ignored the check as his gaze raced quickly over the neatly slanting script on the page embossed with her monogram. *Do not try to contact me. Please be patient. I will come to you. Regina.*

Closing his eyes, he slumped back against the pillows cradling his broad shoulders. She had ended it with three sentences, and her name. He opened his eyes, and the lethal calmness flowing from their depths matched the hardness of his unreadable expression.

He would not contact her. Not now. Not ever.

CHAPTER 14

Regina walked onto the tarmac of the private airstrip at the Mexico City airport, smiling broadly when she saw her father alight from the sleek corporate jet. He had come to take her back.

Racing into his outstretched arms, she flung herself against his solid body, reveling in his protective embrace. "Daddy, Daddy," she murmured over and over as she placed tiny kisses on his chin and jaw.

Martin Cole tightened his grip on his daughter's narrow waist, swinging her up into his arms and carrying her up the steps into the jet. He struggled to control his own emotions when he realized he finally was going to get his firstborn back after a ten-year absence. She was only twenty-seven, but it seemed as if they had been separated more than they had been together.

She had called him crying uncontrollably at 2:00 a.m. Eastern Time, begging him to come and get her. He couldn't understand her need to leave Mexico at that time, when the ColeDiz pilot was scheduled to meet her later that afternoon. He called the pilot, apologizing profusely for waking the man, then called the airstrip to have the jet fueled and ready for their departure within the hour.

They were now seated and belted inside the luxury aircraft. The pilot's voice came through the speakers. "Mr. Cole, I've been cleared for take-off."

Regina held her father's hand, sharing a dimpled smile with him. A casually dressed Martin Cole was breathtakingly handsome at fifty-seven. His close-cropped curly hair was a luminous silver, complementing his sun-browned, olive skin. Perusing his features reminded her that she was truly her father's child, because she had inherited his coloring, dimpled smile, curly hair, large dark eyes, sweeping black eyebrows, high cheekbones, thin delicate nose, and full sensual mouth. Her father was in the full throes of middle age, claiming a network of attractive lines at the corners of his expressive eyes whenever he smiled.

Shifting an eyebrow, he stared at her. "Why the nine-one-one phone call in the middle of the night, Cupcake?"

Pressing her head back against the plush seat, she closed her eyes. "The closer I came to leaving the more I panicked."

What she did not say was that if she had not left when she did, she would not have returned to Florida as promised. Her dependence on Aaron had grown so that she feared not being able to leave him.

"Are you saying you did not want to leave Mexico?"

She hesitated, holding her breath as the plane taxied down the runway before increasing its speed for a liftoff. "Is it ever easy to leave home?"

Martin frowned. "Florida is your home."

She opened her eyes and shook her head. "Florida *was* my home, Daddy. Why do you find it so difficult to accept that I'm an adult now? I was a wife for eight years, and ran my own household in a country I had come to regard as home."

Martin bit back the sharp retort poised on his tongue, leaning over and kissing her forehead. His daughter had experienced what most women twice her age hadn't had to undergo—caring for a sick, elderly husband. She was back, and he did not want to do or say anything that would force her to leave—at least, not for a while. He wanted to hold onto her, knowing instinctively that even though Regina had decided to return to Florida her stay would not be a permanent one.

"Why don't you try to get some sleep? You're going to need it, because I doubt whether you'll get much once everyone realizes you're back."

She closed her eyes, but did not sleep. She did not know why it had taken her ten years to realize home was not a country or a structure, but the people you loved. She loved her family, Oscar, and she had also fallen in love with Aaron.

Aaron was everything his father had been—gentle, considerate, protective, and more. The more was the passion he offered her—a passion that transported her beyond herself, where she felt free to exist without her childhood fears tormenting her.

A wry smile touched her mouth. She would wait until the new year, then travel to Bahia in time for Carnival.

Regina felt a swell of emotion fill her chest at the same time her father maneuvered his favored Jaguar sports coupe into the circular driveway of the sprawling Fort Lauderdale structure that claimed the Atlantic Ocean as its backyard.

She was out of the car before he turned off the ignition, rushing to the entrance to meet her younger sister. Arianna had grown at least another inch since she last saw her. Her parents, brother, and sister had come to visit her in Mexico for her twenty-seventh birthday in July, and while it hadn't been three months, the change in Arianna was startling. It was as if she had grown up overnight.

"Ari! Baby sister," Regina whispered, hugging her tightly and kissing her cheek.

Arianna sobbed softly, clinging to Regina as if she were her lifeline. "If you go away and leave me again, I'll kill myself."

Pulling back, Regina examined her sister's pained expression. Fourteen-year-old Arianna had inherited her parents' best features: towering height, slimness, rich, deep, golden-brown coloring, her mother's green-flecked brown eyes and her mouth, and her father's curly black hair, which she wore in a flattering short style. At five-eight, she hinted of a sensuality which was certain to short-circuit any teenage boy's nervous system.

"I don't want to hear you talk about killing yourself," she

admonished softly. "I just buried my husband, Ari. I came back here to reconnect with my family, not bury my only sister."

Arianna nodded quickly, forcing a tearful s mile. "I'm sorry."

"Where're Mommy and Tyler?"

"Tyler went out for a little while, and Mommy's in the house."

Martin Cole walked up to his daughters, his dark eyes shining with pride and happiness. He extended his arms at his sides. "May I escort my lovely princesses into the castle?"

Regina went completely still, staring at her father. *Princesa*. That was what Aaron had called her. She was thousands of miles from him, and still he haunted her.

"Is there something wrong?" Martin questioned.

Shaking her head quickly, she flashed a smile. "No. Not at all." Looping her arm through her father's, she walked into the home filled with both good and bad memories.

Parris Simmons-Cole lay on a chaise beside Regina, holding her hand tightly as they stared at the foam-flecked incoming tide. It had been a long time since she had all of her children together at the same time.

"You've aged me, Angel."

Regina stared at her mother, her mouth gaping. "You look beautiful. No one would take you for fifty."

And they wouldn't. Her mother's hair had grayed considerably, but her hair stylist had lightened some of the remaining dark brown strands, so the overall effect was that of a frosted look. Her flawless skin was smooth and completely wrinkle-free, and five years ago she had begun an intense exercise regimen that kept her slender body well-toned.

Parris closed her eyes behind her oversize sunglasses. "I'm not talking about how I look. It's how I feel. I've never hidden anything from you, so you know what I had to go through just to bring you into the world. Then I lost you for six days, and when I got you back I swore to myself that I would never let you go. But I had to let you go, or I would've spent the rest of my life hating myself if you did not fulfill your dream. It's not easy for a mother to let her firstborn go—especially since you were so young."

Squeezing her mother's fingers, Regina smiled at her. "But everything worked out, didn't it?"

Opening her eyes, Parris smiled and nodded. "Yes, it did. You made me very proud of you."

A shadow blocked out the strong rays of the early fall sun, and Regina glanced up to find her brother standing over her. She sat up quickly, offering him her hand. He pulled her up in one strong, swift motion.

"Tyler!"

Curving his arms around her waist, he picked her up, holding her aloft effortlessly, then released her. "Welcome home, Sis." He kissed her soundly on her mouth.

Staring at her brother, Regina's eyes were filled with pride as she visually examined Tyler Cole. At seventeen, he was as tall as his father, but claimed a lankiness that made him appear more delicate than he actually was. He flashed a rare smile, his dark eyes too serious for someone so young. He, too, had changed since she last saw him. She ran a hand over his head, feeling the stubble against her palm.

"What did you do, shave your head?"

He nodded. "I joined the swim team at school."

Regina wagged her head in amazement. "I don't believe it. The Coles have two swimmers in the family."

Tyler ducked his head, staring at his shoes. "Arianna swims to compete. I've starting swimming to build up muscle. I feel uncomfortable working out in a gym, so I felt swimming was the next best thing."

His head came up, and he stared down at his older sister. Taking her arm, he led her down to the beach and out of range of their mother's hearing.

"How long are you going to hang around this time?"

"Tyler!" she whispered.

"Answer my question, Regina."

"I can't, because I don't know."

"You can't imagine what Arianna and I have had to go through the past ten years."

Her body stiffened in shock. "What are you talking about?"

"Mom and Dad have us on lockdown. They've tightened the reins so much that we feel like we're under house arrest. They lost you and—"

"They didn't lose me," she countered angrily. "I graduated and I moved away. You still have another year before you complete high school, and Ari has four."

"But you were only sixteen," he argued.

"They could've stopped me if they'd wanted to."

"But they didn't."

"So, what's your beef?"

"My *beef* is that I'm not allowed to apply to colleges out of the state. I want to be a doctor, Regina, and for that I want to go to a college where I can get the best medical training available. And in case you aren't aware of it, Meharry, Harvard, Stanford, and Yale don't have campuses in Florida."

Resting her hands on her hips, she shifted her eyebrows. "So, you really want a career in medicine?" Tyler nodded. "Have you taken your SATs?"

"I took the PSATs last semester."

"What were your scores?"

"I managed a combined score of over fifteen hundred."

She smiled. "My brother, the genius."

"Uncle Josh is the genius in the family. I just study my butt off, that's all."

She sobered quickly. "I had no idea what you and Ari were going through. When you came to Mexico to visit me, why didn't you say something?"

He shrugged his shoulders. "I don't know."

"I'll talk to Daddy about this. I won't let him know that I spoke to you. I'll bring it up casually, and feel him out."

Tyler gave her a wide smile for the first time. "Will you?"

"Of course. And what does Ari want?"

"She wants to be an Olympic swimmer. She's fast," he added quickly. "Very, very fast. Her coach had her try out for a possible spot on the team, and she beat everyone in the one- and two-hundred-meter freestyle competition. You should see her in the four-hundred-meter relay. She's awesome!"

Curving an arm around her brother's waist, she rested her head against his shoulder. "Narrow down the college of your choice, then give me a couple of weeks to see what I can do."

Regina had been in Florida exactly two weeks when she was finally reunited with the entire Cole clan, who had increased appreciably in her absence. Four generations gathered at the family estate in West Palm Beach early one Saturday afternoon.

Her uncle Joshua Kirkland and his wife Vanessa had flown in from Santa Fe, New Mexico, with their son and daughter. Emily had turned twelve, and Michael was now eight. Both children had inherited their father's electric green eyes.

Music producer David Cole and his nurse-wife Serena had doubled their family with a set of twins. Ana and Jason, who had celebrated their first birthday on September twenty-third, joined their older brother and sister, eight-year-old Gabriel and six-year-old Alexandra, adding to the never-ending activity going on at their Boca Raton beachfront home.

Her aunts, Nancy Cole-Thomas and Josephine Cole-Wilson, were grandparents, claiming a half-dozen grandchildren between them. Her grandmother, Marguerite Josephine Diaz-Cole, the family matriarch, had managed to maintain her regal beauty at seventy-eight, while M.J.'s husband of nearly sixty years exhibited signs of aging poorly with his declining health. Samuel Claridge Cole was now eighty-five, and most times now was confined to his bed. A debilitating stroke had left him with limited use of his right arm and leg.

Cradling the twins on either hip, Regina walked across the

expansive lawn where everyone lounged under a large tent to escape the harmful rays of the intense Florida sunshine.

Emily Kirkland approached her, holding out her arms. "I'll take one."

Regina handed her Jason, then cradled Ana to her chest, but the child squirmed uncomfortably in her arms. She smiled at the tiny girl, and much to her surprise Ana returned her smile. She was the image of her father, with the exception of her eyes. Ana, along with all of Serena and David's children, claimed their mother's clear brown eyes and their father's dimpled smile.

"I'll take her if she's too heavy for you."

Turning around, Regina smiled at Serena. "I don't mind holding her. It's time this little princess and I became better acquainted with each other."

"Why don't you come back to Boca with us tonight, and hang out for a couple of days? David and I would love to have you," she added when Regina hesitated.

"You, Uncle David, or Alex?"

Petite Serena Morris-Cole ran a hand through the profusion of short reddish-brown curls sticking to her moist forehead, flashing a knowing smile. She had recently celebrated her thirty-ninth birthday and had given birth to four children, yet could easily pass for someone in her late twenties.

"It's Alexandra. Ever since she realized her cousin was, as she says, 'a moo-vee star' she's been bugging me to ask you if you would come and tell her about your acting career."

"Doesn't the child know I only have two films to my credit?"

"Tell that to a six-year-old."

"I can't go back with you tonight. Arianna and I have plans to do some shopping in the morning. What I'll do is come up to Boca during the week and stay for a few days."

Regina handed Ana to her mother, then spent the next four hours relaxing, eating, laughing, and interacting with her many cousins. Everyone waited for their food to settle before they retreated to the pool house to change into swimwear.

Arianna and Tyler stood at the edge of the Olympic-size pool, their arms hanging limply at their sides as an eerie hush settled over the assembly. Regina glanced at her parents, who stood together, arms around each other. She smiled behind the lenses of her sunglasses, but at the same time an emotion she identified as jealousy welled up in her chest.

Her parents were still in love, and the man she had fallen in love with was thousands of miles away. She had seen Martin and Parris's furtive glances when they did not think she noticed, and on more than one occasion she saw her father caress her mother's body in a way that made her feel she was spying on them. Parris Simmons had been twenty-two when she met Martin Cole for the first time, but had to wait ten years before she could claim him as her husband and a father for her daughter.

Closing her eyes briefly, she tried imagining it was Aaron she had been married to, and not his father. Instead of becoming Oscar Spencer's widow she would be Aaron Spencer's wife, and probably the mother of his child or children. She opened her eyes, frowning. She did not want to think about Aaron, any more than she wanted to love him.

All thoughts of him vanished as she watched her brother and sister dive into the pool. Moving closer, she was transfixed by the form and speed of Arianna as she sliced through the water like a silent torpedo. There was complete silence, everyone watching her swim to the opposite end of the pool, turn, then push off to return. Arianna was halfway across the pool before her brother made his turn.

David Cole extended a hand to his niece, helping her from the water, and handing her a towel. He shook his head in amazement. "Martin, are you certain your daughter doesn't have webbed feet?" he teased with an attractive, lopsided smile.

Arianna blotted water from her short hair, grinning broadly. "Anyone want to race?" Despite the exertion, she was breathing normally. She pointed to her uncle with the silver-blond hair. "How about it, Uncle Josh?"

Joshua Kirkland waved a delicate hand. "Too full."

She snapped the towel in his direction. "Too full, or too frightened?"

Joshua gave her a warm smile. "Too old," he confirmed. "Why don't you challenge some of the younger guys?"

Arianna stalked her young male cousins. "Come on, guys. Don't tell me you're scared of a *girl?*" She encountered silence.

Nancy Cole-Thomas leaned over and whispered in her youngest son's ear and he stepped forward, pulling his T-shirt over his head.

The setting sun glinted off his brown back. "Let's go, Ari," he challenged. He didn't fare any better than Tyler. She beat him by an even larger margin.

Regina saw the exhibition of Arianna's prowess as the perfect opportunity to approach her parents. Moving next to her father, she wound her arm through his free one.

"Ari has the makings of a world-class champion," she said softly.

Martin arched his eyebrows, his impassive expression never changing. "You think so?"

"I *know* so, Daddy."

"What are you suggesting, Cupcake?"

"You should let her compete."

"She does compete."

"She competes locally. That's not enough."

Turning his head, he stared down her, meeting her direct stare. "Say what's on your mind."

"She needs to follow her dream, Daddy. And that dream is to make the next Olympic team."

"You think she could make it?"

"I *know* she could. Think of the publicity she would get, too, being an African-American swimmer instead of a runner, gymnast, or a basketball player in the upcoming summer games."

"That would mean that she would travel with the swim team and—"

"She would be away for a while, but she would always come back home," Regina interrupted. "I did," she added quietly.

Curving his arm around his daughter's waist, Martin pulled her closer and kissed the top of her head. "You're right, Cupcake. You did come back home."

Closing her eyes, Regina prayed for strength. She knew her stay in Florida was to become a short one—she doubted whether she would stay until the end of the year. She had tried filling her days and nights with activity when she redesigned her mother's flower garden and spent hours in her grandparents' formal gardens, but when she least expected it remnants of what she had shared with Aaron filled her thoughts. She felt his invisible pull, binding them together across thousands of miles.

Martin nodded, smiling. "I'll let her compete. Now, before you dance a jig, tell me what Tyler wants."

She stared at her father, complete shock freezing her features. "You knew?"

"Of course we knew," Parris replied, peering around her husband. Her deep, sultry voice was filled with repressed laughter. "We know our children a lot better than they think we do."

Regina hugged her parents, then kissed their cheeks. "You guys are so cool."

Parris affected a frown. "Your father and I aren't that *cool*. What we've come to realize is that Tyler and Arianna are growing up, and we have to do whatever it takes to help them fulfill their destinies. I'd love to have my children with me forever, but that's not realistic. You'll be faced with the same dilemma once you have your own children," she predicted sagely.

I hope I won't, she prayed silently. If or when she ever became a mother, she hoped she would remain objective enough to know when to let go.

CHAPTER 15

Bahia, Brazil

Aaron Spencer lounged on a chair in his study, staring at the images on the television screen. He could not remember how often he had viewed *Silent Witness* since he had ordered a copy of the movie two weeks ago, but after the first half-dozen times he activated the mute button on the remote and only watched the flickering images. There was no need for him to hear the dialogue, because he had memorized every line.

When the camera first captured the image of a seventeen-year-old Regina Cole walking through the AeroMexico terminal, he'd caught and held his breath until a lack of oxygen forced him to release it. It was as if her face and body made love to the camera. He'd been transfixed by the sultry sound of her voice, the way she moved, and her unabashed innocence. He did not know why, but he felt betrayed whenever he watched her love scenes with her co-star, and had begun fast-forwarding those segments.

He had returned to Bahia and fully immersed himself in his work at the hospital, the research institute, and his coffee plantation. His foreman had predicted an excellent yield for an April or May harvest. What he could not do was erase the memory of Regina Spencer from his mind. She haunted his days, as well as his nights, and there were times when he sat up all night, only to fall asleep with the sunrise.

This night was to become one of those.

Fort Lauderdale, Florida

Regina left her bed for the first time in twenty-four hours, showered, shampooed her hair, and changed into a pair of sweatpants with an oversized T-shirt. She was sitting at the kitchen table drinking a cup of tea sweetened with honey and flavored with a slice of lemon when her mother walked in.

Parris gave her a warm smile. "Are you feeling better this morning?"

She nodded, grimacing as a wave of dizziness swept over her, bringing with it chills while leaving a layer of moisture on her brow. "A little."

Parris sat down at the table, peering closely at her daughter and noticing the hollows under her high cheekbones. She had lost weight. Placing the back of her hand against her forehead, she frowned.

"You feel a little warm. I'm going to call the doctor for an appointment."

Regina felt too weak to protest. Whenever her stomach churned and rejected its contents, she was left feeling lethargic and listless during the aftermath of several violent retchings.

"I'm going back to bed," she murmured, pushing to her feet. She met her father as he walked into the kitchen, tightening a silk tie under the collar of a pristine white shirt.

He stopped and kissed her damp hair. "Still under the weather, Cupcake?"

"Yeah," she moaned, moving slowly in the direction of her bedroom.

She flopped down across the bed, willing the tea to stay down. Her stomach settled itself, and she let out her breath slowly. She had been back for six weeks, and during that time she hadn't had a menstrual flow. She hadn't told her mother, but she did not need a doctor or anyone else to tell her that she was carrying Aaron Spencer's child. And she also knew exactly when it had occurred—the night she had offered him her virginity.

* * *

Regina waited until she was seated in the car with her mother, then disclosed the doctor's findings. "Congratulations. You're going to be a grandmother."

Parris's hand froze as she attempted to put the key in the car's ignition. "How? Who? Where?" The three words came out in a staccato cadence. Unbuckling her seatbelt, she turned toward her daughter.

"Which question do you want me to answer first?" Regina replied flippantly, then sobered when she saw a warning cloud settle on her mother's usually pleasant features.

"I'm sorry," she continued in a softer tone. "The who is Aaron Spencer. And the where was in Mexico." Parris's astonishment was apparent when her delicate jaw dropped slightly. "We hadn't planned for it to happen, but circumstances being what they were we became emotionally as well as physically involved with each other."

"Do you love him?"

Closing her eyes, she nodded slowly. "Yes."

"How long have you known him?"

"Not long at all," Regina admitted. "We spent a total of five weeks together."

Letting out her breath in an audible sigh, Parris managed a knowing smile. She had been more than familiar with young love. "You're good. It took me about two weeks to fall in love with your father."

Regina smiled for the first time since hearing the doctor confirm her suspicions. "That's because he saved your life. Daddy was your hero."

Her father had saved her mother's life when her ex-husband tried to drown her after she had rejected his advances for a reconciliation. What she hadn't verbalized was that Aaron had become *her* hero, protecting her from all seen and unseen. With him she was safe.

"And he still is," Parris admitted. "Does Aaron know that you love him?"

"No."

"Why not?"

"I couldn't tell him."

"Do you know if he loves you?"

"He said he did, but I don't know about now. I left him without saying goodbye."

Parris touched her daughter's cheek. "What's going to happen now? I hope you're going to tell him about the baby."

Biting down hard on her lower lip, Regina turned to stare out the side window. "I've decided to tell him in person."

Parris closed her eyes briefly, willing the tears welling up behind her eyelids not to fall. "When are you leaving?"

"In a couple of weeks," she replied noncommittally, twisting the circle of diamonds around her finger.

"What about marriage?"

A slight frown furrowed her forehead as she turned to meet her mother's gaze. A shaft of sunlight highlighted the green in Parris's clear brown eyes, reminding Regina of a pairing of brilliant emeralds and warm golden topaz.

"I'm not going to marry a man just because I'm carrying his child."

Parris opened her mouth, then closed it just as quickly. Whatever impasse Regina would have with Aaron Spencer would be have to be solved by them. She hoped the man her daughter had chosen to father her child would be puissant enough to withstand Regina's formidable personality.

Regina's planned departure from Fort Lauderdale was vastly different than the one of a decade ago. The early morning breakfast she shared with her parents, brother, and sister was filled with laughter and a few ribald jokes about scantily clad women from a normally serious Tyler when he promised to visit her in Bahia during Carnival.

Martin Cole glanced at his watch and stood up. He pushed back his chair. "Let's go, Cupcake. It's time we left." He would drive her to the airport, then return to the offices of ColeDiz International, Ltd. for a monthly board meeting. He looked forward to the meetings because they offered him the opportunity to spend a few days with his half brother. Even though Joshua Kirkland still maintained an apartment in Palm Beach, he preferred living with his family in the southwest. He had relocated to Santa Fe after he retired from a career as the former decorated Associate Coordinating Chief of the Army's Defense Intelligence Agency.

Parris also rose to her feet. "And I have to go into the shop this morning." She had set up an interior design business in nearby Hollywood, Florida, after Arianna entered high school, but had limited her clients to no more than a half-dozen at any given time.

Regina stood up, holding out her arms to her brother and sister. The three hugged tightly while sharing a secret smile, then she walked over to her mother. "I'll call you as soon as I arrive," she promised.

"I pray you find a lasting happiness this time."

"So do I," Regina whispered.

Parris stared at her, tears filling her eyes, then turned and walked out of the kitchen to grieve in private. Tyler and Arianna stared at their mother's departing back and followed her.

Picking up her handbag from the countertop, making certain it contained her passport, traveler's checks, and an ample amount of Brazilian currency, Regina walked out of the house and to the garage, where her father waited beside his car.

Smiling up at him, she said teasingly, "I must have been a Gypsy or a bedouin in another life."

He dropped an arm around her shoulders. "You're a lot like I was at your age. It was as if I was living two lives simultaneously, traveling from country to country on business."

"When did it stop?"

He gave her a smile that reminded her of her own. "After I married your mother."

She shifted an arching eyebrow. "But I *was* married."

Martin's smile faded. "You married the wrong man the first time, Regina."

"Like my mother?"

He nodded. "I know you'll get it right the next time." Opening the passenger-side door, he helped her into the car, then took his position behind the wheel.

Both were silent during the drive to the airport, each lost in their private musings—Martin wishing the best for his willful daughter, Regina trying to imagine Aaron's reaction when he saw her again. He would notice the most obvious change first, leaving her to tell him of the changes going on within her body. What she did not try to predict was his reaction to the news that he was to become a father.

They arrived at the Fort Lauderdale Airport, she hugging and kissing her father once they neared the security sector. "I love you, Daddy."

He closed his eyes, smiling. "And I love you, too, Cupcake." He opened his eyes, his expression sobering. "I want you to take care of yourself and my grandchild."

"I will," she promised.

"If you need me—for anything—I want you to pick up the phone and call."

"I will," she repeated.

Those were the last words they shared before she turned and made her way to the area where she would be cleared to board her flight. Half an hour later she was seated in the private jet, en route to Brazil.

Regina stared out the small window, her eyes widening in amazement as the jet lost altitude in preparation for a landing. She had not been able to fathom the size of Brazil with its magnificent Amazon River and awesome rain forest. Observing

Salvador da Bahia for the first time from an aerial view was something that would stay with her forever. Built on a bluff, Salvador, Brazil's first capital, overlooked *Bahia de Todos os Santos.*

She recalled Aaron Spencer's deep voice when he had spoken of the beauty and majesty of the country he had decided to make his home. He had related that eighty percent of Salvador's two million people were black—as evidenced by the region's music, art, dance, cuisine, and festivals—but she did not understand why he was still an American. Even though he had lived in the South American country most of his life, he had elected not to relinquish his coveted U.S. citizenship status.

Regina felt the intense heat and humidity the moment she walked out of the *Aeroporto Dois de Julho* following the baggage handler, who led her to an awaiting car. It was the middle of November, and in another two weeks the Brazilian summer season would officially begin.

She ignored the admiring glances men threw her way as she passed them, her attention focused on the driver standing beside the car. He nodded, opened the rear door for her, then closed it. Settling back against the leather seat, she closed her eyes and inhaled the cool air coming from the automobile's vents.

Her father's longtime personal secretary had seen to her travel arrangements, from securing a ninety-day visa to reserving a car and driver for the trip from the airport to Aaron's home. Philip Trent, ColeDiz's senior attorney, had made certain funds from her personal account were wired to a Salvador branch of *Banco do Brasil* for her use.

She was prepared to spend three months in Salvador, the capital of the northeast state of Bahia, then return home. The tentative plans she had made to secure her own home and set up a business were delayed because of her impending motherhood.

Thinking of becoming a mother wrung a satisfied smile from her as the driver drove quickly and expertly over cobblestone streets lined with ornate churches from the early sixteenth century.

There were times during her marriage to Oscar when she wished it had been a real one, in which she could actually feel like a wife. She had wanted to share her husband's bed and also his body, and there were times during the eight years that she thought about having a child. She had then dismissed the notion as quickly as it had come to mind. There would have been no way she could have cared for a child and a terminally ill husband at the same time. And it would not have been fair to Oscar, knowing he would never live to see his child reach adulthood.

A part of Oscar would now live on in his grandchild. Closing her eyes, she placed a slender hand over her flat middle, praying silently for a son, a son who would inherit the gentleness of both his father and grandfather. The rolling motion of the car lulled her into a state of total relaxation, and within minutes she succumbed to the drowsiness that seemed to envelop her now when she least expected it. When the driver turned off the local road and onto the one leading to the da Costa property, she missed the many acres of coffee trees putting forth their abundant yield for a May harvest. It wasn't until the car came to a complete stop that she opened her eyes and peered through the glass at the structure Aaron Laurence Spencer called home.

The driver opened the rear door, extended his hand, and pulled her gently to her feet. *"Obrigado,"* she said softly, pleased she had remembered the Portuguese word for thank you. She knew very few words of Portuguese, but her knowledge of Spanish would serve her better than if she didn't understand any of the language.

Standing beside the car, she waited for the driver to make his way across an open courtyard to the entrance of a two-story, stucco farmhouse with a red-tiled roof. There were several smaller buildings constructed in the same Spanish-Moorish architecture as the main house several hundred feet away, and Regina wondered who or what had occupied these buildings over the years.

The driver returned and retrieved her luggage from the trunk of his car, then motioned with his head for her to follow him. *"Por favor, Senhora."*

She followed the man, grateful that he spoke Portuguese and Spanish. Each step she took brought her closer to her destiny, and she knew even if she did not marry Aaron Spencer their lives would always be linked to each other because of the tiny child growing beneath her breasts.

The solid wooden door opened and a petite, dark-skinned woman with crinkling, graying hair pulled back in a tight chignon glared up at her. Observing her, Regina saw every race of Brazil etched on her face: African, European, and Native Indian. It wasn't possible to tell her age, because in spite of the graying hair her skin was flawless and wrinkle-free.

Her dark eyes saw everything, missing nothing—especially the diamond wedding band Regina wore on the third finger of her left hand. She drew in a quick breath, then let it out slowly, turning her attention to the driver. "Tell Senhora Spencer that Senhor Spencer is not here, but she may come in."

The driver translated in Spanish, and Regina smiled at the woman for the first time, nodding. She stepped into the entry and followed the woman through an inner courtyard open to the sky, then into a living room with a vaulted brick ceiling. She was not given time to survey her surroundings, since the woman gestured to her.

They made their way up a curving staircase with a wrought-iron railing, the driver following with her luggage, to the second floor. Thick, bare, white plaster walls and a brick flooring kept the interiors cool, offsetting the intense heat of a country set south of the equator.

The older woman opened the door to a room, and stood aside. Regina walked in, then the driver, who placed her luggage in a corner. A majestic octagonal ceiling rose twenty feet above bare, stark-white walls and a polished wood floor, making it a place of beauty. She knew instinctively it was Aaron's bedroom.

Opening her purse, she withdrew several *reis* notes and handed them to her driver. He thanked her profusely in Spanish before turning to the housekeeper and addressing her in rapid

Portuguese. Whatever he said seemed to affect the woman, who nodded apologetically.

He turned his attention back to Regina. "Senhora Pires will bring you some refreshment before you take your *siesta*. I hope you'll enjoy your stay in our wonderful country."

"I'm certain I will," she replied, successfully stifling a yawn. What she wanted to tell the driver was that she did not want anything to eat or drink as much as she wanted to sleep, because she had eaten lunch during the flight. There was only a two-hour time difference between the eastern United States and eastern Brazil, so jet lag was not a factor.

Waiting until she was left alone, she removed her shoes, slacks, blouse and bra, but left on her panties. Then she pulled back a colorful handmade quilt and slipped under a cool cotton sheet. The scent of Aaron's cologne swept over her as she closed her eyes. Ten minutes later, the smell of coffee and fresh bread wafted in her nostrils, but she did not open her eyes.

If she had, she would have seen the cold fury in the depths of Magda Pires's malevolent gaze.

CHAPTER 16

Regina woke hours later, totally disoriented. Lengthening shadows crisscrossed the room, giving no indication of the hour. Rolling over onto her back, she stared up at the ceiling. Then she remembered. She was in Bahia, and in Aaron's bedroom.

"*Boa tarde,* Senhora Spencer."

Recognizing the deep male voice, she gasped, noticing Aaron's presence for the first time. He sat in a corner, his face hidden in the shadows.

Sitting up, she pulled the sheet over her naked breasts. "Good afternoon," she replied, her voice lower than usual with the lingering effects of sleep.

Aaron closed his eyes, and at the same time his grip on the arms of the chair tightened. He forced himself not to move, not to go to her. His housekeeper had called him at the institute, asking if he would be home for the evening meal because his *wife* had arrived, and he had known she was referring to Regina Cole-Spencer. If she had introduced herself as Senhora Spencer, then Magda would assume that she was his wife instead of his stepmother.

Opening his eyes, he visually examined the woman on his bed. She had changed. Missing was the waist-length curly hair, and in its place was a sleek style with the remaining glossy, black curls swept off her face and long neck. If possible, she was even more beautiful than he had remembered. She appeared older, more sophisticated.

Looping one knee over the other, he crossed his arms over his chest. "Why did you come?"

Her gaze widened. "Why? Because I told you I would, that's why."

"You did not *tell* me, Regina. You left me a note!"

"I left you a note because I couldn't face you."

"Why? Because you were too much of a coward to say whatever you needed to say to my face?"

Regina felt a rush of heat suffuse her face. "It had nothing to do with cowardice. I had to leave when I did or I never would've returned to Florida. I'd been away for eight years—eight long years."

Aaron uncrossed his leg, placing both feet firmly on the floor. "What are you talking about?" he questioned softly, rising to his feet and closing the distance between them.

Regina stared up at him in a stunned silence when she saw his face. If she had changed, he had too. He still wore his hair close to his scalp, but he had added a moustache to his lean, clean-shaven face—a moustache that was an exact replica of Oscar's. Her gaze followed him as he sat down on the bed beside her. She flinched slightly when he laid his right hand along her jaw.

"If I had left Mexico with you I don't think I would've returned to the States," she confessed.

"Why?" He leaned in closer, inhaling the clean, feminine scent that was exclusively Regina Spencer's.

Her gaze fused with his. "Because I had fallen in love with you, Aaron. It was easier for me to leave you at *El Cielo* than have you walk away from me at the airport."

Aaron flashed an easy, open smile for the first time since he had returned to Bahia from Mexico. He arched a sweeping eyebrow. "You love me?" He seemed amazed by her admission.

Regina lowered her gaze in a demure gesture. *"Sí."*

"And I, you," he whispered, pressing her gently back against the pillows cradling her shoulders. His mouth closed over hers, telling her silently how much he had missed her. What began as a tender joining, a series of slow, shivery kisses, became a hot, hungry possession as he devoured her mouth.

Rochelle Alers

Succumbing to the forceful dominance of his mouth, Regina pressed her parted lips to his, capturing his thrusting tongue. The heat in his large, powerful body was transferred to hers, and her hands were as busy as his when she unbuttoned his shirt and pushed it off his wide shoulders.

Their mouths still joined, Aaron quickly divested himself of his slacks and briefs. There was only the sound of their labored breathing and the whisper of fabric against bare skin, followed by the satisfied moans of their bodies joining in a familiar act of possession.

He suddenly went still. His passion for the woman he held to his heart was spiraling out of control, and he wanted to prolong their fulfillment until the last possible moment. It was not to be.

Lowering his head, his mouth closed over an erect nipple, causing Regina to writhe sensuously beneath him. He suckled her breasts relentlessly, the motion sweeping down her body to the secret place between her thighs, her soft whimpers firing his blood. Everything that was Regina—her feminine scent, silken limbs, husky voice, and tight, hot, moist body—pulled Aaron in so that he forgot who he was.

"I've missed you, *Princesa.* I've missed you so much."

She nodded, unable to verbalize how much she missed him as her hands moved over his back and down his hips. Her fingers tightened on the firm muscles of his hips when he began moving inside her.

Nothing mattered, only his comforting weight and the hardness between his muscled thighs sliding in and out of her throbbing flesh and increasing her fever-pitch desire for him.

Her lust for him overrode everything else, and she surrendered to the fiery passion, soaring to an awesome, shuddering climax as the screams in the back of her throat erupted and then faded away in a lingering sigh of sated delight.

Aaron's own pleasure peaked and exploded with a frenzied thrusting of his powerful hips and a deep, rumbling moan of gratification. His heart pounded painfully in his chest as he tried forcing air into his labored lungs. Not only were they man and woman, but she had become heart of his heart, and flesh of his flesh. He loved her; he loved her so much he feared losing himself if she ever left him again. Burying his face between her scented shoulder and neck, he rained kisses across the silken flesh.

Curving her arms around Aaron's strong neck, Regina pressed her mouth to his ear. "I have something to tell you," she whispered quietly.

Pulling back slightly, he stared down at her mysterious expression. "What?"

"Estou grávida," she confessed in Portuguese.

He withdrew from her warm flesh, reaching for her shoulders at the same time and pulling her to sit across his lap. He stared at her, complete surprise on his face.

"What did you say?"

"I'm pregnant," she repeated in English.

Aaron gave her a narrow, glinting look, and she silently berated herself for telling him about the baby. She had made a mistake. She never should have come to Brazil.

Pulling away from him, she attempted to scramble off the bed, but was thwarted when he curved an arm around her waist, not allowing her to escape him. He released her body, then captured her head between his large hands. There was no mistaking the smile of extreme joy lighting up his dark eyes.

"Oh, *Princesa.* You've just made me the happiest man in the world."

Regina collapsed against his chest in relief. "You want this baby?"

Running his fingers through her shortened curls, he wagged his head. "You beautiful, silly goose. What made you think I wouldn't?"

She shrugged a bare, slender shoulder. "I don't know." Her voice was muffled in his chest. "You just seemed so stunned."

He laughed softly. "Of course I was stunned. I'm still stunned."

Her soft laugh joined his. "You hit the jackpot the first time we made love."

"I hit the jackpot the day I met you," he countered.

She curved into the comforting warmth of his body and closed her eyes. "What do you want, Aaron? Boy or a girl?"

"It doesn't matter as long as it's healthy. Speaking of healthy, I assume you've seen an obstetrician."

"Yes."

"When are you due?"

"June twelfth."

"Perfect timing. We'll be harvesting this year's coffee crop in late April and early May."

"I won't be here for the harvesting."

He froze. "Why not?"

"I'm only staying three months."

Easing back, he stared at her as if he had never seen her before. "You can't!"

"I'm here on a ninety-day visa."

"You can always renew the damn visa. We'll travel to Argentina, then reenter the country with another ninety-day visa."

"No."

"You can't go back."

"I have to, Aaron. I want my child born on U.S. soil."

"It won't matter where the baby is born. Both of us are United States citizens."

"I can't stay," she argued.

"If it's a question of citizenship or the renewal of visas, we can always get around that by getting married."

She felt a fist of disappointment squeeze her heart when he mentioned marriage. He claimed he loved her, but had only mentioned marriage when she spoke of leaving him. He had equated marriage to a form of proprietorship. He wanted to hold onto her the way he held onto his coffee plantation—with a license or a deed.

Her gaze did not waver as she caught and held his. "I will stay six months, Aaron. Don't ask me to promise more than that. Then I'm going back to Florida to have my baby. I will schedule my return for the first week in May."

Aaron struggled to control his temper. "Oh, now it's *your* baby," he drawled sarcastically.

"Don't fight me," she warned softly.

"Fight? I'll make you sorry you ever drew a breath if you try keeping my child from me, Senhora Spencer."

Her eyes narrowed as she went to her knees. "Don't ever threaten me—"

"Or what?" he said, cutting her off. "You'll tell your rich and powerful father that I threatened his little girl?"

The very air around them was electrified with a tension thick enough to swallow them whole, neither willing to concede as they stared at each other.

Regina couldn't believe how their red, hot passion had turned to red, hot fury. Tilting her chin in a haughty gesture, she slid gracefully off the bed. Unmindful of her nakedness, she folded her hands on her hips.

"Please show me to a bathroom where I can wash before I get dressed."

Moving off the bed, Aaron towered over her, his arms folded across his bare chest. "This will be your bedroom. The bathroom is the door on the right, and your dressing room is on the left."

He reached for his slacks on the foot of the bed and slipped into them, his gaze never leaving her face. "We usually eat the evening meal at eight, but in deference to your condition we'll dine earlier. I'll tell Magda to expect us in an hour."

He turned and walked across the room, opened the door to the dressing room, and disappeared, leaving her staring at the space where he had been. She glanced at a clock on a table with several framed black and white photographs, noting the time. It was only five-thirty. She had spent the afternoon sleeping, making love, and arguing with Aaron. It was not what she had anticipated for her first day in Bahia. She would take a bath and change for dinner, but first she would call her family and confirm her safe arrival.

Picking up the telephone on one of the bedside tables, she dialed the international code for the United States, then the area code and telephone number for her parents' home. Arianna answered the call. She exchanged greetings with her brother, mother, and father. It was another fifteen minutes before she hung up to prepare herself to face Aaron again. Her delicate jaw tightened when she realized her relationship with him had changed, and it was the new life growing inside her that was responsible for that change.

She had promised him she would remain in Bahia for six months, and she prayed she would be able to fulfill that promise.

Regina took a leisurely bath in a bathroom from a bygone era. Ivy climbed up one wall through the wrought-iron grill-work of the windows, bringing the outdoors inside. The collection of blue glass vials, containers, and vases cradling grooming supplies and plant cuttings were a vivid contrast against the sand-colored stucco walls. The brick floor was nearly worn smooth from thousands of feet wearing down its surface over hundreds of years.

She stepped out of the tepid, scented water and reached for a thick, thirsty towel in a cobalt blue. Blotting her moist face, she walked over to a shelf and peered at a collection of elegant razors with handles inlaid with pearl, onyx, jade, and several semi-precious stones.

Bending down, she attempted to dry her legs and feet and slumped to the floor as the objects in the room began spinning. Gasping, she tried swallowing back a wave of nausea. Crawling on her hands and knees, she made it over to the commode.

At the same time, Aaron walked into the bathroom. He held her gently while she purged the contents of her stomach, then placed a cool cloth over her face and helped her brush her teeth and rinse her mouth before he carried her back to the bedroom.

He placed her on the bed where they had made love less than

an hour before and held her until she rewarded him with a dimpled smile. "*Muito obrigado,* Aaron."

"You're very welcome," he replied, returning her smile. "How much Portuguese have you learned?"

"Just enough to be polite."

"You knew how to say I'm pregnant." She nodded, closing her eyes against his intense stare. "How often do you throw up?"

She opened her eyes. "At least twice a day."

"You're losing weight." It was more of a statement than a question. "When I go to the hospital tomorrow I'm taking you with me. I want Dr. Nicolas Benedetti to look at you."

"I'm okay now," she said, pulling out of his loose embrace. "I'd like to get dressed." Aaron left the bed and returned to the chair where he had sat watching her sleep. Regina stared across the room at him, unable to believe he was going to sit and watch her dress. "Aaron, please give me a little privacy."

"No." He draped one leg over the other. "I'm not moving. You can get dressed with me right here. There's nothing you have I haven't seen before. Try to think of me as your personal physician."

"But, you're not."

He flashed a wide grin. "Oh, but I am, *Princesa.* Very few Bahian doctors make house calls."

She knew he was not going to leave, so she walked over to the loveseat where she had placed the dress and underwear she had selected to wear to dinner.

It was impossible to ignore his dark, burning gaze as she slipped into a pair of dark brown, lace bikini panties with a matching demi-bra. She thought she heard Aaron's intake of breath when she leaned over to pick up a loose-fitting dress made of an airy voile fabric in a soft, eggshell-white. She had just slipped her arms into the sleeveless garment that ended mid-calf when he rose to his feet and crossed the room.

Standing in front of her, he gently brushed her hands away and fastened the tiny pearl buttons lining the front. The heat of his freshly showered body caused her to sway gently, and he caught her shoulders to steady her. He was as casually dressed as she was. He had elected to wear a taupe-colored, short-sleeved cotton shirt with a pair of black linen slacks and loafers.

He smiled, exhibiting his straight, white teeth under his neatly barbered moustache when he glanced down at her narrow feet. "Are you going to take the phrase barefoot and pregnant literally?"

She wiggled her professionally groomed toes. "My shoes are in the smaller bag." She pointed to her luggage in the corner.

"I'll have Magda unpack your clothes and put them away." Walking over to her luggage, he recognized the superior quality of the kidskin leather. "Which pair do you want?"

"Any sandal."

He withdrew a pair of black, patent leather mules with a two-inch heel. Easing her down to the loveseat, he bent down and slipped them on her feet. Staring up at her, he smiled. "Do you need help with your hair?"

Regina wrinkled her delicate nose. "I think I can manage, thank you." Returning to the bathroom, she brushed her hair off her face, then outlined her mouth with a soft orange color. Turning, she saw Aaron standing several feet away, watching her every move. "I'm ready," she replied breathlessly.

He held out his hand, and she caught his fingers. Pulling her to his side, he examined her features intently. "If anyone asks about our relationship I'll tell them that you are my wife." He ignored her sharp intake of breath. "It will save a lot of explaining once your pregnancy becomes apparent." He did not say that if they lived the lie long enough perhaps it would become a reality.

She nodded, acquiescing. It wasn't as if she wasn't a Mrs. Spencer. She just wasn't Mrs. Aaron Spencer.

Regina and Aaron dined alfresco on a terrace garden under an allée of areca palms, which gave the appearance of an encroaching jungle in a civilized oasis. A cooling ocean breeze made eating under the sky possible once the sun traveled overhead in a westward direction.

The outdoor wooden furniture had acquired a natural patina, with a quartet of chairs covered with rush seats. A nearby bench was flanked by large clay urns overflowing with ferns indigenous to the region.

Aaron watched with amusement when Regina's gaze lingered on overgrown sections of the untamed land. He cleared his throat, recapturing her attention.

"What do you think?"

Arching a sweeping eyebrow, she angled her head. "About what?"

"The garden."

"It has a lot of potential. How long has it been neglected?"

"Too long," he replied. "This garden was my aunt's pride and joy."

Regina took a long sip of chilled bottled water, meeting his gaze over the rim of her glass. "Would you mind if I suggested a few renovations?"

"I was hoping you'd ask. Every acre of this land is yours, *Princesa*. Make any change you want."

Placing her glass on the table, she laughed, her low, husky voice floating and lingering sensuously in the warm air. "I don't believe you would actually trust me with your precious coffee plantation."

I would trust you with my life, he said silently. "And why wouldn't I?" he queried aloud. "It's a known fact that ColeDiz International owns and manages several coffee plantations throughout the Caribbean, and I'm willing to bet you know as much about the plant as I do."

"The only thing I'll concede at this time is that I've given up drinking it for the next year."

Aaron was right. She was very knowledgeable about the planting, cultivating, and harvesting of coffee.

His gaze went from her face to her chest. "Do you plan to breast-feed?"

"I would like to."

His eyes crinkled in a smile. "Good."

She picked up her fork and concentrated on finishing her meal, which consisted of a salad, *arroz, feijãao,* and carne— white rice, black beans, and steak—grilled with peppers and spices.

"How many acres do you use for your coffee fields?" she asked after a comfortable silence.

"Eight thousand out of a possible twelve."

"It didn't realize it was that large."

"It's the largest in Bahia. Leonardo da Costa's family was one of the largest landowners in Bahia for several centuries. They controlled the country's sugar industry from the time Salvador was the capital of colonial Brazil until the eighteenth century. After the decline in international sugar prices they lost most of their wealth. My aunt married the last surviving da Costa, and when she failed to produce an heir the bloodline ended with Leonardo."

Regina touched her lips with a cloth napkin. "May I have a brief tour of the garden before it gets too dark to see anything?"

Aaron rose to his feet and came around the table to pull back her chair. "I'll show you the coffee fields at another time. But if you're willing to get up at five, you can come with me when I drive down to meet with the foreman."

"I don't think so, Aaron."

He shrugged a shoulder in the elegant gesture she hadn't seen in a long time. "Just asking."

Holding her hand firmly, he guided her over a slate path to a world of overgrown trees, shrubs, and wildflowers. Ivy and ferns were growing in riotous disarray, spilling over stone walls and benches.

Regina stopped, pointing to a marble figure obscured by a tangle of climbing vines. "There's a fountain."

Releasing her hand, Aaron reached through the vines, trying to pull them away from the figure, which held a pitcher from which water had poured into a small pool many years ago.

He shook his head, sighing heavily. "They are going to have to be cut away. The vines are probably choking an underground pool. Look," he said, pointing to a damp area on the flagstone path. "The pool was over here."

Regina felt her pulses racing. Instead of designing a garden, she would undertake restoring this one to its former magnificence. Working on the garden would give her something to do while Aaron was away from the house during the day.

"Tomorrow I'll begin identifying flowers, vines, trees, and ferns," she said excitedly.

"You're going to have to postpone your project for a day. Remember, you're coming to the hospital with me tomorrow for a checkup with Nicolas Benedetti."

She nodded. "Can you hire an assistant for me?"

His hands slipped up her bare arms, bringing her closer and molding her soft curves to the contours of his body. "What else do you want, *Princesa?*"

Tilting her chin, she gave him a dazzling smile. "That's all for now."

He lowered his head until their lips were only inches apart. "Are you sure?"

She inhaled his moist breath, closing her eyes. "Yes."

"The assistant is yours," he whispered seconds before he claimed the sweetness of her lush mouth. He tightened his hold on her body, moaning slightly when she looped her arms around his neck and returned his kiss. Both were breathing heavily when the kiss ended.

Aaron smiled down at the dreamy expression on her face. "One of these days I'm going to make love to you in your garden paradise, because I want to experience what Adam felt when he made love to Eve."

"But theirs was the Garden of Eden," she argued softly.

"And ours will be the *Jardim da Costa.*"

"I have to see if I can find some fig leaves."

Shaking his head, he laughed deep in his throat. "Forget the fig leaves, Darling. The only concession I'm willing to make is a blanket to protect your delicate little behind."

"You're a wicked man, Senhor Spencer."

"Not as wicked as I'd like to be, Senhora Spencer."

"You have to remember I'm carrying a child."

"That is something I'll never forget."

Regina felt the invisible thread drawing them closer, closer than she wanted to be. What she would not think about was the time when she would be forced to leave Aaron, taking the fruit of their love and passion with her.

CHAPTER 17

Aaron led Regina out of the garden, experiencing a gentle peace he had not felt in years. For the first time in his life everything he had ever wanted was his: a medical profession, his direct involvement in medical research, the promise of harvesting the da Costa plantation's best coffee crop in more than a decade, and the realization that the woman he had fallen in love with was carrying his unborn child.

"Who lives in those buildings?"

Regina's query shattered his pleasant musings. "The larger one belongs to the foreman and his family, and Magda lives in the smaller one."

She glanced up at his distinctive profile, studying the set of his firm jaw. "Why doesn't she live in the main house?"

"After my aunt died I decided I didn't want to share the house with any of the employees. I value my privacy too much to have them lurking about."

"Have you caught them lurking about?"

He shook his head. "No. But I don't want to give them the opportunity, either. Magda comes at seven in the morning and is usually gone before ten at night." He tightened his grip on her fingers. "Come, I'll show you the rest of the house."

Regina followed Aaron in and out of rooms which were added to the original building erected by the first European da Costas, who had sailed across the Atlantic to the New World more than three-hundred-fifty years ago. Terra-cotta, stone, wood, and plaster were the basic ingredients of the traditional sixteenth and seventeenth-country structures. Even with the addition of indoor plumbing and electricity, the magnificent house had lost none of its exquisite beauty, as it claimed terra-cotta-tiled roofs and chimneys, rustic stone walls, vaulted ceilings, and stained glass windows.

Staring out a window on the upper level, she was enchanted by the panorama unfolding before her eyes. Countless numbers of shrubs bearing the fruit which would blossom with cherries containing coffee beans swayed gently in the cooling ocean breeze. She noticed that acre upon acre of trees were planted nearby to shade the coffee trees and developing fruit from the hottest sun.

She felt the heat from Aaron's body as he moved behind her. He curved an arm around her waist and pulled her back to lean against his chest.

"What blend do you grow?" she asked.

"Coffee arabica."

Smiling, she nodded. "My family has perfected a variety of an arabica that is known as San Ramon."

"If they're cultivating a dwarf strain, then they must harvest the Jamaican Blue Mountain."

"They do."

Turning her around in his embrace, he cradled her face between his hands, giving her a questioning look. "All you know about coffee is drinking it?"

She flashed a saucy grin. "I suppose you can say I know a little about the plant." Her grin faded when his expressive face changed, becoming almost somber, and an inexplicable look of withdrawal hardened his gaze. Her hands moved up and curved around his strong wrists.

"Aaron?"

He blinked, seemingly coming out of a trance. "Yes?"

"I'm going back to my room to lie down."

"Are you feeling all right?"

"I'm just a little tired," she admitted truthfully.

His hands dropped. "Do you want anything before you retire for bed?"

"Just water, please."

Leaning down, he pressed a kiss to her parted lips. "I'll bring you the water."

She turned and walked down the hallway to the bedroom Aaron had assigned her, leaving him to stare at her back. She retreated to the bathroom to wash her face and brush her teeth. By the time Aaron walked into the bedroom she had slipped into a nightgown and was in bed with a pile of pillows cradling her back. Light from an exquisite Tiffany table lamp lit up the space with a soft, golden glow.

He placed a carafe of water on the table beside the lamp. Removing the top, he filled it with water. Sitting down on the edge of the bed, he smiled at her.

"I've told Magda to prepare meals for you using only bottled water. Brazil's water can be unkind to those who aren't used to it."

She gave him a dazzling, dimpled smile. "Thank you, Aaron."

"Are you going to be all right sleeping here alone?"

Her lids lowered as her smile slipped away. "I think so."

"If you need me I'll be in the bedroom on the other side of the dressing room. I'm going to leave the doors open, just in case…"

She placed her fingertips over his lips, stopping his words and savoring the feel of hair covering his upper lip. "Stop worrying about me," she chided softly. "I'll be okay."

His fingers curled around her wrist and he pressed a kiss against the silken flesh of her inner arm. "Good night, *Princesa.*"

"Boa noite," she whispered softly.

Her gaze followed him as he opened the door to the dressing room. "Remember, I'll be less than fifty feet away if you need me."

She nodded, then sank down to the pillows and stared up at the unusual ceiling, not seeing Aaron as he lingered in the doorway. Closing her eyes, she placed a hand over her belly. Her breathing deepened and within minutes she fell into a deep, dreamless sleep.

* * *

Sleep wasn't as kind to Aaron as he lay in bed hours later, staring at the half-moon suspended in the nighttime sky. The day had been one of surprises—Regina's arrival, and the news that she was carrying his child.

When she fled Mexico he had thought he would never see her again, despite her written promise that she would come to him. Now she had come, but not alone.

A wide smile split his face. He was going to be a father. It was after he had made love to Regina the first time that he realized it was the only time that he had slept with a woman and had not protected her. It had taken only that one time to get Regina pregnant.

When he offered to marry her she had spurned him. She was willing to share the next six months of her life with him, but would not commit to sharing her future or his child with him.

His fingers curled into tight fists. What was there about her that made him so vulnerable? Why had he permitted her to challenge him over and over? What power did she hold over him so that he thought of her first and himself second?

What he felt for her went beyond love. She had become his obsession.

Regina woke two hours before dawn with a gnawing hunger gripping her stomach. The glowing red numbers on the clock were clearly displayed in the darkness. Her pulse quickened. The room was dark, but she had not remembered turning off the lamp.

Closing her eyes, she counted backward slowly, hoping to quell the rising panic in her chest. She had nothing to fear; she was safe. Aaron was not far away. His words came rushing back, stemming her trepidation. *If you need me I'll be in the bedroom on the other side of the dressing room.*

She did not want to need him, even though she did. Somehow she forced herself to sit up and reach for the lamp. Her fingers grazed the base, moving slowly upward until she pulled the delicate chain. Within seconds the room was flooded with warm, comforting, protective, golden light.

The door to the dressing room stood open, and she smiled. All she had to do was leave her bed, walk across the room, and walk through the dressing room to find Aaron.

Instead of going to Aaron, she made her way to the bathroom to splash water on her face and brush her teeth. The pangs of hunger grew stronger, and she knew she had to put something into her stomach.

Opening her bedroom door, she glanced out into the hallway. A lighted wall sconce at the head of the staircase provided enough illumination for her to navigate the stairs safely. Her bare feet were silent as she went in search of her pre-dawn snack.

She hadn't stepped off the last stair when she noticed the silhouette of someone closing the front door, and she wondered if Aaron had left the house to meet with his foreman. It was only a little after four o'clock, and he said he usually met the foreman at five.

Shrugging a bare shoulder under her revealing silk nightgown, she made her way into the dimly lit kitchen, flicking a wall switch for the overhead lights. Three minutes later she sat at a large oaken table, drinking a glass of chilled milk and eating a banana.

A low whistle punctuated the silence, and she turned and stared at Aaron as he leaned against the arched entrance to the kitchen, his arms crossed over his T-shirt-covered chest. He was casually dressed in a pair of jeans and work boots.

She flashed a shy smile. "Good morning."

He shifted an eyebrow, his lips parting in a mysterious smile. "Good morning back to you. I take it you're hungry?"

"Starved," she confirmed, wrinkling her delicate nose.

He pushed away from the wall and closed the distance between them. Leaning over her, he curved his fingers around her neck and dropped a kiss on the top of her head. "I'll fix you something to eat."

She inhaled the warmth of his clean, masculine body. "Are you going to join me?"

He stared down at her, and she stared up at him with an expectant look in her dark eyes. He usually ate breakfast after he returned from the fields, but that practice would change, along with everything else in his life, now that Regina lived under his roof.

He ran a finger down the length of her nose. "Yes." His mouth replaced his finger.

"Do you need help?"

Hunkering down in front of her, he held her hands loosely in his warm, strong grip. "I want you to sit and relax. I'll take care of you while offering you everything you'll ever need."

Regina studied the lean, dark face with the high cheekbones, slanting eyes, and the strong masculine mouth beneath the neat, clipped moustache. Placing her fingertips over his lips, she leaned over and pressed a kiss at the corner of his mouth, unable to believe she loved him as much as she did.

There was a time she had thought she was captivated by Aaron because he had come into her life when she had been most vulnerable, that he had filled a void no man, including his father, had been able to fill. Closing her eyes, she realized she wanted him to take care of her. In Mexico he had promised to protect her, and she came to a realization that for the next six months she would permit him to do that.

Opening her eyes, she met his penetrating gaze. "I think I could get used to that."

He smiled, but the warmth of the expression did not quite reach his eyes. "Whether you get used to it doesn't matter much, because you don't have a choice."

She inhaled sharply, frowning. "I can't believe your arrogance."

"It has nothing to do with arrogance or what you believe, Regina."

"Then what do you call it?"

Releasing her hands, he stood up and stared at her upturned

face. "I *will* do whatever I have to do to take care of you. And whenever you doubt that, I'll be the first to remind you of it."

A sudden anger lit her eyes at the same time she bit back the acerbic words poised on the tip of her tongue. What was it about Aaron Spencer that set her on edge the way a scrape of a fingernail across a chalkboard sent chills down her spine? Within a span of seconds he could ignite her desire until she vibrated with passion, then without warning douse the flames until she found herself spewing virulent words like a shrew.

It would not happen this morning. He had goaded her for the last time. She schooled her expression to one of complacency. "I'll make certain you don't have to remind me, *Dr. Spencer.*"

His forehead furrowed in an angry scowl. "You just have to have the last word, don't you?"

"What are you talking about?"

"I've warned you about using my professional title."

"Are you or aren't you a doctor?"

"At the hospital, or at the institute. But never in my home."

She lowered her gaze in a demure gesture. "I'm sorry, Aaron."

Reaching down, he pulled her gently to her feet. "Are you really sorry?" His angry gaze softened, moving from her eyes to her shoulders and still lower, to the soft swell of breasts rising above the lace of her nightgown.

Rising on tiptoe, she moved closer, pressing her breasts to his chest. "No," she whispered inches from his mouth.

"I thought not," he murmured softly. His right hand moved slowly down her back until his fingers were splayed over a hip. "Why don't you go upstairs and put on something less enticing while I prepare something to eat, because if you continue to tempt me in that nightgown I'm afraid I'm going to be the only one eating this morning."

"You wouldn't take advantage of me like that." There was no mistaking the thread of disbelief in her incredulous tone.

He released her, his hands going to the waistband of his jeans. His fingers were poised on the zipper when Regina turned and rushed out of the kitchen, his unrestrained, ribald laughter following her departing figure.

She was right. He would never take advantage of her. Yet the lingering image of her slender, swaying hips stayed with him as he opened the refrigerator. The image was not of an erotic nature. Seeing Regina completely nude the day before had sent a warning signal to his brain when she revealed that she was pregnant. Her hips were narrow—much too narrow to allow for an easy delivery if she carried a large baby to term.

Aaron went completely still, his hand reaching for a bottle of milk and halting in midair. He was thinking as a doctor, not as a man who loved Regina and hoped to marry her, but she wasn't his patient. She would be Nicolas Benedetti's patient for the duration of her stay in Bahia. He had to inform his colleague of his concerns for the mother of his unborn child.

Half an hour later he looked up to find Regina striding into the kitchen with a *"Don't mess with me"* mien radiating from her face and carriage. His admiring gaze swept from her damp curly hair to a straight, slender, cotton skirt and matching blouse in a flattering melon-orange down to her well-groomed feet in a pair of leather sandals in the same melon shade.

"You look beautiful." The adoration in his eyes mirrored his statement.

She folded her hands on her hips, flashing a saucy grin. "Beautiful enough to *eat?*"

Pulling out a chair from the table, he bowed from the waist. "Sit down, *Princesa,* and oblige me," he said teasingly.

"Perhaps another time, Sweetheart. Right now your baby and its mother need nourishment."

He seated her, lingering over her head for several seconds. Even though Regina had informed him that he had gotten her pregnant, she had been referring to their unborn child as *my baby.*

"Say it again," he whispered.

She went still. "Say what, Aaron?"

"Tell me it's my baby."

Turning slightly, she looked up at him, her expression softening. "It's not yours or mine, but ours."

Bending, his lips slowly descended to meet hers. "Yes, *Princesa,* it is ours."

Regina caught his hand, holding it tightly, and when their lips parted she pressed a soft kiss to his palm, rewarding him with a sensual smile.

Aaron straightened, reluctantly withdrawing his fingers and moving away to place the plates that he had kept warming on the table. The dreamy intimacy evoked by their kiss lingered far beyond breakfast.

Regina sat in the Range Rover beside Aaron, staring out the window as he drove slowly past acre after acre of coffee fields. He chanced a quick glance at her profile behind the lenses of his sunglasses.

"I divided this year's crop into four varieties, each one encompassing several thousand acres."

She turned to look at him. "Which ones have you decided to plant?"

"Conilon, Typica, Bourbon, and Caturra."

Smiling, she turned her attention back to the passing landscape. That explained why some of the plants were large bushes or shrubs while others were small trees.

"Do you usually get enough rainfall to sustain a good harvest?"

"Most times we do. But I installed a sophisticated irrigation system two years ago just in case the rainfall is lower than usual. Several years back nearly every coffee grower in Brazil suffered enormous losses when a frost swept the country."

Maneuvering off the single-lane unpaved road, he shifted into four-wheel drive and drove up a rutted road until he stopped at the top of a hill. A tall, thin man came out of a small cabin at the same time Aaron stopped and turned off the sport utility vehicle's engine.

A bright smile curved the man's mouth when he spied Aaron getting out of the late-model four-wheel drive vehicle. "*Bom dia,* Senhor Spencer. You are later than usual this morning."

"*Bom dia,* Sebastião," Aaron replied, a mysterious smile parting his lips. He rounded the Range Rover and opened the passenger side door for Regina. Extending his arms, his hands circled her waist as he lifted her effortlessly before setting her on her feet. His foreman's surprise was apparent when he snatched a worn straw hat from his head and crushed it to his chest.

"Sebastião, this is Regina Spencer." His arm tightened around her waist. "Regina, Sebastião Rivas, my foreman and the person most responsible for the excellent quality of da Costa's superior coffee crop year after year."

Sebastião bobbed his head up and down as he clutched his hat tighter to his chest. "*Muito prazer,* Senhora Spencer."

"He says he's pleased to meet you," Aaron translated the Portuguese into Spanish.

Regina inclined her head. "*Muito prazer,* Senhor Rivas," she replied, trying out her limited Portuguese again.

Sebastião's gaze was directed to her left hand, where the rising sun fired the diamonds that made up her wedding band. Aaron saw the direction of his gaze. Regina had not removed the ring his father had given her to symbolize their union, and he was grateful she hadn't, because it eliminated his need to deceive others who assumed they were husband and wife. He wanted to protect Regina from unnecessary gossip concerning what would be obvious with her impending motherhood.

Regina listened intently as Aaron and his foreman lapsed into a serious discussion of the number of laborers needed to harvest the current crop, she understanding less than half of what was said in rapid Portuguese. Her six months in Brazil would be put to good use: renovating the da Costa garden and learning Portuguese.

Aaron, with Sebastião's assistance, had modernized the da Costa coffee plantation. Higher labor costs were offset by using modern techniques, including the use of fertilizers, herbicides, pesticides, mechanization, and irrigation.

He ended his daily encounter with the foreman, shaking his hand. Turning, he directed his attention to Regina, who had walked to the summit of the rise and stared down at countless acres of coffee plants stretching down to the ocean.

Walking up behind her, he curved both arms around her waist, pulling her back to lean against him. "What are you thinking?"

She laid her hands over his and closed her eyes. "It's so beautiful here. So peaceful."

"That's why I live here." His voice deepened until it resembled a sensual growl against her ear.

And as beautiful as it is, I'll have to leave it, she said silently.

Aaron tightened his grip, inhaling the clean, rain-washed scent of her soft body. "Marry me, Regina. That way you won't have to go back to the States. You can stay here forever."

She stiffened in his embrace. "No," she whispered.

Turning her in his embrace, he cradled her face between his hands. Vertical lines appeared between his eyes. "Why not?"

"Why not? I'm surprised you have to ask me that."

"Am I missing something?" he questioned.

"You are, Aaron. I will not marry you just because I'm carrying your child. That is not reason enough for me to accept your offer of marriage."

"But I love you."

"And I, you. But if our love is strong enough, then we can wait until after the baby's born." Rising on tiptoe, she kissed his scowling mouth. "I'm still Mrs. Spencer."

"You were Mrs. Oscar Spencer," he spat out angrily.

"And I'll become your wife if the time presents itself."

He cursed under his breath, coarse, vulgar, obscene curses which surprised even him when they sprang to mind.

His expression changed, becoming impassive. "Let's go. You have an eight o'clock appointment to see Nicolas."

CHAPTER 18

Aaron arrived at Salvador's largest municipal hospital, parking in his assigned space in the staff parking lot. He attached an ID badge to the waistband of his jeans and escorted Regina through the staff entrance and into the elevator and up to the floor for gynecology and obstetrics. Dr. Nicolas Benedetti worked the 3:00 to 11:00 a.m. shift, and had offered to see Regina before he completed his morning rounds.

Knocking on the door bearing the name of his colleague, Aaron pushed it open to find Nicolas rising to his feet behind his desk.

"*Bom dia,* Nicolas. Thank you again for agreeing to see Regina."

Coming from behind the desk, Nicolas extended a large hand covered with a profusion of coarse, black hair. "*Bom dia,* Aaron. Anything for you."

Aaron moved closer to Regina, pulling her gently to his side. "Regina, this is Dr. Nicolas Benedetti. He's the best obstetrician in the country. Nicolas, Regina Spencer."

She shrank from the large, hulking man, who claimed swatches of thick, black eyebrows that grew in wild disarray over his squinting black eyes. Forcing a smile, she extended her hand. "*Muito prazer,* Dr. Benedetti."

Nicolas, momentarily stunned by her dimpled smile, took her slender hand and held it gently. "*Muito prazer,*" he repeatedly as if in a trance. "Please come with me," he continued in rapid Portuguese.

Aaron released her waist. "You'll have to speak either Spanish or English, Nicolas. Her Portuguese is very limited."

Nicolas shifted an eyebrow that looked very much like a hairy caterpillar inching its way up his forehead. "I hardly speak Spanish since living in Brazil," he said to Regina, speaking rapidly in that language. "I don't get a chance to speak English except with my American wife. You can correct me when I make a glaring blunder with my words."

"Then English it is," she confirmed, her smile growing wider.

Nicolas stared at Aaron. "Would you like to stay for the examination?"

Regina felt a wave of heat suffuse her face. It was one thing to share her body with Aaron, but having him present when another doctor conducted an internal examination made her uncomfortable.

He shook his head, relieving her of her increasing apprehension. "I'll be in my office. Call me when you're finished." Leaning over, he pressed his lips to Regina's forehead. "I'll see you later."

Aaron waited until Regina disappeared into the examining room with Nicolas, then made his way down the highly waxed corridor to the elevator. His steps slowed when he saw Dr. Elena Carvalho coming toward him.

She walked over to him, lips drawn back over her teeth. "You cowardly bastard!" she spat out, her voice low and controlled. "Why did I have to hear it from your servant that you are married?"

Reaching for her elbow, he steered her gently away from the elevator and over to the door leading to a stairwell. "We'll discuss this in my office."

Elena pulled back. "We have nothing to discuss, *Dr. Spencer.*" Her hazel eyes filled with unshed tears. "If you couldn't tell me to my face, then you should've called to let me know that you were married. I go out with you one night, and less than twenty-four hours later your servant tells me you can't come to the telephone because you are eating dinner with your *wife.*"

Aaron struggled to control his rising temper. "Magda is not my servant, but an employee, and the only person I'll ever owe an explanation to for *anything* in my life will be my wife. Is there anything about what I've just said that you don't understand, Dr. Carvalho?"

Elena recoiled as if he had struck her. "I understand everything, Dr. Spencer." Tilting her chin, she gave him a smile which successfully concealed her newfound hatred of him. "Have a nice life."

Aaron stood, watching the woman he had seen socially no more than a half-dozen times over the past year walk down the corridor to her office. Elena had achieved everything she had ever wanted in life, with one exception: a husband and children. And for reasons he could not fathom, she wanted to become Mrs. Aaron Spencer.

They usually attended hospital social events as a couple, and there were times when they shared dinner, a movie, or concert, but never at any time had Aaron ever misled her. He could count the number of times on one hand when he'd kissed her, and the kisses were always chaste ones.

He wanted to tell Elena that he had agreed to have dinner with her two nights ago because she had come to his office earlier that morning, threatening to cause a scene if he did not see her. Elena had wanted answers he was unwilling to answer, and she wanted to know the status of their relationship. He had told her firmly that there was no relationship. There never was, and never would be.

Shrugging a shoulder, he took the staircase up the two flights to the floor set aside for pediatrics. He was scheduled to see patients in the clinic at eleven o'clock, which gave him time to review patient records and then drive Regina back to the house before he began his shift.

He recalled Elena's parting words—*Have a nice life*. He shook off the chill that swept over his body. The four words stayed with him until he opened a chart and read the lab results on a child who had been hospitalized with a high fever which had not responded to the powerful antibiotic he had prescribed to combat the infection invading his tiny, six-year-old body.

He stared at the diagnosis and let out his breath slowly. The tests revealed the child had acute promyelocytic leukemia—APL, a particularly deadly form of the disease. Closing his eyes, he mumbled a silent prayer. The child would be spared, because a brand new medicine developed by pharmaceutical company researchers had predicted an eighty percent survival rate with the new miracle drug.

He glanced at his watch, then picked up the telephone and dialed the number of the man who headed a U.S. pharmaceutical company, knowing the child's parents would never be able to afford the cost of the medication, but he could.

Waiting for the connection, he listened to the automated recorded message on an answering machine, then left his message. "Good morning. This is Dr. Aaron Spencer, and I'm calling from the *São Tomé Instituto de Médico Pesquisa* in Bahia, Brazil. I'd like to leave a message for Dr. Charles Sands. Chuck, please call me after noon Brazilian time—"

"Good morning, Aaron," said a male voice with a distinctive New Orleans drawl, interrupting the recording. "How's the research?"

"Slow, but very productive, Chuck," he replied truthfully. "I need a favor."

"Spit it out."

"I have a patient who was just diagnosed with APL, and I need some—"

"Say no more, Aaron," his former classmate interrupted. "I was just walking out the door to go to the office for a breakfast meeting. As soon as I get there I'll FedEx the drug. I'll have it delivered to your institute."

His telephone call lasted less than five minutes, and when Aaron hung up his smile was one of relief. Regina was right. He had executed a marriage of pediatrics and medical research with wonderful results. If only his personal life were as perfectly aligned.

The telephone rang softly, and he picked it up after the first ring before the secretary for the pediatric department could answer it. She waved to him as she walked into the large outer officer and took her position behind her desk.

"Dr. Spencer," he said softly. "Please hold on." He placed the receiver on the desk, stood up, then walked over to close the door. He did not want the secretary to overhear his conversation with Nicolas.

He returned to the desk, picking up the receiver. "Nicolas?"

"She's in excellent health, Aaron, for a woman who is ten weeks into her term. I don't foresee any complications, which means you can expect to become a father anytime between June twelfth and July eleventh."

"Where is Regina now?"

"She's sitting out in the waiting room. Why?"

"I have one concern."

"And that is?"

"The narrowness of her hips."

"You have a right to be concerned, Aaron. But I'll monitor her closely. Bring her back next month and I'll give her an ultrasaound. I want you to watch her to make certain she doesn't gain too much weight during the last trimester, but if the baby is a large one which makes a normal delivery impossible, then we can't rule out her having a C-section."

"Thanks, Nicolas. I'll be there in ten minutes." He hung up, burying his face in his hands.

How could he tell Nicolas that Regina planned to leave Brazil six weeks before she was due to deliver their child? He had openly lied, telling Nicolas that Regina was his wife, and he wondered how many more lies he would be forced to tell before he would actually claim her as wife.

He lowered his hands and stared at a shaft of sunlight pouring into the room. He did not want to think about Regina leaving him and taking their unborn child with her.

Compressing his lips tightly, he shook his head. She had left him once, but it would not happen again—not as long as there was breath in his body....

Aaron drove Regina back to the house, giving Magda specific instructions about seeing to Senhora Spencer's meals, then changed his clothes before returning to the hospital. Regina walked with him to the garage, holding his hand and telling him of the plans she had made for her afternoon. He wasn't disappointed when she kissed him passionately, then turned and made her way back to the house. He stood watching her until she disappeared from view.

Regina's plan to identify and label plants, flowers, and shrubs was thwarted by a torrential downpour. She'd been sitting in an enclosed patio flipping through magazines and watching the falling rain when Magda brought her a midmorning snack of sliced fruit, cheese, bread, and chilled milk. After she ate, a weighted fatigue descended upon her, and she retreated to her bedroom for a nap.

She awoke once to relieve herself and then returned to the bed, where she slept through the afternoon and into the early evening. The second time she woke up it was to the now familiar feeling of gnawing hunger and the solidness of Aaron's body as he lay beside her on the large bed.

Light from the table lamp illuminated his smiling face. *"Boa tarde."*

She tried sitting up, but he eased her down to the pillows. "What time is it?"

He took a quick glance at the clock on the bedside table. "Five forty-seven."

"Aaron, I've slept the day away," she moaned, burying her face against his warm throat. "All I do is eat and sleep."

He laughed deep in his chest. "That's what you're supposed to do." Releasing her, he leaned over and offered her a glass of milk. She drained the glass. At the same time, he picked up a bowl filled with stew. "It's called *cozidos*," he explained, spooning small portions into her mouth. "It's made with a variety of boiled vegetables with different cuts of beef and pork."

"It's good," she said between bitefuls of savory vegetables and tender cuts of meat. "Where's yours?" she questioned after Aaron handed her a cloth napkin.

"I'll eat later."

Placing the bowl beside the glass, he turned back to her, smiling. "How was your day?"

Lying down beside him, she visually examined his face. There were lines of fatigue she hadn't noticed before. They were etched around his nose and mouth, and closer inspection revealed newer, deeper lines around his slanting eyes.

"Very uneventful. I watched the rain, read an old magazine, and slept. How was yours?"

"Hectic. I vaccinated at least a dozen infants against the most common childhood diseases, admitted an eight-year-old for pneumonia, diagnosed one child with PKU, and treated a little boy for impetigo." He did not tell her that a little girl died in his arms of dehydration because her parents had neglected to bring the child to the hospital after three days of vomiting and diarrhea from an intestinal infection.

"What are impetigo and PKU?"

"Phenylketonuria, PKU, is a rare, inherited disease that affects the body's ability to break down the amino acid phenylalanine. If it is allowed to accumulate in the body, phenylalanine damages the nervous system and results in mental retardation."

Regina's hand went to her belly. "What about our child?"

Aaron covered her hand with his. "Don't worry, Darling. PKU will be inherited *only* if both parents carry the PKU gene."

Her eyes widened. "Do you carry it?"

Lowering his head, he kissed the tip of her nose. "No."

She let out an audible sigh of relief. "What about the impetigo?"

"Impetigo is a bacterial skin infection most often seen around the lips, nose, and ear, even though it can occur anywhere on the body."

"What causes it?"

"Common skin organisms like streptococcus and staphylococ-cus, which are carried in the nose and on the skin."

"What does the infection look like?"

"The rash starts as small blisters, which break and crust over to become yellow-brown scabs that look a lot like particles of brown sugar."

She shuddered, moving closer to him. "Yuck."

He forced a smile, telling himself this would be the first and last time he would discuss his patients with Regina. He did not need or want her agonizing over unfounded fears for her unborn child when her only concern should be carrying a healthy baby to term.

Pulling away from Aaron, Regina rolled over and sat up. "I need to take a bath and change my clothes." She hadn't bothered to remove her skirt and blouse, which she had put on earlier that morning when she lay down to take a nap which had stretched into more than six hours of a deep, refreshing slumber.

"I'm going to shower and change, too."

Leaning forward, she pressed her lips to his, lingering and enjoying the taste and feel of his moustached mouth. "I'll see you later."

Aaron left the bed and picked up the tray with the empty bowl and glass. He winked at her as he made his way across the bedroom. Regina sat staring at the space where he had been, a comforting feeling of calm and confidence filling her entire being.

She loved him, loved him so much that she wanted to cry from the joy and passion he aroused in her. She thrilled to the touch of his hands whenever they grazed her body, and to the taste and feel of his lips on her own. When she least expected it she craved his possession, wanting to take him into her body so that they ceased to exist as separate entities. Joined, they became one in the same manner that the child growing beneath her breasts symbolized the blending of their ancestors.

She slipped off the bed and walked into the bathroom. Instead of turning on the electric lights, she lit several scented candles and positioned them on the tables under the windows. The fragrance of lavender blended with the powerful scents of damp earth and blooming flowers coming in through the windows.

She emptied a capful of scented bath oil under the flow of warm running water, filling the tub with her favorite fragrance as she brushed her teeth. The tub was half-filled when she stripped off her clothes and eased her naked body into the relaxing waters.

"Very nice. Very nice indeed."

Her head came up quickly, and she stared at Aaron standing in the doorway smiling at her. He was naked, with the exception of a towel covering his loins.

A rush of heat swept over her face and settled in her chest. "What are you doing?"

He arched an eyebrow. "Getting an eyeful."

Sinking down lower in the water, she tried escaping his penetrating stare. "Aaron!"

His smile widened as he walked into the space, his gaze never leaving her face. "I've come to share your bath."

"Men don't share women's baths," she protested, her voice lowering to a seductive octave.

"How would you know?"

Aaron's hands went to his waist, and the towel fell to the brick floor. "I want your first bath experience to be a memorable one."

Regina wanted to pull her gaze away from his naked form, but couldn't. The rich darkness of his coloring was shadowed in the flickering candlelight. However, the definition and planes of his powerful upper body stood out in bold relief in the golden light.

She hadn't realized she was holding her breath until he stepped into the oversize tub behind her and pulled her back until her spine was pressed against his chest. The oil-slicked water lapped over her thighs and up to her belly.

Closing her eyes, she smiled. "You're going to smell like me," she crooned, enjoying the warmth and hardness of Aaron's body molded to her back.

"That's okay," he replied. There was a hint of laughter in his deep voice. His arms tightened around her waist and his hands moved up and cradled her moist breasts. "The smell of you lingered in my nostrils for weeks," he continued quietly. "Even after I'd returned to Bahia it seemed as if I could still smell you. And there were times when I imagined I could taste you in my mouth. So many weeks had gone by, but everything about you stayed with me. There was never a moment during the day or night that I didn't think of you."

Tears welled up behind her closed eyelids and slipped down her cheeks at his erotic confession. "I didn't want to leave you, Aaron."

His fingers tightened on her breasts, the thumbs moving up and down in a soft, sweeping motion over the erect nipples. "I know, *Princesa.* You did what you had to do." She gasped aloud, and his fingers stilled. "Do they hurt, Baby?"

Breathing heavily through her parted lips, she nodded. "They're very sensitive."

Aaron's hands went to her waist and he lifted her so that she faced him. Sitting up straighter, he settled her thighs until she straddled his. Long and short shadows flickered over her face, highlighting the sensuous smile curving her lush mouth.

Leaning closer, Regina pressed her breasts to his broad, hard chest and touched her lips to his. "I love you, Aaron Spencer," she whispered reverently.

Aaron cradled her face between his palms, increasing the pressure of her mouth on his at the same time his ardor escalated. He lifted her with one arm, while his other hand eased his sex into her body.

Regina did not have time to stifle a gasp when she felt Aaron's hardness filling every inch of her body without any pretense of foreplay. She stared up at him and detected an expression she couldn't quite identify lurking beneath the surface of his rising desire.

There was something feral, almost savage, in his gaze that aroused and frightened her at the same time. Something foreign, unknown, indicated that this coming together would be different than any other they had shared.

She did not know whether it was the atmosphere created by the candles in the darkened space, the intimacy of their sharing a bath, his passionate confession, or the physical changes in her body because of her pregnancy, but she knew she would recall the scene over and over for the rest of her life.

Curving her arms around his neck for support, Regina began moving over his aroused flesh. It began with a slow up and down motion, then increased to a frenzied rocking, and Aaron's upward thrusting splashed water over the sides of the tub and onto the brick floor.

Without warning, he reversed their positions, supporting her body, and his lower body pumped with the velocity of a piston as he wordlessly communicated his masculine dominance.

"Marry me," he gasped, his breath hot and heavy against her ear.

Sharking her head, she swallowed to relieve the dryness in her throat. "No, Aaron. I can't."

"Marry me," he repeated.

"No!"

"Marry me, *Princesa,*" he intoned, the supplication becoming a litany which rang in her ear like a chant.

Passion, desire, and rage surged through Aaron, one emotion fusing with the other until he did not know who he was. Claiming Regina Spencer's body wasn't enough; her carrying his child still wasn't enough. What he wanted was to claim her as his own, and that would not become possible until he made her his wife.

Without warning, he withdrew from her, rose to his feet, and stepped out of the bathtub. He reached for her, knowing he had startled her when she emitted a cry of surprise as he lifted her effortlessly and carried her across the bathroom and into the bedroom.

It had taken less than sixty seconds before he placed her on the bed where she had spent the afternoon, fastening his rapacious mouth to her sensitive breasts. Her keening cry fired his blood as his mouth journeyed down her body, tasting every inch of her silken flesh.

The primitiveness of the act awakened a primal hunger in Regina as she writhed under the sensual assault, her husky voice begging him not to stop.

"I can't stop, Baby," he countered, moving up her wet, trembling limbs and joining their bodies.

Her fire spread to his, dissolving both in an inferno from which there was no escape. His tongue slipped into her mouth, keeping perfect rhythm with his hips as he drove into her over and over.

One hand moved over the curve of a breast and slid down her taut stomach and still lower. Arching his lower body, his finger found the tight nodule hidden in the downy hair at the apex of her thighs. The pad of his thumb massaged the engorged flesh, and she cried out shamelessly with the spasm of pleasure shaking her from head to toe.

Increasing the circular motion, Aaron bit back his own moans of pleasure, which threatened to drown him a maelstrom of ecstasy from which he did not want to escape.

Regina felt herself sinking further and further into the morass of immeasurable ecstasy as their bodies met in exquisite harmony with one another.

Her moans of erotic pleasure became unrestrained screams of ecstasy when she stiffened with the explosive rush of orgasmic fulfillment sweeping through her. The screams subsided to long, surrendering moans of physical satiation as she closed her eyes and registered the rush of Aaron's release bathing her throbbing flesh.

Tears leaked from under her lids. Aaron Spencer possessed the power to assuage her physical need for him, but unknowingly he also had the power to tear her soul apart. She prayed he would not ask her to marry him again, because at that very moment she would have consented.

They lay together on the bed until their breathing resumed its normal rate. Then Aaron picked her up again and returned to the bathroom. They were silent as they shared a shower, watching each other warily and knowing that the single passionate physical act had changed them—forever.

CHAPTER 19

Regina blotted the back of her neck with a linen handkerchief she had taken from an ample supply nestled in a drawer in one of the two massive armoires occupying the dressing room she shared with Aaron. The intense Brazilian summer forced her to work more slowly than planned. She had spent less than two hours in the late Alice Spencer da Costa's garden, and had uncovered an herb garden containing petunias, moonflowers, daturas, brugmansias, four o'clocks, and nicotianas.

A large field of pungently perfumed, colorful lavender grew in wild abundance, reminding her of the scent of the candles she had lit in the bathroom the night she shared the unforgettable bath with Aaron. He had shared her bath and her bed that night, establishing a ritual which would determine their relationship for the duration of her stay in Bahia.

Slipping the handkerchief into the pocket of her loose-fitting cotton dress, she squinted up at the sun through the lenses of her sunglasses. It was directly overhead, indicating the noon hour. She would take her *siesta,* then return to the garden once the sun passed over in a westerly direction.

She hadn't taken more than a dozen steps when she saw Aaron striding toward her, holding a package in one hand. Vertical lines appeared between her eyes, and she went completely still. What was he doing home in the middle of the day? He was committed to working three days at the hospital in Salvador, and usually put in another three at the research institute.

Rochelle Alers

Her pulse quickened as he quickly closed the distance between them. "What's the matter, Aaron?"

His quick smile allayed her fear. "Nothing, Darling. I just came home to bring you a package that was delivered at the institute this morning. The return address on the label bears the ColeDiz logo."

He handed her the package, and she stared at the familiar handwriting on the label. It was from Parris Cole. "I wonder what my mother sent me." She had celebrated her twenty-seventh birthday in July, and even though it was late November it was still too early for a Christmas gift.

Curving an arm around her expanding waist, Aaron pulled her to his side. "Let's go into the house. It's not good for you to be out in the heat."

He was right. She was at the end of her first trimester, and her body was beginning to show signs of her pregnancy. Her breasts were noticeably fuller, and she had discovered that many of her fitted garments were too tight in the waist. Aaron had driven her to Salvador, where she spent an afternoon shopping for clothes which artfully camouflaged her physical condition. Shopping for a new wardrobe served a twofold purpose. She and Aaron had received their first social invitation as a couple. They were invited to attend a surprise birthday party for Nicolas Benedetti's American-born wife Saturday evening.

Aaron led Regina into his study, seating her on the comfortable chaise they shared whenever they watched television. She did not know why, but this room was her favorite in the large house. Books filled the built-in shelves from floor-to-ceiling, Aaron's desk was covered with papers stacked in neat piles, and a profusion of live plants was nestled in every corner and any available surface large enough to hold a clay pot.

It was into this room that Aaron usually retreated after dinner, entering notes in his computer or communicating electronically with researchers from all over the world. It was also into this room that he came to watch videos or movies with her, translating the dialogue whenever some of the Portuguese totally eluded her comprehension.

She had been in Bahia for three weeks and, despite Aaron's urging she had not redecorated the house—not when she planned to leave in five months.

Her fingers were steady as she peeled the paper off the package to reveal an exquisite, black-lacquered box. As she turned a key in the lock, the top opened to reveal a collection of silver-framed photographs nestled between bubble wrap.

Her eyes brightened in amusement. "She sent me photographs from our last family reunion." Picking up the one on top, she studied it closely, then handed it to Aaron. "This one shows my grandparents and their children. My dad is behind Grandpa, and my grandmother is standing between my uncles Joshua and David. The two women are my aunts."

Aaron stared at the professionally shot photograph. "Everyone resembles your grandmother, except one of your uncles."

She nodded. "That's because he's my grandfather's son from an illicit affair with a young woman who was in his employ."

He gave her a questioning look. "I suppose the Coles have their family secrets like everyone else."

"They *are* like everyone else. Having money does not exempt them from having skeletons in their closets." She kept her features deceptively composed as she removed the next photograph. "Here's me with my mother, father, sister, and brother."

Aaron took the photograph, staring intently at the two people who were responsible for creating the woman he had fallen hopelessly in love with. "I see where you get your beauty. Your mother is gorgeous."

"She is," Regina agreed. "But my sister Arianna looks more like her than I do." She removed the next two photographs. "These are my aunts, their husbands, children, and grandchildren."

Whistling softly, Aaron shook his head as he counted the number of people in the two photographs. "Your aunts are the prolific ones in the family."

Regina removed the next photograph. "My uncle David is gaining quickly. He and his wife have four children, and I don't think they're finished. He complains he was cheated when his wife delivered twins."

"You have twins in your family, too?"

She touched her slightly rounded belly. "Don't even go there, Aaron Spencer. You know I'm carrying one child." A recent ultrasound had verified a single birth, even though it was too early to detect the sex of the tiny baby.

"I was thinking about the next time," he explained.

"There may not be a next time," she murmured softly as she removed the last remaining photograph. "Here's Uncle Josh, his wife Vanessa, and my cousins Emily and Michael."

Aaron had felt a fist of fear squeeze his heart with her statement. *There may not be a next time.* Was she warning him in advance that they would never have another child—that when she left him she would never return?

His lean jaw tightened. "Have you thought of any names?"

"No," she admitted.

He forced a smile he did not quite feel. "Do you think it's too soon to start thinking about names?"

Regina shrugged a shoulder. "Not really. We can list a few for boys and a few for girls. Then we can wait and see what he or she looks like, then make a decision."

"I don't know about that," he stated, shaking his head. "I don't believe a child can actually resemble a name."

"Sure they can. Look at my brother and sister." She pointed to the photograph of her immediate family. "Tyler and Arianna fit their names perfectly."

He nodded. "I like those names. Look, *Princesa,* why don't we compromise? You select the name if it's a boy, and I'll select one for a girl."

Arching a sweeping eyebrow, she gave him a skeptical look. "You won't mind if I name our son?"

He shrugged his shoulder under a crisply laundered pale-blue shirt. "I trust you to come up with something befitting, where he won't spend half his life punching people out because his mother decided to name him Percival."

"Percival isn't that bad," she teased.

"Tell him that each time he's suspended from school for fighting."

Regina peered into the box and withdrew a sheet of paper. She smiled when she read what her mother had written: *A little something to remind you that we love and miss you. Mom.*

Moving closer to Aaron, she angled for a more comfortable position. "Whose decision was it to name you Aaron?"

There was a swollen silence before he answered. "It had been my mother's choice." He flashed a quick smile. "And you?"

"My mother."

"Your father agreed with her decision?"

Closing her eyes, Regina drew in a deep breath. She had to tell Aaron. She had to tell him of the family secret so jealously guarded by the Coles, because the child she carried beneath her breasts claimed the blood of the Coles and the Spencers.

"My father wasn't aware that he had fathered a child until I was nine years old."

He went completely still, his gaze narrowing. "Why?"

"Because my mother was forced to leave him before she could tell him that she was pregnant. She was threatened with death if she did not leave Florida, and my father."

"But why?"

She opened her eyes and stared at the puzzlement on Aaron's face. "Because a very powerful, very wealthy man did not want his son to marry my mother. He paid someone to blackmail her, while threatening her with death if she ever returned."

A shadow of alarm touched Aaron's features when he analyzed what she had revealed. "Was that man your grandfather?"

"Yes, it was. He had had an extramarital affair when he was a young man, which resulted in the birth of Joshua Kirkland. My grandmother forgave him for his indiscretion, but apparently my grandfather couldn't forgive himself for turning his back on his own flesh and blood. So when my father began seeing my mother, Grandpa confused her with the kind of woman whom he had loved more than his own wife."

"How were your parents reunited?"

"Daddy got his half brother to look for us."

"Your grandfather finally accepted his illegitimate son?"

"That wasn't until years later. Uncle Josh was a career officer in military intelligence, so he knew where to look for us. My parents were finally married, then Daddy went into politics. The people Grandpa hired to get rid of my mother tried a few more times to kill her, and failed. One of the men needed money to pay off loan sharks who were looking for him, which led to me being kidnapped. You know the rest of the story."

She stared at Aaron staring back at her in stunned silence. "Now you know all of the Coles' dirty little family secrets. And after many years of bitterness they've declared a truce. My grandfather has had a lot of time to repent for his sins because he's been a semi-invalid for the past fourteen years. I still find it difficult to believe that he was once one of the most feared African-American businessmen in the world whenever I see him sitting in a wheelchair just staring into space."

Aaron shook his head in disbelief. "Have you forgiven him?"

"Yes, I have. You have to forgive in order to be forgiven."

He knew she was right. It had taken him twelve years to forgive Oscar for claiming the first woman he had fallen in love with. And Oscar had redeemed himself, because he had given him Regina in return.

His expression grew serious as he studied her intently. "You're luckier than I am, because I was never given the opportunity to tell my father I was sorry for turning my back on him," he said quietly.

"Tell him now," Regina urged softly. "He's listening, Aaron."

He lifted an eyebrow. "You think so?"

"I know so. There are times when I feel his presence, or I imagine I hear his voice. I had a dream about him several weeks ago in which he told me that he was overjoyed that I was carrying his grandchild."

Aaron wanted to laugh at her childish beliefs but did not, because he realized Regina had exhibited a maturity far beyond her years.

"My father forgave me before I forgave him."

Her brow furrowed in a frown. "When?"

"When Oscar told you to contact me. When he left his money to the institute so I could continue my research. And when he brought us together."

She shook her head. "Oscar had no way of knowing that we would end up together."

"But he did, *Princesa.* My father and I were more alike than dissimilar. The woman who was Oscar's second wife was engaged to me first." He ignored Regina's gasp. "She slept with me, then slept with my father. She told him she was pregnant to get him to marry her."

Regina's lids fluttered wildly. "But—she could've been carrying your child."

"That was highly improbable. I never slept with Sharon or any other woman without using a contraceptive. You were the first woman who did not fall into that category."

She blushed, nodding. "Was she actually pregnant?"

"No, and it did not take Dad long to realize that she had used him to further her acting career. But the damage had been done. I told myself that I didn't have a father, and after a while I came to believe it. Now you know the Spencers' dirty little family secret."

And now I know why you want to marry me, Regina countered silently. It had nothing to do with possession or ownership, but revenge. Oscar Spencer had married the woman Aaron loved above all others, and now he wanted to marry the woman Oscar had claimed as wife.

Her delicate jaw hardened with determination. "What we've shared today will stay between us. I don't want our child's life influenced by the heinous behavior of its decadent ancestors. It's time we begin anew."

"You're right," he agreed, leaning closer. His mouth covered hers, sealing their oath with a passionate kiss.

Regina surveyed her face in the mirror for the last time, her fingers smoothing back a gel-covered curl from her forehead. She walked out of the bathroom at the same time Aaron made his way through the connecting dressing room into their bedroom. He stopped short, his eyes widening appreciably when she stood in front of him.

Successfully concealing a smile, she watched him as he walked slowly around her while staring at her over his shoulder. His body language called to mind a matador challenging a motionless bull.

Tilting her chin, she smiled down the length of her nose at him. "Do I pass inspection, Senhor Spencer?"

Aaron found breathing difficult as he surveyed her tall, ripening body in a sheer, gunmetal-gray sheath dress lined in black silk, with shimmering, floral beaded designs from neckline to hem. His gaze was fixed on an expanse of one pale-gray-covered leg from a thigh-grazing slit. The garment fit loosely at the waist, artfully disguising the slight swell of her belly. Her narrow feet were encased in a pair of gun-metal-gray, silk-covered, sling-strap heels with narrow ties encircling her slender ankles. The high heels put her within three inches of his own towering height.

He moved closer and stood behind her. She shivered slightly as his warm breath swept over the back of her neck. "You are perfect," he murmured.

Closing her eyes, Regina leaned back against his solid chest, savoring the warmth and the haunting scent of his aftershave. Even with her eyes closed she still could see the smoothness of his shaven jaw, the shimmer of hairdressing clinging to the shortened strands of his close-cropped graying hair, and the contrast of the whiteness of the wing collar of his dress shirt against the rich darkness of his strong throat.

"I suppose that means you approve?" she whispered.

"I more than approve," he confirmed, his hands moving up and covering the fullness of her breasts over the sheer fabric. A jolt of white-hot heat swept through his groin when he appraised the weight and size of the flesh filling his large hands.

His fingers tightened slightly, squeezing gently. "You are the most enchanting woman I've ever seen in my life." Lowering his head, he pressed his mouth to the side of her neck. "And you're going to become even more stunning in the coming months."

Breathing heavily through parted lips, Regina felt the heat of his body course down the entire length of hers. One of Aaron's hands moved over her belly, and a moan of ecstasy slipped through her lips. "I'm going to be fat in the coming months," she slurred.

"You're going to become the most beautiful mother-to-be in existence." His hand inched lower, lingering over the warm area between her thighs.

"No, Sweetheart. Please," she pleaded. "We have to go out."

The passion clouding Aaron's mind lifted, and his hands went to her bare shoulders, turning her around to face him. For what seemed like the hundredth time he found it hard to believe he had fallen in love with a woman so exquisitely beautiful and passionate. It was as if fate had rewarded him for his patience.

"You're right," he replied reluctantly.

He released her, and Regina moved over to the bed. She picked up a small, sequined bag and the jacket matching her dress, while Aaron retreated to the dressing room to retrieve his white dinner jacket.

He returned, grasped her left hand firmly, and removed the diamond ring his father had slipped onto her finger eight years ago, replacing it with a wider band designed with alternating white and yellow round diamonds set in platinum.

Her temper flared, fingers curling into fists, but Aaron was ready for her quick temper. "My mother would've been honored for *her daughter* to wear her ring," he explained in a deep, soothing tone.

Lowering her gaze, she nodded in acquiescence. The virulent words poised on the tip of her tongue died quickly. She knew Aaron resented the fact that she hadn't taken off his father's ring. She would humor him and wear his mother's ring. But only for the one night.

Holding out her hand, she stared up at him, and wasn't disappointed when he dropped the circle of diamonds into her outstretched palm. She dropped it in the bottom of the small evening purse.

Aaron hadn't asked that she marry him since the night of their passionate bathtub encounter, and she hoped he would not broach the subject again until after she delivered. She did not doubt that he loved her, but she could not ignore the notion that his wanting to marry her was motivated more by revenge than that love.

Aaron offered Regina his arm, and she placed her hand over the pristine sleeve of his white jacket. He led her out of the bedroom, down the staircase, and out to the courtyard, where he had parked a low-slung, silver-gray sports car. Opening the passenger side door, he helped her in and waited until she was comfortably seated on the black leather before closing it. Removing his jacket, he placed it in the space behind the front seats, then slipped into the car beside Regina.

A liberal sprinkling of stars littered the navy-blue Bahian summer nighttime sky as he drove quickly and expertly along the unlit roads. He felt the heat of Regina's gaze on his right hand each time he shifted gears.

A glint of determination filled his eyes as he concentrated on navigating the dark road. A feeling of satisfaction filled his chest after he had gotten Regina to accept his mother's ring. It wasn't the ring he had purchased for their wedding, but that no longer mattered because she wasn't wearing the one his father had given her.

"I am thinking about buying you a car so that you can get around without waiting for me to take you into the city," he said after a while, breaking the comfortable silence.

Turning her head, she stared at his strong profile. "Save your money, Aaron. I don't need a car."

He gave her a quick glance. "My last name may not be Cole, but I'm a long way from being labeled a pauper, *Princesa.*"

"It's not about money," she retorted. "I go into the city only twice a month. You take me in to see Nicolas, and I usually spend the rest of the day at the beauty spa. The only other time I go in is to have an occasional manicure and pedicure. Having a car is a waste for me."

Shrugging a shoulder, Aaron smiled at her. "I thought you were bored hanging around the house and wanted a change of scene."

She laughed softly. "I spend more time in the garden than in the house. I've completely identified every plant in your aunt's garden from fern to herb, flower to lichen. Next week I'm going to create a blueprint design to lay out what I want to move."

"How is your assistant?" He had recruited a young man who usually worked in the coffee fields to help Regina in her garden.

"Christôvão is wonderful. He's teaching me Portuguese."

"He's supposed to be helping you with your work."

"He *is.*"

"He can't be, if he spends the day flirting with you."

Her mouth dropped open as she stared at Aaron, her eyes widening in surprise. "Don't tell me you're jealous of a boy, Aaron."

"He's not a boy. In case you haven't noticed, he's very much a man."

"He's only twenty-two."

"He's a *man,* Regina."

"And he believes I'm the wife of the man who pays him his salary. I don't think he would do anything that would jeopardize his employment."

"He'd better not," Aaron countered in a dangerously soft voice. "Losing his job will be nothing compared to what I'd do to him if—"

"Stop it, Aaron!" she admonished, cutting him off. "What's with your unfounded jealousy? And why would any man be interested in carrying on with a pregnant woman? In case you haven't noticed, I've lost my waistline."

"What I've noticed is that you're more beautiful now than when I first met you."

Glancing away, she stared out the window. "That's because it's your child I'm carrying."

"I'm not quite that vain, Senhora Spencer."

"But you do admit to being vain," she teased.

He shrugged his shoulder in the elegant gesture she loved to see. "A little."

"Mentiroso," she said accusingly.

"I'm not a liar."

"Yes, you are, Aaron Laurence Spencer. Aren't we living a lie?"

His fingers tightened on the leather steering wheel before he shifted into a higher gear. The racy car picked up speed as it seemed to fly over the uneven surface of the unpaved back road.

"Only temporarily," he ground out between clenched teeth.

Those were the last two words they exchanged until Aaron maneuvered into the courtyard of the sprawling Spanish Colonial-style home belonging to Dr. Nicolas and Jeannette Benedetti.

CHAPTER 20

Regina noticed raised eyebrows and startled expressions, and she registered questioning whispers as to her identity, when she and Aaron were ushered into the expansive Benedetti living room by a young man hired by the party planner to greet the invited guests. Another, acting as a parking valet, had parked more than a dozen cars on a remote section of the property and out of sight of anyone approaching the house.

Aaron nodded, smiling at the people waiting silently in the room, then settled Regina on a straight-back chair. Her loose-fitting dress artfully designed her ripening body. He stood behind her, his right hand resting possessively on her bare, scented shoulder. She smiled over her shoulder at him, then crossed her legs gracefully, giving him and everyone in attendance a glimpse of her long, smooth, shapely legs encased in shimmering pale gray. There was an eerie silence as the gazes of all the invited guests were fixed on the tall couple trading mysterious smiles.

The front door opened and then closed behind an attractive couple who laughed softly, as if sharing a private joke. The woman's dark red hair was swept up off her neck in an elaborate twist. The color was the perfect foil for her clear, hazel eyes and honey-gold complexion.

Regina's eyes narrowed in concentration as she tried placing where she had seen the man before. Running various categories through her mind, she enumerated: actor, singer, athlete. Athlete! He was Fragancio Solis. As Brazil's most popular *futebol* player, he had attained superstar status similar to Pele, who had retired more than twenty years ago yet was still revered by all Brazilians as a national hero.

Fragancio Solis glanced around the room, acknowledging his renown as if it were his due while his red-haired date glared at Aaron, her golden eyes hardening like cold jewels.

Regina held her breath when she felt Aaron's fingers tightening on her bare shoulder. Reaching up, she covered his hand with her left one, and he eased his punishing grip on her tender flesh. She did not want to look up at him, but knew instinctively that things did not bode well with the man whose child she carried and the provocatively attired woman with the auburn hair.

Her obsidian gaze met and fused with one of gold, neither willing to concede, and Regina knew that during her tenure in Bahia she would never call the woman *friend*.

The parking attendant opened the door, slipped quietly into the room, then closed it quickly. "They're coming," he whispered excitedly.

Within minutes the front door opened again and a formally dressed Nicolas Benedetti walked into the living room. His dark gaze swept over the people sitting or standing quietly in his home, his solemn expression brightening.

"Come help me look for my wallet, Jeannette," he called out in heavily accented English. "It will go quickly if we both look."

Jeannette Jackson-Benedetti mumbled angrily under her breath as she stepped into the living room. Her scowl vanished, replaced by an expression of shock when she saw her husband's friends and colleagues smiling at her. Turning, she walked out of the house, Nicolas a half-dozen steps behind her.

"Come back, *Querida!*"

"No. You *didn't!*" Jeannette whispered harshly. "How could you, Nicky?"

Nicolas pulled his protesting wife back into the living room amid applause and hooting. "Are you surprised?"

Resting a hand over her heaving bosom, Jeannette smiled up at Nicolas. "Very."

She permitted him to lead her to a chair festooned with stream-ers of pink, white, and red ribbon. Sitting down, she lowered her head, forcing a smile. Her dark eyes were shimmering with bright tears when she finally glanced up.

"I don't know what to say," she began slowly, searching for the equivalent words in Portuguese, "except thank you all for coming to help me celebrate my thirtieth birthday." She shot her husband a lethal glare. "I'll take care of *you* later," she threat-ened in English.

Crossing his arms over his chest, Nicolas displayed a Cheshire cat grin. "How?"

"You'll find out soon enough." Jeannette stood up. "It looks as if everyone came to party," she continued in Portuguese. "So, let's have some fun!"

Two silent, efficient waiters escorted the dozen couples filing out of the living room and into a formal dining room to their assigned seats while another filled crystal goblets and glasses with wine and water.

Aaron helped Regina to her feet, guiding her toward the guest of honor. Jeannette's expression softened as she offered Regina an infectious, friendly smile. Jeannette was average height and favored a fashionable, close-cropped natural hairstyle. Her flawless cinnamon-brown skin, perfectly round face, slanting eyes, and high cheekbones made her an exotically beautiful woman.

Jeannette extended her right hand, the overhead light from a chandelier catching the blue-white brilliance of the enormous square-cut diamond on her finger. "I suppose you know I'm the birthday girl," she said in a laughing voice.

Regina took the proffered hand, flashing a dimpled smile. "Happy birthday, Jeannette. I'm Regina Spencer."

Jeannette's gaze widened, and she hugged Regina. "I don't believe it. A sister girl!"

Regina returned the hug. "Florida."

"I'm from North Carolina." Her grin widened. "We have to get together and talk."

Holding onto the sleeve of Aaron's jacket, Jeannette smiled up at him. "While you and Nicky are busy healing mankind, your wife and I are going to hang out together."

He returned her smile. "That sounds like a wonderful idea." He'd hoped Regina and Jeannette would bond quickly. He didn't like leaving her alone so much.

Nicolas curved an arm around his wife's thickening waist. "Come sit down, *Querida.* You must eat or you'll be sick."

When Jeannette placed a hand over her slightly rounded belly, Regina realized she was pregnant. The exquisitely designed gunmetal-gray-and-back dress had artfully concealed her own condition from anyone who hadn't been aware that she had just begun her second trimester.

Aaron saw the direction of Regina's gaze. "You two have a lot more in common than just being sister girlfriends from the States."

Satisfaction pursed her lush mouth as she looped her hand over the bend of his elbow. "Something tells me we're going to have a lot of fun."

Lifting his broad shoulders in an elegant shrug, Aaron nodded. "That's what I was hoping." Lowering his head, he pressed his mouth to her hair. "It's time we go in and sit down."

Regina sat on Aaron's right and opposite the soccer player and his date, successfully avoiding her malevolent glare as she listened to the conversations in Portuguese floating around her.

Nicolas, sitting at the head of the table, rose to his feet and raised a glass of burgundy-red wine. His thick, black, wiry hair had been tamed with the efforts of a styling gel, and he managed to look very elegant in formal wear despite his bulk. Most people who met him for the first time thought he looked more like a professional wrestler than a doctor.

"I'd like to propose a toast to my lovely wife in celebration of her birthday. I want to thank you for the happiness you've given me these past two years. Happy birthday, *Querida.*"

Rising to her feet, Jeannette raised her goblet of water. "I'd like to thank Nicolas and everyone for helping me celebrate what will become a very special year for me. I extend my sincerest appreciation to all of my old friends, and the new ones to come." She glanced at Regina, giving her a bright smile. "God bless you all." A spattering of applause was followed by Nicky nodding to the caterer to begin serving.

Regina lost count of the number of dishes she had sampled as Aaron leaned toward her, quietly describing the contents and ingredients of each course. She found herself leaning against his solid shoulder or touching his hand when she least expected it, but the gestures were not lost on the other diners.

Nicolas waited for the end of the fourth course, then stood up again. "Most of us know one another, but there are a couple of people here for the first time. Aaron, would you like to make your introduction?"

Placing his damask napkin beside his plate, Aaron rose to his feet. His gaze was fixed on the short, black glossy hair Regina had brushed off her forehead. The sophisticated style displayed the perfection of her delicate features.

"The beautiful lady sitting beside me is Regina Spencer—my wife, soon to be the mother of my child."

Flashing a shy smile, Regina accepted the congratulations and good wishes of everyone in the room as Aaron took his seat.

Nicolas took a sip of wine. "Jeannette and I thank the Spencers for gracing our table." He turned his attention to Elena Carvalho. "Elena, will you please introduce your guest?"

Fragancio Solis pulled back Elena's chair, assisting her as she stood up, and towered above her by at least six inches. She inhaled, causing a swell of golden breasts to rise precariously from her dress's revealing décolletage, then let out her breath in a soft whisper.

"I'm certain this man needs no introduction," she began slowly enough for those who weren't fully conversant in Portuguese, "but for those who are not familiar with the celebrities in *our* country..." Her words trailed off as she glared across the table at Regina. "I'd like to introduce my very good friend, Senhor Fragancio Solis."

Fragancio inclined his head in acknowledgement, his gaze meeting and fusing with Regina's. A slight smile played at the corner of his sensual mouth, and as he sat back down he winked at her.

She felt waves of anger radiating from Aaron, even though she hadn't glanced at him. Placing her hand over his clenched fist, she leaned closer. "I have to use the lavatory," she whispered in Spanish.

Pushing back his chair, Aaron stood up, excusing himself. His hand cupped Regina's elbow as he eased her to her feet and led her out of the dining room.

Regina waited until they were concealed behind the closed door of an ultra-modern bathroom, then asked angrily, "What is going on back there?"

He went completely still. "You tell me."

Her gaze narrowed. "No, Aaron, you tell me. Your redhaired girlfriend has been throwing daggers at me from the moment she laid eyes on me, and I don't like it. I suggest you handle your business," she warned softly.

"There's nothing to handle, because there's nothing going on between Elena and me."

"Then what was her snide remark about those not being familiar with *our* country all about? She doesn't know me or anything about me, yet that doesn't stop her from being downright bitchy. Muzzle her, Aaron, or I won't be responsible for what I just might say. After all, these people are your esteemed colleagues, not mine."

She brushed past him, opening the door and leaving him to follow her. She hadn't taken more than a half-dozen steps when he caught up with her, his fingers curving around her upper arm.

"Calm down," he ordered, holding her fast. His grip tightened as he pulled her against his chest in a comforting embrace. "Relax, *Princesa.*" She went limp against his body. "Are you all right now?"

Closing her eyes, she smiled. "Yes."

His nose nuzzled her ear. "Do you know something?"

"What?"

"You're magnificent when you're angry."

Easing back, she couldn't help herself when she burst out laughing, and much to her surprise his low, rumbling laugh joined hers.

Winding her arm through his, she brushed her mouth over his. "Let's go back before they send out a search party for us."

They returned to the dining room, holding hands while sharing a secret smile. The rest of the evening sped by quickly as Aaron and Regina withdrew to their private world where no one or nothing could penetrate the invisible thread binding them even tighter than before.

They were silent on the return trip home. Aaron smiled to himself, concentrating on the uneven surfaces of the road illuminated by the car's headlights. After their confrontation in the Benedetti bathroom and he and Regina had declared a temporary truce, Elena had transferred her undivided attention to her flirtatious jock for the remainder of the evening.

Jeannette and Regina made plans to visit each other, and he was pleased Regina had found a friend. She needed more than her garden to keep her occupied.

They arrived home after midnight, and Regina hesitated going inside as she stood in the veiled blackness, inhaling the scent of Brazil.

"I can't believe the vastness of this country," she whispered softly to Aaron.

"It is mind-boggling, isn't it?"

Leaning back against his body, she stared up at the star-littered sky, placing a delicate hand over the mound of her belly. "I have a name for our son."

"What is it, Darling?"

"Clayborne Diaz Spencer."

Turning her around to face him, Aaron tried making out

her features in the dark. "He would carry his grandfathers' middle names."

She nodded and moved closer. "Something tells me he's going to be very much like his grandfathers."

Bending slightly, Aaron curved an arm under her knees and the other under her shoulders. "If that's the case, then he'll become a man who should make us very proud."

Holding onto his neck, she buried her face against his throat, inhaling his sensual male scent as it mingled with his cologne. "I'm sorry about going off on you in the bathroom," she whispered as he pushed open the door beyond the inner courtyard and headed for the staircase. "I just couldn't sit there and watch Elena—"

His mouth swooped down on hers, stopping her words. "Shhhh, *Princesa*. Don't ever mention her name in this house again," he warned softly between light, nibbling kisses.

"I won't," she whispered back.

As he lifted her higher, she gasped as the tiny purse she held in one hand fell to the floor. "Stop, Aaron. I dropped my bag."

He continued up the staircase. "Don't worry about it. You can get it in the morning."

And she did forget about it, and everything else, once she lay in bed with Aaron, welcoming him into her arms and into her body. Their lovemaking was a prolonged, tender joining, and when they finally released their dammed up passions both were filled with an amazing sense of completeness they had never experienced before.

Regina left the bed at sunrise and managed to complete her morning toilette without waking Aaron. It was Sunday morning, and she wanted to prepare breakfast for him for the first time.

Her step was light and carefree as she practically skipped down the staircase, stopping only to pick up the small sequined bag she had dropped the night before.

She walked into the kitchen and stopped abruptly. Magda was there, filling a coffeepot with water. It wasn't seven o'clock, and she hadn't expected to see the housekeeper before that time. The petite woman turned and stared at her, her gaze widening in surprise.

Regina gave her a warm smile. "*Bom dia,* Magda."

"*Bom dia,* Senhora Spencer."

Walking across the kitchen, Regina placed her evening bag on a countertop. "You don't have to make breakfast for Senhor Spencer this morning. I'm going to do it."

Magda stared at her, unmoving. "I always make Senhor Spencer's breakfast."

"Not this morning. I'd like to surprise *my husband*—" The instant the two words were out of her mouth she knew she thought of Aaron Spencer not only as the father of her unborn child, but as the man she would exchange vows with.

Magda shook her head as if she did not understand. "I'm sorry, Senhora, but I will make the breakfast."

Regina knew the housekeeper understood what she was saying. She had learned enough basic Portuguese from the young man who helped her in the garden to communicate with most Brazilians.

"I *will* cook," she said firmly. "You may go back home."

Magda put down the coffeepot, at the same time mumbling angrily under her breath. Regina stared, her mouth gaping when she recognized a curse she had heard two men exchange during a heated argument when she'd walked down a street in Salvador.

"What did you say?"

Magda spun around, her dark eyes narrowing with resentment. "*Nada,* Senhora Spencer." There was no mistaking the facetiousness in the title.

"Senhora Pires, I would like to see you—alone!"

Both women jumped at the low, angry sound of Aaron's voice. Neither had heard him when he walked into the kitchen.

"*Agora.*" Even though he hadn't raised his voice, Magda flinched. He wanted to see her *now!*

Regina took a step toward Aaron, hoping to explain to him that Magda probably hadn't understood her, but he shot her a warning glance which shouted *Don't interfere,* and she wouldn't.

Her gaze softened as it met Magda's when she followed Aaron out of the kitchen.

Aaron waited for the housekeeper to walk into his study before he closed the door. He gestured to the chair beside his desk. "Please sit," Magda nodded, taking the chair.

Waiting until she was seated, Aaron sat down behind the desk and laced his fingers together as he stared from under lowered lids at the woman who had come to work for the da Costas the year he turned twenty. He had always found her cooperative and efficient, and there was never a time since his stepmother-aunt had passed away that he'd ever found fault with her household duties.

Except now.

"Did you not understand Senhora Spencer when she said she would prepare breakfast for me?"

Magda kept her gaze fixed on her folded hands on her lap. "I understood, Senhor Spencer."

His forehead furrowed in a frown. "Then why did you not do as she asked?"

"But I always prepare your breakfast for you."

His frown deepened. "That was in the past, Magda. If Senhora Spencer elects to prepare breakfast, then I don't want you to challenge her. She is mistress of this house, and her word is final. Do you understand?"

She nodded, raising her head and giving him a direct stare. "Yes."

He offered her a gentle smile, his eyes crinkling attractively. "I've been thinking about giving you more time off." Her eyes widened with this disclosure. "From now on you will work from Monday through Thursday."

"You do not need me on Fridays?"

He shook his head. "No." He had decided to cut back his own work schedule. He was committed to the three days at the hospital, but now he limited his involvement with the research institute to one day. Medical research was an ongoing laborious task, and his need to care for Regina was much more immediate.

What he did not want to acknowledge was his fear—a fear that she, like his mother, would not survive childbirth. The fear surfaced when he least expected it, leaving him shaking and feeling powerless despite his medical training.

Magda forced a smile. "Thank you, Senhor Spencer."

"You're welcome, Magda."

He waited for the tiny woman to leave, then sat for several minutes staring at the closed door. A foreign emotion had not permitted him to fire Magda though he registered the slur she made about Regina. It was as if something had swept away the red-hot fury, temporarily paralyzing his tongue.

He suspected Magda resented Regina's presence. For more than three years no other woman had occupied the house, and she had probably come to think of herself as mistress of the da Costa estate.

Aaron closed his eyes, shaking his head slowly. If Regina Spencer did not become mistress of his house, no other woman would ever claim that status.

CHAPTER 21

Regina sat at the dressing table in the expansive dressing room, outlining her lips with a brown liner before filling them in with a flattering, orange-brown color. A gleam of anticipation glimmered in her dark eyes as she looked forward to spending the afternoon with Jeannette Benedetti. They had agreed Jeannette would come to the da Costa estate for brunch for their first social engagement.

Surveying her face, Regina was pleased with the results. She had had her hair trimmed the day before, when she went to Salvador with Aaron for her monthly checkup with Dr. Nicolas Benedetti. Her trip to the hair salon was followed up with an afternoon of shopping for Christmas gifts for family members, and instead of waiting for Aaron to drive her back home she had secured the services of a taxi for the return trip. She offered the overly polite, friendly driver a generous tip, prompting him to propose his services as an on-call driver. She accepted his pager number, promising to call him whenever the need arose. Having a private driver at her disposal would eliminate the need for Aaron to purchase a car for her personal use.

The light from a lamp on the dressing table glinted off the stones on the ring on her left hand, and she stared down at Arlene Spencer's ring. She had promised herself she would only wear it the night of Jeannette's surprise party, but two days had passed since that event. Twisting the wide band around her finger, she pulled it off and left it on the table.

Rising to her feet, she made her way over to the armoire where her clothes were stored, opening one of many small drawers. The sequined purse she had carried to the dinner party lay beside another covered with a profusion of black bugle beads. She picked up the purse, retreated to her bedroom, and poured its contents out on the antique quilt covering the large bed. A jeweled compact, tube of lipstick, and a small sable brush lay on the bed covering. Vertical lines appeared between her eyes as she shook the purse vigorously. The ring was missing!

Closing her eyes, she tried remembering the events wherein Aaron had removed Oscar's ring from her finger. He had given it back to her, and she had dropped it into the purse, she was certain. But then she remembered dropping the purse on the staircase when he carried her up the stairs to their bedroom later that night.

She opened her eyes. However, she had found the purse the following morning in the exact place where she had dropped it, and she was sure it hadn't opened to spill its contents on the staircase.

A lump rose in her throat. The ring was her last inanimate link with Oscar Spencer, and she wasn't ready to let him go—not yet. There were times when she wondered why she had not accepted Aaron's marriage proposal, rationalizing there was no rush to marry him because she was carrying his child. On the other hand, there were occasions when she believed the enmity between Aaron and Oscar continued despite the latter's death. After all, Oscar had married the first woman Aaron had ever loved. And the memory of a first love usually did not fade—not even with time.

Her jaw hardened as she returned to the dressing room and retrieved Arlene's ring. It was safer on her finger than lying around. She intended as soon as Aaron returned from the hospital to ask him if he had removed the ring from her purse.

She made her way down to the kitchen to solicit Magda's assistance to set the table on the pergola. After their Sunday morning confrontation Magda had come to her and apologized profusely. She accepted the apology, with a promise it would never occur again.

Taking several steps back from the table in the pergola, Regina surveyed her handiwork. The round wooden table was set with a sunny, yellow linen tablecloth with matching napkins. Blooming yellow tea roses entwined with ivy, climbed over the trellis, filling the warm air with their delicate floral scent.

A closet off the kitchen contained century-old sets of china, silver, crystal, and linens, and she had selected a place setting of bone china with sprigs of yellow flowers circling the edges and sterling silverware with heavy handles designed with an elaborate baroque design.

She had spent the morning preparing a menu which was certain to surprise her guest, hoping to bring a touch of the American South to Bahia, Brazil. The sound of voices filtered in the warm summer air, and Regina turned to find Magda escorting Jeannette into the pergola.

"What's up, Girlfriend?" Jeannette asked, grinning broadly.

Regina hugged her new friend, returning the smile. "We're having soul food for lunch," she whispered close to her ear.

Jeannette pulled back, her mouth gaping in surprise. "Oh, no you didn't!" she exclaimed once she found her voice. "What did you make?"

"Oven-fried chicken, cornbread, sweet potatoes, and steamed kale. I couldn't find any collard or mustard greens, so the kale was the next best substitute."

Jeannette's head bobbed up and down in slow motion as she wrinkled her nose. "Did you slip any smoked meat in the kale?"

"I put just a sliver in, for seasoning purposes only," she confirmed, feeling like a conspirator. "You know your husband's warnings about sodium intake."

Waving a hand, Jeannette glanced at the table set with the heirloom china, crystal, and covered silver serving dishes. "Nicolas can be a pain in the behind when he wants to. My blood pressure is normal, and my feet and legs haven't swelled, so I don't know why he monitors my diet so closely." She glanced down at the ballet slippers on Regina's narrow feet. "And judging from the spikes you were wearing Saturday night I know you haven't been retaining fluid."

Regina nodded. "I'm giving myself until Christmas for the heels, then I'm going to put them away for a while." Taking Jeannette's hand, she led her to the table. "Let's sit and eat before everything gets cold."

Jeannette Benedetti sat down, visually admiring her hostess. This Regina Spencer looked vastly differently from the one she had met at her dinner party. She looked younger, almost too young for Aaron Spencer. A pair of slim, black Capri pants she had paired with a tailored, white linen smock concealed her physical condition. Pregnancy agreed with her. Her skin was clear, her eyes bright, and her coiffed hair full and lustrous. Jeannette had been as surprised as her husband when Nicolas revealed that Aaron had married and his bride was expecting a child.

Jeannette took a forkful of each portion, shaking her head in reverence. Girl, you can cook for me anytime. Where did you learn to cook like this?"

Regina raised her goblet filled with chilled lemonade and took a sip. "My father. He won't admit it, but he's always been a frustrated chef. I don't know how he does it, but he manages to make grilled franks taste wonderful."

Smiling, Jeannette stared at Regina over the rim of her own goblet of lemonade. "Does Aaron cook?"

"Yes. And very well."

"It seems as if you married a man like your father."

Regina's expression sobered when she analyzed Jeannette's statement. Aaron was more like her father than she realized. Both were tall and powerfully built. And whenever Aaron sat and draped one leg over his knee the motion was the same graceful movement she had seen Martin Cole execute over and over.

Even their personalities were more similar than dissimilar. Aaron saw to her every need in the manner that her father had taken, and continued to take, care of her mother. The most important factor was that they were honorable men, and she knew if she married Aaron it would be for a lifetime.

"You're right about that," she confirmed with a bright smile.

"I don't like spreading gossip, but you have to know that Aaron was quite the bachelor before he married you." Jeannette had lowered her voice. "I don't mean that he ran around with a lot of women, because he didn't. Some women were just downright shameless whenever they tried coming on to him."

"What did they do?" Regina did not know why she'd asked the question, but a part of her always wanted to know more about the man she now shared a house with before he had come into her life.

"It wasn't so much a *they* as it was one person in particular."

"Elena?"

Sitting up straighter, Jeannette stared directly at her. "You know about Elena?"

"What I do know is that we will never become friends."

Wiping a corner of her mouth with the napkin, Jeannette frowned. "I'm surprised Dr. Elena Carvalho hasn't come at you with a scalpel."

Regina felt a flicker of apprehension race up her spine. "She's a doctor?"

"Aaron didn't tell you?"

"Aaron and I do not discuss the *lady*."

Jeannette registered the sarcasm immediately. "Nicolas and I have had long, heated conversations about her. She's one of the best surgeons on the continent, but she's also obsessed with Dr. Aaron Spencer. She had a prestigious position at a major hospital in Rio, but transferred to Salvador about eighteen months ago after she met Aaron at a medical conference. He was dating someone else, but that ended a week after Elena joined the staff."

"Was the other woman also a doctor?"

Jeannette shook her head. "No. She was a television news commentator."

"What did Elena do to her?"

"No one knows. The word was she handed in her resignation and left the country. I really can't say that Aaron and Elena were ever a couple, because the few times I saw them together I realized there were no sparks, no passion. I watched him with you Saturday night. Seeing the way he touched you and looked at you said more than a spoken admission of love. We had no idea that when he took a personal leave of absence for more than a month it was to get married."

"Aaron is a very private person," she said truthfully—so private he would not permit his full-time household staff to reside under his roof.

It was apparent Aaron had not told his friends and colleagues that he had left Bahia to bury his father—subsequently seducing his father's widow.

"How did you find your way to Bahia via North Carolina?" she queried Jeannette, smoothly changing the topic.

Jeannette's expression brightened. "I came here for Carnival three years ago and met Nicky. I was a partner with three of my college soros in a travel agency, and each year one of us visited a different place to update our travel packages.

"We offered trips to Rio for Carnival, then decided to add Bahia. I was chosen to cover the festivities, and after several hours of dancing and mingling with local Bahians and visitors I was literally cooling my heels in a small restaurant. I had taken my sandals off and put my aching feet up on a chair when Nicolas Benedetti walked in with two of his friends. They were seated at a table next to mine. He kept staring and smiling at me while I tried ignoring this hulk of a man who looked like the *after* for a Rogaine ad. I much preferred his taller, darker friend, whom I later discovered was Dr. Aaron Spencer."

Regina shifted a naturally arching eyebrow at this disclosure. She remembered Aaron saying that he stayed away from Carnival because it had become too boisterous for him.

"How did you finally meet Nicolas?"

"He walked over to my table, sat down, and began massaging my bare, dusty, aching feet. I was too shocked to do anything but stare at this gentle giant while he whispered softly in Portuguese about how much he liked my face. He said it reminded him of a beautiful sculpture he had on a wall in his house."

"You understood Portuguese?"

Jeannette nodded. "I was a language major in college. At that time I spoke fluent Spanish, French, and Italian. My Portuguese was limited, but my knowledge of Spanish helped a lot. I've lived here for two years, and there are times I still have to grope for the words because I find myself thinking in Spanish. Nicky was talking about me coming to his house to see his sculpture when most guys I knew would talk about taking a girl home to see the etchings on their ceilings."

Leaning forward, her eyes shining with anticipation, Regina said, "What happened after that?"

"I turned him down, but hadn't noticed that his two friends left the restaurant without him. When I told him why I was in Bahia, he offered to act as my tour guide. We spent the next six hours together, talking and laughing. He took me back to my hotel, and as we stood outside the door to my room his beeper went off. I let him in to use the telephone to return the page, and when he hung up I saw a very different Nicolas Benedetti. Gone was the smiling, joking man, and in his place a very serious Dr. Benedetti. He told me he had to get to the hospital to deliver a baby."

"He hadn't told you he was a doctor?"

Shaking her head, Jeannette said, "No."

"What happened after that?"

"He came back to the hotel around four o'clock the next morning, exhausted. His patient had been unable to deliver vaginally, and he'd had to perform a C-section. He laid across my bed and slept for six hours without waking up. When he woke up I ordered breakfast for us and we spent the day together until he left to go back to the hospital.

"I saw him every day until it was time for me to return to the States, and in all of the time we spent together he never tried to touch or kiss me. At first I thought that he hadn't found me attractive, but a month later he called me and he said he was sorry he let me go without kissing me. I told him that I would give him the opportunity when I came back to Bahia for the next Carnival."

"Did you?"

"No. I came back sooner. Nicky called me every Sunday night for four months, and we'd talk for hours. Then one day without warning I decided to fly down and surprise him. I told myself I was crazy, but I didn't care. I walked into the hospital, went to his office, and asked to see him. His bushy eyebrows shot up so far on his forehead that I thought they would never come down. I stared at him, realizing he looked nothing like the men I had ever dated in the States, but at that moment I didn't care because I had fallen in love with him.

"I spent the week with him at his house, and before I left Bahia to fly back to Winston-Salem, North Carolina, I had accepted his proposal to become Mrs. Nicolas Benedetti. My girlfriends thought I had lost my mind until Nicky came to the States to see me that Christmas. I invited them over to my apartment for a Kwanzaa party, and showed them my engagement ring. Needless to say, my three very beautiful, unattached girlfriends left later that night just a tad jealous."

"Where were you married?"

"We decided to marry in Bahia. My sister was my matron of honor, and Aaron was Nicky's best man. Aaron paid for the reception dinner at *Tempero da Dadá,* one of the more popular restaurants in Salvador. It was a very small gathering with my parents and Nicky's, who had flown up from Buenos Aires."

Regina sighed softly. "It sounds like a fairy tale romance."

"And it has been," Jeannette confirmed. "Earlier this year we decided to start a family, and I finally conceived in August."

"Which means we should deliver a month apart."

"Which means our children will grow up together. Our husbands are good friends, and I'm hoping you and I will also become good friends," Jeannette said, flashing a bright smile.

Reaching across the table, Regina squeezed her hand. "I'm certain we will."

She wanted to tell Jeannette that she had never had a girlfriend. Her female cousins did not count as girlfriends, and while in school she had never cultivated a friendship with any girl she felt comfortable enough to confide in. After her kidnapping she had found it hard to develop a closeness with anyone outside her family, and when most girls were flirting and hanging out in the malls with adolescent boys she had immersed herself in her studies, excelling, accelerating, and graduating a year ahead of her contemporaries.

She'd moved in with Oscar at seventeen, married him at nineteen, and spent the next eight years caring for her elderly, sick husband. She planned to spend six months in Bahia, and during that time she was certain she would call Jeannette Benedetti friend.

Aaron reread the newspaper article, the smile playing around his mouth widening as his gaze moved swiftly over the words.

"Good news?" questioned Dr. Dennis Liu.

"It has to be, or why would we be sitting here with chilled champagne?" asked the doctor who headed the research team.

Nodding, Aaron glanced up at the brilliant young microbiologist. "Very good news."

"Then share it with us, Aaron," a female research assistant pleaded softly.

Smiling at the eight people sitting around the conference table, Aaron lowered his gaze and began reading.

"Doctors at the *São Tomé Instituto de Médico Pesquisa* in Bahia, Brazil, have developed a new way to test fetuses for a potentially fatal blood problem known as RH incompatibility.

"The procedure, which is not yet in general use, is safer and faster than existing tests. Instead of inserting a needle through the mother's abdomen and into her uterus, the doctors draw blood, with test results available within a day rather than a week or more.

"RH incompatibility can cause anemia, swelling, and brain damage. The current tests for RH-factor incompatibility use a needle to extract amniotic fluid or tissue from the placenta. These tests are accurate, but there's a small risk—one percent to two percent—of their causing a miscarriage.

"The testing determines whether what is called the RH-factor in the baby's blood is compatible with the mother's. If not, the mother's immune system may create antibodies that attack the baby's blood.

"In a study to be published today in the *New England Journal of Medicine,* Dr. Aaron Spencer, the institute's director, said he found that the mother's blood carries enough of the fetus's DNA to determine the baby's RH-factor as early as fourteen weeks into pregnancy."

Folding the newspaper, he offered each person sitting at the table a warm smile. "Congratulations."

The man who headed the research team stood up and applauded as the others in the room followed suit, applauding one another.

The young doctor from China, who had joined the research staff a year ago, reached for the open bottle of champagne chilling in a container on the conference table, and one by one each person held out a flute to be filled.

Dr. Dennis Liu filled a glass, extending it to Aaron. "To you, Aaron. For believing in us, and for signing our paychecks."

"Hear! Hear!" the assembled chorused.

Aaron took the proffered glass and raised it. "To the finest research team in the world. This recognition could not have come at a better time, because this Christmas will become one that I will remember for a long time. And before we end this research year for our holiday recess I'd like to invite everyone to my home for a little celebratory soirée next Saturday evening. You may bring your wives, husbands, partners, or significant others." There was a stunned silence during which the eight exchanged questioning glances. "The festivities will begin at seven," he continued smoothly. Draining his glass, he savored the bubbles on his tongue before swallowing the premium champagne. "Excuse me, ladies, gentlemen. I'm taking the rest of the afternoon off."

Dennis Liu glanced at his watch. It was only two-thirty. He might have been the newest member of the research team at the *São Tomé Instituto de Médico Pesquisa,* but he was more than aware of the in-house rumors of Dr. Aaron Spencer regularly spending as many as three nights a week at the institute until he took a leave of absence several months ago.

He had returned to Bahia a changed man, and since his wife arrived he had exhibited another facet of his personality no one had ever seen before. He seemed more relaxed, smiled more often, and there were times when he seemed more human, not an automaton who existed for medical research. Yes, Dennis mused, getting married had had an amazing effect on the man who headed the *São Tomé Instituto de Médico Pesquisa.*

Aaron parked the Range Rover in the garage, then made his way toward the garden, where he was certain to find Regina. He slowed his pace, noting the obvious changes. All of the overgrown portions of the flower and herb gardens were cleared away, turning the garden into a civilized oasis. Water poured from the fountain into a pool, which flowed into a long runlet.

Walking along a wide avenue of stone, he noticed that the many flowers were living works of art. He touched the dewy petals of a dainty iris, and inhaled the distinctive fragrance of orchids growing in extravagant abandonment.

He had played hide-and-seek in his aunt's garden during his youth, usually ignoring its haunting beauty. Regina had painstakingly begun its restoration, and like a phoenix it now rose anew.

Making his way up a flight of stone steps, he smiled at a statuary swathed in palm fronds. He ran his fingers over the cool marble, tracing its smooth curves.

Movement caught his attention and he went completely still, listening.

He heard Regina's low, sultry voice then that of Christôvão's. Aaron did not know why, but he felt like a cuckold husband spying on his unfaithful wife. He waited until they emerged from the overgrowth of trees, startling both when they saw him.

"*Boa tarde*," he announced quietly, inclining his head.

Christôvão offered him a half-smile. "*Boa tarde*, Senhor Spencer." He gave Regina a shy smile. "I'll see you tomorrow."

Regina gestured to him. "No, Christôvão, don't leave."

"Let him go," Aaron commanded when the younger man quickened his pace and walked away.

Rounding on him, Regina glared at Aaron. "What are you doing? Spying on me?"

Folding his arms over his chest, he tilted his head at an angle. "Is there a reason why I should?"

Heat flooded her cheeks. "Of course not." She gave him a long, penetrating stare. "What are you doing home so early?"

His upper lip curled under the neatly barbered moustache. "I came home to share *siesta* with my wife."

"You delude yourself, because I'm not your wife," she shot back angrily.

His temper rose to match hers. "And what keeps you from becoming my wife, Senhora Spencer?"

Her gaze widened. "There are a number of reasons."

"Enumerate."

"I don't want to become a possession, Aaron. I don't want to feel as if you own me the way you own this land. And I don't want you to think I'm beholden to you because I'm carrying your child. Years from now I don't want you to throw it in my face that you married me because you didn't want your child to be illegitimate. I also don't want you to use me to pay your father back for marrying your fiancée. And, last but not least, I don't need your money to provide support for this baby, nor do I need your name, because I'm already a Spencer."

"Are you finished?" he questioned in a dangerously soft voice.

Raising her chin in a haughty gesture, she turned her back. "Yes, I am."

"Good." Taking two steps, Aaron swept her up in his arms and carried her into the allée of palms closing in around them. She struggled in his embrace, and he tightened his grip. "The only time you aren't verbally abusing me with that whip you call a tongue is when I make love to you, Senhora Spencer."

Her gaze widened as she froze. "You're not going to make love to me in—"

He stopped her words when his mouth descended on hers, robbing her of her breath. Pulling back, he drew in a lungful of air, then recaptured her soft, throbbing mouth.

Day merged into night the farther he retreated deep into the garden, the towering trees blocking out the brilliant Brazilian afternoon summer sun.

Regina, caught up in the dizzying spell of rising passion, remembered Aaron lowering her to the cool, damp earth, but nothing beyond that. It was later, much later that she found herself nude, lying on Aaron's shirt as he lay beside her breathing heavily. When his respiration returned to normal, he had plucked a flowering shell ginger and tucked it behind her left ear.

The cool earth absorbed the heat from her moist body as she closed her eyes, reveling in the aftermath of their passions having spiraled out of control.

"What are you doing to me, Aaron?"

Turning on his side, he smiled at her thoroughly kissed mouth. "I'm loving you, *Princesa.*"

"No, you're not," she slurred.

"Oh, yes I am," he insisted.

"You're taking advantage of me. You're bigger, stronger, and—"

"And I love your life," he confessed, pressing his mouth to hers.

There was a low rumble as the earth vibrated under their

bodies and both went completely still. It was thunder. They were lying naked in the garden while the threat of imminent rain threatened to cool their wanton coupling. There was another roll of thunder, followed by fat, warm drops dotting their fevered flesh.

They sprang to their feet, pulling on articles of clothing to cover their nakedness as they raced out of the garden toward the house. Aaron managed to slip on his slacks and Regina her slacks and top, both leaving underwear and shoes behind.

She clutched Aaron's hand, while holding her unbuttoned blouse together with her other. "Slow down!" she screamed to be heard above the intermittent rumbling.

He slowed enough to swing her up into his arms and raced the remaining feet to the house. Staring down at her flushed face, he smiled, his gaze moving down to her exposed breasts. The lush darkness of her distended nipples renewed his passion all over again as he pushed open the door to the inner courtyard.

Magda walked across the living room, staring at the rain-soaked couple, her knowing gaze taking in their state of half-dress. "Is Senhora Spencer all right?"

Regina pressed her face to Aaron's bare chest when she heard the housekeeper's voice. She wanted to tell Magda that she was wonderful. Aaron had just made love to her in the garden, and all she wanted to do was spend the rest of her life in his arms.

"She's fine, Magda," Aaron said, taking the stairs two at a time. He moved down the hallway, smiling at Regina. "Now, are you ready to take *siesta* with me?"

"Ummm," she moaned, angling for a more comfortable position.

He placed her on the bed, removed her damp clothing, then removed his slacks and lay down beside her. "I love you, Regina Spencer," he whispered as he closed his eyes and joined her in a sleep for sated lovers.

CHAPTER 22

Regina awoke to a blue-veiled sky and an orange-colored full moon as the backdrop for a profusion of twinkling stars. She moaned softly as she turned away from the window.

"Did I hurt you?" questioned a deep voice in the velvet darkness.

"No. I'm just a little stiff from pulling up weeds."

Aaron sat up, reached over, and flicked on the table lamp. Turning back to Regina, he frowned at her. "What are you doing weeding? Isn't that why I hired Christôvão?"

She let out her breath in an audible sigh. "I was helping him."

Moving closer, he place a hand over her hip, massaging the tender muscles in her lower back. "Next time let the man do *his* job."

"I will," she promised. She moaned again. "That feels wonderful, Aaron."

Going up on his knees, he leaned over her prone body and massaged her back and legs, his strong fingers working their healing magic.

"I want to host a Christmas party for the staff at the institute," he stated firmly.

There was a noticeable pause before Regina responded. "Where?" Her low, sultry voice floated up and lingered in the quietness of the room.

"Here."

"When?"

"Next Saturday."

A slight smile softened her full lips. "You're not giving me much notice, Aaron. I have to prepare a menu and decorate the house."

He ran his forefinger down the length of her spine. "We'll have a caterer provide the food. Meanwhile, Magda and I will help you with whatever else you'll need in the house."

Shifting, she sat up and pressed her back against the massive, carved headboard. "How can you help when you're working?"

Aaron moved over and sat beside her. His admiring gaze lingered on her delicate profile. "Tomorrow will be my last day at the institute for two months. And—"

"Two months?" she queried, interrupting him. It was apparent she was shocked at this disclosure.

"We always recess for two months. It gives everyone a chance to return to their native countries, or go on holiday. You'll get to see a lot of me until mid-February."

"Speaking of February, would you mind if I invited my brother and sister to come for Carnival?"

Curving an arm around her shoulders, he pulled her head to his chest. "Of course I don't mind. Invite whomever you want."

She smiled up at him. "You wouldn't be so generous if I decided to invite the entire Cole clan."

"Oh, yes I would," he said teasingly. "I don't know where everyone would sleep, but I'm certain we could figure out something."

Regina stared at her left hand splayed over his muscled chest, her gaze lingering on the white and rare yellow diamonds in the wide band on her finger. Pulling back, she gave him a direct stare. "Did you take my ring from my evening purse?"

He frowned. "What ring?"

"The ring Oscar gave me."

"No, I didn't. Why?"

"I can't find it."

"When was the last time you saw it?"

"The night we went to Jeannette's party. You took it off my finger, but I put it in my bag."

"Do you think it could've fallen out?"

She shrugged both shoulders. "I don't know. I dropped the purse on the staircase, but when I picked it up the next morning it was still closed."

Moving off the bed, Aaron stood up. "After I shower I'll ask Magda if she found it."

Regina went to her knees and held onto his wrist. "Don't. I'll ask her. I don't want her to think you're accusing her of stealing it."

His eyebrows met in a frown. "I'd never accuse her of being a thief."

"Let me handle it?"

"Okay," he conceded. "I won't say anything." He extended a hand. "Come share a shower with me."

She grasped the proffered fingers. "Only if you promise to behave, Aaron Spencer."

Pulling her gently from the bed, he swung her up in his arms. "I can promise you anything but that."

"*Aaron,*" she wailed.

"Okay. But just this time." Walking across the bedroom, he shifted her ripening body, smiling. She was gaining weight. "I've come up with a name for our daughter," he said mysteriously.

Her eyes brightened with amusement. "What is it?"

"Eden."

Lowering her gaze, lashes brushing her sun-tanned cheeks, Regina flashed a shy smile. "It would be very appropriate for a girl, but—" Her gaze moved up and locked with his.

"But what?" His voice was barely a whisper.

"But it's going to be a boy."

"How do you know that, Senhora Spencer?"

"I just know."

"We'll see."

"Promise me you won't ask Nicolas to see the ultrasound pictures."

"Have you seen them?" he countered.

"No. And I don't want to. Promise me, Aaron." His mouth

tightened beneath his moustache. "Please, Darling," she pleaded, offering him one of her irresistible dimpled smiles.

"All right. I promise," he said between clenched teeth.

"I will finish bringing out the dishes and show the caterers where you want them to set up when they arrive, Senhora Spencer."

Regina smiled at Magda, nodding. "Thank you for your help. Everything looks beautiful." She and Magda had prepared all of the appetizers for the cocktail hour.

Cold fish dishes, along with other platters filled with assorted cheeses, a Mediterranean salad, a five-tomato salsa, stuffed tomatoes and mushrooms, chicken salads, oven-roasted artichoke slivers with thyme and marjoram, and prosciutto-stuffed figs all lined the tables set up in the courtyard, which was brightly illuminated with more than three dozen lanterns positioned around the perimeter. Strings of tiny electric lights cast an ethereal glow on the garden and beyond.

Regina had planned for an outdoor buffet dinner for twenty, followed by dancing under a navy-blue, star-littered sky. The oppressive daytime temperatures were alleviated by the setting sun, and a nighttime temperature of seventy-five with a warm summer breeze had helped create the perfect setting for a holiday gathering.

Magda offered Senhora Spencer a sincere smile for the first time since she had come to the da Costa estate. Her smile was still in place as she watched Regina retreat to the house to dress before the arrival of her guests.

Even though she resented the younger woman's presence, she had to admit she had treated her kindly. When Regina had questioned her about her missing wedding ring, she had readily accepted her response that she hadn't seen it.

She'd lied smoothly; it was she who had taken it from the small purse lying on the staircase. Discovering the ring had been divine providence. She had waited two days, then taken a rare trip to Salvador and sold it for a fraction of its worth. She could have haggled and gotten more money, but what she received was enough—more than enough to pay someone to make certain Senhora Regina Spencer and the child she carried in her womb would not survive the next harvest.

Aaron squeezed Regina's fingers, then smiled down at her as the first of the invitees walked into the courtyard. The invitation had indicated casual dress. The men arrived *sans* jackets and ties, and the women favored colorful sandals they had paired with dresses that revealed the maximum amount of bare flesh without being vulgar.

Regina felt almost overdressed in her silk ensemble of slacks and softly flowing top with a scooped neckline. She wore red, and Aaron had elected black: linen slacks, shirt, and imported Italian loafers.

She felt the excitement the moment she had descended the staircase. Every room in the house was filled with flowers, bringing the ethereal enchantment of her resplendent garden indoors.

The caterers and the musicians had arrived, and had set up quickly and expertly before their guests crossed the boundary line marking the da Costa property.

"Everything looks beautiful," Aaron whispered. "You look beautiful."

Returning his smile, she nodded. "Thank you, Darling."

Lowering his head, he pressed his mouth to her ear. "No, *Princesa,* thank *you.*"

"I'm truly wounded, Aaron. You throw a party and forget to invite me."

Aaron's head came up quickly when he heard a familiar male voice. A bright smile crossed his face as he released Regina's hand and pulled Marcos Jarre into a quick, rough embrace.

"If you wanted an invitation, you should've let me know you were back."

Marcos Jarre's black eyes narrowed in concentration as he

ignored the man who was more like a brother to him than his own brother, his gaze softening when he stared at the tall, slender woman standing beside Aaron Spencer.

Aaron did not miss Marcos's interest in Regina. Curving an arm around her waist, he smiled. "Regina, this gypsy is Marcos Jarre, our closest neighbor. Marcos, Regina Spencer."

Regina extended a slender hand, offering Aaron's friend a warm, dimpled smile. "My pleasure, Marcos."

He took her hand and pressed a kiss to her knuckles. His steady gaze did not waver behind the lenses of his round, wire-rimmed glasses when he catalogued every inch of her face and body. "No, Regina. The pleasure is mine. I can't believe my friend has been holding out on me."

"I wouldn't have to hold out on you if you called me more than once a year," Aaron teased. "Marcos has spent the last ten years of his life studying and teaching in Europe and Africa. And I must admit that he is a brilliant teacher and scholar," he explained to Regina.

Marcos shook his head, smiling. "You've changed, friend. Old age and marriage have humbled you."

"Old age!" Aaron retorted. "I'm only a day older than you are."

Regina examined the man who would be her neighbor during her stay in Bahia. She eclipsed his height by several inches, but his slender body made him appear taller than his five feet, eight inches. He affected a close-cropped haircut, while a neat goatee added character to his narrow face. His coloring reminded her of a polished pecan with rich, gold-brown undertones. His English was flawless, and she wondered whether he was a native Brazilian or had learned the language during his travels.

"In case you're not aware of it, your husband is also an excellent teacher," Marcos stated with a wide grin. "He taught me English—"

"And you taught me to speak Spanish," Aaron countered.

"And I taught you how to ride a horse, *amigo,* and you became a better horseman, even though I had grown up around them all of my life."

Aaron nodded. "That's because books were your passion, not horses. How long do you plan to stay in Bahia this time?"

"I've taken a sabbatical. I'll be here for a year."

As he placed a large hand on Marcos's shoulder, Aaron's expression softened. "Good. Welcome home, friend."

"Thank you."

"I hope you're going to join us," Regina offered in a quiet tone.

"I thought you'd never ask," Marcos teased, winking at her.

"He's seems very nice," she said to Aaron after Marcos made his way across the courtyard to where a portable bar had been set up.

"He's the brother I never had," Aaron admitted. "He's truly brilliant, *Princesa*. He has become an expert on African history. He has lived in most African countries, and has lectured at every prestigious university in the States and Europe. He just spent the past two years at Oxford."

Curiosity and anticipation lit up her eyes. "I'd love to invite him for dinner."

"Knowing Marcos, he won't wait for an invitation. Chances are you'll get to see a lot of him now that he's going to remain in Bahia for more than a few months."

She inhaled, then let out her breath slowly. "I think it's time you introduced me to your guests."

"*Our* guests," he reminded her, spying Nicolas and Jeannette as they made their way into the courtyard.

Regina spent the cocktail hour meeting and socializing with the people who worked at the research institute. She thought them too formal, stilted, until each had sampled a cup of potent rum punch. After their second drinks inhibitions were shed, and everyone exhibited a liveliness that was infectious.

The frivolity continued well into the night with drinking, dancing, and a nonstop consumption of food. Regina shared her first dance with Aaron, then with every man present. A few of the doctors from the institute flirted shamelessly with her, but she laughed and ignored some of the more ribald comments, attributing the loose tongues to the intoxicating effects of the punch.

Near the midnight hour she found herself in the arms of Marcos Jarre, once the pulsing musical numbers had slowed to a classic, Brazilian love ballad. He had pulled her into a close embrace, then gone completely still once he registered the slight swell of her belly artfully disguised under the red silk.

"You're expecting a child?" His voice was a hoarse whisper.

She shifted an eyebrow, smiling. "Yes."

He whistled softly. "My friend has really changed."

Her smile faded, replaced by a questioning frown. "Why would you say that?"

Marcos shook his head. "There was a time when Aaron took a solemn oath that he would never marry or have children."

She forced a smile she did not feel. "I suppose anyone can change."

"That's true, Regina. But I just remember Aaron being so adamant about not wanting to get married." He swung her around in an intricate step, she following easily. "However, I can see why he did change his mind. You're stunning," he murmured in a velvet tone.

Easing back, she stared at him. "Are you flirting with me, Marcos?"

"Of course," he replied flippantly.

She was forced to laugh even though she did not feel like it. Marcos and Jeannette had remarked how much Aaron had changed, and she wondered who was the real man she had reluctantly pledged her future to.

Had he proposed marriage because he truly did love her, or was revenge his intent? The question nagged at her until Marcos's voice shattered her musings.

"How much of Bahia have you seen?"

"Not too much. I visit Salvador several times a month. I'm

currently spending a lot of time at home because I'm restoring the garden."

Marcos tilted his head at an attractive angle, flashing a knowing smile. "I know Aaron is probably up to his eyeballs with his work at the institute and at the hospital, so I'm going to appoint myself as your personal guide. And if you're willing to give up a few days working in your garden I'll show you a place unlike any other on the continent. A thorough tour of Salvador will take about five days, while I can also plan a few day trips to Caldas do Jorro or Lençóis. One thing you must see is a *candomblé* ceremony."

"What is *candomblé?*"

"It is a religious ceremony that is wholly African in origin. The participants worship various divinities called *orixás.*"

Regina gave him a skeptical look. "Brazil is a Catholic country, yet you're saying the people practice *candomblé?*"

Marcos nodded. "It's fascinating. I'll take you to a *candomblé* ceremony, and let you judge for yourself. All I'll say is that Salvador is known as the most deeply religious of Brazilian cities, and has about one hundred-sixty churches and approximately four thousand *candomblé terreiros,* or temples."

"I can't wait."

"Wait for what?" questioned a deep, velvety voice.

Regina turned to find Aaron standing less than three feet away, watching her dance with his friend. "Marcos has promised to take me to a *candomblé* ceremony."

His expression became a mask of stone. "I'd prefer that you stayed away from those places."

Stepping away from Marcos, she moved over and wound her arm through Aaron's. "Why, Darling?"

"We'll talk about it later." He had addressed Regina, but his angry gaze was trained on his friend and neighbor.

Recognizing the warning look in Aaron's eyes, Marcos nodded to Regina. "Thank you for the dance."

"You're welcome," she called out as he walked away.

Aaron turned to look at her, his hands cradling her face. "What do you say we send our guests on their way, then go to bed?"

Her fingers curled around his strong wrists. "Before you do that I'd like to know something."

He gave her a sensual smile. "What is it?"

"This pretense of masquerading as husband and wife." He nodded. "Who are you trying to protect? Me, or yourself?"

His smile faded quickly. "What do you mean?"

She leaned closer, her gaze widening in the shadowed light from the minute bulbs hanging from the branches of a nearby tree. "I think it's your reputation you want to protect, not mine. It was you, Bahia's eminent Dr. Aaron Spencer, who swore he would never marry or father a child. But all of that has changed since—"

"Stop it, Regina!" He hadn't raised his voice, but the three words cut through the night like the crack of a whip.

"Stop what, Aaron? Stop wanting to live a lie? What's the matter with you that you can't accept the truth?"

"And what do you think is the truth?"

"That I've become a willing victim in your scheme to punish your father for marrying your fiancée."

He dropped his hands and turned away from her. "You're back to that again."

"I can't let it go, Aaron."

He turned slowly to face her, his impassive expression masking the rage threatening to explode. "And why not?" he questioned softly.

"You lost Sharon to Oscar, and you had to accept that. But why has it taken you twelve years to commit to marrying? Why me and not Elena, or some other woman? More importantly, why your father's widow?"

"You're asking questions I'm not able to answer, because there are no answers."

"You expect me to believe that?"

"Yes."

"Well, I can't, Aaron."

"Then you have a problem, Senhora Spencer. A very serious, personal problem."

"You're right about that," she confirmed. "Marcos told me about your oath that you would never marry or—"

"Marcos talks too much," he interrupted.

"But did you say it?"

Aaron silently cursed his friend for his loose tongue. He had never lied to Regina, even though they continued to live a lie. What Marcos revealed was true. After his aborted engagement he had returned to Bahia and confided in Marcos, leaving nothing out. And it was then he took a solemn oath that he would never marry or father children. He hadn't kept the oath because now he wanted to marry, and he looked forward to holding his child within the next six months.

"Yes, I did say it."

Closing her eyes, she nodded slowly. "Thank you for the truth."

It was Aaron's turn to close his eyes briefly, and when he opened them Regina had disappeared. He waited several minutes, trying to sort out what had just occurred between them. Marcos's return should've signaled a joyous reunion, but it hadn't. His friend had revealed a part of his past he had buried when he symbolically buried Oscar Spencer.

He had to get Regina to understand that his wanting to marry her had nothing to do with revenge. It was because he loved her, and wanted to share his life with her.

Exhaling, he let out his breath slowly. He would give her time and the space she needed to come to terms with their future. Then he would try to make amends for Marcos's careless comments.

CHAPTER 23

Regina felt the warmth of a hard body molded to her back; she opened her eyes, encountering darkness. Her eyelids fluttered before lowering as exhaustion descended on her like a warm, heavy blanket, but something about the darkness jolted her into a startling awareness as she sat up, blinking. Her gaze, fixed on the window closest to the bed, narrowed in concentration. A wavering orange glow dissected the night, growing brighter the longer she stared at it.

Her heart pounded uncontrollably in her chest, making it difficult for her to draw a normal breath. "Aaron!"

He came awake immediately, reaching out for her in the obscure shadows. "What's the matter?"

Her breath was coming faster as a momentary panic rendered her speechless. "The fields are on fire," she gasped, her voice sounding abnormally loud in the heavy silence.

Aaron was out of bed and turning on the table lamp in one motion. Reaching for the telephone, he pressed a button. Seconds later he shouted, "Turn on the sprinklers!"

Regina was still on her knees, staring out the window, when she heard Aaron pull on a pair of slacks and race barefoot out of the bedroom. Then she was galvanized into action, reaching for the bathrobe thrown over the arm of the chair in the sitting area.

Not waiting to search for her own shoes, she made her way down the staircase, out of the house, and across the courtyard to the garages. She shouted to Aaron as he shot past her in the Range

Rover, but he did not see her or chose to ignore her as he drove in the direction of the coffee fields.

The orange glow glimmered brightly against the blackness of the night, along with the distinctive smell of smoke. All she thought of was the fire spreading quickly, incinerating everything in its wake.

And Aaron had gone out into the night to meet the inferno. Fear snaked its way up her body, tightening around her throat so that she couldn't make a sound. How could he fight a fire without equipment?

"Fool!" she screamed when she finally found her voice. "Let the damn fields burn!"

It did not matter if he lost this year's crop. She would offset his losses from the assets she had not drawn from since receiving her trust fund at her majority. She wanted to go after Aaron and tell him, but she couldn't. Even though he always parked his cars in the garage with the keys in the ignition, she did not know the landscape well enough to maneuver in the dark. She had only accompanied Aaron once to the coffee fields, preferring instead to remain close to the house or in the garden.

The child she carried in her womb was heir to the house, land, and coffee plantation, yet she had not bothered to connect with any of it because she hadn't planned to remain in Bahia. She lived under Aaron's roof, shared his bed, but had yet to commit to share her future or that of his child with him.

The acrid smell of smoke increased as the orange glow dimmed until a wall of blackness shrouded the nighttime sky once again. She murmured a silent prayer that Aaron and Sebastião had managed to extinguish the fire. Moving slowly to a chair, she sat down and waited for Aaron's return.

Something startled Regina, and her head jerked up. Pink and yellow streaks of light crisscrossed the sky, heralding the beginning of a new day. She stared at Aaron as if she had never seen him before when he hunkered down beside her, smiling.

"Bom dia," she whispered, stretching her arms upward and returning his smile.

"Good morning to you." He arched an eyebrow at her. "There are at least a half-dozen beds in the house, yet you prefer sleeping on a chair in the courtyard where anyone can see you in a state of undress."

Glancing down, she realized the bodice of her robe hung open, revealing a generous amount of breast spilling over the lace of a matching nightgown.

She pulled her robe closer to her body, her eyes widening when she remembered why she was in the courtyard. "Did you put out the fire? Was there much damage?"

Rising to his feet, Aaron swept her up from the chair, and headed toward the house. The smell of smoke clung to his clothes and flesh. "It's out. And thanks to you, we managed to contain it to less than ten acres. Sebastião activated the underground irrigation system, keeping the ground wet enough so that the flames did not spread."

She tightened her arms around his strong neck. "What do you think caused the fire?"

"I don't know."

Her gaze met his. "Have you ever had fires before?"

"A few times," he replied softly. "We had a fire three years ago that destroyed the entire crop. That year we never had a rainy season, and everything was as dry as paper. A flash of lightning hit a tree, setting it afire. By the time we put it out we had nothing left to harvest. After that disaster I decided to put in the irrigation system."

His bare feet were silent as he mounted the staircase slowly. He walked into the bedroom and placed Regina on the bed. Leaning over, he kissed her forehead. "I have to shower. Don't run away," he teased, forcing a tired smile.

"I won't," she whispered, pulling his head down and pressing her parted lips to his. "Thank you for coming back safe."

Aaron gave her a questioning look before he removed her arms from his neck and walked toward the bathroom. She lay on the bed, staring up at the vaulted ceiling, knowing that when the time came it would not be easy to leave Aaron Spencer—he had become so much a part of her existence that she did not know when he hadn't been in her life—but she could not afford to let romantic notions control her just because she loved him.

And she did love him, but more than love was the realization that she had come to depend on him. It was as if the life she shared with Oscar had been reversed. Oscar had needed her, and she needed Aaron.

No, a silent voice whispered to her. She had to curb her need and dependence. And for the first time since she had stepped foot on Bahian soil she wanted May to come quickly, so that she could return to the United States.

Thinking of the States prompted her to pick up the telephone and dial her parents' number.

"Good morning," she said softly after hearing her mother's voice.

"Regina? Are you all right?"

"I'm fine."

"Then why are you calling me this early?"

She heard the repressed panic in her mother's low, sultry voice. "It's only early in Bahia, not Fort Lauderdale." Her gaze noted the numbers on the clock on the table alongside two small black and white photographs of Aaron's mother and stepmother-aunt. His features were an exact replica of the identical twin sisters. "I just wanted to talk to you."

"Don't fool with me, Regina," she warned. "We just *talked* two days ago. What's going on between you and Aaron?"

Staring at her bare feet, she noted a film of dust on her toes. When Aaron finished in the bathroom she would take her own shower. Her mother wanted to know what was going on between her and Aaron, and if she answered truthfully she would say nothing, because the problem wasn't Aaron but herself.

"It's me," she whispered.

There was a noticeable pause before Parris Cole responded. "What's wrong, Angel?"

"I don't know, Mommy. I don't know what's wrong with me."

"There's nothing wrong with you," Parris replied in a comforting tone. "You're pregnant and—"

"It has nothing to do with my physical condition," she interrupted. "It's more emotional." She hesitated, trying to form the phrases to explain how she felt about her relationship with Aaron. "I love him, Mommy. I love him more than I ever thought I would love a man."

"Loving him bothers you?"

"No. It's—it's a feeling of not trusting him that bothers me."

"Has he been unfaithful to you?"

"No. At least, I don't believe he has."

There was no way she could tell her mother that her libido was stronger than it had been before she slept with Aaron, matching and at times surpassing his fervid passion, which meant she gave him no reason to seek out another woman or women.

"I feel as if he's using me," she finally confessed.

"How?"

Taking a deep breath, Regina told her mother about Aaron's and Oscar's estrangement, then related what Jeannette and Marcos had revealed about the man whom she had fallen in love with.

"He's very possessive," she concluded.

"And probably just as controlling," Parris added.

"He will not control me. I will never permit any man to do that." She smiled when she heard her mother's husky laughter come through the receiver.

"He's possessive because he's fears losing you. Remember, he lost one woman he loved, and I'm certain he doesn't want history to repeat itself."

"What I want him to be able to do is trust me. Trust me enough to return to Florida to have my baby before I come back to Bahia."

"You're asking a lot from him. It was different when you left him in Mexico, because he did not know you were carrying his child."

"Why are you taking his side, Mommy?" She felt the rush of hot tears well up behind her eyelids.

"I'm not taking sides, Angel. I've been down the road you're now traveling. For more than nine years your father did not know he'd fathered a child. And once he found you it was always his fear that he would not have you for long. And he was right, Regina. He had you for a very short time. I remember him voicing his fear one day when we were sitting by the pool and he was watching you swim. *'She's growing up so quickly, it's frightening. Every time I see her she's changed. I'll have her for such a short time. In eight years she'll be eighteen, and by then I won't be the only man in her life.'* I knew he was praying for at least eight years, but his prayers weren't answered. I withheld the first nine years of your life from him, and then you left home before your seventeenth birthday.

"I've learned a lot about Martin Diaz Cole in the almost thirty years since my first meeting him, and his love is strong and deep—his love for his family and his children. And something tells me that Aaron Spencer is a lot like your father. You did not call me this morning just to talk, but for advice. And I'm going to be a meddling mother, grandmother, and mother-in-law-to-be and tell you to give Aaron a chance to love you and his child."

"Are you saying I shouldn't come home in May?"

"I'm saying that your home is in Bahia with Aaron."

"But I thought you did not want me to leave."

"I want you to be happy, Angel."

"I am happy," she argued.

"No, you're not. If you were we would not be having this conversation. Stay in Bahia and have your baby. Give Aaron the chance to prove himself. And whenever you're ready to come to Florida for a visit, I'll have your father send the jet for you."

Regina's delicate jaw tightened in annoyance. "I suppose you want me to marry him, too."

"That must be your decision, not mine. I also lived with your father for several months before he proposed marriage. I turned him down, while committing to living with him. Living with a man is very different from being married to him. I don't have to tell you which is more fulfilling."

Letting out her breath slowly, Regina closed her eyes. "I'll think about what you've said. Thank you, Mother."

"Mother!" Parris repeated, laughing. "What ever happened to Mommy?"

Opening her eyes, Regina smiled through her tears. "I'm going to be Mommy, and you're going to be Grandmother, or whatever you want this baby to call you."

"Grandma will do just fine, thank you."

"I love you, Mommy."

"And I love you, daughter."

"Bye."

"Until the next time," Parris said, repeating her usual parting statement.

Regina replaced the receiver in its cradle. Turning around, she saw Aaron standing less than six feet away from the bed. He had reentered the room so silently that she had not been aware of his presence—but she had no doubt that he had overheard a portion—maybe even all—of her conversation.

He stood over her, resplendent in his male nakedness, long fingers splayed over slim hips. His face was a glowering mask of rage. "I am committed to you, Regina. I am committed as any man could be without being married to you. I don't know what you want from me, but whatever it is I can't give it to you at this time."

His gaze narrowed as he took a step closer. "You don't trust me. Well, right now I don't trust myself to be with you."

Her initial shock wore off as she rose to her knees. Tilting her chin, she glared up at him. "I hope you're not threatening me, Aaron Spencer."

He shook his head. "There's no need for threats, because I'm going to make this easy for you. No more lies, Regina. Our only connection will be that you're carrying my child. Your life is your own to control, and for the duration of your stay in Bahia we don't have to share a bed. However, I'll make certain you'll always know where to contact me if you ever *need* me."

She watched, paralyzed, as he picked up his watch from the bedside table, then walked out of the bedroom, closing the door. He hadn't bothered to use the connecting dressing room. The separation was not only profound, but complete.

The tears which had welled up in her eyes during her telephone conversation with her mother now fell, staining her cheeks and the silk fabric of her nightgown. Aaron's shower had not lasted long enough. If he hadn't overheard her telephone call she would have told him what he had been waiting to hear the first day she arrived in Bahia.

She would have consented to become Mrs. Aaron Laurence Spencer.

Regina woke up late Christmas Eve morning, not wanting to get out of bed, but the pressure on her bladder and the need to eat surpassed her lethargy. Pushing aside the sheet, she left the bed and walked to the bathroom. It had taken a week for the realization to set in that Aaron intended to keep his word about allowing her to control her own life. If she saw him, it was only at a distance.

He rose early, conferred with Sebastião, then—on Mondays, Wednesdays, and Fridays—he saw patients in the pediatric clinic at the municipal hospital in Salvador. His Tuesdays, Thursdays, and Saturdays were spent at the research institute, despite the fact that all of the staff were on holiday for two months. On Sundays she caught a glimpse of him whenever he entered or exited his study. Most times, he looked through her as if she were a stranger, but whenever they chanced a face-to-face encounter he usually acknowledged her with a smile.

Each morning he left a schedule of his whereabouts, along with telephone numbers, on a bulletin board beside the wall phone in the kitchen, but knowing where he was did little to assuage her feelings of loss and alienation.

Her stubborn pride would not permit her to go to him and tell him that she wanted to share his bed, his name, his life, and his future. She had promised him that she would stay one hundred-eighty days, and she would. Then, she would leave him and Bahia to await the birth of her baby.

Half an hour later, dressed in a daffodil-yellow sundress with a loose-fitting waist and matching leather mules, Regina descended the staircase. She stopped before she stepped off the last stair, staring at Aaron as he was making his way up the staircase. Moving aside, she noticed the difference in his appearance immediately. His face was leaner, and his eyes appeared sunken in their sockets. As he neared her she felt the warmth of his large body. Her gaze widened when she saw the layer of moisture dotting his forehead.

Without thinking she reached out and touched his forearm. The heat of his dry flesh burned her fingertips. "You're sick!"

He jerked his arm away. "Stay away from me."

Regina flinched at his angry tone, but recovered quickly. "You need a doctor."

His upper lip curled in a sardonic sneer. "I *am* a doctor."

"But not a very smart one," she snapped. "You should be in bed."

Closing his eyes, Aaron supported his sagging body against the banister. "That's where I was going."

She stood aside, watching him literally drag himself up the stairs. "Have you taken any medication?"

Aaron shook his head, chiding himself for attempting the motion. Every bone in his body ached, along with a pounding headache that would not permit him to think clearly. He knew what he had contracted. It was the flu.

Regina continued her descent, raced into the kitchen, and picked up the telephone. She called the Benedetti residence, apologizing profusely to Nicolas for disturbing him at home. He promised to come to the da Costa estate within the hour.

She hung up, then busied herself brewing a pot of green tea, at the same time nibbling on fresh pineapple, mango, and guava slices. Temporarily assuaging her own hunger, she prepared a tray with a cup of tea, freshly squeezed orange juice, and a small portion of applesauce.

Aaron was in bed, asleep, when she walked into his bedroom. This bedroom was an exact replica of the one she slept in, except that it was smaller and claimed an adjoining half-bath instead of a full one.

Placing the tray on a bedside table, she walked into the bathroom and soaked a small cloth with cold water. Returning to the bedroom, she placed the cloth over Aaron's head, and he came awake immediately. She noticed he hadn't shaved, and a coarse stubble of hair covered his lean cheeks.

He pushed her hand and the cloth away. "Go away, Regina. I don't want you to get sick."

She slapped at his hand. "I'm not going to get sick."

Closing his eyes, he let out his breath in a shuddering sigh. "Think about the baby," he slurred.

"It's not the baby that's sick," she retorted. "It's his father."

"*Her* father," he moaned, throwing a muscled arm over his forehead.

"*His* father," she insisted. "Move your am, Aaron."

"No."

Leaning over his prone body, she pulled his arm down and replaced it with the cloth. "Don't fight with me. You can't possibly win."

A slight smile softened his jaw. "You're taking advantage of me because I don't feel well."

"When you're feeling better I'll offer you a rematch."

Opening his eyes, he stared up at her. "I don't want a rematch."

"What do you want?" Her husky voice had lowered to a velvet whisper.

"You know what I want."

"Say it," she challenged.

He closed his eyes again, a frown creasing his forehead. "No. I will not ask you again."

She wanted to tell him that she would marry him, but swallowed back the words poised on the tip of her tongue. She had time. They had time. They had five months to learn to trust each other before she boarded the flight which would take her back to the United States.

She managed to get him to take in half a cup of tea, several ounces of orange juice, and three tablespoons of applesauce before he drifted off to sleep. Then she lay down beside him, holding him close to her ripening body until Nicolas arrived.

Regina sat on an armchair in the corner of the bedroom while Nicolas checked his patient's vital signs, glancing away when he swabbed an area on Aaron's hip before injecting him with an antibiotic which was certain to bring down his high fever.

"How is he?" she asked after Nicolas motioned for her to step out of the room with him.

"He'll feel more like himself in a couple of days. I gave him something that will make him more comfortable, even though it will not speed his recovery. Only bed rest will do that."

"What's wrong with him?"

"He probably has a virus. Several of my patients have come down with the same malady." He handed her a vial filled with capsules. "Make certain he takes one of these twice a day. Give him the first one around nine o'clock tonight. If he's not feeling any better tomorrow morning, call me."

"I'm sorry I had to call you at home—"

"If you hadn't called, I would have been very annoyed with you," Nicolas said, stopping her apology.

She offered him an attractive, dimpled smile. "Thank you, Nicolas."

Leaning over, he kissed her cheek. "I want you to take care of yourself. You're much more vulnerable to the flu than Aaron."

She saw Nicolas to the door, then returned to the upper level and Aaron. She sat at his bedside, reading and watching him sleep, leaving only to eat. At nine o'clock, she forced a capsule between his lips and got him to drink a cup of water. When she lay down beside him, she noticed his skin was cooler than it had been earlier that morning.

Closing her eyes, she slept, one arm thrown over his flat belly.

CHAPTER 24

Regina and Aaron celebrated Christmas a week late. He left his bed before sunrise, but had not gone to the coffee fields.

They sat together at a table in the pergola, sharing breakfast for the first time in two weeks. He'd lost weight, the evidence reflected by the gauntness of his face. He had removed the week's growth of whiskers from his lean jaw, but had not trimmed his moustache to its former clipped precision. It was thicker, fuller, concealing most of his upper lips.

"Marcos stopped by yesterday with an invitation to a New Year's Eve party," she stated, breaking a comfortable silence. "His parents decided at the last possible moment to throw a little something to welcome him home."

"What did you tell him?"

"I declined the invitation."

Aaron shifted an eyebrow. "Why?"

"You're still recovering from the flu."

"That shouldn't stop you from attending."

Regina stared at him for a long moment. "I know I don't need your permission to accept an invitation. I declined the invitation for you because I didn't want you to relapse. I declined for myself because I did not want to attend without you."

Aaron was not successful when he tried concealing a satisfied grin. "Should I accept your not wanting to attend without me as a compliment?"

She felt a warm glow flow through her. "Yes."

He inclined his head. "Thank you."

Removing a slender, foil-wrapped box from the large patch pocket of a flowing smock, she pushed it across the table. "It's a little late, but Merry Christmas."

He grew still, staring at her over the rim of his coffee cup. "I wasn't expecting anything."

Lowering her head, she flashed a shy smile. "I bought it before you…" Her words trailed off.

Aaron placed his cup on the saucer. "Before I started acting like a horse's ass." Her head came up, her eyes crinkling in laughter. "Don't say anything, *Princesa,*" he warned softly. "I've called myself every name imaginable for being Bahia's biggest fool."

"Open it, Aaron."

"Don't you want to talk about it?"

"No, I don't. It's the past, Aaron. Let it remain in the past."

But he wanted to talk about it. He wanted to allay her fears, gain her trust, and offer her his name and protection for the rest of her life.

"Let me get your gift, and we'll open them together," he said instead.

Regina waited for Aaron to go into the house to retrieve the gift he had selected for her. She inhaled, then let out her breath slowly. They hadn't resolved their differences, but at least they were talking to each other.

Aaron returned to the pergola and handed her a gaily wrapped gift. Leaning down, he pressed his mouth to the side of her neck. "Merry Christmas."

She shivered noticeably, savoring the brush of silken hair on her sensitive flesh. "Thank you."

Her fingers were shaking slightly as she peeled away the paper covering a large, square velvet box. Even without lifting the top, she knew it contained a piece of jewelry.

Shafts of sunlight filtering through overhead trees caught the fiery brilliance of a necklace of graduated diamonds the instant she raised the cover. Tilting her head, her startled gaze met Aaron's amused one.

"Oh, Aaron. It's beautiful."

"I hope you like it."

"I love it. Thank you." Removing the necklace from the box, she handed it to him. "Help me put it on."

He draped the length of diamond around her neck, securing the clasp. Pulling her gently from her chair, he smiled down at her. "They are almost as beautiful as you are."

Her fingers caressed the flawless, blue-white stones. "I'll treasure it—always."

Cocking his head at an angle, Aaron studied her animated expression. He knew she was upset when she lost her wedding ring, and had felt the need to replace it with another dramatic piece of jewelry. He had considered giving her a bracelet until the jeweler showed him the necklace. Seeing the brilliant stones resting below the delicate bones of her clavicle verified he had made the right decision.

Moving closer, Regina curved her arms around his neck, burying her face against his shoulder. His arms came up, circling her waist and pulling her to his middle. Oh, how he'd missed her. He missed her more than he could have ever imagined.

The few times he had woken he'd found her asleep at the foot of his bed, but had been too ill to reach for her. Even in his weakened condition he had wanted to hold her, kiss her, love her. And his love for her frightened him, because he feared he loved Regina more than he loved himself.

"Open your gift, Aaron," she urged softly, her warm breath caressing his throat.

He released her, feeling her loss the moment she pulled out of his embrace. He sat down and unwrapped his gift, closing his eyes briefly after he'd glimpsed the exquisite, solid gold razor with his name engraved on its gracefully curved handle, resting on a bed of navy-blue velvet.

He opened his eyes, smiling at her. "How did you know? Where did you get it?"

"Oh, Aaron, how could I not know?" she laughed. "You only

have a half-dozen of them on the shelf in the bathroom adjoining the master bedroom. I called my mother and asked her to pick it up for me."

He sobered quickly. "I collect antique razors, but none of them are solid gold. You should not have spent so much—"

"Did I give you a limit on how much you could spend on my gift?" she countered, cutting him off.

He managed to look sheepish. "No, ma'am."

"I thought not," she crooned, giving him a smug smile.

The exchange of gifts signaled a change, a change which offered them a glimpse of what they had shared before mistrust and doubt had come between them.

They spent the evening in the garden, enjoying the ethereal setting when they sat on a stone bench near the gurgling fountain. The instant the clock tolled the twelve o'clock hour, heralding the advent of a new year, Aaron dropped an arm around Regina's shoulder; they watched the sky light up with fireworks set off by the revelers at the Jarres.

He stood up, smiling and extending his hand. "Will you share a dance with me to celebrate the new year?" She placed her hand in his, and he pulled her gently to her feet. "Thank you, Senhora Spencer."

"You're quite welcome, Senhor Spencer," Regina whispered, enjoying his closeness and masculine strength.

He cradled her waist, one hand splayed over her rounded belly, waltzing her around and around the fountain until she pleaded fatigue. Bending slightly, he picked her up and carried her across the courtyard and into the house. There was only the sound of their breathing when he climbed the staircase to the second level.

Holding her breath, Regina met and held his direct stare as he lowered her to her bed. She exhaled, closing her eyes when he pressed his mouth to her forehead.

"Happy new year, *Princesa*. I hope this is the year all of your dreams come true."

She managed a tremulous smile. "So do I, Aaron." *So do I, my darling,* she repeated silently.

Aaron hesitated, his penetrating gaze sweeping over her composed features. They had declared a truce; a very fragile truce for the beginning of a new year.

Regina did not move, not even her eyes, when her gaze fused with his. She knew he was waiting, waiting for her to invite him into her bed. She wanted him, she had missed him, but there was no way she could fall into his arms and offer him her body until they resolved their differences. And that would not happen with just a passionate session of lovemaking, because after a physical release the doubts would still remain.

They had time; she had time; she had months to commit to spending the rest of her life with Aaron Spencer, or walk away from him—forever.

Regina's new year began with a whirlwind frenzy of social activity. She spent time with Jeannette Benedetti. They shared lunch or shopping excursions. And she toured Bahia with Marcos Jarre. She suspected Aaron wasn't too pleased with the amount of time she spent with Marcos, but he had yet to voice his annoyance.

That all changed when she strolled into the house half an hour before midnight in late January.

He walked out of his study at the same time she headed for the staircase. "Where have you been?"

She stopped suddenly, staring at him, her forehead creasing in bewilderment. "If I was not here, Aaron, then wouldn't I have to have been *out?*"

He ignored her curt retort. "Out with Marcos?"

Her frown faded. "Yes. Why?"

Aaron struggled to control not only his temper but a surge of red-hot jealousy. "Is it not enough that he monopolizes your days? Must that also include your nights?"

"Lençóis is not around the corner. It was a six-hour drive, each way, from Salvador."

"I'm aware of the geography of Bahia, Senhora Spencer."

"Then what exactly is the problem, Aaron?"

"I want you to spend less time with Marcos."

Regina closed her eyes, sighing heavily. She was tired, bone tired, and she needed to take a bath to soak her tired and aching feet and legs before she fell into bed.

Opening her eyes, she stared up at Aaron glaring down at her. He still had not gained back the weight he'd lost when he had come down with the flu. The bones in his face were more pronounced than when she had first met him; she now thought of him as lean and dangerous-looking with the thick moustache.

"I wouldn't spend so much time with Marcos touring Bahia if you had offered to take me around. You close the research institute for two months, yet you still go in as if it were open."

"Why didn't you tell me you wanted to see Bahia?"

"I shouldn't have to ask you, Aaron," she countered angrily.

"I don't read minds," he argued, his voice rising slightly. "I offered to buy you a car so that you can get around independently, but you refused it. You said you wanted time in the garden. If you're afraid of driving by yourself, then you should've said something."

"I'm not afraid to drive."

"Then what is it?"

"Nothing," she replied wearily. "Look, Aaron, I'm exhausted, and I have to go bed." What she did not tell him was that she did not want any tokens of permanence, because when she left Bahia she would leave with only her clothes and personal items.

He inclined his head. "We'll continue this in the morning."

She gave him a tired smile. "Thank you. *Boa noite*."

"Boa noite, Princesa."

She climbed the staircase slowly, one hand resting over her belly. She stopped, her eyes widening in shock. A dreamy smile softened the lines of fatigue ringing her generous mouth.

Aaron saw her stop and was beside her in seconds. "What's the matter?"

Her head came up slowly as she rewarded him with a tearful smile. "I felt the baby move, Aaron." Reaching for his hand, she placed it over the area where she had felt the slight fluttering.

"It's called quickening." He could not disguise the hoarseness of his own voice.

"He just moved again," she whispered, leaning into him.

Aaron curved an arm around her shoulders and led her up the staircase to her bedroom. "You're practically falling asleep on your feet. I'll fix your bath and wash you—"

"No," she cut in, shaking her head.

"Yes," he stated firmly. "Don't fight with me, Regina. Even though you've put on a little weight over the past few months, I'm still bigger than you are."

"You're a bully."

"Wrong," he countered, sitting her gently on the bed and removing her shoes. "I'm the man who loves your life."

He took off her slacks, smock top, and underwear, leaving her briefly to fill the bathtub. A quarter of an hour later, she lay on the bed, her scented body tingling from the light pressure of his magical fingers as he massaged the tight muscles in her legs and feet.

"Aaron?"

"What is it, *Princesa?*"

"I'd like to make a request."

Covering her nude body with a sheet, he sat down beside her. "What is it?"

"Stay with me tonight."

Leaning closer, his mouth grazed an earlobe. "Are you asking me to share your bed?"

"Yes." She slurred the single word, and within seconds she was asleep.

Aaron watched her features relax as she succumbed to the exhaustion she had valiantly fought and lost. He combed his fingers through the raven curls falling over the top of her ear, his former anger fading.

Her outings with his childhood friend had begun innocently enough when Marcos offered to take her to the historical churches, forts, and buildings of colonial Salvador. After two weeks their excursions escalated to day-long outings to Cachoeira, Ilhéus, and Caldas do Jorro. He was pleased that Regina enjoyed Marcos's company and his vast knowledge of African history, but he did not like Marcos's obvious obsession with the woman who was carrying his child.

He had planned to confront Marcos, warning him to stay away from Regina before she revealed that she saw Marcos because he had not been there for her. And she was right. Even though the institute was closed, he still went into his office like clockwork. Regina had always been so fiercely independent and solitary that he had not thought of spending more time with her. Now that would change. Moving off the bed, he headed to the bathroom to shower, then returned to lie down beside her.

She felt the power of his large body as it settled against her back. Stirring slightly, she moved toward the source of heat.

"Go back to sleep," a deep voice crooned close to her ear.

"Te amo," she whispered in Spanish.

"And I love you," Aaron confessed, pulling her closer.

Regina stopped pacing long enough to give Aaron a tortured look. "Where could they be, Aaron? The jet landed more than an hour ago."

He stood up, took her hand, and eased her back down to the seat beside his. "Sit down and relax. They're probably being held up in customs. It's Carnival time, and the whole world comes to Brazil to party."

"But my father always has us pre-cleared before we arrive." Aaron gave her a look that said he did not believe her. "I never wait with other passengers when I fly on the corporate jet."

Money and rank have their privileges, Aaron mused silently. "Don't worry, *Princesa,* they'll be here." Nodding, she rested her head against his shoulder.

Aaron was not as relaxed as he appeared. Two days ago Sebastião woke him up with the report of another fire. This time more than a hundred acres were destroyed before the fast-moving blaze was extinguished.

When the people who worked in the fields reported to work that morning, he gathered them all together and lectured them sternly about smoking. No one—and he reiterated, *no one*—was allowed to smoke anywhere on the da Costa property. A single infraction was cause for immediate dismissal.

"There they are!"

Aaron stood up, staring at a tall, attractive couple as they followed a baggage handler. Their resemblance to Regina was startling—especially her brother.

Arianna Cole spotted her sister and raced ahead of Tyler, her arms outstretched, while he slowed his pace and stared over his broad shoulder at a beautiful, dark-skinned Brazilian girl who flirted shamelessly with him as they passed each other.

Regina hugged her sister, then kissed her cheek. "I've been pacing the floor waiting for you guys. Welcome to Bahia."

Arianna pulled back, her clear, green-flecked brown eyes surveying her older sister. "You look beautiful."

Regina wrinkled her nose. "I look fat."

"Pregnant women are suppose to gain weight." She examined Regina's rounded face, softly curling short hair, fuller breasts, and the hint of a rounded belly under an exquisitely tailored bright orange linen smock over a pair of slim black slacks. "You look better pregnant than not."

Arianna's gaze shifted to the tall man standing several feet behind her sister, arms crossed over his chest. Her eyes widened when she noticed that there was something about the man that reminded her of her own father. "Is that Aaron?" she whispered *sotto voce*. Regina nodded, smiling. "Good grief! He's hot!"

Shaking her head in amusement, Regina directed her sister over to Aaron. "This is Arianna. My very talented sister just earned a spot in our next Olympic swim team."

Aaron smiled at the teenage girl, his teeth showing whitely under his moustache. Leaning over, he placed a kiss on her cheek. "It's a pleasure to meet you. Congratulations on making the team."

Arianna flashed a bright smile. "Thanks."

Tyler walked over to Aaron and extended his right hand. "Thanks for having us, Dr. Spencer. Tyler Cole."

Aaron shook the proffered hand, then pulled Tyler to him in a rough embrace. "None of that Dr. Spencer business, Tyler. It's Aaron."

Tyler nodded, offering him a smile so reminiscent of his older sister's. "Okay, Aaron."

Dropping his arms around the shoulders of the Cole siblings, he smiled at them. "Welcome to Bahia. Regina and I will give you time to settle in, rest up, and get used to the heat. Then after that it's party time."

"When does Carnival begin?" Tyler asked.

"It starts up around Friday, but by Saturday it's in full swing. And for four full days all business stops for what becomes a street party."

"Is it only at night?" Arianna questioned.

"It's all day and all night," Aaron replied.

"Hot damn!" Tyler whispered under his breath.

Aaron gave him a sidelong look. "Did you come to party, or did you come for the girls?"

"Both," he said, flashing his attractive shy grin.

Regina laughed. Her very serious brother had finally discovered the opposite sex. She had begun to give up on him, because in the past he'd much preferred reading a book to interacting with girls his own age. Tyler was his father's son. He had inherited his height, astounding masculine beauty, and the famous male Cole charm.

Her brother and sister had planned to stay a week, and a week was enough for Regina, because having them with her would counter her occasional spells of homesickness.

CHAPTER 25

Aaron helped Regina and Arianna into the Range Rover before directing the baggage handler to store the Coles' luggage in the cargo area. He tipped the man, then slipped behind the wheel beside Tyler.

Slipping on a pair of sunglasses against the rays of the fiery Brazilian sun, he waited patiently until he could maneuver out of the traffic jam at the Salvador airport. The area's population had almost doubled with the influx of tourists for Carnival. While the festivities surrounding Rio's Carnival had waned over the years, the reverse had not been true for Bahia. It had become one of the most spontaneous street festivals on the face of the earth. It was not only spontaneous, but uninhibited, and unadulterated fun. He had stayed away for the past three years because seeing everyone celebrating with such fervid abandonment had reminded him of how empty his life had become. He had existed for his medical research, and nothing more. But now he awaited the birth of his child; a child who would give him a purpose for existing beyond his career.

He took a quick glance at Tyler Cole's perfect profile. "Your sister says you're thinking of a career in medicine."

Tyler smiled. "I am."

"What schools have you considered?"

"I'm thinking of applying to the big ones—Harvard, Yale, Stanford. Where did you go?"

Aaron smiled. "Johns Hopkins. If you think about attending, let me know and I'll write you a letter of recommendation."

"Would you do that?" There was no mistaking the excitement in the younger man's voice.

"Of course. It's the least I could do for the uncle of my son or daughter."

"Do you know what sex the baby is?" Arianna asked from the backseat.

"No." Regina and Aaron had spoken in unison.

"Why not?" she asked.

"Regina doesn't want to know," Aaron replied, glancing up at the rearview mirror.

Arianna sucked her teeth. "I think I'd want to know."

"So would I," Aaron concurred.

"It's going to be a boy," Tyler predicted.

Reaching forward, Regina patted her brother's shoulder. "I think you're right."

"If it is a boy, then Daddy is going to lose his mind," Arianna stated with a big smile. "He's already set up a stock portfolio for the baby. All he's waiting for is the name."

Aaron wanted to tell Arianna that he could afford to provide for his child, but swallowed back the words. He had to remember that his son or daughter was also a Cole, and the Coles had established their own traditions. On the other hand, he intended to establish a few Spencer traditions which would be handed down from one generation to another. The land he owned was still known as the da Costa estate, even though the last of the da Costa line ended with Leonardo. After the birth of his son or daughter he would officially change the deed to read Spencer.

Regina showed Arianna to her bedroom. "This is it," she said, gesturing with a slender hand.

Arianna walked slowly into a room where a massive, four-poster iron bed dominated the space. Panels of antique ivory lace floated around the bed, offering furtive glimpses of lace-trimmed pillows, shams, and bolsters. A pedestal table cradled a vase filled with a profusion of fragrant white and pale pink flowers.

A Chippendale-style chest-on-chest and a burgundy brocade armchair and matching footstool were nestled in a corner near a door which opened to a full bath.

"This house and everything in it is magnificent, Regina. I hate to say it, but you're a better decorator than Mommy."

"Bite your tongue, Ari," Regina teased. "I can't take credit for anything you see here. Aaron's aunt was mistress to these treasures long before I arrived."

Closing the door softly, Arianna leaned against it. "When are you going to become the mistress?"

"Say what?"

"When are you going to marry Aaron?"

Regina felt a rush of heat suffuse her face. "Who told you to ask me that? Mommy? Daddy?"

"I'm not going to answer that. You can tell me to mind my own damn business—"

"Arianna Cole!"

Pushing off the door, Arianna threw up both hands. "Don't act so shocked. I've said worse. Back to my question. When are you going to marry Aaron? Even though I'm not sexually active, I know when a man loves a woman. I've seen Mommy and Daddy together enough to know. And your Dr. Spencer has it real bad."

Tilting her chin, Regina stared down the length of her nose at her younger sister. "If you know so much, then you'd see that I love him."

"Love him enough to marry him?"

"Yes."

"What's stopping you?"

"He hasn't asked me—lately."

Arianna's mouth dropped open. "Lately?"

"We've had a few squabbles, and even though we live under the same roof we've been somewhat estranged."

"Which means?"

"He sleeps in his bedroom, and I sleep in my bedroom."

Rolling her eyes upward, Arianna shook her head. "You're both too old to play games."

"And you're not old enough to understand the dynamics. I suggest you take *siesta,* because we're going to Salvador later tonight to eat. Then tomorrow night we're throwing a pre-Carnival party. Our neighbor has cousins visiting from the Dominican Republic who are around your age. They will probably want to hang out with you and Tyler."

"Cool!"

Regina wrinkled her nose. "Yeah, cool. Did you bring something to party in?"

"I have a few outfits."

"How would you like to go to a beauty spa with me tomorrow morning? You can have your hair trimmed, get a manicure, pedicure, facial, and massage. And if we have time we can always visit a few boutiques to pick up a few more party outfits. Remember, Carnival is four days of nonstop fun."

Arianna executed a dance step, spinning around on her toes. "Yes!"

Aaron sat across from Tyler Cole, silently admiring the younger man's enthusiasm. Tyler had elected to forego *siesta* when he urged him to talk about his research projects.

"What are you working on now?"

"We have two projects going at the same time," Aaron replied. "Several of the doctors have developed an oral antiviral agent which has been used experimentally in children and adults with meningitis to shorten the course of the disease."

Leaning forward on the sofa, Tyler rested his elbows on his knees. "But viral meningitis, unlike the bacterial version, is not life-threatening."

"You're right about that. But the picornaviruses are small viruses that, once inside the body, can travel to many different tissues, causing disease, inflammation of the heart muscle, otitis media or inflammation of the middle ear, meningitis, and the common cold. And viral meningitis also causes incapacitating headaches that can last two weeks or more."

"What's the drug's reaction time?"

"Most patients feel better on the first day, and many had their painful headaches disappear within a week. Most patients in the study recovered within nine days instead of taking the usual fourteen for the infection to run its course."

"That sounds exciting."

"It is for infectious-disease doctors," Aaron confirmed. "I'm personally involved in a project where we have successfully developed a bandage that can stop severe bleeding in seconds, potentially saving thousand of lives on battlefields and highways. I received a grant two years ago from the US Army after I'd sent a proposal to the Pentagon for funding to develop the experimental bandage and a related foam and spray that contain freeze-dried clotting agents in concentrations fifty to one hundred times greater than human blood."

Tyler wagged his head in amazement. "Have they begun using it?"

"Clinical trials are to begin in a couple of months at an army hospital in Texas, where the bandage will be applied to the gushing wounds from prostate removal surgery."

"What will the foam and spray be used for?"

"The foam is intended for bullet wounds and other punctures that bleed from deep inside the body, while the clotting spray is for seeping wounds like severe burns and torn muscle."

Tyler continued with his questioning. "What did you use for the clotting process?"

"A protein called fibrinogen and the enzyme thrombin."

"Isn't thrombin derived from plasma?"

Aaron nodded, smiling. There was no doubt Tyler Cole was a brilliant student and would probably gain admission to any college he selected. "When the fibrinogen and thrombin come in contact with blood, they instantly begin forming a sticky lattice called fibrin that adheres to live tissue and eventually becomes a scab."

"Oh, man, that's incredible."

"We are pretty excited about it. By the way, what branch of medicine are you interested in?"

Tyler shifted his sweeping black eyebrows. "I don't know yet. I've thought about obstetrics, but I keep vacillating between that and epidemiology."

"Have you considered pediatrics?"

Tyler registered Aaron's smug expression. "You're a pediatrician, aren't you?"

Smiling broadly, he nodded, then glanced at his watch. "We have some time before we have to be ready to go out for dinner tonight. How would you like a tour of the hospital and research institute? Maybe seeing everything up close and personal will help you make up your mind."

Tyler sprang to his feet, then seemed embarrassed by his eagerness. "I'd love that, Dr....Aaron," he said, correcting himself quickly.

"Wait here for me. I have to let your sister know where we're going."

Aaron took the stairs two at a time, then made his way down the hallway to Regina's room. Knocking lightly on the door, he pushed it opened. A tender smile curved his mouth when he saw her lying on her side, facing the open window.

"Have you come to share *siesta* with me?" Her sultry voice sent a warming shiver down his spine.

He walked around the bed and sat down beside her. "You should've asked me before I promised Tyler that I'd take him on a tour of the hospital."

She placed a hand over his. "I'll take a rain check."

"Will that rain check be valid for other than *siesta?*"

She lifted an eyebrow. "What are you asking?"

Leaning over, he pressed his mouth to hers. "How about tonight?"

"I'll let you know," she whispered against his parted lips.

"When?"

"Tonight."

Increasing the pressure on her mouth, he cradled her head between his palms and drank deeply, temporarily assuaging a gnawing thirst he had been forced to endure for weeks.

"Tonight," he repeated, reluctantly pulling away. Running a finger down the length of her delicate nose, he winked at her. "I'll see you later, *Princesa.*"

Regina stared at him, holding his gaze as he stood up and backed away from the bed. She waited until he closed the door behind his departing figure, then closed her eyes. She lay motionless, enjoying the feel of the tiny life moving in her womb. A feeling of peace invaded her as she imagined holding a nursing child to her full breasts. Then she fell asleep, a gentle smile mirroring the peace she had discovered since Aaron Spencer had walked into her life.

"Aaron, please help me put my necklace on."

He took the length of glittering diamonds from her fingers and looped it around her neck, securing the clasp. "We wouldn't be late for our guests if you hadn't wanted to stay in bed," he whispered close to her ear.

"Oh, now it's my fault *you* wanted to spend the afternoon in bed."

Curving an arm under her breasts, Aaron eased Regina back to lean against his chest. "It's your fault that I've had to undergo a long and agonizing period of abstinence. So don't blame me if I got carried away. Do you want to have another go at it?"

"Behave, Aaron," she chided softly.

"I am."

Turning in his loose embrace, she raised her face for his kiss, and she wasn't disappointed when he left her mouth burning with a passion that rekindled her desire all over again.

Pushing gently against his chest, she moaned softly. "Go and greet our guests. I'll be down as soon as I repair my makeup." She had to run a comb through her hair and reapply her lipstick.

Aaron had waited twenty-four hours to redeem his *rain check.* They had shared *siesta,* and each other's bodies, for the first time in more than a month. She had been humiliatingly conscious of his scrutiny when he stared at her naked body before placing a large hand over a pendulous breast. She looked very pregnant, with and without her clothes. There were times when she did not feel very attractive, and she feared Aaron would not find her attractive or desirable. Her fears were unfounded, though, when he closed his eyes and traced every curve of her body with his fingertips as if he were a sculptor idolizing his creation.

Their lovemaking was tender, passions tempered, until it finally exploded in a soaring ecstasy that had been building for more weeks than she could remember. The rush of sexual fulfillment had rendered her unable to move as her breath had come in long, surrendering moans of amazing completeness. Then she slept for hours, long past the time when she had allotted to prepare herself for the pre-Carnival party she and Aaron planned to host for her brother, sister, their friends, and neighbors.

She retouched her mouth with a shimmering copper lip color, then ran a comb through her professionally coiffed hair. The image staring back at her reflected a woman in love. She literally glowed: her eyes and flawless skin competed with the length of flawless diamonds draped around her neck.

She had elected to wear midnight-blue silk—sleeveless top with a scoop neck banded in satin, and matching silk slacks. Her shoes were low-heeled, navy-blue patent leather pumps with satin bows. Her jewelry was Aaron's mother's wedding ring, his Christmas gift necklace, and a pair of diamond stud earrings she received from her parents to celebrate her sixteenth birthday.

Checking her reflection for the last time, she went downstairs to join her guests.

Taped music blared from a sound system set up around the courtyard and pergola. Regina and Aaron had catered a sit-down dinner for twelve following a buffet where platters of fish and meat appetizers and potent drinks to wash down the spicy fare were served by silent, efficient waiters.

Dinner included grilled meats and chicken and *feijoada,* a dish consisting of black beans, sausage, beef, and pork served with rice, finely shredded kale, orange slices, and *farofa.* Regina had quickly developed a taste for *farofa,* which was manioc flour that was fried with onions and egg. She avoided most dishes prepared with coconut milk, dende oil, and the fiery malagueta pepper. Certain foods she had been able to consume before becoming pregnant were now shifted to a DO NOT EAT list.

Throughout dinner she watched Tyler interact with Marcos Jarre's female cousin and her sister flirt with his two male cousins. Arianna had elected to wear a black tank dress that showed off more flesh than Regina had ever displayed, creating a stir among the younger males, who were stunned by the perfection of her strong, lean athletic body. Dinner was a leisurely affair, lasting nearly three hours before everyone retreated to the courtyard to dance or walk off the ample portions of food that were followed by a number of rich, sweet desserts.

Marcos approached Aaron and patted him on his back. "Excellent party, friend. Good food, good music, and perfect weather for a gathering of old and new friends." He gestured with a hand holding a glass filled with a well-made *caipirinha.* The concoction of *cacahaça*—a high-proof, sugarcane alcohol—lime, sugar, and crushed ice, was Brazil's national drink. "Your niece and nephew seem to have hit it off well with my cousins."

Aaron took a sip of his own *caipirinha* as he watched Tyler lean closer to whisper in the ear of the sixteen-year-old girl from Santo Domingo. Tyler and Arianna, like Regina, were also fluent in Spanish.

"What can I say, Marcos? They are teenagers."

Marcos nodded, withdrawing a slim cigar from the pocket of his jacket. He snapped open a lighter, and within seconds the flame caught and lit the fragrant tobacco.

His hand tightening around his glass, Aaron stared numbly at Marcos. "When did you start smoking?"

Taking several more puffs to ensure the cigar was lit, Marcos blew out a stream of smoke, watching it curl in the air. "About a year ago. I took a side trip to Turkey and decided to sample one of their renowned blends. After a couple of puffs, I was hooked." He held the cigar between his thumb and forefinger. "It's not Turkish, but it's the best Brazil has to offer."

"Be careful where you put it out. I've had two fires in my fields this season."

"I thought I smelled smoke the other night."

"You did. I've lost a little more than a hundred acres. I've banned all smoking on the property."

"I'll be careful." Even though Marcos had spoken to Aaron his gaze was fixed on Regina as she laughed at something his Dominican-born mother had said.

Aaron saw the direction of his gaze, and a shadow of annoyance settled onto his features. Since he had spoken to Regina about spending so much time with Marcos she had curtailed her outings with him, but apparently that had not stopped his boyhood friend from seeking her out.

Marcos had called one morning asking to speak to her, but was disappointed when Magda informed him that Senhora Spencer had gone to Salvador with her husband.

"I've been meaning to speak to you about Regina," Aaron began in a dangerously soft tone.

Marcos lifted his head alertly, but did not look at Aaron. "What about her?"

"I want you to stop seeing her so often."

Turning, Marcos glared at him from behind the lenses of his glasses. "Are you telling me to stay away from her?"

"That's not what I said."

"What you are asking is impossible."

"And why the hell not!"

"Because I love her, Aaron."

"Don't even go there, Marcos."

"And why not? We wouldn't be having this conversation if you paid more attention to her."

Aaron's left hand shot out, his fingers grasping the front of his neighbor's shirt. Tightening his grip, he jerked Marcos closer. "I'll forget you ever said that because I've always regarded you as a brother. But if you ever cross the line and try to come between me and Regina, I'll forget the oath I took when I became a doctor and take your life." His chest rose and fell heavily as he tried curbing the rage coursing throughout his body.

Marcos had seen Aaron angry once, and that one time was enough. He would not test him further. He had told him the truth. He loved Regina—her beauty, intelligence, sensitivity, and her enthusiasm for learning—but he wasn't *in* love with her, at least not enough to test his lifelong friendship with Aaron or his volatile temper.

"I would never disrespect you or Regina," he offered in apology. "At least, not the way you think." He let out a sigh of relief when Aaron released him. "You're a lucky man, Aaron, because you have what most men spend all of their lives seeking. You have a beautiful, intelligent woman who loves you selflessly. You are the heir to lands whose history is documented in books written about this region, while the woman you love is carrying a child who will eventually inherit not only his property, but also a heritage which he or she will be able to trace back to the powerful and mighty kingdoms of ancient Africa."

Aaron took several steps, then stopped and stared up at the clear summer sky. He was losing it. He hadn't realized how close he had come to injuring Marcos until after he had grabbed him. If he hadn't been holding a glass in his right hand he was certain he would've hit him.

For several seconds it had become déjà vu. He had loved Sharon, and so had Oscar. Now, he loved Regina, and so did Marcos. He had lost Sharon, but he had no intention of letting

Regina go. He would fight to keep her, and if necessary give up his own life in the struggle.

"I'm sorry." The two words came out in a hoarse whisper.

Marcos closed the distance between them, placing a hand on Aaron's shoulder. "No, friend, *I'm* sorry."

Glancing over his shoulder, Aaron smiled at him. Seconds later the two men were hugging and thumping each other's backs. Marcos extended his glass, touching it to Aaron's before they drained the contents.

Grimacing, Aaron shook his head. "I should test this stuff at the lab. I'm certain it's responsible for minimal brain damage."

Marcos nodded in agreement. "I think you're right. Let's get another glass to make certain."

The two men returned to the small crowd of people talking, dancing, and sitting on chairs under the clear, nighttime Brazilian sky as they anticipated the start of Carnival.

CHAPTER 26

Regina survived the first night of Carnival, but declined Tyler and Arianna's offer to accompany them the following evening. She could still hear the nonstop, ear-shattering music coming from live bands atop trucks packed with musicians, singers, and gyrating dancers.

After several hours of dancing, she had been swept along in a sea of people, losing Aaron and the others in their party in the crowd until she took refuge in a restaurant and waited for them to search each establishment until they found her. She was jostled without regard to her physical condition, and there had been a time when she feared for the life of her unborn child.

Marcos, Tyler, Arianna, and the Jarre cousins decided they hadn't partied enough, so she and Aaron returned home. The sky had brightened with the beginning of a new day when the Cole siblings stumbled in and fell across their beds fully dressed.

"What's the matter, Sis? Can't hang?" Tyler teased.

Cradling her belly with both hands, she squinted at him. "You've got that right. Do me a favor. Try not to come in with the sun."

Arianna's head jerked up. "You sounded like Mommy."

"She's just practicing," Tyler teased.

"I'm serious." Her expression mirrored her statement.

"She's right," Aaron concurred, speaking for the first time. "Your parents entrusted us with your safety, and as long as you're under our roof you'll follow the rules."

Tyler sobered quickly. "What time do you want us to come home?"

Regina stared at Aaron and inclined her head. She would let him establish the curfew.

"Tell Marcos I want you in before one."

Arianna and Tyler shared a smile of relief. That would give them at least six hours to party.

"Thanks, Aaron. One it is," Tyler confirmed.

Waiting until the teenagers left the living room, Aaron moved over to sit beside Regina. "I'm not even a father and already I'm setting curfews."

Resting her head on his shoulder, she closed her eyes. "I don't even want to think about it. I just hope and pray I'll survive weaning, toilet training, and teething."

"You'll do okay, *Princesa.* You'll be a wonderful mother."

I hope you're right, she mused. The more she advanced in her term the more doubts she had. Would she be able to breast-feed? Would she have enough milk for the baby? Would the baby be colicky? Would she undergo a period of postpartum depression?

"Princesa?"

"Yes, Aaron."

"We are going to have to go to Argentina next week."

Her eyes opened and she stared up at him. "Why?"

"You have to renew your visa," he reminded her.

"I can't believe I've been here for almost ninety days. Time has passed so quickly."

Too quickly. Aaron did not look forward to the next time when her visa expired. This time he would have to prepare to put her on a plane for her return to the States. He hadn't proposed marriage again since the time he made love to her in her garden. Each time she rejected him he gave up a little piece of himself. One more rejection, and he would cease to exist. And he had to survive—not only for himself, but for Regina and the child kicking so vigorously in her womb.

Regina stood at the window in her bedroom, staring at the ripe coffee plants stretching for acres and beyond her range of vision.

Within two weeks the workers would begin harvesting the crop, while she would prepare to leave Bahia.

She inhaled, holding her breath when the baby did what she imagined was a somersault inside her. She had just entered her eighth month, and her overall weight gain of fifteen pounds made her feel large and lumbering whenever she walked up the staircase. It was time she considered occupying one of the first-floor bedrooms.

She missed Aaron. He had been gone only three days, but it seemed more like three months. He had been invited to lecture at the Walter Reed Army Institute of Research on the process that was used to produce the bandage that miraculously minimized blood loss.

He had been reluctant to leave her, but she gently coerced him into going, saying she would be waiting for his return. She expected his return the following afternoon, and she had managed to keep busy in his absence.

She was nearing completion of restoring the garden. Her greatest satisfaction had been uncovering a kapok tree concealed by the overgrowth of other trees and shrubs. The tree, native to Asia, had probably been planted before Alice da Costa had passed away. They were known to survive centuries and grow to heights of more than a hundred feet. Its massive twisted trunk and branches would provide a canopy of shade for generations to come.

The soft chiming of the telephone shattered the silence, and she moved over to the table to answer it.

"*Olá.*"

"Hello, yourself. How's it going?"

Her eyes crinkled in a smile. "I'm here, Marcos."

"How would you like to go to a *candomblé* ceremony tonight?"

"I don't know."

"Didn't you enjoy the last one?"

"Yes," she agreed reluctantly. She had enjoyed it, even if her baby hadn't. Hours after she left the temple and returned home the baby moved and gyrated as if he still heard the rhythmic passion of the drummers beating out the sounds of Africa.

"How about I pick you up and we go into Salvador for dinner. We'll hang around for a while, then head over to the *terreiro*. If we get there early we'll be able to get a good seat."

She did not want to share dinner with Marcos, even though she wanted to see another *candomblé* ceremony before she left Bahia. The ancient religion mimicked the Catholic worship of saints with their own native gods. At first she associated *candomblé* with the voodoo ceremonies of the Caribbean, but Marcos quickly reminded her that there was a major difference between the two. Unlike voodoo, *candomblé* was not aimed at producing bad luck for one's enemy. *Candomblé* was used only to produce positive results for the worshiper. There were no dolls with pins sticking in them in any of the ceremonies.

"I'll meet you there."

"Don't you want to eat out?" he insisted.

"No. I'm on a very bland diet nowadays." Recurring heartburn and indigestion made it impossible for her to ingest anything with the spices indigenous to the region.

"What time should I expect you?"

"I'll call my driver and tell him to pick me up around eight-thirty."

"Then I'll expect you at nine-fifteen."

"I'll see you later, Marcos."

Regina walked into the kitchen to get several bottles of water to take with her. Magda glanced up, halting stacking dishes in the dishwasher.

"Are you going out, Senhora?"

"Yes, Magda. I should be back around midnight."

"With Senhor Spencer gone, would you like me to stay in the house until you come back tonight?"

"That won't be necessary. But thank you, anyway."

She retrieved the bottles from a shelf in the pantry, slipped them into a large woven tote, then walked through a door at the back of the house and made her way around the courtyard to wait for her driver.

The driver pulled up within minutes of her arrival. He jumped out of the large, battered sedan and opened the rear door for her.

She stepped into the car and settled back against the aged leather seat, closing her eyes. The driver shifted into gear and the car rolled smoothly across the courtyard and down to the main road leading to Salvador.

They hadn't been on the road for more than five minutes when Regina sat up straight and opened her eyes. Sniffing, she turned and glanced out the rear window. An orange glow lit up the sky. Fire! Someone had set the coffee fields on fire again.

"Turn around!" she screamed at the driver. She shouted at him again, then realized she had spoken English.

"Stop and go back!" she demanded in Portuguese.

The driver hit the brake, the car skidding dangerously off the road, sliding precariously into an embankment. Panic spurted through her when she was slammed against the door of the car and fell to the floor. Pain ripped through her middle as she stifled a cry of agony.

The driver put the car in reverse and accelerated, and the vehicle eased back onto the solid road surface. Meanwhile Regina crawled onto the seat and lay down, fighting the waves of pain washing over her.

She lost track of time when she concentrated on the waves of pain slicing through her abdomen. The acrid smell of the smoke drifted through the open windows the closer they came to the coffee fields.

The car stopped in the courtyard, and when the driver helped Regina from the car she forgot her pain when she saw the orange glow that illuminated the night sky.

"The world is on fire," she whispered to herself.

"Senhora?" the driver asked, his voice trembling.

Reaching into her tote, she grabbed a handful of bills and threw it at him. "Get help," she ordered.

She did not wait to see what he would do as she made her way toward the house, both hands cradling her belly.

As she walked into the house, the telephone rang. Her hand was trembling uncontrollably when she picked up the receiver.

It was Sebastião. He was shouting into the phone, and she could not understand what he was saying. She thought she heard something about water, but any and everything around her faded with the next wave of pain, which brought her to her knees.

She knelt, staring at the widening circle of liquid pouring onto the floor. She had lost her amniotic fluid. "No," she moaned. The baby couldn't come now. It wasn't time. It was not full term.

Somehow she crawled across the floor and made it to one of the bedrooms on the first level. The contractions were coming faster when she pulled herself up to the bed. If she delivered on the bed, then maybe her baby had a better chance of surviving than on the floor.

Regina had no idea of how long she lay on the bed as waves of pain washed over her in measured intervals. One time she opened her eyes to find Magda standing over her.

Reaching out, she caught the housekeeper's hand. "Help me," she pleaded.

Magda's mouth curved into a sneer. "*Puta!* You need me to help you birth your brat, don't you?" She leaned closer, and Regina saw her own death in the woman's eyes. "You will die, and so will your baby. I will see to that."

Falling back to the pillow, she could not stop the tears that flowed down her cheeks. "Why?"

"Why, *puta?* Because you took the man who was supposed to marry my daughter. She should have been mistress of this house, not you."

"I don't know what you're talking—" She could not finish the sentence because another contraction seized her, this time stronger and longer than the others.

"Elena, *puta*. Elena Carvalho is my daughter. The beautiful child I had to give up because the woman in whose house I worked could not bear a child. So like Hagar, I lay with my Abraham and gave him a child his wife could not have. Elena had everything she could ever want—all except Dr. Aaron Spencer. And she did not believe me when I told her that I would get him for her."

Clenching her teeth against another contraction, Regina sat up and swung at Magda, her fist grazing her cheekbone.

Magda reacted quickly, pushing Regina away and slapping her across her mouth, cutting her lip and drawing blood. She slapped her again and again until the stinging in her face matched the pain in her belly.

Then it stopped abruptly. Someone pulled Magda away from the bed. There was a resounding thump, followed by a whimper of pain and the keening sound of someone sobbing.

Biting down on her cut lip, Regina stifled a moan when a contraction threatened to tear her in two. "Aaron." His name came out in a trembling moan.

"I'm here, *Princesa*."

She was dreaming. Aaron couldn't be in Bahia. He wasn't expected to return until the next day.

Between contractions, she opened her eyes to find him sitting beside her on the bed. "The fields are burning," she mumbled tearfully.

"It's all right, Darling."

"You'll lose everything."

"No," he countered in a soft tone. "Only if I lose you, I will have lost everything."

Aaron worked quickly, expertly, as he relieved Regina of her clothes. He had to examine her to find how her labor had progressed before he called Nicolas.

"My—my water broke."

"It's okay, Baby."

She drew in a sharp breath as another contraction gripped her.

Aaron slipped two pillows under her hips, then pulled a table lamp closer to the bed. She was dilated, but he prayed the baby was facedown in the pelvic cavity.

Leaning over her, he touched the side of her battered face. "*Princesa,* listen to me. I'm going to leave you for a few minutes. I have to call Nicolas. Then I'm going to wash up. If Nicolas doesn't get here in time, then I'm going to have to bring our baby into the world. And for that I need your help."

"Okay," she slurred between contractions.

He kissed her forehead before he moved away from the bed, stepping over the prone figure of Magda Pires, who lay motionless on the floor.

Regina drifted in and out as she heard voices floating around her. She detected the familiar fragrance of Aaron's aftershave and savored the gentle caress of his hand on her distended belly.

She opened her eyes once and found him kneeling on the floor at the foot of the bed as he eased her gently toward him.

"Aaron?"

"When I tell you to push I want you to bear down and push. Push, Regina! Push harder."

She tried pushing, but gave up quickly. "I can't."

"Yes, you can. Pretend you have to go to the bathroom. That's it, Sweetheart. That's good."

Aaron waited until another contraction gripped her before he ordered her to push again. She did, and minutes later she heard the wavering cry of an infant.

Tears of joy and relief filled her eyes and flowed down her bruised cheeks. "It's a boy, isn't it?"

"Yes! Yes! Yes!" Aaron said, blinking through his own tears.

"Nice job, Aaron."

Still holding his son, Aaron glanced over his shoulder to find Nicolas Benedetti standing several feet away. Putting down his medical bag, Nicolas slipped on a pair of latex gloves.

"Put the baby on his mother's belly. I'll take over now."

Aaron complied, then removed his bloodstained gloves. He sat down on the bed beside Regina, holding her hand while Nicolas cut the umbilical cord and removed the mucous from the baby's nose and mouth. He wrapped the tiny, shivering boy in a blanket and handed him to Aaron.

"You can clean up your son now, Doctor."

Cradling the baby to his chest, Aaron took him to the kitchen, placed him on the counter next to the sink, and washed him gently with warm water.

The baby let out a frantic cry when the water touched his face. "Shh, Clayborne Diaz Spencer. This is as bad as it is going to get for a while. Right now I have to clean you up before you meet your mother," he crooned softly. "You must remember that you always have to look nice for the ladies."

He ran a finger along the infant's cheek and instinctively he turned his head in that direction. His son was small, but he was perfect—as perfect as the woman who had carried him.

The smell of burnt coffee beans wafted in through the windows, but Aaron could not think of anything but the woman who could have been lost to him if he hadn't returned when he did. Walking over to the window, he stared out into the night and whispered a prayer of thanks. A haze lingered, concealing the full moon. A gentle breeze blew in from the ocean, and the sky brightened as a silvery glow illuminated the earth. The moon appeared larger and brighter than at any other time of the year. It was then that he realized it was the night of a harvest moon, as well as his own birthday. His son had arrived in time to help his father celebrate his thirty-eighth birthday.

Lowering his head, he kissed Clayborne on his forehead, then returned to the bedroom, where he would introduce him to his mother.

Aaron returned to the bedroom to find Nicolas kneeling beside Magda, waving a bottle under her nose.

Regina sat up in bed, a gentle smile creasing her battered face as she reached for her son. Aaron sat down on the side of the bed and kissed her bruised mouth.

"Thank you for the birthday present."

Her eyes widened when she registered what he had said. "You came back early to celebrate your birthday?"

Nodding, he watched Regina guide the baby's mouth to her breast. After a few misses, he found the nipple and began sucking vigorously.

"Aaron, I can't imagine what would've happened if you hadn't come back when you did."

"If anything *had* happened to you, I probably would spend the rest of my life in jail, because I would've done more to Magda than just slap her."

"She tried to kill me because she thought having me out of the way would make it easier for Elena to marry you."

He frowned. "I never would've married Elena. Why would Magda think I would?"

Regina related what Magda had told her about being Elena's mother, watching disbelief freeze Aaron's features. "I wonder if Elena even knows Magda's her birth mother. I doubt that, because last week Elena announced her engagement to her *futebol* player."

"So now Magda will go to jail for nothing."

"No, *Princesa,* it will not be for nothing. She will be charged with attempted murder and arson. Those are pretty serious charges in Brazil."

The sucking motion stopped and Regina smiled down at her son. His last name might have been Spencer, but his features said he was a Cole.

Her head came up slowly as she gave Aaron a seductive look. "Do you think you can make an honest woman out of me, Aaron Laurence Spencer?"

He leaned closer. "I think I can."

"When?"

"As soon as you're better."

"Better how?" Her gaze was fixed on his sensual mouth.

"As soon as your doctor gives you the okay that you can travel."

"Where are we going, Darling?"

"Florida, *Princesa*. We'll have a double ceremony. We'll have a priest marry us, then baptize the baby."

She laid her head on his shoulder. "It sounds as if we're going to have quite a party."

"I'm ready," he crooned, sealing his pledge with a kiss that promised forever.

EPILOGUE

Parris Cole held her grandson, tears filling her green-flecked brown eyes when she watched her husband lead her firstborn down the aisle where Aaron Spencer waited to make her his wife. The tiny baby slept peacefully, unaware of the danger that had threatened his very existence.

Her gaze shifted from the tall man reaching for and grasping her daughter's hand to the baby who represented another generation of Coles. Clayborne was his mother's child, from his black curly hair to his delicate features and the twin dimples that were passed down from his Cuban-born great-grandmother.

Parris had to admit that Regina had chosen wisely. Aaron would be a good husband and father. The wedding ceremony ended with the exchange of vows, rings, and kisses. Then Regina, Aaron, and the priest, along with Tyler and Arianna, moved over to the baptismal font.

Rising to her feet, Parris handed Tyler his nephew. Clayborne wailed—his cry joining the voice of the priest intoning the prayer washing away original sin—then water was poured on his head. His crying continued until Tyler handed him to his mother. At six weeks of age, he had bonded quickly with her.

Martin moved closer to his wife, holding her hand gently. "We will have her for such a short time," he whispered close to her ear.

Parris saw the shimmer of tears in her husband's eyes. Regina and Aaron had planned to spend a month in Florida before they flew on to Mexico. They had promised to return to Florida to visit with the Coles at least twice each year: after Aaron harvested his coffee crop, and during the Christmas holidays. It wasn't much, but she would take it. She would take any time given her from her children.

Regina led Aaron through the formal gardens at her grandparents' estate, pointing out the differing plants and flowers. She had fed Clayborne, and he now slept in the nursery where many a Cole baby had slept over the years.

Aaron stopped and smiled down at the face of his bride. "Do you know what I was thinking, *Princesa?*"

She arched a naturally curving eyebrow, shaking her head. "No, Aaron. This is not our garden."

"No one will see us?" he whispered.

"I don't care."

"How about a kiss, Mrs. Aaron Spencer?"

"One kiss coming up," she crooned, putting her arms around his neck.

Six weeks had passed quickly. Magda and her accomplices were in jail, awaiting trial for attempted murder and arson. Sebastião had activated the irrigation system, saving more than half the crop.

She and Aaron would spend a month in Florida, then fly to Mexico to introduce Clayborne to his paternal grandfather. Then they would return to Bahia, to begin to live out their dreams without demons lurking in the background to thwart their happiness.

Pulling back, Regina glanced around her husband's broad shoulder. "I don't think we're the only ones making out in the garden," she whispered.

"She looks a little young—"

"Emily!" Regina hissed, startling her twelve-year-old cousin.

Emily Kirkland's dark green eyes widened in surprise. "Please don't tell my father," she pleaded as she approached the newly married couple.

"Who were you with?" Turning, Emily pointed to a tall,

handsome young man who strolled casually from behind a wall of hedges.

Regina arched an eyebrow at Matt Sterling's stepson. "Chris?"

He cleared his throat several times before saying, "I would never touch her, Regina. Her father would kill me."

Regina gave him a knowing look. "I'm glad you realize that. I think the two of you should go back and join the others before your fathers come looking for you."

Christopher Delgado extended his hand to Emily Kirkland, who hesitated and then placed her hand in his. Regina and Aaron watched until they disappeared from view.

"Young love," he said softly.

"Dangerous love," Regina countered. "His sister is my cousin's best friend."

"Is her father your uncle with the silver hair and green eyes?"

"The same."

"That boy likes living on the edge, doesn't he?"

"You've got that right."

"Right now I feel like living on the edge, Mrs. Spencer," he crooned, pulling her deeper into the boxwood garden.

There was only the sound of their laughter before it ended abruptly with the exchange of a passionate kiss.

Hand in hand they returned to the house, smiling at everyone who had come to help them celebrate the harvest of their lives.

* * * * *

*Now that you've enjoyed these stories in
the* HIDEAWAY LEGACY *series,
here is a preview of the first chapter in
Rochelle Alers's latest installment of her
popular* HIDEAWAY *romance series*

STRANGER IN MY ARMS
Coming next month.

CHAPTER 1

Three knocks on the bedroom door in rapid succession stopped Alexandra Cole as she prepared to slip her feet into a pair of three-inch, silk-covered, midnight-blue pumps.

A frown furrowed her forehead as she stood up. This was the second interruption that had thwarted her getting dressed for her cousin's wedding.

The first time it was Ana, who, in the full throes of PMS, had experienced a temporary meltdown when she couldn't zip up the dress she'd chosen to wear for the New Year's Eve ceremony. She and Ana were the same height, five-three, but Alex outweighed her younger sister by a mere five pounds. The crisis was resolved when she offered Ana one of the two dresses she'd brought with her.

"Who is it?" she called out.

"Jason."

Alex rolled her eyes. Now it was her younger brother. "What's the matter, little brother? Do you need me to tie your tie?"

"Very funny, Alex," he drawled sarcastically from the other side of the door. "I came to tell you that one of your loser ex-boyfriends just showed up uninvited, and Uncle Martin's security people won't let him in. What do you want to do?"

Crossing the carpeted bedroom on bare feet, she opened the door. Jason Cole stood before her in a dark blue suit, white shirt and white silk tie. It wasn't often that she saw him in a suit, but Alex had to admit that her twenty-four-year-old brother cut a very handsome figure in tailored attire.

Jason was the quintessential Cole male: over six foot, olive coloring, black curly hair and a dimpled smile. And in keeping with a family ritual that dated back to the marriage of their grandparents from which the prospective groom was exempt, any male who claimed Cole blood affected light-colored neckwear.

"Who is he?"

Jason lifted sweeping black eyebrows. "The message was 'Tell her Donald is here.'"

Her large clear gold-brown eyes narrowed. "Donald," Alex repeated. She knew two Donalds. One who'd been her study partner in undergraduate school and another she'd dated only twice before she handed him his walking papers. "Did he leave his last name?"

Crossing his arms over his chest, Jason shook his head. "He also said, and I quote, 'She'll know who I am,' end quote."

Realization dawned. He had to be Donald Easton. "That arrogant SOB," she whispered. "Tell them to let him in and have him wait for me by the refreshment tent."

A sardonic smile parted Jason's lips. "If you want, Gabe and I can give him a blanket party."

Her brow furrowed. "What are you talking about?"

"We'll throw a blanket over his head, then kick his ass. And I'm willing to bet that if he wasn't getting married in an hour Michael would also want to get his licks in."

Alex stomped a bare foot. "Stop it, Jason! There will be no brawling tonight or any other night. Donald Easton has a problem with the word *no*. I'll take care of him."

"Are you sure, Alex?"

Forcing a dimpled smile, she patted her brother's arm. "Yes, I'm sure. Now go so I can finish dressing."

Jason flashed a wolfish grin so reminiscent of their father's. "Okay. By the way, you look great."

"Thanks."

Alex closed the door and crossed the expansive bedroom she shared with Ana and two other female cousins whenever they gathered in West Palm Beach.

Slipping her feet into her shoes, she wondered why a man she hadn't seen in nearly a year had come from Virginia to see her. Unfortunately she'd told Donald that she always celebrated Christmas and New Year's in Florida with her extended family; it was apparent he wanted to surprise her.

Well, the surprise would be on him because she had no intention of resuming what had been doomed from the start.

A member of Martin Cole's private security detail took a glance at the SUV with West Virginia plates and entered the number into his PDA. Smiling, he nodded at the man behind the wheel.

"We'll park your vehicle for you, Mr. Grayslake." He gestured to a parking attendant before returning his attention to Merrick Grayslake. "Once you walk through the gates and make a right someone will escort you to the Japanese garden."

Merrick nodded. "Thank you."

Reaching for the suit jacket resting on the passenger-side seat, he got out of his vehicle, slipped his arms into the sleeves, then as directed made his way through a set of iron gates that protected the property that made up the Cole family West Palm Beach compound.

He hadn't taken more than half a dozen steps when he spied a small camera attached to the upper branches of a tree. Security personnel and surveillance equipment monitored everyone entering or leaving the property.

He'd left Bolivar, West Virginia, at dawn, stopping twice to refuel and stretch his legs. The drive south had taken longer than expected because of bumper-to-bumper holiday traffic along I-95. It was New Year's Eve and motorists were heading either home or to clubs or restaurants where they'd ring in the coming year with their families and/or friends.

At thirty-five, Merrick Grayslake had lost count of the number of countries where he'd welcomed in a New Year. Whether in Central or South America, the Middle East, Southeast Asia, or in his last assignment as a CIA covert field operative—Afghanistan—for him it had become just another uneventful holiday.

Now, for the first time in more than two years, he wouldn't be alone or engaged in an undercover mission when the clock struck midnight. It had taken the wedding of Michael Kirkland, a man who'd saved his life, for Merrick to temporarily forsake his reclusive way of life and leave what had become his sanctuary, a modest two-story home near the Allegheny Mountains.

He'd checked into a local hotel and asked the front desk for an eight-thirty wake-up call. His head had barely touched the pillow when the ringing telephone woke him from a deep, dreamless sleep. He'd drunk a pint of water from the wet bar to offset dehydration before he readied himself to attend a New Year's Eve wedding.

When U.S. Army captain Michael Kirkland had come to him to solicit his help in protecting his social worker fiancée, Merrick experienced a long-forgotten shiver of excitement that always preceded a new covert mission. But the feeling was short-lived. He'd helped Michael identify Stanley Willoughby, the man behind a conspiracy to kill Jolene Walker; he'd remained in the Washington, D.C., area for several weeks following the arrest and subsequent indictment of the D.C. power broker before returning to his adopted home state.

Merrick still didn't understand why he'd decided put down roots in West Virginia, but there was something about the topography that suited his temperament. The panoramic views, the rugged splendor of the mountains, and the small towns that predated the Revolutionary War and still bore the scars of the Civil War had remained virtually untouched architecturally since the 1950s.

The slate path widened to a lush, manicured meadow where an enormous gauze-draped white tent protected cloth-covered tables from insects. A smaller tent, less than fifty feet away, doubled as a portable bar. The weather had cooperated: clear skies, full moon and nighttime temperatures in the low sixties. His pace slowed as he joined a small crowd milling around the entrance to a garden.

A young woman sporting a white blouse and black skirt approached him. As she came closer he saw the earpiece in her left ear; he found it ironic that whenever he left Bolivar his surveillance instincts kicked into high gear. It was as if he went into hunter mode, watching, listening and mentally recording everything around him.

She flashed a professional smile. "Your name, sir?"

"Grayslake."

"Please follow me, Mr. Grayslake." She led him into a large tent in the middle of a Japanese-inspired garden; organza-swathed chairs were lined up in precise rows like soldiers at a military parade. She indicated a chair with a Velcro tag bearing his name. "The bar is open for appetizers and liquid refreshment."

Merrick was grateful for the offer. He hadn't eaten anything in eighteen hours. "Thank you." Nodding to the woman, he went back the way he'd come.

The light from the full moon competed with strategically placed floodlights and thousands of tiny bulbs entwined in the branches of trees and lampposts. With the artificial illumination it could've been ten in the morning rather than ten at night.

Merrick had received an engraved invitation that read that Michael Blanchard Kirkland and Jolene Walker were scheduled to exchange vows at eleven, followed by a midnight reception dinner and a New Year's Day brunch.

He would remain in West Palm Beach for the wedding and reception. He'd decided to skip the brunch because his plans included spending a few days in Miami before heading down to the Keys. He hadn't told Rachel he was coming, praying she wouldn't seek retribution because he hadn't kept his vow to keep in touch.

A hint of a rare smile played at the corners of Merrick's mouth as he neared the bar. He was never one to make resolutions, but the events of the past three months had forced him to rethink his monastic existence. Since reuniting with Michael Kirkland, he'd socialized more than he had in years.

The sound of voices raised in anger caught his attention. As he turned around, his gaze caught and held the petite figure of a woman in a dark-colored dress with a revealing décolletage. Light reflected off the sparkle of diamonds in her ears, several delicate strands gracing her slender neck and in her dark hair. Merrick only saw her profile, but what he saw held him captive.

Alexandra glared at Donald. He'd downed one glass of champagne while holding another flute filled with the bubbly wine. She couldn't believe he'd come—unannounced—to her uncle's house and proceeded to get drunk.

"What are you doing here?" She didn't bother to disguise her annoyance.

Donald tilted the glass to his mouth and swallowed the imported champagne in one gulp. "What does it look like, Miss Alexandra Cole?" He spat out her name. "I came to ring in the New Year with my snobby, bitchy girlfriend."

She wrinkled her delicate nose in revulsion as the odor of something stronger than wine wafted into her nostrils. Donald Easton, the brilliant computer programmer, Donald the arrogant egotist yet always the consummate gentleman, had shown up at her family's estate drunk!

"I am not your girlfriend, Donald," she said, raising her voice above its normal tone. "I never was, never will be. Now I want you to leave."

"What if I don't want to leave!" he shouted. Those close enough to hear his outburst turned and stared at him.

"I think you should do as the lady says," warned a deep male voice filled with a lethal calmness that sent a chill over Alex despite the comfortable nighttime temperature.

She shifted to her right. A slender man with brilliant silver-gray eyes stood less than a foot away from her and Donald. Her gaze caught and held his; she was hard-pressed to pinpoint his age or ethnicity. His close-cropped hair was an odd shade of red-brown that complemented his khaki-brown coloring. His lean face, with smooth skin pulled taut over the elegant ridge of prominent cheekbones and the narrow bridge of his aquiline nose and firm mouth, hinted of a Native American bloodline.

Donald, weaving unsteadily in an attempt to maintain his balance, squinted at Merrick. "And who the hell are you?"

Merrick took a step and forcibly wrested the flutes from Donald. "You don't want to know." He handed the glasses to Alex. "Take care of these while I take care of your boyfriend." His request was a command. His right hand caught Donald's neck, fingers tightening on his carotid artery. "Let's go, buddy, while you're still able to breathe." He loosened his grip when Donald clawed at his hand.

"He's not my boyfriend," Alex said to the stranger's back as he led the interloper away.

Her hands were trembling when she placed the flutes on the bar. One of the bartenders came over to her. "May I get you something to drink, Miss Cole?"

"I'll have sparkling water." She asked for water when she needed something stronger to calm her jangled nerves. When she'd told Jason she would handle Donald she hadn't thought he would be intoxicated. The last thing she wanted was for her brothers to confront him when he was unable to defend himself. It would've been better for Donald if her uncle's security staff escorted Donald off the property than for her male relatives to get involved. She'd always teased them, saying even though they were trust fund babies, they were a whit above thug status. They generally did not go looking for a fight, but none were willing to back down from one if a situation presented itself.

Jason was right about Donald being a loser, and it had taken her two dates to come to that realization. His insistent bragging about his accomplishments and a need to tell her how to live her life had been his undoing. However, Donald wasn't a man who took rejection lightly. After their second date she refused his telephone calls, text messages and letters that continued long after she'd left Virginia for Europe, where she'd enrolled in an accel-

erated graduate program for a master's in art history with a concentration in European architecture and pre-Columbian art. She'd
completed the first half of the program wherein she'd spent six
months studying and traveling throughout France, Spain and Italy.
And in another three weeks she would leave the States for Mexico
City to complete her course and fieldwork for the program.

"Here you are, Miss Cole."

Alex accepted a goblet filled with ice and carbonated water.
"Thank you." She took a sip welcoming the chill bathing her
throat as the man who'd come to her rescue returned. As he
closed the distance between them she noticed, for the first time,
his height. He was tall, as tall as her father and brothers.

However, there was something about the stranger that disturbed her more than Donald's unexpected appearance. She wasn't
certain whether it'd been his eyes, the lethal calmness in his voice
when he'd spoken to Donald, or the speed with which he'd
grabbed the man's throat. Everything about him radiated danger.

She forced a smile, dimples deepening as she extended her
right hand. "I'd like to thank you, Mr. …"

"Grayslake," he said, reaching for a hand that was swallowed
up in his much larger one. "Merrick Grayslake."

Alex's smile did not slip. "Thank you, Mr. Grayslake, for diffus-
ing what could've become somewhat embarrassing for my family."

Merrick gave her fingers a gentle squeeze before releasing
them. He angled his head, his penetrating gaze taking in the perfection of her small, oval face in the bright light. Her eyes weren't
as dark as he believed they would've been given her nut-brown
coloring and inky-black hair, hair piled atop her head in sensual
disarray and secured with jeweled hairpins. He fixed his gaze on
her face rather than her petite, curvy body in a provocative halter
dress with a generous front slit showing a liberal expanse of
shapely legs. Her heels and upswept hairstyle put the top of her
head at his shoulder.

"Please call me Merrick." His voice was low, calming. "And
whom do I have the pleasure of rescuing from the big bad wolf?"

A soft laugh escaped her parted lips. "Alexandra Cole. But everyone calls me Alex."

Merrick's dark eyebrows lifted with this disclosure. "Well, because I'm not everyone, I hope you don't mind if I call you Ali. Alex is for a boy." And there was nothing about Alexandra Cole that even hinted of *boy*. Not with her curvaceous little body.

It was Alex's turned to lift her eyebrows. Over the years, she'd been called Alexa, Lexie and Zandra, but never Ali. "No, I don't mind." Merrick moved closer and she felt his heat, inhaled the haunting fragrance of his cologne that was the perfect complement for his natural body's scent.

"I can think of a way where you can really thank me, Ali."

Alex went completely still. Merrick had gotten rid of one nuisance only to become one himself. "I don't think so, Mr. Grayslake. I don't date."

It was Merrick's turn to recoil from her unsolicited frankness. A shadow of annoyance crossed his face. "I wasn't going to ask you out, because like you I don't date."

She tilted her chin, the gesture obviously challenging. "Are you married?"

Merrick's impassive expression did not change. "No."

"Engaged?"

"No."

"Do you prefer men?"

He blinked once and forced back a smile. "No. And to put your mind at ease, I absolutely have no interest in you romantically."

A becoming blush darkened her face. Alex didn't know whether to be annoyed or embarrassed. Her quick tongue had gotten the better of her—yet again. She closed her eyes for several seconds as heat singed her cheeks. "I'm...I'm sorry, Merrick, but I—"

"It's all right, Ali," he interrupted. The smile he'd struggled to hide softened the angles in his rawboned face. "There's no need to apologize. I can assure you that I'm not like your boyfriend."

Her delicate jaw tightened when she clamped her teeth together. "Donald is *not* my boyfriend."

"That's not what he said."

"What did he say?"

"You were lovers."

Alex's eyes conveyed the fury racing through her. She should've let her brothers take care of the drunken liar. "He was never *my* boyfriend or *my* lover."

Merrick felt a strange numbed comfort with her disclosure; he'd thought Alex and Donald were having a lovers' spat. "Good for you."

"Why? Even though you're not interested in me romantically you think you'd be better for me than Donald?"

He was momentarily speechless in his surprise. Alex Cole was as outspoken as she was beautiful, a trait he wasn't used to in the women with whom he'd been involved.

"No. That's because I've never been a good boyfriend."

Alex took another sip of water, staring at Merrick over the rim of her goblet. "Do you realize you're an anomaly?"

"Why would you say that?"

"Most men would never admit to being less than perfect in the romance department."

"That's because some of them are either liars or fools."

"And you've been neither?"

Attractive lines fanned out around Merrick's luminous silver-gray eyes when a natural smile slipped under the iron-willed control he'd spent most of his life perfecting. "Wrong, Ali. I've been a fool a few times."

He'd become a king of fools when he trusted a woman whose duplicity had cost him a kidney and a career with the Central Intelligence Agency.

What he didn't tell Alex was that whenever he'd gone under-cover he became a liar—someone with a fictitious background. He'd become an actor in a role wherein one slip would compromise his mission. His focus hadn't been the risk that he would forfeit his life, but completing the mission. And it was always the mission.

A server approached with a tray of appetizers. She handed Merrick a napkin and he took several puff pastries, offering them to Alex. She shook her head. "No, thank you. I'm saving my appetite for dinner."

"Speaking of saving, I'd like you to save me a dance."

His request surprised Alex. "You want to dance with me?"

Slowly, seductively, his silver gaze slid downward before it reversed itself. "Yes."

She felt a tingling in the pit of her stomach she found disturbing. Merrick Grayslake was disturbing her in every way she didn't want. She would dance with the man, and after tomorrow she would never see him again.

"One dance," she crooned, flashing her enchanting dimpled smile. She wiggled her fingers. "I'll see you later."

Merrick stared at Alexandra Cole as she lifted the hem of her dress and walked out of the tent.

He'd come to West Palm Beach for a wedding and unwittingly found himself bewitched by a slip of a woman who just happened to be the groom's cousin.

CONNIE BRISCOE

is a *New York Times* bestselling author of five novels, including *Can't Get Enough, P.G. County, Big Girls Don't Cry, Sisters and Lovers* and *A Long Way from Home*. Her work has hit the bestseller lists of *USA TODAY, Washington Post, Essence* and many others. Profoundly deaf by thirty, Briscoe's hearing was restored recently through cochlear implant surgery. She lives in Maryland with her family in a quiet community with beautiful pastoral views.

LOLITA FILES

is the author of six bestselling novels: *Scenes from a Sistah, Getting to the Good Part, Blind Ambitions, Child of God, Tastes Like Chicken* and *sex.lies.murder.fame: A Novel*. She currently lives in Los Angeles, California, where she is developing projects for television and film.

ANITA BUNKLEY

is the author of nine successful mainstream novels, two novellas and one work of nonfiction. A Blackboard bestselling author, she was inducted into the Texas Institute of Letters in 2004 and was an NAACP Image Award nominee in 2000. A full-time novelist, she lives in Houston, Texas, where she also conducts writers' workshops for aspiring authors.

Pleasure SEEKERS

Part of the Hideaway Legacy

A sizzling, sensuous story about Ilene, Faye and Alana—
three young African-American women whose lives are
forever changed when they are invited to join the
exclusive world of the Pleasure Seekers.

Rochelle Alers

NATIONAL BESTSELLING AUTHOR

"Fans of the romantic suspense of Iris Johansen,
Linda Howard and Catherine Coulter
will enjoy [*Pleasure Seekers*]."
—*Library Journal*

Available the first week of January wherever books are sold.

sepia™

www.kimanipress.com   KPRA0360107TR

A special Collector's Edition from
Essence bestselling author

KAYLA PERRIN

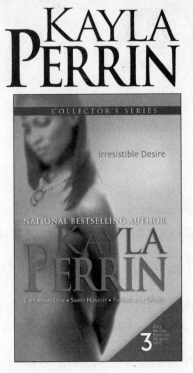

Three full-length novels

From one of the most popular authors for the
Arabesque series comes this trade paperback volume
containing three classic romances. Enjoy warmth, drama
and mystery with EVERLASTING LOVE, SWEET HONESTY
and FLIRTING WITH DANGER.

"The more [Kayla Perrin] writes, the better she gets."
—*Rawsistaz Reviewers* on *Gimme an O!*

Available the first week of January wherever books are sold.

KIMANI PRESS™
www.kimanipress.com

KPKP0530107TR

KIMANI
tru
™

A dramatic story about cultural identity, acceptance and being true to oneself.

The Edification of Sonya Crane

JDGuilford

When Sonya Crane transfers to a predominantly black high school, she finds that pretending to be biracial makes it easier for her to fit in and gives her the kind of recognition and friendships that she's never had before. That is, until popular girl Tandy Herman threatens to disclose her secret....

Look for it in March!